COBRA TRAP

COBRA TRAP

Peter O'Donnell

SOUVENIR PRESS

First published 1996 by
Souvenir Press Ltd.,
43 Great Russell Street, London WC1B 3PA
and simultaneously in Canada

Reprinted 2000

ISBN 0 285 63332 5

Typeset by Rowland Phototypesetting Ltd
Bury St Edmunds, Suffolk

Printed in Great Britain by Biddles Ltd
www.biddles.co.uk

CONTENTS

BELLMAN

It was a warm day in Tangier, but Willie Garvin was very comfortable in the discreet grey summer-weight suit he wore as he crossed the reception hall of the Hotel Malaurak to the lift marked *Private—Staff Only*. This gave access to offices on the top floor of the hotel, which was owned by *The Network*. Willie pressed the call-button and maintained the air of a serious young executive until he was in the lift with the doors closed. Then he allowed himself a grin.

Being a criminal organisation *The Network* did not advertise its name or activities, but these were well known to the Tangier police, and Inspector Hassan was more than content with the situation. So he ought to be, Willie reflected. Since the war of the four gangs which had followed the creation of *The Network* by Modesty Blaise three years ago, Tangier had become notice-ably more law-abiding.

When the lift stopped on the fifth floor Willie got out and walked along the corridor to Garcia's office, thinking about Modesty Blaise. As always when he thought about her, which was often, he felt a touch of awe. At no more than seventeen she had taken over the small-time Louche group, saved it from destruction by more powerful gangs, and begun the setting up of an organisation that now operated on a near worldwide basis. In doing so she had wiped out several dealers in drugs and vice from Tangier to the Levant, and had established herself as an in-valuable source of the kind of information that enabled Inspector Hassan to take preventive measures against crime on his own patch.

She had also won the respect of certain intelligence authorities in a number of countries and established a useful relationship with them. Like Inspector Hassan, they were well aware that she was herself making a fortune from a variety of ingenious rackets on an international scale, but it seemed they could live with that, perhaps because *The Network* was run under her own strange but rigid rules and these were found acceptable by those whose position allowed them to be more concerned with justice than with laws.

Willie recalled a conversation with Inspector Hassan at the conclusion of an unpleasant matter Modesty Blaise had instructed Willie to deal with because it was beyond Hassan's legal writ. 'There are three kinds of crime, Mr Garvin,' the inspector had said. 'There are dirty crimes, very dirty crimes, and fairly clean crimes. As a policeman I disapprove of all categories. As a citizen and a father I have some respect for any person who assists in reducing the first two, even if she—even if that person is professionally engaged in the third. Thank you for your assistance these past two days, Mr Garvin.'

'I'll tell Miss Blaise. I'm acting on 'er behalf, Inspector.'

'That is understood. And I imagine you are happy in her employ?'

Willie had smiled at the impossibility of finding an adequate answer. Then he had just said, 'Yes, I'm 'appy.'

But now he felt a touch of unease as he tapped on Garcia's door and entered, for he had sensed something unusually troubled in Garcia's manner when he phoned for Willie to call at the office. Garcia had been with Modesty Blaise from the first day and was her right-hand man, yet like the rest of her lieutenants he never failed to behave towards her with deference. No man addressed her or referred to her other than as 'Mam'selle' or 'Mam'selle Blaise'—except Willie Garvin, who had come to *The Network* in circumstances so remarkable that she had allowed him the *cachet* of addressing her in the way he had first used on the day she bought him out of a gaol in the Far East. It was then he had addressed her as Princess.

Garcia closed a file on his desk and nodded. 'Sit down, Willie.

What are you doing about that pimp and his minders who've been bothering Claudine?'

Willie took a chair. 'I'm sorting that out today, Mr Garcia. Can I 'ave Sammy Wan and draw a thousand dollars for expenses? It's a bit expensive, but worth it long-term I reckon.'

'What have you got in mind?'

Willie told him, and Garcia's chuckle became a full-throated laugh. 'Marvellous. We'll see the story gets around, it'll discourage others from taking liberties with our people.' Garcia got up and moved to the window, his smile fading. There he turned and looked at Willie soberly. 'Now I've got something difficult to say.'

Willie froze. 'I 'aven't stepped out of line, Mr Garcia? Mam'selle's not giving me the elbow?'

'Good God, no.' Garcia's expression softened. Being dismissed by Modesty Blaise was the one thing in the world that frightened Willie Garvin. 'Look, I'll leave the difficult part to the end and deal with the good bit. You know this is an anniversary?'

Willie hesitated. 'Well, it's a year today since Mam'selle took me on, but I didn't think anyone else would remember.'

Garcia gave a short laugh. 'All her top men do. It was a very good day for *The Network*.'

Willie relaxed, exhaling a long breath. 'It was an even better day for me, Mr Garcia.'

'I know. But you've done well, Willie. A damn sight better than well, and Mam'selle knows it. You're right up there in her class when it comes to action, but like her you've got muscles in your head, too, and that's where it counts.' He studied Willie curiously for a few seconds. 'It's strange. I thought when you started making your mark that some of her top men might get jealous, men who've been with her from the start—Krolli, Nedic, Sammy Wan.'

Garcia shook his head. 'But it didn't happen. They respect you, Willie, but they like you, too, and we're men who are pretty choosy about who we like.' He shrugged and made a small gesture with an open hand. 'Maybe it's because you respected them and never got pushy, never traded on that time you dropped Saafi

during the fracas with his mob down in El Golea when he was
set to blast her with a Uzi. Or maybe it's because they know
you're *her* man, just like they are. That's important to us, Willie.'

Garcia moved to his desk and sat down. He said gently, 'I
guess that's why she's given orders that you're to work in tandem
with me from now on. *We're* her right hand now, you and me.'

Willie stared. 'Me? With you, Mr Garcia?'

'That's what she said, and that's what I want. And you stop
calling me Mister. My name's Rafael. Rafa to you, okay?'

Willie ran a hand through his hair. 'You reckon I'm up to it?'

'Yes. What's more important, Mam'selle does, so you'd bloody
well better be, hadn't you?'

'Well . . . yes, if she says so. What about Krolli and the others?'

'They have no say in it, Willie. But I've told them, and they're
pleased. It's good for *The Network*, and they're all in favour of
that. It's our living, isn't it? Oh, and don't worry about the
paperwork.' Garcia gestured around the office. 'I take care of all
administration and office staff. You'll be in charge of training,
planning and operations—all under Mam'selle's supervision, of
course.'

Willie got up, pacing across the big office and back to the
desk. 'Rafa . . . ?'

'That's me. Go ahead.'

'I reckon you put in a good word for me. Thanks.'

Garcia grinned. 'Self-interest. I confirmed her opinion, that's
all.' The grin faded. 'Now let's get to the difficult bit, and for
that we go back a couple of years. Did you know that Moulay
used to have a daughter?'

Moulay was the man in charge of Modesty Blaise's house,
Pendragon, among the hills west of Tangier, a combination of
chef, butler and general factotum, with two or three staff who
lived out. Willie shook his head, surprised by Garcia's question.
'I didn't even know Moulay was married.'

'His wife died some years ago. When Mam'selle bought *Pendragon* and engaged Moulay she took his daughter on as a personal maid. Her name was Lisette, and she was sixteen.' Garcia
gave a wry smile. 'I suppose about three years younger than

Mam'selle herself at the time, but I think Mam'selle sometimes felt as old as God in comparison. You wouldn't wonder. Anyway, Lisette was a really nice kid, and Mam'selle liked her a lot.'

Willie said, 'That figures. She 'as to come on like 'ickory and steel to run us lot, but she's still feminine gender. Needs someone to relax with sometimes—who doesn't? Be nice if she could let 'er hair down with another girl once in a while. Can't do it with us.'

Garcia regarded him with interest. 'I thought I was the only one who could see that. But maybe you're only almost right, Willie.' He seemed about to follow the trend of his last words, then frowned and said briskly, 'Anyway, the girl meant a lot to Mam'selle, and one afternoon in the Rue Picard she was stabbed to death by a couple of junkies for the few francs in her purse.'

Willie said, 'Oh, Jesus. Then what?'

'Two policemen chased and cornered them. One of the junkies went for the policemen with a knife, and they shot him dead. The other's in gaol for ever. But they were nothing, Willie. Even victims, maybe. Bellman was the real killer.'

'Bellman? The Port Said drug pedlar? But I 'eard Mam'selle took Krolli and a task force there to sort 'im out just before I joined.'

Garcia said, 'She did. And the year before that he was operating out of Tangier. He specialises in organising teams to get young kids hooked, and he had a monopoly at this end of the Mediterranean. So Mam'selle smashed the whole set-up. It wasn't easy, and she had to kid herself a little. I mean she won't risk Network people unless it's for the safety or benefit of the organisation— which was true concerning Bellman because it gave us a healthy credit with Inspector Hassan. Anyway, Bellman moved to Port Said and in about a year he'd got a new organisation running. So like you heard, she took a team and smashed that too.'

Willie smiled. 'Safety of *The Network*?'

Garcia looked hard at him. 'We have an office there, and if she did have to kid herself a little more, so what? Isn't she entitled to a few little whims, for Christ's sake?'

Willie said, 'I wasn't knocking 'er, Rafa. I was enjoying what you told me. Whatever whims she's got, I love 'em. I wouldn't want 'er different.'

Garcia relaxed. 'Okay, then. So she's chased Bellman out of North Africa and Middle Eastern territory, but he's still alive and you haven't asked why.'

Willie scratched his cheek thoughtfully. 'Well, we don't do assassinations. She wouldn't mind putting the bastard down if he came at 'er, but she wouldn't do a cold killing and she wouldn't order one. So I suppose Bellman left 'is muscle to fight it out, and when they cracked he just 'ad it away on 'is toes.'

'Right,' said Garcia. 'Bellman probably kills a few thousand people a year with drugs, but he doesn't get his hands dirty. And now he's moved to new territory where we can't as yet claim to have an interest. He's settled in Peru, operating from a base near Lima, and next week Mam'selle is going after him again. Solo.'

Willie stiffened, the normally amiable blue eyes suddenly hard and alert. 'To do what?'

Garcia spread his hands. 'God knows. She says it's a personal matter. I'd guess she means to force him to come at her somehow, and then put him away, but I don't know how, and I'm worried sick. So I'm relying on you, Willie. I want you to see her and persuade her to take you with her.'

'*Me* persuade 'er?' Willie shook his head anxiously. 'I'll go with 'er all right, but you'll 'ave to fix it. You *can't* let 'er go solo on this, Rafa, we could lose 'er.'

'I've tried,' Garcia said quietly, 'and she won't listen.' He moved round the desk to face Willie, looking at him intently. 'There's something special about you, young Garvin. Something she can see in you. I can't name it, maybe neither can she. It's not your bright blue eyes and manly figure but it's there. I think you're the only one who can do this for us, and you've got to try. I can't tell you how, just go away and figure it. You've got an instinct, so use it.'

Willie Garvin opened his mouth to speak, then closed it again. Garcia went back to his chair. A minute passed in silence, then Willie said in a low voice, 'Christ, we mustn't lose 'er.'

He moved to the door, and as he reached it Garcia said,

'Willie.' When he turned, waiting, Garcia went on, 'I wasn't going to say this now, but I will. If she lives, *The Network* will thrive. We'll all get richer than we've ever dreamt of. But sometime in the next ten years, maybe less, she'll close this organisation down. Between now and then she's going to need a friend, a close friend. It can't be me or any of the others. Our relationship is set. But it could be you. It could well be you because your relationship is developing. She does combat workouts with you, and I think the chemistry's right.' He glared suddenly, chin thrust forward. 'Don't read anything bloody stupid into what I'm saying. Don't start getting fancy ideas. She's untouchable. You understand me?'

Willie was looking at him, open-mouthed. 'Me? Jesus, Rafa, you gone off your trolley? I couldn't even think of 'er like that.' His shock became tinged with anger. 'What she's done for me, she's given me a *life* to live. She's ... I mean, she's ... you know.' He gestured helplessly.

'She's the Princess,' Garcia said softly. 'That's fine, Willie. Keep it so, and remember what I said. The Princess needs a friend.'

*   *   *

The villa stood on a hillside, facing down a pine-clad slope to the sea. When Modesty Blaise bought it she had renamed it *Pendragon*, a name from the Arthurian legends. This was in memory of Lob, the old Jewish professor from Budapest, a refugee with whom she had roamed the Middle East throughout her teens, protecting him, providing for him, and being educated by him.

She was thinking of him now as she rose from the desk in her study and moved to the window overlooking the gardens and the pool. Three years and more since she had buried him in the desert, but she still missed him, for since losing Lob she had been without a companion. For a female of her age to create and control *The Network* had called for a rigid distancing of herself from the men who served her. This was the price of survival and she had paid it willingly, but there were times when she would have been deeply thankful for a chance to relax, to talk easily and without having to maintain her Network persona, as she had talked with Lob throughout the long days and nights of their wanderings.

It was early evening, the air was warm and the pool inviting. Weary of the paperwork on her desk, she was tempted to forget it and spend half-an-hour in the pool when she saw a small car take the curve in the road that ran past the gates of *Pendragon*. It was Willie Garvin's car, and she felt surprise tinged with pleasure at the sight of it. He had made no appointment to see her here at the villa, yet she found herself hoping that he was not just passing but in fact had some reason to call.

She was at her desk when the intercom buzzed a minute later and Moulay's voice said, 'Mr Garvin is here, Mam'selle. He apologises for the intrusion but would be grateful if you could spare him a few minutes on an urgent matter.'

She decided that a pretence of annoyance was unnecessary, and said, 'All right, Moulay. Send him up, please.'

While she waited it occurred to her that Garcia would have told him of his promotion and he might wish to thank her . . . but no, Willie Garvin was far too intelligent to describe that as urgent. There came a tap on the door, and when he entered in response to her call she once again found herself marvelling at the difference between this man and the man he had been when she bought him out of a Thai gaol only a year ago. Despair had been replaced by zestful confidence, and he had given her brilliant service in a variety of Network operations.

She nodded to the easy chair facing her desk and said, 'Hallo, Willie. Sit down.'

'Thanks, Princess. I 'ope this isn't putting you out.'

'Well, not so far. I like dealing with urgent matters before they get worse.' She studied him, intrigued to see that he was nervous, as he had not been from that moment a year ago when she had given him a place in *The Network*. 'I take it Garcia's told you you're to run in tandem with him from now on?'

'He told me this morning. I'm really grateful.'

'You've more than earned it. Now what's come up to bring you here in a hurry?'

He rubbed a hand across his mouth in a troubled gesture. 'It's difficult. I don't know 'ow to . . .' he broke off, shaking his head. 'Well, I need a favour, Princess. A big one.'

She felt surprise and disappointment. 'Money?'

'Oh blimey, no. You pay me 'andsomely, and then there's the bonuses, and I don't spend a lot. I—um—well, I need your permission for something.'

She leaned back in her chair, not allowing her puzzlement to show. So it wasn't money. Good. But what then? An idea for a Network job? If so, why the obvious unease? She said, 'Permission for what?'

He started to speak, stopped, looked away, then sat in troubled silence. After a while she said, 'Willie?'

He sighed, and looked at her again. 'It's no good, Princess. I'd better leave it.' He got to his feet. 'I shouldn't 'ave come. I'm sorry.'

She said sharply, 'Sit down, please.' When he slowly obeyed she sat looking past him, her mind racing as she sought a decision. Impossible to guess what the favour he wanted might be, but of two things she was utterly certain. First, that it would not be to her personal detriment, and second, that it would not be to the detriment of *The Network*. After thirty seconds she came to a conclusion and said, 'All right, you've got your favour. Now what is it?'

He seemed taken aback for a moment, then said quickly, 'I just want to go to Lima with you to sort out this creep Bellman.'

For a brief instant she was simply a very young woman suddenly startled and indignant, then Modesty Blaise of *The Network* was back, staring at him, tight-lipped and narrow-eyed. 'You *conned* me, Garvin!'

He made an apologetic gesture. 'No. I would've done, but I couldn't figure a way. Honest.'

'Did Garcia put you up to this?'

'He just told me the Bellman story.'

'And you decided to interfere in my personal affairs?'

Willie Garvin drew in a long breath, as a man might do before throwing dice on which his life depended. He said doggedly, 'I just think it's barmy for you to go after Bellman on your own, saying it's personal and not Network business. If you get signed off *The Network* dies. Worse than that, it turns bad because you're not there to set guidelines.' His words came ever more quickly as if he feared she might stop him. 'Look, it's important to a lot of people that you stay alive, and that's why I wanted a favour so I can be there with you in Lima for back-up.'

Modesty Blaise stood up, and he was immediately on his feet as she moved to the window and stood there with her back to him, holding her elbows, a posture he had often seen when she was thinking intensely. Watching her now, he closed his mind to the dread that she might send him away, he simply stood watching her for the pleasure of it, a pleasure that held not the slightest shadow of desire.

She wore a pale yellow blouse, a denim skirt, and sandals, her legs bare. The raven-black hair was coiled in a chignon to reveal the splendid column of her neck, and her only jewellery was an amethyst pendant. She was not particularly tall, perhaps five feet six, but he knew the elegant proportions of her body for she wore a leotard when they met twice a week for a technical combat workout in the gym attached to *The Network*'s small private hospital. The workout was an hour-long and very businesslike affair, greatly intriguing to her front-line men such as Krolli, Nedic and Sammy Wan, who often found excuses to be in the gym at those times.

Remembering, Willie marvelled again at her speed and mastery of timing, above all at her unique combat ability while in retreat. This was a gift acquired during her childhood struggles no doubt, but one that made her as dangerous an opponent as any he had faced.

Two minutes had passed when she said, 'Were you faking when you got up to go without telling me the favour you wanted?'

'No, Princess. I just realised I couldn't expect you to make a blind promise, that's all. It was genuine.'

'So you were giving up?'

'Well, not exactly. I reckoned on tailing you to Lima so I'd be on hand for when you tackled Bellman. Or maybe I'd get to 'im first.'

'Keeping me alive for the good of *The Network*?'

A pause. Then, 'No. For me own sake. You're my lifeline.'

There was another long silence. At last, without turning, she said, 'Have you any Network business to attend to this evening? Garcia mentioned a job he wanted done.'

'Oh, that was sorting out a couple of heavies working for a pimp who was trying to get Claudine on his books, but I cleared that up this afternoon.'

'Young Claudine? One of our couriers?'

'Yes.'

'What did you do?'

'Picked up the heavies and the pimp, then hired a plane and flew them down to Tahala. Old man Saad's got 'em, and he's leasing them to Fuad's tribe for six months. Some of those nomads 'ave unusual tastes, so they'll find out what it's like. I told Saad you weren't asking for any commission.'

She turned to stare at him, and he saw amusement in her eyes. 'Danny Chavasse is always telling me that you have style—not that I need much telling. But I didn't know you were licensed to fly.'

'Five years ago, Princess. An American lady financed it so I could spring 'er useless son who was doing fifteen years in a slammer north of Duranzo, in Uruguay. She picked me up when—' he broke off. 'No, it's a long story. Sorry. Anyway, that's 'ow I got licensed, and I've done crop-dusting and a bit of gun-running since.'

She moved to the desk and said, 'Do you have anything personal on this evening?'

He smiled. 'Any time you want anything done I'm free, Princess.'

'Well ... there seems to be a lot I don't know about you, Willie Garvin, because you haven't been handing it out. Useful stuff, maybe. I'd like you to have dinner with me here this evening so we can talk. Nothing special. Just talk as it comes.' For a moment he thought he saw her almost smile for the first time. 'I don't get much chance for that, I'm afraid,' she said, and lifted a hand as he started to speak, 'but this isn't an order. I don't give orders outside Network business.' A dark eyebrow lifted in query above a midnight blue eye. 'Well?'

For a moment he stared in blank incomprehension, then gave a shaky laugh. 'When I came 'ere just now I thought I might end up getting the elbow, and I'll never be more scared. Now this. I don't know what to say, Princess, except yes please. It'll be a privilege.'

She pressed the intercom on her desk, and when Moulay answered she said, 'Two for dinner, Moulay. Mr Garvin is joining me.'

'Very well, Mam'selle. In half-an-hour?'

'That's fine.'

As she released the button Willie said with a touch of anxiety, 'And it's all right about me coming to Lima with you?'

There was a hint of warmth in her voice, something he had never detected before, as she said, 'It's very much all right. You've put a new perspective on it, and I'll be glad of your company. Now let's walk in the garden and talk till Moulay's ready for us.'

*   *   *

At nine-thirty Modesty Blaise poured fresh coffee and passed Willie his cup. She noted with satisfaction that throughout the leisurely meal he had drunk only two glasses of wine and that his manner had been as she would have wished, increasingly at ease but with no hint of presumption. A few moments ago, when Moulay had brought in a large envelope and a pair of surgical gloves, Willie had shown a touch of surprise but asked no questions.

Now she said, 'When you're ready I want you to put the gloves on and take out the report you'll find in that envelope. It's about fifteen pages long, and I don't want any fingerprints on it. Not yet.'

The document was in Spanish, but she already knew that he spoke four languages, including Arabic, with fair fluency and had a useful smattering of two more. With only an orphanage education he was remarkably knowledgeable in a wide variety of fields. 'I seem to pick things up fast,' he had said almost apologetically, 'and they stick. I don't forget anything.'

She knew this was true. In the middle of a large-scale Network battle with the Saafi mob she had heard him deliver an entertainingly appropriate quote from the Psalms, giving chapter and verse. The insouciance of it had inspired confidence at a critical moment. Later she learned from Danny Chavasse that in his youth Willie Garvin had spent several months in a Calcutta gaol with only a psalter to read. He knew the Psalms by heart, and could produce a quotation for every occasion. The humour of his choice was much appreciated by his peers in *The Network*.

Now he finished his coffee without haste, then put on the gloves and took the stapled sheaf of paper from the envelope. Modesty said, 'Take your time. I'm going to phone Garcia.'

He rose with her, waited till she had left the room, then sat down and began to read. Twenty minutes passed before she returned, and he was standing by the French windows, looking out over the moonlit gardens. The envelope lay on the table. She gestured for him to take one of the two armchairs that stood on either side of the windows, and seated herself facing him in the other chair.

'I've decided,' she said, 'that I can't tempt Bellman into trying to kill me. If he did try I could react and put him down, but I've been through that scenario before and he just runs. So now I'm hoping to get him put away officially for a long stretch. It's too good for a mass murderer like Bellman, who specialises in getting children hooked, but it'll have to do.' She paused, and when he made no comment she went on, 'I was waiting for you to say that someone else will take his place.'

Willie shrugged. 'It doesn't need saying, Princess. You know it, I know it, but I'm all for putting Bellman away so I'm not coming up with arguments against it.'

'Good. Well, let's suppose you're an area chief of police in

the Lima Department, where Bellman now lives. You're no doubt
on the take from various racketeers, including him, so you won't
put him away for any ordinary criminal offence. But you're under
a strict military government, so what would you think if you read
that document?'

Willie said, 'It's a lovely job. I'd think Bellman was the key
man in a powerful underground movement dedicated to over-
throwing the government in a lightning coup. I'd see a realistic
scenario with a network of thirty-odd cells funded by Bellman.
If I was chief of police there I'd run to the military boss of the
area fast as I could go, and I'd reckon on Bellman being arrested
within an hour of the military seeing that document. If he's lucky
he'll end up in a labour squad.'

She said, 'No questions?'

'Well, I take it the paper's of local manufacture and you've
got the typewriter. You'll be aiming to plant them both on Bellman with 'is prints on 'em. I don't know 'ow, but you must've
'ad someone out there to do a close recce of the set-up for you.'

She nodded. 'Danny Chavasse has been working on one of the
maids. You'll like his report, it's a masterpiece of detail.' Willie
grinned. Danny Chavasse was a genius with women and had
been away for the past six weeks. Deservedly he ranked high in
The Network, and he had been a good friend to Willie.

Modesty said, 'I plan to leave next week, so we'll spend quite
a bit of time going over Danny's report and working out our
options. Are you clear for that?'

'Yes, Princess. You spoke about maids just now. Do they live
in?'

She looked at him with approval. 'Right. We don't scare
women if we can help it, but in fact there's no live-in female
staff. However, there is a female, a girl about nineteen called
Sandra. She's been with Bellman for years now, but according
to Danny she's not his mistress. The maids assume she's his
daughter, so maybe she is, except there's no record of his ever
having been married.'

Willie said, 'What do we do about 'er?'

'We'll just try to leave her out of any activity, but whatever her status she's connected to Bellman, so if she gets a fright, tough. We won't harm her, but we can't pussyfoot around.' Modesty got to her feet. 'Time you went home, Willie. Collect a copy of Danny's report from my office first thing in the morning, start thinking, and I'd like you to be here tomorrow evening, same time.'

'Sure, Princess.' He had risen with her. 'One thing. You wouldn't use Network people but you put Danny Chavasse in.'

For a second time she almost smiled. 'Danny was never at risk, never even in the house. He's a bedroom warrior, and there's nobody can match him in that. I would never have put in a combat man—well, not till you twisted my arm this evening.'

'I was worried,' Willie said gently. 'Really worried.' He stood looking at her uncertainly for a moment, then, 'Thanks very much for 'aving me to dinner. It's been great.'

She inclined her head in acknowledgement, then moved with him to the hall and the front door.

'Goodnight, Willie.'

' 'Night, Princess. Thanks again.' She watched till he had moved out of sight on the way to his car, then closed the door and stood holding her elbows, gazing absently across the hall. Moulay, passing through to the dining-room, glanced at her but did not speak. He knew she might stand lost in thought for ten minutes or more.

She was still there and he was unloading a second tray of crockery and glasses in the kitchen when she roused from her reverie at last. 'And thank *you*, Willie Garvin,' she murmured thoughtfully.

*   *   *

The house stood four miles from the centre of Lima. It had been built only a hundred years ago but was in Spanish Colonial style with large grounds and a high perimeter wall pierced only by heavy wrought-iron gates opening on to a drive. A strong chain secured the gates.

At three in the morning security lights on the walls would

normally have reacted to any movement, but Willie Garvin had shorted out the circuit activating the sensors. Now, with rope and grapnel, he and Modesty were on the balcony that ran round three sides of the house. Both were in black combat rig, wearing a small backpack and ski-mask. Neither had spoken since coming over the wall. They knew the layout of the house and grounds, knew the security system and the guard arrangements, knew that Bellman and the girl who might be his daughter were in the house. They also knew that situations could change and that in spite of careful preparation there could always be unforeseen problems.

One had already arisen. It was routine for a man to patrol the grounds and another to patrol the balcony. Tonight, for whatever reason, both men were on the long balcony at this time, and one had turned a corner just as Modesty was climbing over the balustrade in the belief that a single guard was at the far corner as she did so. Because she had abnormal speed of reaction she had reached him before he could cry out or draw his gun, dropping him with a strike from the kongo, the small mushroom-shaped piece of hardwood gripped in her fist, a weapon Willie had made for her that was devastatingly effective used against nerve-centres.

She was giving the man a shot of barbiturate that would keep him asleep for an hour as Willie came up the rope to join her. Together they moved to the corner where the balcony turned and peered warily round. The second guard was twenty paces away, leaning on the long balustrade, smoking. Willie touched Modesty's shoulder and gestured to something he held, something dark and limp hanging from cords or thongs. He stepped back and began to twirl it round his head very fast, then stepped out from the shelter of the wall. The limp object seemed to double in size with a thong flying free. Willie nodded to her, and she moved out to see the guard lying unconscious on the balcony floor.

Understanding dawned, and she whispered, 'Sling?'

He nodded again, his voice low. 'Lead-shot moulded in a ball of wax. It's quiet and doesn't kill.'

Together they moved to where the man lay. She knelt, opening the little leather box holding half-a-dozen charged syringes, wondering at what she had just seen. A sling? She knew his ability with a thrown knife and with the little wooden clubs he sometimes used, but in the year since he joined *The Network* he had never spoken of being skilled with a sling. This was something new to intrigue Krolli and his men.

A minute later they were at the French windows of a spare bedroom according to Danny Chavasse's plan. Bellman appeared to place great reliance on his guards, for the windows simply had interior bolts and these caused no delay when Willie had cut a small quadrant from the glass. Using a pencil torch, Modesty led the way across the room and out into a corridor where a low-wattage wall-lamp burned. She halted, handed a syringe to Willie, and moved off to the right, towards the bedroom used by the girl called Sandra. Willie moved left towards Bellman's room. She had given him the job of dealing with Bellman because a glimpse of a female figure, though masked, would identify Modesty Blaise for Bellman, and this was better avoided.

Willie paused at the door and very carefully eased the handle round. As he inched the door open a hinge squeaked. He stopped, waited, then began again. As he crossed the threshold the light went on, and he was gazing at a girl with luxuriant dark brown hair who lay in a double bed. Her feet were towards him and she was almost prone, but with her head turned to look over her shoulder towards him, one arm reaching out to a light-switch set in the bed-head.

Her eyes were wide and startled as she stared for a bare moment at the masked figure, a moment in which Willie knew that Danny's information regarding the bedrooms was wrong, or there had been some change. This was the bedroom of Bellman's girl. She had woken at the creak of the hinge and now she was flinging aside the bedclothes to free herself as she lunged towards the bedside cabinet where an automatic lay.

Evidently Bellman's reliance on his guards was less than total after all, and the girl's hand was almost on the gun when Willie's forward dive brought him within reach of her foot and he hauled her back across the bed on her stomach, the nightdress rucking up to her waist.

He pushed the ankle he held down behind the knee of her other leg, bending that leg back towards her buttocks so the ankle was trapped in the crotch of the knee-joint and he could hold her in position with one hand. She was struggling and panting now as he said quietly in Spanish, 'Do not be afraid, señorita. You will not be hurt.'

The needle went into her buttock and she gasped, head turned to glare back at him with mingled rage and shock, both transformed to bewilderment as he went on reassuringly, 'Let us count backwards from ten to one, señorita. It prevents insomnia.' She began to struggle again as he started counting, but then her eyes glazed, her head drooped to rest on the bed, her body went limp.

Willie heaved a sigh of relief, pulled her nightdress down, eased her to a sleeping position in the bed, and drew the bed-clothes up about her. He put out the light and went from the room, closing the door after him. She would sleep for a full two hours, perhaps longer.

The door of a room along the corridor was open and the light was on. When Willie entered he found Modesty putting away a hypodermic. She had taken off her ski-mask, and now he pulled off his own. A man in his middle forties lay unconscious on the bed, a good-looking man with dark hair and a strong square face. Willie said, 'Did he see you, Princess?'

She shook her head. 'I woke him up with the torch shining in his eyes and put him out with the kongo when he lifted his head.' She put the syringe-case away in her small pack. 'Not that it really matters. He'll guess.' She stood looking down at Bellman. 'It was a surprise finding him here. Danny got the rooms wrong.'

'Well, making sense of what a Spanish maid says when you can't ask straight questions . . .'

He let the words fade as she gave him a look that seemed almost to hold a touch of affection. 'I know that, Willie. You don't have to defend him. How did you manage with the girl?'

'Okay, but I gave 'er a fright. The door creaked and woke 'er up, then the light went on and she saw me and dived for a gun, but I got to 'er in time and hauled 'er back before she could reach it.'

'She's all right?'

'Asleep, but fine.' He thought for a moment. 'Got a nice bottom.'

She looked at him, amusement sparkling in her eyes, and for a moment he thought he might see her laugh for the first time. Then she shook her head, patted his arm and said, 'Let's get on with it.'

Ten minutes later Bellman lay on the floor in his study. He now wore a dressing-gown over his pyjamas and a slipper on one foot. Another slipper lay nearby as if it had fallen off. He was close to one end of a pedestal desk, an arm outstretched with the hand hidden beneath the pedestal. Clutched in the hand was a slightly crumpled document of fifteen pages. A portable type-writer, carried in Willie's backpack and now bearing Bellman's fingerprints, stood on a side table.

Modesty watched as Willie crouched by the big safe set in one wall of the room, securing a thick ring of plastic explosive round the lock. When he was satisfied he inserted a small detonator and unreeled thin flex across the room to a power point, plugging the transformer at the end of the flex into the socket. Modesty rolled up the thick rug by the fireplace and together they arranged it carefully over the safe. Willie moved a heavy filing cabinet across the study and stood it against the rug.

When he switched on at the power point the explosion was surprisingly muffled and undramatic. He moved the filing cabinet away, the rug fell to the floor, and the safe door opened easily when he pulled on the handle. 'We're in luck,' he said. 'Can't always get it right first time.'

'You earn your luck,' she said. 'Nice work, Willie.'

'My pleasure.'

They went quickly through the contents of the safe, taking the few thousand American dollars and a number of significant records, scattering other material between the safe and where Bellman lay. Modesty crouched to put the selected papers in her pack. 'I'll pass these on to a man called Tarrant I've done business with,' she said. 'He can circulate the drug enforcement agencies, maybe nail some other distributors.'

She looked round the study. All was arranged as planned. She and Willie had worn surgical gloves and left no fingerprints. An observer of the scene would readily deduce that Bellman had been attacked and robbed, and that he had been trying to hide an important document when he passed out. She said, 'All right, make the call now. Here's Captain Candela's home number.' She passed him the telephone pad on the desk.

Two nights earlier Willie had climbed a telegraph pole fifty yards from the western wall of the grounds and fixed a radio bug to the wires serving Bellman's house. For several hours next day he and Modesty had lain hidden with a small receiver in woods bordering the road. Bellman had made several calls out, giving Willie an opportunity to listen carefully to his voice. As an unexpected bonus, one of the calls had been to Captain Candela, the area Chief of Police, revealing that Bellman addressed him by his Christian name.

Captain Candela was sound asleep when his bedside phone rang. He stirred irritably, and his wife jabbed him with an elbow. 'It's the phone, Javier.'

'I know, I know.' He rolled on his side and groped for the instrument. 'Candela here. What is it?'

A voice he recognised, urgent with panic, said, 'It's Bellman ... there's been a raid, Javier ... they've blown my safe, taken papers—' the voice dropped to a shocked whisper, 'Oh God, they're still *here*! I'll try to—'

Captain Candela, wide awake now, heard a clattering medley of sound, a hoarse cry, then the line went dead. He rattled the cradle without effect, then threw back the bedclothes, put on the bedside light and began to dress. If somebody had taken papers from Bellman's safe, Candela was extremely anxious to know if his name appeared in any stolen document.

Four miles away Willie dropped the phone on the floor near Bellman. Modesty knelt to fix a bug on the underside of the desk, then stood up to survey the scene. Willie said, 'I reckon he'll be along with a posse in about fifteen minutes. He'll be sweating cobs about there being anything in that safe to compromise 'im.'

She nodded. And when Candela saw the subversion document he would surely jump at the chance to distance himself from Bellman and gain kudos by shopping him. She said, 'Let's go and listen, Willie. We'll leave the front door open.' They were in the woods with the small receiver when three police cars drew up at the gates. Bolt-cutters severed the chain and the cars moved on up the drive. Soon they heard a medley of voices from the study where Bellman lay. At first there was a confusion of over-lapping dialogue, but then a voice other than Candela's, from a man who must have been standing close to the desk, said, 'He had papers in his hand, Captain. It is as if he took them from all the rest scattered here and was trying to hide them when he passed out.'

Candela's thin, distinctive voice said, 'Let me see.' There was a long silence. Rustling. Heavy breathing. Background sounds. Then, 'Is the telephone working, Sergeant?'

'Yes, Captain.'

'Clear this room. I must call Colonel Turina at once on a confidential matter of state security.'

Colonel Turina was the area Military Commander, and on Candela's mention of his name Modesty switched off the receiver. 'It seems to be working,' she said, 'and there's nothing more we can do. Thanks Willie. Let's go home.'

*   *   *

The seasons turned, *The Network* thrived. There were many and varied operations. Some were trouble-free, some proved highly dangerous. Neither Modesty Blaise nor Willie Garvin came through unscathed, for there were times when rival gangs, dealing in what Inspector Hassan called very dirty crimes, dealing in death and drugs and flesh, tried to move in on *The Network*. It was then that Modesty Blaise led her people to war, with no quarter asked or given, and in those times she and Willie Garvin were *The Network*'s most deadly weapons.

During those years there were changes in Willie Garvin. There

were changes in Modesty Blaise. A strange and rich companion-
ship developed between them, incomprehensible to many. Garcia,
who had been with her from the first day and loved her like a
daughter, understood completely and was a very happy man.

At last there came a time, as Garcia had predicted, when she
wound up *The Network* and retired to England—to a penthouse
in London and a cottage in Wiltshire. Willie Garvin bought a
pub called *The Treadmill* on the Thames near Maidenhead, 'My
favourite name for a town,' he had announced, and watched the
laugh-lines crinkle at the corners of her eyes, the laugh-lines that
were his gift to her. But to live without risk was not long endured,
and within a year they had been willingly coaxed into an
unofficial mission for the head of a British Intelligence department, a mission that came close to costing their lives, and in
which Willie had been wounded.

Sir Gerald Tarrant was thinking of that occasion, concluded
only a few weeks ago now, as he stood with binoculars to his
eyes, gazing down from the stand at Epsom. Willie Garvin was
walking towards the paddock with an elegant auburn-haired girl
in a green dress. He moved easily, so it seemed the flesh-wound
in his thigh had healed quickly, as Modesty had said it would.
Tarrant lowered the glasses and made his way down the steps.

Leaning on the paddock rail, watching the horses parade round,
Willie said to his companion, 'They call it the sport of kings,
but the truth is if they stopped all the betting today there'd be a
glut of cat's meat tomorrow and you could build a supermarket
'ere.'

The girl smiled. 'I believe you. Do you usually win?'

'Only the bookies usually win. I sometimes get lucky, though.
Mind you, it 'elps if you can read the tic-tac, but I mainly come
for the day out . . . and because you can get talking to people
easily.'

'As you've shown. And I won fifteen pounds on the last race,
so thanks for the tip.'

'My pleasure,' said Willie, then looked past her with mild
surprise. ''Allo, Sir G. Didn't expect to see you at the Spring
Meeting.'

'I have my vices, Willie. Am I intruding?'

'No, we just got chatting.' Willie looked at the girl. 'This is a friend of mine, Sir Gerald Tarrant, and you're Sandra . . . ?'

'Thorne.'

'Sandra Thorne.'

Tarrant raised his hat to her. 'Good afternoon.'

She smiled politely and inclined her head. 'A very good one at the moment. Will you excuse me while I go and see a man about some money?' She looked at Willie. 'Don't go away, I owe you a drink.'

She moved off, and both men watched her go, then Willie took out his programme and began to study it. 'I don't wonder the country's in a bad way,' he said, 'people taking a day off work to go racing.'

'It's a disgrace,' Tarrant agreed. 'Have you backed a winner today?'

'I'm not sure yet, but I'm 'opeful.'

'She's very attractive.' Tarrant gazed idly about him, then said quietly, 'I'd like to find a man called Bellman.'

'Look in Peru,' said Willie, still engrossed in his programme. 'Political prisoner with a labour squad in the emerald mines. Been there six years.'

Tarrant said, 'He got out last year when the government fell. I'm looking for him closer to home.'

'Not your field is it, Sir G.?'

'There's a lot of overlapping these days. My minister has asked me to give all possible help to the Drug Enforcement Agency, which I'm glad to do.'

'Well, if Bellman's out, the sooner you find 'im the better. He's quite a genius in 'is own nasty line.'

'Indeed. I was wondering if you might help.'

Willie looked up and grinned. 'Talk to my agent.'

'You no longer work for Modesty, she's made that very clear. Why refer me to her?'

'Up till she found me,' Willie said amiably, leaning back against the rail, 'I was a loser. From then on I got lucky. Okay, we're retired now, but I'd like to *stay* lucky, see?'

Tarrant sighed. 'I take the point. She's your talisman. All right, perhaps I'll talk to her but I doubt that she'll be helpful.' He saluted with his rolled umbrella and turned to move away.

Willie said, 'Try Sammy's Star in the fifth if you want a flutter.'

Three minutes later, when Sandra Thorne returned, she said, 'I see your friend's gone. Are you ready for that drink?'

'Parched.' He put the programme away and studied her curiously. 'Funny . . . I just 'ad a feeling I'd run into you before somewhere.'

'It must have been in another life.' She took his arm and they began to walk towards the bar.

*   *   *

It was the next day when Modesty stood with a gun to her shoulder and called 'Pull!' The voice-operated trap Willie Garvin had devised for her threw two clay pigeons at a diverging angle of forty degrees. The gun sounded twice and the clays shattered. She lowered the gun, opened it, and turned to the man who stood a little behind her on the clay pigeon layout.

Her cottage lay a hundred yards away across pasture she owned. Beyond was a winding lane that led to the nearby village of Benildon. She was casually dressed for shooting, as was her companion, Paul Crichton, a ruggedly impressive man in his late thirties with the look of one who had lived much in the sun. His gun, open, hung over one arm.

Modesty said, 'We're still level. Would you like another dozen each?'

He half-smiled and shook his head. 'I might find it more interesting if the clays could hit back.'

'Ah. Big white bwana prefer charging lion?'

He shrugged. 'Just something that adds a little spice to the game.'

She looked towards the cottage. 'Then let's go. You won't find much in Wiltshire to give you an interesting hunt.'

He surveyed her with raised eyebrows. 'No?'

She did not react, and they moved away together in silence.

Unseen beyond a tall hedge, a car was halted on the road
bordering the pasture. A driver sat at the wheel, and Sir Gerald
Tarrant stood by a five-barred gate that was flanked on each side
by the hedge. Again he was using binoculars, focusing on the
man and woman moving towards the cottage from the clay pigeon
shoot. He adjusted the focus, studied the two faces and muttered
an oath. Lowering the glasses he returned to the car and got in
the back. The chauffeur said, 'You're not calling on the lady
then, sir?'

'No. I've changed my mind.' *Or had it changed for me*, he
thought unhappily. 'Back to London, Reilly.'

As Modesty and Crichton reached the stables and outbuildings
she said, 'I'll fix an early lunch before we leave for town.'

Crichton said pleasantly, 'Fine. It'll save having to stop on the
way.' When they came to the cottage he left her to go to his car,
opened the boot and put his twelve-bore in its case. Closing the
boot, he glanced towards the cottage to check that she had gone
in, then opened the offside front door and leaned across to run
the palm of his hand over the surface of the passenger seat.
Reaching under the dashboard he threw a small switch, then
pressed a button set in the fascia. A fine needle sprang up through
a minute hole in one of the leather seams, ejected a clear liquid,
then vanished. Crichton wiped the seat dry with a clean rag,
closed the door and walked towards the cottage.

As he entered by the kitchen door he made an effort to maintain
an amiable demeanour and avoid showing anger at her Big White
Bwana remark. It had affronted Paul Crichton's macho self-image
and he would very much have enjoyed hitting her, but took
comfort in the reflection that a far more permanent and profitable
revenge lay ahead.

Three hours later Sir Gerald Tarrant sat at his desk looking at
two photographs lying side by side, one of a man, the other of
an attractive young woman. His assistant, Fraser, stood watching
him, a file under his arm. Fraser was a small vinegary man in
his early fifties who had two personas, a false one as an ingratiating wimp, a true one as a case-hardened cynic. The combination
had made him a very dangerous operative during his active years

as an agent in the field. At this moment he was in his second persona, gazing sourly at his chief.

'So you went down there and didn't see Modesty Blaise after all?' he said.

'Only at a distance. I changed my mind about speaking to her, Jack. Now observe a curious fact.' Tarrant touched one of the photographs. 'We know that Paul Crichton has had recent contact with the elusive Bellman. We also know that Miss Sandra Thorne, as she now calls herself, has a connection with Bellman going back many years. And at this moment Crichton is squiring Modesty Blaise and Miss Thorne is being squired by Willie Garvin.'

Fraser grunted assent. 'Which means?'

'Which means our friends Modesty and Willie don't know it, but they're in trouble. Bellman is after them for some reason. He's setting them up.'

Fraser sniffed. 'You're suggesting we warn them?'

Tarrant kept his eyes on the photographs. 'For anybody with an ounce of decency and self-respect it's the only course.' He looked up and shook his head irritably. 'I wish we could afford such luxuries, but I *want* Bellman. If he's going for our friends Modesty Blaise and Willie Garvin he might well run into problems that force him into the open. Have a close watch kept on them, Jack. Put it in hand right away.'

'Will do.' Fraser moved to the door leading into his own office. 'If it's not too late,' he added.

Tarrant put the photographs aside, wishing he didn't dislike himself so much at this moment. 'There's always that possibility,' he said bleakly. 'In which case we can only hope they survive Bellman's attentions.'

Fraser opened his door. 'That's their problem.'

Next morning found Tarrant in the foyer of a penthouse overlooking Hyde Park, speaking to Modesty Blaise's houseboy, Weng, who was also her chef and chauffeur. It was Tarrant's opinion that the young oriental could well have become a captain of industry had he so wished, and had he not so clearly preferred to remain in service to his highly unusual employer who trusted him with many large and demanding responsibilities.

'No, Sir Gerald,' Weng was saying politely, 'Miss Blaise was due home last night but did not arrive. May I take your hat and umbrella, sir? Miss Blaise would wish me to offer you coffee, tea, or perhaps—'

'No, no thank you,' Tarrant broke in hastily. 'Have you rung her at the cottage?'

'Yes, but she is not there, sir. I have also rung Mr Garvin, but it seems he did not return home to *The Treadmill* last night, as expected.'

'I see.' Tarrant hesitated. 'I—um—think they may have some trouble on their hands, Weng.'

'So I assumed, sir. It is not the first time. I shall wait, and listen out.'

'Listen out?'

'We have radio communication here, sir.'

Tarrant said unhappily, 'I feel their chances of calling you on it may be rather slight.'

'It is the routine laid down by Miss Blaise, sir.'

Tarrant gazed at the houseboy with some annoyance. 'You don't seem particularly worried, Weng.'

A bland, expressionless look. 'Certainly I am worried, Sir Gerald, but I am also inscrutable. I do not allow my manner or my expression to reveal that I believe you have dropped them in it again.'

Tarrant stared, then nodded and put on his hat, turning to the private lift which would carry him down to the reception hall of the block. 'How considerate of you, Weng,' he said.

* * *

Willie Garvin opened his eyes warily, then lifted hands to his aching head, discovering by so doing that his wrists were in handcuffs. Slowly he sat up on the bunk where he had been lying. Looking down at his much rumpled clothes he noted that he was still wearing the dress shirt and dinner jacket he had been wearing when he called to take Sandra Thorne to a charity film première followed by a dinner and dance. He had a feeling that this had been quite a long time ago now.

As the muzziness in his head began to clear he realised that the room was rising and falling very gently. Not a room, then, but a small cabin, dimly lit and well below luxury class. On first sitting up he had registered that Modesty Blaise lay sprawled on her back on another bunk barely an arm's length away across the cabin. She wore a grey skirt with a tartan shirt under a soft leather jerkin, flat shoes and dark tights. In view of his own situation Willie felt little surprise at seeing her. Clearly they were jointly in trouble. Sandra Thorne had arranged his own transfer to wherever he was now, but he had no idea who had done the same for Modesty.

Quietly he got to his feet and thumbed open one of her eyelids. He checked her breathing, felt her pulse, straightened the skirt rucked at her thighs, then looked about him. The cabin contained a small wash-basin, lockers, a door and a porthole. He moved to the porthole and looked out across a calm grey sea. It was a little before dawn, he judged, with a thin overcast of broken cloud. He could make out land no more than a few hundred yards from the anchored ship. No lights gleamed from the shore, and the line of land seemed to terminate when he peered to the right. An island, perhaps.

There came the sound of a key being put into the lock of the door, and in a moment he was back on the bunk, sprawled as if unconscious. Somebody opened the door and entered. He caught a hint of perfume, and knew it was Sandra Thorne. Then she spoke to somebody outside. 'Tell Mr Bellman they're still asleep.'

The door closed and he heard her move to Modesty's bunk. A few seconds passed, then her hand touched his face as she made to lift an eyelid. He caught her wrist, jerked hard so that she fell towards him, and chopped with the edge of his handcuffed hands to a point just behind her ear. Her sudden indrawn breath was exhaled with a barely audible grunt and her body went limp upon him.

He rolled her over on the bunk, got to his feet, lifted Modesty and put her over one shoulder, then moved to the door and opened it carefully. Best move was to get ashore for a start. Not much chance of being able to launch a dinghy, but if he could get overboard with Modesty she would soon revive in the sea. Once on land they could try to deal with the 'cuffs. She might have something to use as a lock-pick. Even a hair-grip might do.

He had barely stepped into the passage when a man came down a companionway ten paces away, a man with long dark hair and a band round his forehead, dark-eyed, with deep-bronze skin. He wore a grey shirt, jeans, and soft leather boots. There was a knife in a sheath at his belt, and he carried a carbine levelled from the hip. Willie nodded a casual greeting and turned to look the other way. A second man had emerged from round the corner of the passage, a bigger man, perhaps forty, with cold unblinking eyes. He wore a camouflage tunic and a baseball cap, and carried a 9mm. Uzi sub-machine gun with a folding stock, slung so that it rested at his hip for immediate use.

Willie gave him a friendly smile and went back into the cabin, emerging a few seconds later with Sandra cradled in his arms and muttering dazedly. With great care he propped her against the passage bulkhead. She gazed at him with bleary, uncomprehending eyes while he held her until her straddled legs gathered enough strength to support her. Then he let her go and smiled winningly at the big man with the Uzi.

'She 'ad one of her turns,' he explained, and went back into the cabin, closing the door. Seconds later he heard the key turn in the lock. Taking a handkerchief from his pocket he soaked it at the wash-basin, hauled Modesty into a sitting position on her bunk, and slapped the wet pad on the back of her neck. Then, awkwardly because his hands were 'cuffed, he began alternately to shake her and pat her face quite sharply.

'Come on, Princess,' he said firmly, 'this is no time to sleep it off. We've got to 'ave a talk. Wake up, there's a good girl.' Her eyelids flickered and she began to turn her head feebly to avoid his pats. 'Come on, where are we?' he demanded. 'Let's see you do your 'uman compass trick. Where's north?' She muttered something, and moved her 'cuffed hands to indicate a direction.

'There's a clever girl. Now tell Willie where you went to sleep.' He gave her a shake. Eyes half open now, frowning irritably, she pointed.

'South-east?' She muttered assent. 'So we could be somewhere off the west coast of Scotland? Is that what it feels like?'

She stiffened slowly in his grasp, drew in a long breath and opened her eyes wide. She looked at Willie, at her 'cuffed hands, then round the small cabin. He watched her begin controlled breathing as she drew on her deeper energies to bring her to full alertness, and a minute later she said in her normal voice, 'Yes, that's about what it feels like. How did we get here?'

'Don't know about you, Princess. I got picked up by a girl called Sandra who slipped me a mickey in a drink she gave me at 'er flat.'

Modesty said slowly, 'Paul Crichton . . . I was in his car, and . . . oh God, yes.' She winced at the memory and tried to feel her buttock. 'Needle in my backside. Last thing I remember is thinking I'd sat on a wasp.' She got to her feet and moved to the porthole. 'This was planned well in advance and with no expense spared, Willie. I'd say we're on a motor fishing vessel somewhere north of Glasgow, and they brought us up here by helicopter under sedation.' She turned to look at him, and he was glad to see that her colour was good and her eyes clear as she said, 'Do you know who they are?'

He nodded. 'It's Bellman.'

She stared. 'Lima? Six years ago?'

'That's the one. He got out of the mines when the government fell. Tarrant's looking for 'im, and I just 'eard my friend Sandra say 'is name.'

'You've seen her, then?'

'Yes, she came in to check 'ow we were doing.'

'Did she say anything?'

'Not to me. I'd been awake a couple of minutes, but I made like I was out and gave 'er a chop. Then I was carrying you out to see if I could find a dinghy, or if not make a swim for it, but I ran into a Red Indian with a carbine and a mercenary-type with a Uzi, so I brought you back in and took Sandra out.'

She smiled and moved to sit beside him, giving him a pat on the knee. 'You've been a busy lad, Willie love.'

'And stupid, too, letting meself get picked up at Epsom.' He frowned. 'Who's Paul Crichton? I don't remember you mentioning 'im.'

'I met him only a few days ago. And don't brag, I'm just as stupid as you are. He's from Kenya. I asked him to come to the cottage, then wondered why. He's very macho. A hunter—' She broke off.

Willie said, 'A hunter?' They looked at each other with new speculation.

After a while Modesty said, 'Well, I don't suppose it'll be long before we find out.'

*   *   *

Crichton sat at the wardroom table polishing the steel butt-plate of a hunting rifle, already burnished by years of use. A little way from him sat the big man with the Uzi, smoking, his gun lying on the table in front of him. Occasionally he glanced at Crichton with a shade of contempt. On the port side of the wardroom was a man in a wheelchair with a blanket over his knees. His hair was white, his face lined and the colour of putty. He sat with hands clasped in front of him, sunken eyes fixed on the door.

It opened, and Modesty Blaise came into the wardroom followed by Willie Garvin with a carbine at his back. The redskin moved to one side and stood watching them, the carbine at his hip. Modesty and Willie surveyed the wardroom thoughtfully, then stood with eyes on the man in the wheelchair. After a moment or two he said in a throaty voice, 'Well . . . ?'

Realisation came with a shock. They looked at each other, then at the man again, and Willie said cheerfully, ' 'Allo, Bellman. How's your luck?'

Bellman spoke in a voice that was shaken by weakness and passion. 'Hard to recognise me, is it? A few years of hell in the mines and I'm an old man. *An old man!*'

Modesty said, 'I've seen junkies a lot younger who looked worse. Your clients.'

For all the reaction he showed, Bellman might not have heard. He said hoarsely, 'I've waited a long time for this. It was all that kept me alive. Now you're going to *die*, God damn you!' He did not take his eyes from Modesty as he went on, 'These are your hunters. Charlie Brightstar, Choctaw Indian. Best hunter in the States. Sooner kill a paleface than a bear. Van Rutte. Seven years a mercenary in black Africa. Good killing machine. Crichton . . . big game. A hunter with all the trophies—except a man or a woman.'

The door opened and Sandra came in. Bellman said in a gentle voice, 'Are you all right now, darling?'

'Just a headache.' She moved to face Willie, her eyes hostile. 'You still don't recognise me?'

He looked at her searchingly. 'Wait a minute . . . ah, yes, you've changed your hair colour. Lima, wasn't it? The girl on the bed.' He smiled apologetically. 'I didn't get much of a look at you that night. Not your face, anyway.'

She looked at him coldly, then turned away and moved across the wardroom to stand beside Bellman, a hand on his shoulder. He reached up to rest a hand on her own, eyes dark with hate as he stared at Modesty. 'You hunted me,' he said with bitter rage. 'You hounded me across the world . . . and then you *framed* me! I was innocent!'

'Innocent?' Modesty shook her head. 'You want us to bleed for you, Bellman? You handled three-quarters of a ton of heroin every year. You ran a training school, teaching your pushers how to get the kids hooked.' Willie saw Sandra stiffen, and it seemed to him that fury and shock were at odds within her as she looked uncertainly down at Bellman, then at Modesty again as she went on: 'You've killed them by the thousand, Bellman . . . but slowly. You rotted their souls. But you wouldn't ever see that end of it. You were just the big supplier. You didn't see the kids crawling to your pushers for a fix, ready to lick boots, steal, kill, anything—'

'*Stop the bitch!*' cried Bellman in a quavering scream, and

Crichton came out of his chair fast, hitting Modesty hard across the mouth with the back of his hand, eyes alight with pleasure. Her lip was cut, and she lifted her hands, pressing the back of a wrist against her mouth to stem the bleeding.

Willie looked at Crichton and said mildly, 'What was the name again?' In contrast to the voice there was something so truly chilling in his eyes that Crichton stepped quickly back. Then he recovered and forced a laugh. 'You won't come looking for *me*, Garvin. I'll soon be looking for *you*.'

Van Rutte said, 'And he won't be the only one. Here's your gear.' He picked up a haversack beside his chair and emptied it on to the table: a colt .32, a bowie knife, a waterbottle, and handcuff keys on a string.

In a voice trembling with malice and self-pity Bellman said, 'You hunted me! Now you'll learn what it feels like. You'll be put ashore on an island at ten. It's small, nobody lives there. You'll have your favourite weapons, Colt thirty-two for you, Blaise, a knife for Garvin. A bottle of water. Keys for the hand-cuffs.' Van Rutte put the items back in the haversack as they were named, and Bellman went on, 'You'll have two hours, then they'll be coming to hunt you down . . . *and kill you!*' His voice cracked on the last words and he swayed in his chair, panting, looking about him with crazed eyes. Sandra held his shoulder to steady him, deeply troubled.

Modesty said quietly, 'It wasn't the labour squad that ruined you, Bellman. It was having no guts. You just gave up, because you're a whinger and a quitter.'

Bellman tried to speak, but no word emerged. Sandra looked at the two captives with savage anger, then at Charlie Bright-star. 'Take them away,' she said. 'I don't want to hear any more lies.'

*   *   *

Modesty Blaise and Willie Garvin stood on a flat stretch of rock that made a natural landing place, watching the small launch as it headed back towards the ship anchored off-shore. On leaving her they had noted that she carried a Panamanian flag and was called *Ambato*. They were still handcuffed, and Willie was carrying the haversack. For a few seconds they studied their surroundings, noting the lie of the land, the distance to the ship, the set of the current, and estimating the time it would take to swim to the *Ambato* if at some stage they so decided.

Modesty gave a little nod, and together they turned and moved inland, up a short rocky slope then down into a hollow where they would be hidden from anyone watching with field-glasses from the ship. Willie took keys from the haversack and unlocked Modesty's 'cuffs, eyebrows lifting with a touch of surprise. 'I thought Bellman might be 'aving us on,' he said. 'Wrong keys.'

'They could well have been.' Modesty took them from him and freed his wrists. 'Bellman's half crazy. Eaten away inside.'

'Like a few thousand of 'is old customers, if they're still alive.' Willie took out the Colt and passed it to Modesty. As she checked the cylinder to see that it was loaded he rested the bowie knife across one finger to assess the balance. 'How d'you want to play it, Princess?' he asked.

'The long way, I think. Find a hole and disappear, maybe for a couple of days while they get swivel-eyed and impatient. Alternatively, we might swim to the ship after dark and take it over, leaving the Three Musketeers on the island. We don't want to prove anything, do we?'

'Well . . . not exactly.'

He spoke reluctantly, and when she saw him glance at her badly swollen mouth she knew his mind and said, 'Well, let's find a hole first, then see how things go.'

'Okay. We've got the best part of two hours.' He put the handcuffs in the haversack, the keys in a pocket of his dinner jacket.

Modesty said, 'We can pick up a little food to keep us going. Just easy stuff. Rock seaweed, shellfish, and maybe some nettles or dandelions.'

Willie grimaced. 'I might go on a fast. I was the least squeamish kid in the orphanage, but I wish I 'ad your stomach.'

She smiled and picked up the hem of her skirt. 'I had early

training in diet. Hack this off short for me, Willie. It's a pity I wasn't wearing slacks.'

He dropped to one knee and began to cut the skirt to above mid-thigh. There might be no immediate need for this if they were going to ground, but she was taking nothing for granted, and if action came sooner than expected she wanted no skirt to hamper her movements. When he had finished Willie put the cut fabric in his haversack on the principle that it might be useful. In circumstances like these, you could never tell.

* * *

At noon the ship's launch headed for the shore, an Asiatic seaman at the tiller. Brightstar sat with the carbine across his knees, silent and impassive. Crichton carried his hunting rifle and wore a wide-brimmed hat with a strip of leopard skin round the crown. Van Rutte nursed his Uzi and had changed his baseball cap for a camouflaged steel helmet.

On the deck of the *Ambato* Bellman sat in his wheelchair with Sandra beside him. A pace or two away, watching them uneasily, was the ship's master. Captain Ricco Burrera was a worried man with an ingratiating manner. He was well aware that whatever was about to happen was entirely illegal, in fact that it almost certainly involved a double killing, and he was concerned that this might, if discovered, be held against him.

He cleared his throat noisily to make his presence known and said, 'I hope there will be no troubles afterwards, señor.'

Bellman did not put himself out to turn and look at the man as he said, 'I own you, Burrera. You and your miserable ship. Go away and don't bother me.'

'Of course, señor. Thank you.' Burrera made a placating gesture and moved unhappily away.

Gazing towards the island, Bellman said, 'Soon be over now, my darling. Do you think I'm a wicked man to take revenge like this?'

'No!' She took his hand and spoke fiercely. 'You've been good to me since the day I came to you all those years ago, and they did *this* to you. They destroyed you. They're evil, and I hate them.' She hesitated, then went on with fading vehemence. 'I want them to know how it feels. I want them hunted and destroyed.'

There was a silence, and Bellman reached out to pat her hand. After a moment she said, 'It wasn't true, was it? I mean, what they said about you. About drugs.'

He turned his head to look at her, smiling a little. 'Can you even begin to believe it of me?'

She leaned over to rest her cheek against his. 'Oh, I'm sorry, please forgive me. It was just ... he seemed not the way I'd always imagined. Willie Garvin, I mean. Well, both of them.'

He nodded and squeezed her hand. 'Yes. They're very clever, you know.'

She straightened up and sighed. 'Of course. I was being stupid.'

*   *   *

Only by courtesy could the hide-away be called a cave. It was a broad, tapering slot running through a low spur of rock that projected into a valley bottom. The entrance was perhaps three feet high and twice as wide. Within, the roof rose briefly to five feet, then sloped down, and the width gradually narrowed to a smaller opening into the valley some twenty feet away on the far side of the spur.

Willie Garvin lay asleep, head pillowed on his folded dinner jacket. Modesty sat cross-legged near the mouth of the cave, holding the Colt in her lap, the haversack and bottle of water beside her. Willie stirred, opened his eyes and was immediately awake. He sat up and straightened his bow-tie. 'I feel a bit over-dressed for this caper,' he remarked. 'You fancy another little cat-nap for 'alf-an-hour, Princess?'

'No, I'm well rested now, thanks. Have you got a comb, Willie?'

He produced one from his jacket and crawled forward to sit beside her. She took the comb, pulled pins from her chignon and began to comb out her hair. 'Where had you been in that rig?'

'The dinner jacket? Oh, I bought a couple of tickets for us. That charity film première you fancied, with the dinner and dance after.'

She looked puzzled. 'You didn't tell me.'

'No, I rang Weng and he said you'd got a gentleman in the offing so I left it. Then when Sandra cropped up, I asked 'er along.' He grinned suddenly. 'Did Weng mean Crichton?'

Modesty frowned, tugging hard at her hair. 'I suppose so. Yes.'

Willie chuckled, and she said, 'Ha! Big joke! You got conned by Sandra, anyway.'

'Don't remind me. *And* I'd seen 'er before. Well, back view.'

Modesty sighed and began to plait her hair in two short pigtails behind her ears. 'I met Crichton three nights ago at a party and he made himself pleasant. He came to the cottage for some shooting yesterday morning, and by the time we left for town I was off him.'

Willie moved to kneel behind her. 'I'll do it, Princess. You 'ang on to the gun.'

She felt him take over the combing and plaiting, and remembered the first time he had done this for her, years ago in *The Network* days when she had been wounded and he had sick-nursed her. She said, 'Bellman's destroyed himself with hating us. It would have been better to put him down.'

'Much. Better for 'is customers and for us, too. But he wouldn't fight.'

'That was the trouble.' She was silent for a few moments, then, 'We never did find out who that girl is. It's just a feeling, but I don't think she was for sleeping with.'

'I 'ad the same notion.' He completed a plait and tied it with a thin strip from the off-cut of her skirt. 'D'you mind if I cut your jerkin up?'

She looked surprised for a moment, then understanding dawned. 'No, it's a good idea.'

A quarter of a mile away Crichton moved along the foot of a low ridge, rifle under his arm. Binoculars hung from his belt, and an object like a small radio was suspended from his neck so that it rested on his chest. From the top of it a twelve-inch loop aerial projected. Crichton halted and turned the aerial slowly, watching a dial set in the chassis beside it. A needle moved up the dial to a mid-point on it, began to fall, then rose again as he fine-tuned the direction of the loop. He looked up, sighted along the loop, then moved on.

In the cave, her plaits completed, Modesty sat watching from just within the entrance. Willie had cut a triangle and several thin thongs from the soft leather of her jerkin and was fashioning a sling. She said, 'I think we can have a mouthful of water each now,' and reached for the waterbottle. She uncorked it, moistened two fingers and tasted, then corked the bottle again. 'Willie, he's given us strong salt water.'

Willie knotted a final thong to a corner of the leather triangle. 'Well, if he's playing it that way . . .'

'Yes.' She broke open the Colt, shook out the cartridges and passed one to him. As he examined it she lifted the gun to look down the barrel. 'Don't bother, Willie, they'll be live all right. The barrel's blocked solid halfway down. He was hoping I'd blow a few fingers off.'

Willie started to speak, but she stopped him with a quick hand on his knee, then edged back and lay on her stomach. He eased down beside her, looking out into the sunshine. A hundred yards away at the top of a slight incline Crichton stood fiddling with a small black object that hung from his neck. After a few moments he took binoculars from his belt and looked directly towards the cave entrance.

They lay still, using material cut from her skirt as cowls to mask their faces, confident that they could not be detected in the deep shadows. Modesty whispered, 'He's using some sort of gadget and he's found us much too damn quickly.'

'Could be a little direction-finder. But we'd 'ave to be carrying something for it to home in on.'

She said, 'The water was salt, the gun was booby-trapped. That leaves the knife.'

He looked at the bowie knife, in his hand now. 'A homer, fixed inside the 'ilt.'

'And big white bloody Crichton didn't fancy clay pigeons

because they can't hit back,' she said, tight-lipped. 'Don't throw that knife, you might break the homer and it's too useful to waste.'

'That's what I was thinking.' He laid the knife on the ground. At the top of the slope Crichton had put down the mini d.f. He checked his rifle carefully, then began to move towards the cave, crouching, taking cover behind a boulder or in a shallow gully of the seamed ground as he moved.

Modesty said, 'He's putting on a nice act. Wants me to take a shot when he's close.'

'Then you get your 'and blown apart and he comes in quick over the last bit and blasts us while we're wondering what 'appened.'

She said softly, 'I really hate that bastard. All right, I'll play bait. You slip out the back way and take him from the flank.'

Crichton lay behind a low outcrop of rock, enjoying himself as he visualised what would be happening in the cave. They would have seen him, of course, but she was far too smart to use the Colt at long range. They would be watching his approach, confident that she could drop him before he could sight her, and then they would have his rifle to use against Brightstar and Van Rutte. He peered round one end of the outcrop, the binoculars to his eyes. Adrenalin was pumped into his bloodstream as he saw her hand and forearm resting on the ground fifty yards away, just clear of the cave's shadows. The Colt was in her hand, aimed in his general direction, but she would not fire yet.

He prepared for a quick dash forward to the next piece of cover, a low hump in the ground, then set off at a crouching run. This would bring him to within a dozen paces of the cave, and when he made the next dash she would surely fire. This would leave her hand shattered and Garvin briefly frozen by shock. Then it would be easy—

Crichton's thought ceased abruptly, for his senses were splintered and he was sent sprawling to the ground, stupefied by a savage blow from nowhere. Watching from the cave, Modesty caught her breath in surprise as she saw the missile that fell with him—not a pebble from a sling, but the full and heavy waterbottle, which had hit him squarely on the side of the head. Willie Garvin's accuracy in throwing was not confined to knife or club. He was equally capable with anything from a coin to a felling-axe.

The waterbottle was less damaging, less potentially lethal than a pebble sling-shot, and as Willie came into her field of vision, running hard, she knew he had chosen it simply to disarm Crichton for long enough to reach him. *Yes*, she thought, touching fingers to her bruised and swollen mouth, *that figures.*

Crichton had got to his knees and was peering about for his fallen rifle when a hand of frightening strength took him by the back of the neck. He was hauled to his feet and spun round to face a man in a stained and crumpled dress shirt, looking at him with blistering blue eyes.

Willie Garvin said, 'The name's Crichton, I believe?' Then his arm swung in a shattering back-hand blow across Crichton's mouth and the man was flung sideways as if by a silent bomb blast, unconscious before he hit the ground. Willie heard Modesty's approach and turned to face her, palms raised in placatory protest. 'Don't go on at me, Princess. The bastard 'it you while you were 'cuffed. I 'ad to get that off me chest.'

'You could always have had counselling,' she said solemnly, then smiled. 'I know, Willie love, and I'd smile more if it didn't hurt. You're so old-fashioned.' She looked at Crichton. 'D'you think his neck's broken?'

'Well, I wasn't trying for that, but I wouldn't shed tears.' Willie moved to examine the limp form. 'No, he's okay. Might need a bit of dentistry sometime, that's all.'

'Some people have all the luck. Let's get him into the cave.'

Two minutes later the bowie knife lay near the top of the slope where Crichton had first appeared. In the cave, Modesty lay with Crichton's rifle covering the area where the knife with its concealed homer had been planted. Behind her Crichton lay face-down, still unconscious, wrists handcuffed behind him. Willie sat beside her studying a hand-drawn map he had found in a pocket of Crichton's bush-jacket.

'It's a nice map,' said Willie. 'Relief shading and contour lines, but three straight lines dividing the island into three separate sections marked B, C and V. I reckon that means separate 'unting grounds for Brightstar, Crichton and Van Rutte, with us in Crichton's patch.'

Modesty relaxed slightly but kept her eyes on the ridge. 'That figures,' she said. 'We have to assume that Brightstar and Van Rutte also have d.f. gadgets, so they'd have been here by now if there were no restrictions. But why set it up like this?'

Willie frowned at the map. 'I wish we knew. It could be a big 'elp.'

Crichton groaned faintly and began to stir. Modesty turned her head to look back at him thoughtfully. 'Willie,' she said, 'I've just had a bit of an idea.'

A little under a mile away, Bellman sat in his wheelchair staring towards the island. Sandra came from the galley with a tray of cold meats and salad, setting it down on the small table beside him. He shook his head impatiently and lifted binoculars to his eyes.

Sandra shivered. 'I wish it was over,' she said in a low voice, and seated herself in the canvas chair beside him. After a brief silence she went on, 'May I ask you a question? It's strange, but I've never asked you this over all the years.'

Bellman lowered the glasses. 'What is it, darling?'

She gazed out over the sea, eyes focused on memories. 'I was . . . how old? Eleven, I think, when you bought me on the virgin market in Buenos Aires, child of an English-born prostitute recently murdered, father unknown.' She shook her head. 'I was so scared, but you never touched me. You just treated me as if I were your own daughter. Educated me, looked after me. And when I grew up you were never jealous about men, only caring and protective. Even while you were in the mines you made sure I was in safe hands with a good family. All the time you just gave, and you seemed to want nothing in return. Can you tell me why?'

Bellman gazed blankly at the far horizon. 'I suppose,' he said slowly, '. . . I suppose I needed somebody. Needed a friend.'

'You?' She was bewildered.

He smiled weakly. 'Somebody to care for. Somebody who would care about me, as you have done.'

'But you know hundreds of people. All kinds, all over the world. I don't understand.'

'All business acquaintances, Sandra. It isn't the same, you know.'

She bit her lip, looking towards the island with a troubled air as she put a hand on his. 'Do you have to go through with . . . what you're doing? Is it too late to stop? I just feel it isn't the kind of thing you've taught me. Oh, I thought I wanted it too, but now that it's real I feel different. This thing . . . it isn't *like* you.'

'Sandra, look at me.' His voice was ragged. 'Look at me and remember. I'm *not* like me any more, am I? Remember how I was? Do you want them to have done this to me and go laughing on their way?'

After a little while she said wearily, 'No. I hate them for it. But then I hate them all . . . Charlie Brightstar and Van Rutte and that Crichton creature.' She closed her eyes and leaned back in the chair. 'Maybe myself, too.'

*   *   *

Crichton was conscious again, and very unhappy. The fact that his face hurt intolerably was overshadowed by apprehension of worse to come. He had been searched by Willie Garvin who had taken his pipe, matches, wallet, keys, tobacco pouch and handkerchief. He lay on his front now, wrists handcuffed behind him, head turned to watch Willie's hands as they used one end of a thin leather thong to form a small slip-noose round the trigger and trigger-guard of the Colt, drawing the noose almost tight so that any further pressure would pull the trigger.

'Interesting, isn't it?' said Willie. He laid down the Colt, grasped Crichton's left ankle and bent the leg so that from knee to foot it was vertical. Craning his neck, Crichton saw him tie the other end of the thong round the raised ankle. He picked up the gun, thumbed back the trigger, and next moment Crichton felt the weapon being pushed down his back under the bush-jacket he wore. There was very little slack between the ankle and the point where the thong disappeared over Crichton's collar.

Willie turned to Modesty. 'The gun's not much cop for shooting,' he said, 'but it makes a ducky little bomb.' He smiled cheerfully at Crichton. 'You know something, bwana? You're definitely on our side now, because if we don't come back your leg's going to get tired and the gun'll go bang and you'll get a slipped disc or something.'

Sweat beaded Crichton's face as he croaked, 'For God's sake . . . !'

'Just don't wriggle,' Willie advised earnestly, adjusting his bow-tie, 'and keep your fingers crossed for us.' He picked up the map and haversack. 'It might 'elp if we knew how your mates are working, but I wouldn't ask you to grass on 'em.' He moved at a crouch towards the cave entrance. 'All set, Princess?'

'Let's get on with it.' Holding the rifle, Modesty made as if to leave the cave.

Crichton said desperately, 'Wait!' She paused, looking back at him impatiently, and he hurried on. 'We surveyed the island last week. Split it in three sections. We hunt independently, Bellman's orders. No poaching. You're in my area.'

Modesty gave him a hostile glare. 'He's playing for time, Willie. Use that knife to gut the bastard and let's get going.'

Willie nodded. 'Okay, I'll just disconnect the gun first—'

'*For Christ's sake it's true!*' Crichton broke in, his voice a screaming whisper. 'It's bloody *true*! We're being paid all expenses and five thousand each for the job. There's a bonus of another five thousand for whoever makes a kill. *Each* kill.'

Modesty said, 'Anything else?'

He gave a very minimal shake of the head, terrified to move. 'Nothing, I swear! But watch out for Brightstar.'

Willie said, 'There. I knew you wanted us to come back.' Modesty turned, crouching, and moved out of the cave.

Crichton panted, 'Oh Jesus, don't leave me like this!' From the entrance, Willie looked back at him. 'Like this you've got a chance,' he said grimly. 'And you were set to kill us. Don't tempt me.'

Outside the cave Modesty was squatting on her haunches studying the map. As Willie joined her she put a finger on it and said, 'Suppose we plant the knife-homer there?'

'Let's 'ave a look. Ah, yes. Just where Charlie Brightstar's shooting rights join Van Rutte's. Seems to be a long gully running across the demarcation line there.'

She nodded. 'So they should come from opposite directions, north and south, and we can lay for them.'

'Sounds fine.' They stood up and he said casually, 'I'll take Brightstar, then?'

'Willie, we're on a caper,' she said gently. 'That's when you stop being a courteous and protective gentleman. You've done enough of that for today. We think Brightstar is the sneaky one, and we have a rifle and sling between us. I can't use a sling or throw rocks. Whoever has the rifle must take Brightstar.'

Willie sighed. 'You're right,' he acknowledged. 'Sorry.'

'That's better. But let's not rush this. We're safe here in Crichton's territory so we'll let the others tramp about their patches for a few hours while we relax and they get frustrated.'

Willie grinned. 'You're a hard-'earted lady. But I'd better take that bomb off Crichton's back until we're ready to go.'

*   *   *

Van Rutte sat with his back to a rock in a shallow basin on a hilltop. The direction-finder stood beside him, the Uzi rested on his knees. He stubbed out a cigarette, adding to the six or seven butts scattered nearby. Van Rutte felt he was close to losing a bonus of five or possibly ten thousand pounds, and he was not pleased.

Two minutes later he reached out again for the hundredth time to swivel the aerial, but this time his eyes widened as the needle on the dial suddenly kicked. He picked up the instrument and stood carefully adjusting the aerial for maximum response, then moved off along the line indicated.

Almost half a mile away, Charlie Brightstar showed no sign of emotion as the needle on his d.f. moved for the first time since he had come ashore long hours ago. Without haste he adjusted the aerial, studying first the dial and then the map that lay to one side of the instrument. A few moments later he rose to his feet and moved without a sound from the patch of dry brown grass in which he had lain perfectly camouflaged for the past hour.

Van Rutte was moving warily along a broad gully some ten paces wide and with walls rising almost vertically to well above the height of a man. Its sides were seamed and broken, with many niches and crevices. A few minutes ago his d.f. had given such a strong signal that he was sure the homer Garvin carried could be no more than a hundred and fifty yards away.

Van Rutte moved warily, keeping close to one side, his Uzi cocked. Rounding a slight bend, he froze at sight of something lying in the middle of the gully, something black and fawn with . . . his eyes narrowed in puzzlement. That was the dinner jacket Garvin had been wearing, and on top of it was Crichton's bush-hat with the leopard-skin band.

Crichton? Was that bastard poaching? Surely not. That was a no-pay offence, and there had been no shot. But could he have taken Garvin silently? Rifle-butt at close quarters? Van Rutte edged slowly forward, the Uzi poised.

Lying prone amid low scrub on top of the gully wall, Willie Garvin frowned. It was, he felt, inconsiderate of Van Rutte to have changed his baseball cap for a steel helmet. It may well have been that he did not wholeheartedly trust his colleagues, but the effect was to disrupt Willie's plan of taking Van Rutte out with a sling-shot from above, for the helmet protected him from a downward-angled missile.

In the past, studying Modesty Blaise and her ways with great intensity when he first came to *The Network*, Willie Garvin had acquired a quality he lacked before. He had discovered, with much pleasure, the virtues of forethought. Today, as he moved into position for tackling Van Rutte, he had pondered the various options that might confront him. His quarry had lethal fire-power, and it might well be necessary to improvise some means of distracting his attention in order to get into sling-shot range.

The lure of the jacket and hat was a move in that direction, but Willie had not relied on that alone. Wriggling back from the edge he took Crichton's handkerchief from his pocket. The four corners of this were now attached to thin leather thongs cut from Modesty's jerkin to form a crude parachute. With some reluctance Willie unfastened his bow-tie, saddened to lose it, for till now he had felt that the black tie and dinner jacket gave a rare touch of style to recent events. It wasn't often these days, he reflected, that one could smite the ungodly while attired in faultless evening dress. Well, not exactly faultless, perhaps . . .

He attached one end of the tie to where the thongs of the parachute joined, held a match to the other end until it was smouldering nicely, then clipped that end in Crichton's box of matches so that it rested halfway down with the tie covering the heads. Carefully he rolled the matchbox and two pebbles in the handkerchief, then wriggled back to the edge of the gully. Van Rutte was standing by the jacket and bush-hat now, peering down at them, his back to Willie. After a moment or two he kicked the hat aside and stared north along the gully.

Willie stood up and hurled his little package high in the air beyond Van Rutte, then dropped amid the scrub again, watching. He had achieved a good height with the parachute, and as soon as it began to fall it opened nicely, the tie dangling from it with the matchbox attached. The two pebbles dropped to the ground, and at the small sound Van Rutte froze, head cocked as he tried to locate the source. The parachute drifted slowly down at an angle and was within twenty feet of the ground when Van Rutte saw it. The Uzi came up, covering the far wall of the gully beyond the parachute's descent. He was nailed, and Willie lowered himself quietly down to the valley floor.

Be nice if the matches lit now . . . he thought, and began to whirl the sling. Another quality he had long ago acquired from Modesty Blaise was a belief in the idea that inanimate objects could be perverse or co-operative according to one's attitude towards them. Don't curse the recalcitrant screw, give it a little affection. In consequence he had fashioned his parachute contraption with benign care and good vibes. If it failed him he would not complain, but he was cheerfully hopeful . . . and cheerfully grateful when the matchbox erupted in flame, engulfing the parachute as it fell the last ten feet, and holding Van Rutte's baffled attention.

During that time Willie walked steadily towards him as he stared at the dying flames, and was within five paces when the spell broke suddenly and Van Rutte swung round as if at some slight sound. He had barely completed the turn when a stone the size of a tomato struck like an iron fist to the solar plexus. The Uzi dropped and he doubled forward, mouth agape as he fought for breath. Willie reached over his back, grasped him round the waist, hoisted him up head-down, then dropped to his knees.

Van Rutte's steel-helmeted head hit the ground with considerable force, wiping out his already blurred senses and ramming the helmet down crushingly round his brow.

* * *

The homer-knife lay some three hundred yards north along the gully. About the same distance further on was a short broad branch running off the main gully, blind after twenty paces. The bottom was thinly grassed and surrounded on three sides by shoulder-high rock, opening into the main gully on the fourth side. Here Modesty Blaise stood close against the rock wall near the junction, Crichton's rifle held in the port position. She hoped Brightstar's d.f. had picked up the homer and that he would now be moving down the gully from the north, just as Van Rutte should be moving up from the south to where Willie lay in wait.

She stood relaxed, her mind empty except for tight focus on sight and hearing for the first hint of approach. She did not distract herself by speculating on what might be happening with Willie, and she knew he would not be wondering about her own task. For the time being her whole world consisted of waiting for Brightstar to appear. He would surely come along the valley bottom, for he was a hunter and would never move along the top, where he could so easily be seen.

Seconds later shock sent her pulse-rate leaping as a flat, unem-
phatic voice from somewhere behind and above her said, 'Freeze,
lady. Twitch and you're dead.'

Brightstar. She stood very still, using all her mental techniques
to subdue the self-contempt that welled within her and to waste
no energy wondering how he had located her. The unasked question was answered as the voice murmured, 'I'm Choctaw. Picked
up your smell at twenty yards. Where's Garvin? Just breathe it,
lady.'

'He's around.' She spoke barely above a whisper.

There was a tinge of satisfaction in the flat voice as Brightstar
said, 'That gives me head money on the two of you.' A brief
pause. 'Okay, we don't want any noise, so keep hold of the butt
and just lower the barrel. Easy now. Right down till it's touching
the ground. Don't let that rifle fall.'

She obeyed, holding the weapon at an angle with her hand on
the butt, the barrel resting on the ground. There came a faint
sound behind her and she knew that Brightstar had dropped down
from the gully wall. By moving the angle of the rifle fractionally
she was able to pick up his reflection in the polished steel butt-
plate. He was half-a-dozen paces away, his carbine aimed from
the hip. In a low voice she said, 'I'll double Bellman's price.
Ten thousand.'

He was edging slowly forward. 'For you and Garvin I get that
anyway.'

Watching the reflection she said, 'You haven't got him yet,
and I'm offering ten thousand each.'

'Cash? Now?' A hint of mockery.

'You'll get it. I keep a promise.' He was within two paces
now, changing his grip on the carbine, lifting it horizontally to
smash the butt against her head.

He said, 'I'm a redskin, lady. We had too many promises.'

'I know. I saw the movie—' She ducked as he took the final
step and swung the carbine in a crushing hook to her head. The
butt skimmed her hair as she let the rifle fall and stepped back,
twisting to drive an elbow into Brightstar's stomach. He gasped,
losing his grip on the carbine, and she thrust backwards into him

as he doubled forward, reaching over her shoulder to hook a hand round his neck, then jack-knifing forward to bring him over her shoulder with a head mare.

His speed of recovery was astonishing, for he twisted like a cat, landing on one foot, staggering, then snatching a knife from the sheath at the back of his belt. She had been lunging for the fallen carbine but glimpsed the move and flung herself sideways and down, the thrown knife passing above her neck to hit the rock wall behind her.

Brightstar dived at her as she started to come to her feet, his hands reaching for her throat. She fell back, feet lifted and crossed at the calves, catching him by the neck in the V between her ankles, twisting her feet to hold him, straightening her legs to thrust him back and in the same instant turning on her front with hands on the ground, pushing down to lift her body, then using her arms like legs to run forward in the way that children used to play wheelbarrow racing, pulling Brightstar off-balance behind her, his neck locked between her ankles.

In a second she was close to the gully wall, ducking head and shoulders in a forward roll, heaving Brightstar over her doubled-up body to ram the wall with the crown of his head. He fell limply on top of her and she pushed him aside, panting as she extricated herself and got slowly to her feet, lips compressed now as she allowed self-recrimination to flare within her.

There came a polite cough from above and she whirled to see Willie Garvin looking down. Beside him was Van Rutte, hand-cuffs on his wrists, a steel helmet jammed down so low on his brow that he could barely open his eyes. Willie was holding the Uzi. Nodding towards the sprawled figure of Brightstar he said, 'I just caught the end bit. You ruined a good scalp there, Princess.'

She sniffed, looked at a badly grazed elbow, flexed the arm and winced. Moving to Brightstar she checked that he was breathing, then turned and picked up the carbine, limping a little. Willie said, 'You all right?'

She looked up at him and grimaced. 'A lot better than I deserve. He had me cold but he got greedy. Wanted to sign me off without shooting so he could nail you for your head money too.'

Willie turned to speak to Van Rutte, emphasising his words
with rhythmic raps of the Uzi on the steel helmet. 'There. D'you
'ear that, Van Rutte? *Let the wicked fall into their own nets.*
Psalm 'undred and forty-one, verse ten.'

Modesty looked up at the sky. 'Sundown in half-an-hour. Let
Bellman hear what he's waiting for.'

Willie thought for a moment, then switched the Uzi to single-
shot and fired once. He returned to automatic, counted to ten,
and fired two short bursts in the air. Modesty was on one knee,
tying Brightstar's hands with his head-band. Looking down from
above, Willie felt a touch of concern. From the set of her shoulders he could tell there was something amiss. Tentatively he said,
'You really okay, Princess?'

She stood, turning her head to glower up at him. 'No I'm
bloody not!' She pointed to the unconscious redskin. 'He said
he could *smell* me at twenty yards!'

Willie suppressed a grin and gazed down at her with infinite
affection, vastly entertained by her outraged femininity and knowing it would never have surfaced for a millisecond if the caper
had still been running. 'Why shouldn't he, Princess?' he said.
'It's peaches and pomegranates warm in the sun, rose petals and
the bouquet of Chateau d'Yquem, honey and exotic spices.'

She laughed, all tension gone. 'That's lovely, Willie. Who said
it?'

Willie looked hurt. 'I just did,' he said.

*   *   *

On the deck of the *Ambato* Sandra had jumped at the sound of
the shots. Beside her, Bellman tensed for a moment, uttering a
wordless sound, then relaxed as if all energy were draining out
of him.

She said, 'Is it over? Both of them?'

He nodded slowly and it seemed an effort for him to speak.
'Both. They wouldn't have split up, not those two. They must
have been on Van Rutte's patch. The gun blew up in her hand,
then he finished them off.'

Two large canvas sacks, heavily weighted, now lay on the deck. Sandra looked at them and shivered. 'Are you really going to have them put in those sacks?'

'I thought of coffins . . .' his voice was dreamy, faraway, 'beautifully polished . . . brass handles, and plates with their names. Too good, though. Over the side in sacks. Much better. The sea shall have them . . .'

Captain Ricco Burrera came along the deck and saluted. 'I heard the—ah—noise from the island, señor. When do you wish for me to send the launch for your friends?'

Bellman gazed absently through him, and it was Sandra who eventually answered. 'In an hour. They'll need time to assemble and they have . . . things to carry.'

The captain inclined his head in acknowledgement, and as he did so Bellman suddenly focused upon him and spoke briskly. 'Ah, there you are, Salzedo. How did it go in London and Amsterdam?'

Bewildered, Burrera glanced at Sandra but she was looking anxiously at Bellman, a hand to her lips. Burrera cleared his throat and said, 'Excuse me, señor. I am not Salzedo and I have not been to London or Amsterdam. I am Captain Ricco Burrera— you know me well.'

Bellman's head began to nod foolishly. 'Good. Good,' he said, slurring the words. 'I'll see the supplies keep coming. Your job is to get them hooked, Salzedo. Get them hooked . . . what was I saying? Yes, always the young ones, the children, that's our basic training. Easy to get them on the needle . . . and they last longer as customers . . . as customers . . .' His voice faded and the nodding head became still as he sat gazing with empty eyes.

Burrera looked at Sandra, baffled. She was trembling. With an effort she took a grip on herself and said, 'He's been under a big strain. Help me take him to his cabin.'

*   *   *

An hour later Modesty stood by a low crag near the landing point, Brightstar's carbine cradled in one arm. The sun had set and a deep twilight lay over the sea. From where she stood she

could see the lights of the *Ambato* at anchor and the shape of
the launch creaming through the water towards her. A few paces
away Willie stood facing Crichton, Van Rutte and Brightstar.
The two pairs of handcuffs had been used to link the three men
together with Brightstar in the middle. Van Rutte's head was still
jammed in his helmet. Half Crichton's face was one huge bruise.

'Remember that cave where we picked you up, Crichton?'
Willie said conversationally. 'I left the 'andcuff keys on the
ground there somewhere. You'd better all go and 'ave a look.'
He smiled a cheery smile. 'Might as well say our goodbyes now.
We'll 'ave the ship under way long before you're back.'

Crichton tried to hold his voice steady as he said indistinctly
from swollen lips, 'What happens to us?'

Willie said disapprovingly, 'Well, Miss Blaise 'as got a nicer
nature than me, and she says we'll leave you the ship's dinghy
and a couple of oars. The rest's your problem.' He moved closer
to them, lowering his voice, and the humour was suddenly wiped
from his face. 'By Christ, you're lucky. Any of you come near
'er again and I'll rip your guts out, no messing.'

*   *   *

Sandra was sitting at the table in Bellman's cabin, her head in
her hands, her back to the door, when there came a polite tap
and Ricco Burrera entered. 'The launch is on its way back, señorita,' he said. 'Shall I instruct the gentlemen to report to Señor
Bellman here?'

She said wearily, 'Get out, Burrera. Just get out.'

Offended, Burrera looked across the cabin to where Bellman
lay on a low bunk, a blanket covering him to the shoulders. For
a moment the captain considered putting the question to Bellman,
then decided against it and went out. Moving along the deck he
muttered to himself indignantly. 'I am the captain of this ship.
One does not say *get out* to the captain of a ship. It is a position
of great authority. If I was not a man of iron control I would
have—'

He stopped short, his stomach contracting with fear, for on

turning a corner of the deck-housing he found the barrel of a carbine close to his nose, held by the woman he believed dead. Even in the dusk her eyes were very frightening. Beyond her was the big fair man who should also have been dead but who had a hunting rifle slung and was holding a sub-machine gun aimed at two seamen who were standing very still with their hands in the air.

Burrera drew in a deep breath, conjured up a sickly smile and spread his hands in a gracious gesture. 'Welcome back, señorita, señor. I am Captain Ricco Burrera at your service. If you wish to charter my ship it will be a pleasure to arrange most economical terms.'

Modesty said softly, 'The terms are that if you put a foot wrong you go over the side.'

The smile was maintained but became even more sickly. 'I am not a man to haggle, señorita. Agreed.'

'You've made a wise decision. How many crew?'

'Eleven, apart from myself.'

'Your men or Bellman's?'

'Mine, señorita, and cowards to a man. You need have no worry.'

'I haven't. What's your ship's radio?'

'A one kilowatt Telefunken.'

'Where are Bellman and the girl?'

'In his cabin. He is unwell.'

She glanced at Willie. 'We'll deal with them when we've got things moving.' Then to Burrera, 'Put a dinghy ashore with oars, and as soon as your men return you get under way for Greenock. That's the nearest port?'

'It is, señorita.' Burrera drew himself up and saluted. 'I will give orders at once.'

Twenty minutes later, when the engines began to throb, the girl in Bellman's cabin was sitting at the table with head pillowed on her arms, half-asleep, emotionally drained. As the ship stirred she lifted her head then let it fall again, unable to care what was happening. Behind her the door opened and closed. She said dully, 'What is it now, Burrera?'

A man's voice with a Cockney accent said, 'Nothing special.'

She sat up slowly, turning to see Modesty Blaise and Willie Garvin. Both were dishevelled and incongruous, she with her skirt hacked off to well above mid-thigh, he in his once-white shirt and soiled dinner jacket. Both were armed with the weapons of the men who had been sent to kill them. Already numb from shock, Sandra could feel only feeble surprise. She looked from one to the other, then said slowly, 'You won't believe me, and it doesn't matter anyway, but I'm . . . relieved.'

Modesty nodded towards the figure on the bunk. 'Does that go for Bellman?'

'No. It was being glad that killed him.'

Modesty and Willie exchanged a look, then he moved to the bunk and rested two fingers on the side of Bellman's neck. After a moment or two he pulled the blanket up over the man's face.

Sandra said, 'He thought you were dead when he heard the shots. Then he died happy.'

Modesty moved to the table and sat down, rubbing a bruised knee. The sleeve of her shirt was torn and there was blood on her arm. 'I wouldn't begrudge anyone that,' she said. 'Not even him.'

Sandra said, 'The others . . . did you kill them?'

'No. We've left a dinghy. If they row east they'll hit Scotland.'

Sandra absorbed this slowly, trying to comprehend, but the effort was too great and she let it go. Not looking towards the bunk where Bellman lay she said, 'His mind slipped at the end. He babbled things . . . about getting the young ones hooked on the needle.' She shivered, and tears began to run down her cheeks. 'It was true, then? He . . . he really did those things?'

Willie said, 'They don't come any worse than Bellman in that game. It's why we put 'im away.'

For a moment resentment flared in her. 'Who gave *you* the right?'

Modesty said without heat, 'About ten thousand junkies in general and a teenage girl murdered by two of them in particular.'

The spark of anger died, and Sandra wiped tears from her

cheeks with her fingers. 'I didn't know,' she said in a whisper. 'He was always so good to me. Always.'

Modesty gave a tired shrug. 'Maybe when you're destroying people at the rate he was, you need something or someone to keep your mind off it.'

Sandra drew in a deep breath, trying to steady herself. 'Yes. He said something like that himself.' She looked from one to the other of them. 'What happens now? To me?'

Modesty stood up with the carbine and moved a little stiffly to the door. There she paused to look back at the girl with something of compassion. 'What happens now is your problem, isn't it? We have nothing against you. Might be a good idea to go away for a while. Lie in the sun and think about how you start a new life. Not easy, but at least Bellman will have left you well provided for.' She looked at Willie. 'I'll go and call Weng. He can sort out some clothes for us and fly up to Glasgow, meet us in Greenock.'

She flexed her grazed arm gingerly. 'Sometimes I get sick of losing skin. Still, we can't blame Tarrant this time.' She opened the cabin door. 'Look after her, Willie.'

When the door closed there was silence for a while. Sandra sat with knuckles pressed to her cheeks, trembling a little, shaken by moments of weeping but trying to suppress it. Willie picked up a spare blanket and put it round her shoulders. She muttered a word of thanks but did not move. He said, 'Come on, Sandra, you can't stop 'ere. Let's get you to your cabin, then I'll rustle up some brandy and 'ot coffee.'

She rested her hands on the table and gazed down at them, perplexed. 'Nothing against me?' Her voice still wavered from shock. 'What did she mean? I was part of it, wasn't I? Part of having you killed?'

Very gently Willie took her arm and helped her to her feet. 'It's past, Sandra. All over.'

At the door she stopped, turning her head to look at him. 'I did. I took part in trying to kill her. Kill you both. And she just says go away and start a new life. Don't you hate me? Don't you want to *do* something . . . for revenge?'

Willie scratched his ear, searching for an answer. Then he glanced towards the bunk where Bellman lay. 'No,' he said. 'Look where it gets you.'

THE DARK ANGELS

The stretch of road where the killing was to take place formed one of the long curves that wound through the Sierra de Yeguas on the way to Malaga. Two miles north, an open Land-Rover moved steadily through the dusk shrouding the wooded hills. The driver, Macanaz, was an experienced minder who had lived in Chicago for fifteen years and learnt his craft there. For the past two years he had been employed by the man who now sat in the passenger seat beside him.

Kaltchas was fifty years old, half Greek, half Spanish and wholly cosmopolitan; a short square man, enormously rich, who had lost his wife and family to a poorer and less busy man ten years ago. Since then he had lived a reclusive life in one or other of his homes in different parts of the world, using the modern wonders of electronic communication to carry out the various business operations that were his sole interest now.

Half an hour ago he had left his home and staff of servants in the remote and beautiful house he had built outside the small village of Vanegas. His presence was required in Brussels next day, where his financial backing would ensure the four billion-pound hostile takeover by a European consortium of British Chemicals Ltd, the largest corporation of its kind outside the United States.

Kaltchas was a suspicious man, mistrustful, slightly paranoid. Aware of strong opposition to the takeover, he did not put it past his opponents to attempt some sort of delaying action by preventing his arrival at the Brussels meeting. Matters were finely balanced, and even a twenty-four hour delay could shake the market and create uncertainty in the consortium. It was for this reason that he had chosen to disguise his departure by travelling to the airport in the hired Land-Rover rather than in one of his limousines. Being a man who thought well ahead, he had made the arrangement some days ago, but was unaware that it had quickly become known to parties who were deeply interested in his travel plans though unconnected with the threatened corporation.

At the wheel, not taking his eyes from the unlit road, Macanaz said, 'Are you okay, boss?'

'I'm okay.' Kaltchas pulled the cap down more firmly on his head and buttoned the collar of the bomber jacket he wore.

The road was winding downhill now, with the rock from which it had been cut rising sheer on the right, the ground on the left sloping steeply down from the edge, thick with scrub and bushes. Across several curves of the road ahead as it dropped steadily down, Macanaz could see the four red lamps marking the stretch where the road was being widened by cutting deeper into the rock, for at the far end was a dangerous bend where the drop on the left became long and sheer.

Here, in the newly widened strip, an immobilised bulldozer was parked, tools were stored in locked metal sheds, and a mobile crane stood at each end of the working area. Macanaz slowed to thirty k.p.h. as he approached, headlights on beam, alert for any sign of movement amid the cover provided by the roadworks equipment. Beside him, Kaltchas slid a finger through the trigger-guard of the revolver on his lap. It was as they passed the first crane, its derrick leaning out over the road, that a figure dropped from the top of the derrick, a black-clad figure wearing a ski-mask.

The timing was perfect. Ropes attached to the ankles brought the falling figure to a halt in the same instant that two arms wrapped round Macanaz's neck and snatched him bodily from the moving vehicle. Kaltchas, peering to the nearside, heard nothing and was unaware that Macanaz had vanished until the Land-Rover began moving towards the edge and he turned his head to give warning.

Unbelievably for him, the driving seat was empty. The shock was huge, and he snatched at the wheel with one hand, trying to steer a safe course while he manoeuvred himself into position to reach the brake. Then came new shock as he passed the metal tool-sheds, for he glimpsed a dark figure seeming to soar over one of the sheds and drop towards the vehicle, landing behind him as it moved on down the slope.

The second nightmare shock was the last emotion Kaltchas was ever to know, for a hand with a hardened edge struck him sharply on the back of the neck. As he slumped, barely conscious, the man who had hit him leant forward and took the wheel with gloved hands. Macanaz had put the Land-Rover in a lower gear for the descent, but with the increased slope at this point it was steadily gaining speed. When it reached the second crane it was no more than thirty paces from the bend where the ground fell away sheer.

A third figure, identical to the others, dropped from the derrick, ropes strapped to ankles, hands reaching down. The man in the back of the Land-Rover released the wheel and reached up at the precise moment his companion fell. Hands locked on wrists and the vehicle sped on with its lone occupant, smashed through the light wooden barrier and seemed to leap out over the edge of the drop. Seconds later there came the sound of an explosion and the darkness was lit by a glare from below.

The man who had steered the Land-Rover dropped to the ground. His companion doubled forward, pulled himself up one of the ropes hand over hand, sat at the top of the derrick to unstrap his ankles, then came down to the road carrying the ropes. Together the two men moved back to the tool-sheds, where the man who had snatched the driver from his seat now waited. One of them said to him, 'Macanaz?'

'Alive as per contract,' came the answer, 'but unconscious. He will not know what happened.' They spoke in English but said no more as they moved behind the sheds and disassembled the small trampoline used by the second man for his soaring leap. With its pieces distributed between them they moved across the road and set off down the steep scrub-covered slope, heading across country to the car they had left hidden in woods two miles away.

* * *

They called themselves The Dark Angels. This was not for pub-licity reasons since it was vital that their existence should not be known. They called themselves The Dark Angels and thought of themselves as The Dark Angels as a means of establishing their self-image, which in turn was a means of enhancing their special abilities to a remarkable degree.

When planning or executing an operation they took on their professional personas and used only names suited to those per-sonas, names from the hierarchy of demonology—Asmodeus, Belial, and Aruga. They were men in their middle twenties, highly trained in combat and first-class gymnasts.

If it is possible to be strong in character without affection, compassion or humanity, then they were strong in character, but they were also rejects from the elite units of the armed forces, whose psychologists had classified them as psychopaths.

They worked exclusively for a small non-profitmaking organis-ation in the City of London.

* * *

It was mid-afternoon of a spring day when the phone in Modesty Blaise's penthouse bedroom rang. She was under the shower in the bathroom and her houseboy, Weng, was food-shopping in Soho. Turning off the water she picked up a towel and called, 'Danny, answer that for me, please.'

In the bedroom, fresh from his shower and dressing now, Danny picked up the phone and said, 'Can I help you?'

A man's voice said, 'Oh, I'm calling Modesty Blaise. Is that you, Weng?'

Danny said, 'No, I'm a friend, and I'm afraid she can't take a call just now. Would you like me to give her a message?'

'Thank you. My name is Tarrant and I'm invited to Modesty's

cottage in Benildon next weekend. There's something I'd like to ask her if she'd be so kind as to call me.'

Danny started to speak, then broke off as she came from the bathroom, still damp, a towel round her waist. 'Hang on,' he said, 'she's here now so I'll hand you over.' He gave her the phone and said quietly, 'Tarrant.'

'Thanks, Danny.' She sat on the bed, naked to the waist, the towel rucked to her thighs. 'Hallo, Sir Gerald, I hope nothing's cropped up to prevent your visit.'

'No, no, I'm very much looking forward to seeing your country retreat. I simply wanted a word of advice as to the best route from London when I drive down next Friday. It'll be early afternoon, I prefer countryside to motorways, and I recall your telling me of an attractive drive you normally use if you're in no hurry.'

She said, 'Yes, if you've a pen ready I'll give you the route I'll be using myself when I go down today.'

As she went on speaking Danny Chavasse buttoned his collar and put on a tie, watching her, remembering the days when he had worked for her in *The Network*. Their relationship had been very different then, for like her other lieutenants he had not only admired her but had also been somewhat in awe of her for her extraordinary achievement in creating that organisation and controlling the men who served it.

They were hard, dangerous men, yet to them her word was law, for her reputation was unique and they were proud to have the cachet of serving Modesty Blaise. In those days there had been times when *The Network* was beset by powerful and murderous opposition, yet by her combat skills and unconventional methods she had ensured that what she had created never suffered defeat. Danny Chavasse had not been one of her warriors, nor one of her various technicians. He was a key man in her intelligence section and his function was unique, for Danny had a rare gift. He could, when he chose, be almost irresistible to a woman.

Danny was thirty-two, of no more than pleasant appearance, easy of manner and slightly slow in speech. There was nothing obvious about his gift, neither was there a shred of insincerity in it, for he had a huge affection for and empathy with all women of any age, and when he focused this feeling upon one of them it was to her as if she constituted his whole world. This was no less than true at the time. Modesty Blaise had used him to get information from women for Network operations, women in high positions and women attached to men of power in politics, industry or crime, for such men were prone to confide in their women.

It was towards the end of Danny's fourth year with *The Network* that she had sent him on a job to seduce a woman called Jeanne Fournier at a hotel in the Canaries. He was to leave for Lanzarote in three days, and instructions as to the information she required would be awaiting him there. He had flown to the island, settled in at the hotel, and contrived an encounter with the woman, but she was not Jeanne Fournier. She was Modesty Blaise, all authority stripped away, stressed, frightened, vulnerable, and she had said, 'I'm the job, Danny.'

Because it was his gift to understand women, he had perceived her need, and it was only later in the month they spent together there that he learned of the Achilles heel she had hidden from the world, not a flaw in her power but in her womanhood. Two rapes in her early teens when she was wandering the Middle East had left her emotionally crippled in a vital area. She did not fear men, or hate them, but shrank from contact with them yet was torn by normal longing and bitterly aware of the unhealed wound within her.

It was the greatest challenge Danny had ever faced, and the one whose success gave him the greatest pleasure. Eight days passed before he felt the moment had come when they could sleep together, but from then on her cure was startling to him. He knew this would mean the end of his Network days, for the new relationship would be unworkable, but he had no regrets. And once she had wound up *The Network* and retired, he had been an occasional and very welcome guest of hers. He was well aware that there were two or three other men who were equally welcome, but this was pleasing to him, for he knew that it was his gift to her and to them. He had made her complete.

Danny came back from his reverie to realise that she had finished the phone-call and was towelling herself dry, watching him with amusement in the midnight blue eyes. 'Where were you, Danny?' she asked.

He laughed. 'Back a few years, mainly in Lanzarote.'

She dropped the towel and came to him, standing before him and linking her hands behind his neck. 'I wish I could repay you.'

He held her gently by the waist. 'You're my friend. I've shared your bed most joyously for the last couple of weeks and I'm a grateful recipient of a handsome Network pension. I'm very well repaid.'

She shook her head. 'I just mean . . . something as important as what you did for me. A change-your-life sort of something, except you don't need your life changed.'

'I'll tell you what. If I ever find myself tied to railway lines with an express thundering down on me I'll send for you.'

She began to laugh, then looked at him strangely. 'I had a funny feeling when you said that. Look, take care of yourself, will you, Danny?'

He smiled. 'You're a fine one to talk.'

'I know, but . . . things happen. Do you really have to fly to America on Wednesday? You're welcome to stay on for a while.'

'The great secret is never to outstay your welcome. Anyway, I'm between jobs at the moment, so I plan to mix with some stinking rich people who might provide one. There's a billionaire called Paxero who's gathering a bunch of equally rich mates for a cruise on his yacht out of Miami shortly. What's more, I've been asked by a Fleet Street friend to write an inside piece on the cruise, so that fits in nicely.'

'You've been invited by this billionaire?'

'Not yet, but I've seen the list of passengers, and Julie Boscombe, the micro-chip tycoon's daughter, is on it, so I thought I'd try to go as her boyfriend.'

'Julie Boscombe? When did you meet her?'

'I haven't yet, and I've only got three weeks before the cruise, so I really do have to get over there and stumble across her path.'

She stared, then burst into laughter and hugged him. 'Oh Danny, she'll love you. Wait a minute.' She let him go and moved to her dressing-table, taking a small leather pouch from one of the drawers, then returning to put it in his hands. 'It's a thank-you present, but for God's sake don't let Julie Boscombe see it.'

She moved away and began to put on pants and bra. Danny opened the press-stud of the pouch. From within it a most beautiful watch, a Breguet, slid into the palm of his hand. He drew in a long slow breath and flicked open the back, a thin disc of gold. The inside was inscribed *To Danny from Modesty*.

*   *   *

At six that evening as Modesty was driving through the village of Netherstreet with Danny beside her, he said, 'Is Tarrant the Intelligence chap you did that Gabriel job for last year?'

She nodded. 'Yes, he's the one.'

'You should stay away from people like that, you know. They can get you killed.'

'He's a nice man with a nasty job, and I owed him, Danny.'

'For what?'

'Willie's life.'

'I see. That's different.'

'Yes, but we're not making a habit of it. If he asks me again I'll say no. Okay?'

'Okay, I'll shut up. I'm quite happy to sit here dreaming about your legs.' He laughed suddenly. 'Do you know there was a time when I didn't dare let myself register that you'd *got* legs?'

'Ah, Danny. "That was in another country, and besides, the wench is dead"—that wench, anyway.'

'I'm not so sure,' he said slowly. 'Up to a point, maybe. No more Networks, but . . . I doubt you'll ever stop attracting trouble.'

'Oh, come on now. I'm a respectable spinster lady who—' she broke off and began to brake. They were clear of the village now, and ahead on a slight bend a car had pulled off the road near a pond. The bonnet was raised and one man's head and shoulders were out of sight behind it. Another man stood at the edge of the road waving her down with a hopeful air. 'I'm also a Good Samaritan,' she said, and pulled on to the verge, halting a few paces behind the other car.

Both men moved towards her. They were in their late thirties, she judged, a little too well-dressed in a casual way, a little too confident in manner now that they saw clearly who was driving. One had dark curly hair and wore a sports jacket, cream shirt and pale yellow cravat. The other was fair, wearing a fine check shirt, suede jacket and corduroys.

As they stopped by her car, gazing down at her with a hint of quizzical speculation, she said, 'Would you like me to send someone from the next garage?'

The cravat man cast an eye over Danny, who sat looking blandly inoffensive, then smiled at her and said, 'Well, hallo there, nice lady. You've made it worth our breaking down, hasn't she, Adrian?'

Adrian of the suede jacket said, 'Absolutely.'

'Do you want a breakdown van or not?' Modesty asked.

Adrian frowned. 'Steady on. We're just being matey, aren't we, Tarquin?'

Modesty put the car in gear and said, 'No thanks.'

As she started to let in the clutch the man called Tarquin said quickly, 'Hang on. Do you have a screwdriver we could borrow for a few minutes?'

She considered for a moment or two, then switched off, gave the key to Danny and murmured, 'Stay in the car.' When he nodded she got out and went to the boot. From a toolbox there she took a screwdriver, then walked back and offered it to Adrian, noting that Tarquin had moved to stand in front of her open door. 'You can keep it,' she said, 'I have another.'

Tarquin said, 'Look, I've got a better idea. Instead of tinkering with Adrian's heap we'll leave it to be picked up and you could give us a lift.' A dismissive glance at Danny. 'You and your friend.'

Adrian grinned hopefully and said, 'Why not? We can stop at my place for drinkies. Charming little cottage. You'll love it.'

Danny Chavasse thought, *Here we go. She's walked into*

trouble again. How the hell does she do it? He was not worried for her, simply intrigued to see how far these two Hooray Henries would go, and with a guilty hope that they might push things too far. It was a long time since he had seen her in action.

Still offering the screwdriver Modesty said, 'Do you want it?'

Tarquin chuckled. 'Want *it*? Now there's a question!'

She turned back to the boot and put the screwdriver away. When she moved to the open door Tarquin was still blocking her way. She felt a wave of irritation sweep her and said sharply, 'Move.'

His flirtatious air faded. 'Manners, ducky. Don't we say please?'

A voice spoke from behind her, a voice with the strong drawling accent of one of the southern states of America. 'I reckon you better do like the young lady said, Mister.'

She half turned. He stood near the rear offside wing, a man of perhaps sixty, not very big, wearing a shabby black jacket, trousers tucked into calf-length boots. A bootlace tie hung over an old-fashioned frilled shirt; a black hat, round-crowned and broad-brimmed, was pushed back on thick grey hair above a weatherbeaten face. He stood glowering, thumbs hooked in his wide leather belt.

His appearance in this setting was so extraordinary that for a moment Modesty and the two men simply stared, taken aback. He gave Danny a cold glare, then moved forward to stand beside Modesty, gazed balefully at Adrian and Tarquin, and said, 'Git movin'.'

Tarquin shook his head in disbelief and laughed. 'My God, it's Dangerous Dan McGrew!'

Modesty said, 'Thank you, but it's all right, you needn't worry.'

The stranger turned his head to look at her. 'Where I come from, ma'am, a feller always figures he's got to worry about a lady.' He touched the brim of his hat and moved forward to stand between her and the two men. Confronting Tarquin, who was a head taller, he said, 'Any feller behaves bad to a lady like you done, he's dirt. You gonna move or do I have to whip the hide off'n you?'

Tarquin said contemptuously, 'Ah, get lost you bloody old fool or—'

The stranger slapped him across the face before Modesty could intervene and said, 'Don't get lippy with me, feller.'

Tarquin swore and his fist swung, hitting the older man on the side of the jaw so that he staggered sideways and fell. Coldly furious, Modesty said, 'You bastard!' and moved forward.

The face above the pale yellow cravat began to show anxiety, and a hand was raised in warning. 'Now don't you start, ducky!'

She feinted to slap his face, and he jerked up both hands defensively. At once her other hand drove stiffened fingers hard into his solar plexus in a spear-head strike. He gasped and doubled forward. She seized his wrist as Adrian started towards her, reaching out for her, when suddenly she was gone, sliding feet first between Tarquin's straddled legs and coming up behind him, still grasping his wrist with both hands. Now he was bent forward with one arm hauled back between his legs in the classic hold of the Bouncer's Wheelaway.

When she pulled and lifted, he had to run awkwardly ahead or fall and hit the ground with his face. A quick foot-strike sent Adrian staggering back, then she was running her victim towards the pond, right to the edge before putting a surge of power into an upward heave that sent him somersaulting into eighteen inches of water.

It had all happened in five seconds, and Danny sat turned in his seat, watching with happy admiration. The small American sat with a hand to his jaw, gazing in stunned delight, then let out a whoop of triumph. 'Yahoooo—!' He broke off abruptly. 'Watch out, Missy!'

Adrian was running at her, his face ugly with rage. 'You bitch!' He lunged for her, and she seemed to make a very small evasive movement, yet he grasped only air, and then she had turned, with one of his arms drawn over her shoulder as she snapped into a forward bend, shaping his momentum to her own design so that he flew somersaulting over her back to land beside his companion.

She grimaced, and felt round behind her thigh with one hand, pulling up her skirt and craning her head round to look down.

There was a broad ladder in one leg of her tights. She said, 'Blast!' and let the skirt fall. When she turned, the grey-haired westerner was on his feet, holding his hat, face averted, very clearly not looking in her direction.

He said, 'You hurt someplace, Missy?'

She laughed. 'No, just laddered my tights. Excuse me.'

He came towards her, shaking his head in wonder, grinning despite the trickle of blood from a corner of his mouth. 'I'll be gol'durned! They cotched 'emselves a cougar with you, Missy.' He turned his head to glare at Danny. 'Can't say that young feller helped much.'

Danny composed his features and said with dignity, 'I am Madam's butler, sir, and she instructed me to remain in the vehicle. I may also say she is better than I at dealing with such matters.'

'Heh-heh-heh! You can say that again, son!'

Modesty looked at her elderly champion with friendly exasperation, took a handkerchief from a pocket of her skirt and held it against the cut by his mouth. 'Don't you know better than to tangle with lippy dudes half your age?' she asked.

He took over holding the handkerchief. 'Feller's gotta stand up for a lady. Ain't too old till he's dead.'

She studied him curiously. 'They don't make too many like you these days. What's your name and where did you spring from?'

'I'm stayin' down the road a piece at a little pub place, and I jest took a walk. My friends call me Gus.'

She watched the two men wade miserably from the pond, void of aggression now, avoiding her eye. Then she took the old American's arm and walked him to her car. 'All right, Gus,' she said, 'I'll see you home.'

Fifteen minutes later they were sitting together at a low table in a corner of the lounge in a three hundred-year-old hostelry. The table was set for three with a plate of scones, jam and cream, and a pot of tea. Danny, now trapped in his role of butler, sat looking dignified and was not presuming to join in the conversation. Modesty, amused by the set-up and intrigued by her new friend, was pouring tea and saying, 'Well, you're a long way from home, Gus.'

He nodded. 'Yup. They run these here package tours, so I come across for a few weeks.' He took the cup she passed him, thanked her, and put several knobs of sugar in it, stirring as he said, 'My folks was from this village around a coupla hundred years back, so I figured spending a day or two here, seein' if I could find any of 'em in the churchyard or the register thing. Where you from, Miss Modesty?'

'Oh, nowhere special. What do you do back home, Gus? Or maybe you're retired?'

'No, I got a general store.' He frowned with a touch of embarrassment. 'Everybody's gotta come from somewhere, but maybe you reckoned I was nosey, askin' you?'

She shook her head in friendly reassurance. 'It's just that I don't know the answer. I think my folks may have been refugees who didn't make it, but the first thing I can remember is wandering through the Middle East on my own.'

He had picked up his cup, but now he set it down and looked at her wonderingly. 'How old?'

'Seven, eight maybe. Everything before that seems to have disappeared.'

'And you was on your own? Just roamin' about?'

'I was on my own at first. Then I met an old man in a Displaced Persons camp—well, he seemed old to me then but he was probably under fifty. He'd been a professor in Budapest until he had to run for his life. He knew just everything.'

'And he looked after you?'

She smiled. 'No, I looked after him, Gus. He knew everything, but he was hopeless in my kind of world, so I had to fight for us and steal food and do whatever had to be done. I never knew his real name, I just called him Lob. Anyway, that's where I come from.'

'But . . . where d'you go from there, Miss Modesty?'

'Well, we roamed all over the Middle East and North Africa, and he was my teacher. He gave me my name, and I loved him. When I was about sixteen he died one day in the desert. I buried

him, and cried, and went on alone. What came next is much too
long to tell, Gus.'

He sat staring down at the table, his tea untouched, not meeting
her eye, and she had the strange impression that he was struggling
with a feeling of shame. At last he said in a low voice, 'I jest
can't figure how a kid girl could get by all those years.'

She wanted no sympathy for what had been, and said, 'Hey,
lighten up, I didn't tell you to make you feel bad. You've lived
rough yourself, haven't you?'

He seemed to take hold of himself, and grinned. 'Yup. Plenty.
Was twice I sure enough nearly didn't git back alive when I was
a young feller prospecting. But I warn't a kid girl.'

'It's the same for anyone. As long as you don't starve and
don't die of exposure you get by.'

'Sure. But there's more'n being hungry or gitting froze. There's
people. Bad people.'

She had no intention of telling about the occasions of horror
she had gone through, and said, 'What did you do about people
like that when you were a young feller?'

'Me? Well, I ain't big but I used to be real sneaky. I'd kick
'em in the belly, then stomp 'em.'

'I thought it would be something like that. I used to run until
I got big enough and sneaky enough to do it your way.'

'That figures. Ain't no wonder you give them fancy-pants a
surprise just now.' He sighed, turned his head to look at her
directly, and said with curious formality, 'It's been a real pleasure
meetin' you, Miss Modesty. A real pleasure.'

She dipped her head. 'Thank you, Gus. I've enjoyed it too, so
if you come up to London give me a call.' She turned to Danny
Chavasse. 'Give the gentleman my address and number before
we go, Blenkinsop.'

Danny nodded gravely. 'Certainly, madam.'

*   *   *

Two men and a woman sat at a boardroom table in the City of
London. There was no secretary to take minutes. The woman

was Harriet Welling, forty-eight years old, director of three large companies and committee member of several charities. She wore a neat suit, had a round face and forgettable features, an appearance that belied her character, for she had risen from pool typist to become a figure of substance in the City.

There was silence in the room as all three sat reading copies of the same report. First to finish was George Sumner, a lean, eagle-faced man, a brigadier who had been among those axed from one of the county regiments during the last slimming down of the armed forces. He got up, moved to feed his copy of the report into the shredder, then resumed his seat, and said, 'In my view The Dark Angels are getting too damn theatrical. What's the point of all these acrobatics? They just have to kill someone. Don't have to carry on like—who is it?—Batman or somebody.'

The second man, Timmins, was heavily built, square-jawed and with thinning black hair sleeked back from a wide brow. He said, 'You miss the point, Sumner. The theatricality of The Dark Angels is essential to their success. It's essential to *them*, because that is their common character. I'm sure your brigade had a character that you created and which caused it to operate in a particular way—*your* way, and therefore in some degree different from the way another brigade would operate. The Dark Angels are the elite among the executive groups we employ, and we interfere with their methods at our peril.'

Sumner sat gazing into space for perhaps half a minute, then nodded and said abruptly, 'Point taken.' He looked towards the woman, who had laid down her report. 'Your view, Mrs Welling?'

Harriet Welling always spoke slowly but without hesitation, her voice cool and amiable. She said, 'I agree they're theatrical, Brigadier, but if we use psychopaths we have to accept psychopathic behaviour. The Dark Angels revel in their role. To them it's god-like. When they operate, not only does nobody know who was responsible, nobody even knows there's been a killing, because the Angels create perfect accidents,' she tapped the report in front of her, 'as they did for Kaltchas. What's more, although one hundred per cent successful, they're content to remain anonymous, which is greatly to our advantage. Most assassin groups give themselves a name and publicise it. That's the last thing we want if we're to be effective.'

Timmins said, 'Thank you, Mrs Welling. We must also take on board the fact that, unlike lesser contractors we hire, The Dark Angels know our identity.' He glanced at the other man. 'That was inevitable since it was Sumner who had to select them from army records and arrange covert training. My point is that, given their particular mentality, it would be unwise and bad security to subject them to needless criticism. Their work for us has been impeccable. Let us not disturb the relationship in any way.'

Sumner nodded briskly. 'Agreed,' he said. 'I recall anxious moments during the van Doorn business, when other contractors failed twice and we had finally to bring in The Dark Angels. It's just . . .' he paused with a wry smile, 'it's just that they *are* so damn theatrical, and with my own training that sets my teeth on edge. But you've provided convincing reasons why I should put up with it, so I won't raise the matter again.'

Timmins looked at his watch, then at an empty chair where an agenda paper lay on the table in front of it. 'Beckworth's late, but I think we should leave item three until he arrives. Item four—Future Operations.' He looked up. 'This depends on what forewarning we may have of proposed large-scale takeovers affecting this country. I have my usual lines of inquiry out, but nothing to report at present. Mrs Welling?'

Harriet Welling said, 'I believe there is a possible hostile takeover of one of our larger industrial companies being planned, but I would rather wait till I have further intelligence on this before reporting fully.'

Timmins said, 'Thank you. Brigadier?'

Sumner shook his head. 'My sources are very narrow compared with yours and Mrs Welling's. Perhaps Beckworth has—' he broke off as the door opened and a man entered. He wore a city suit and was carrying a bowler hat and umbrella.

Sumner said, 'Ah, Beckworth.'

The man said, 'Sorry Mrs Welling, gentlemen.' He hung up

his hat and umbrella, moved to the empty chair and sat down, a man with a fresh complexion, a chubby face and bright blue eyes, his hair greying at the temples, a neat moustache still dark.

Timmins said with a touch of sarcasm, 'Good of you to come.'

Beckworth answered without resentment. 'I'm on eight boards of directors, Timmins, most useful to our enterprise, and the traffic's hell today. Where are we up to?'

'Item three, please.'

Beckworth studied the agenda. 'Choice of contractor for disposal of Mr Howard A. Keyes. Well, what's the feeling?'

Sumner said, 'I recommend using The Dark Angels right away.'

Harriet Welling said gently, 'As treasurer I feel I must point out that our funds are low following heavy expenditure last year. The Carter group or the Albanian group would be cheaper.'

'Not if they fail,' said Timmins. 'We don't want to pay half in advance and then fall back on the Angels anyway.'

Sumner said slowly, 'We four are the only source of funds. We are dedicated to the sole purpose of keeping British industry British-owned by preventing the steady takeover of our industrial base by foreign corporations. Surely there must be others of our mind, others who foresee the loss of sovereignty and death of Britain as we know it if this continues. Can we not recruit a few carefully selected persons of reasonable substance who would join our enterprise?'

Beckworth fingered his moustache. 'Our enterprise involves killing people.'

'Of course. But we take great care to ensure that only the selected person dies. You'll see from the report on the Kaltchas operation that his bodyguard suffered no harm.'

'A minor torticollis, perhaps,' Harriet Welling suggested.

'I beg your pardon?'

'A stiff neck, Brigadier.'

'Oh. Quite. But I don't think that invalidates my point. We do what has to be done in an extremely responsible manner.'

Beckworth leaned back in his chair and looked round at his

companions. 'My own feeling is that any attempt at recruitment would be dangerous. However, we may have to consider it and I therefore recommend that we leave Sumner's suggestion on the table for future discussion. Now, according to our latest intelligence Mr Howard A. Keyes shouldn't be very difficult to kill. I suggest that to save expense we put the job out to the Carter group first, but with a cash on delivery proviso, no deposit.'

Timmins said, 'Certainly we lose nothing that way. I'll second the proposal. Mrs Welling?'

'Yes. A good compromise.'

Sumner said, 'Agreed.'

There was silence as they looked at their agenda papers, then Beckworth said, 'Items one and two are routine, and no doubt you've dealt with them. Shall we proceed to item four now?'

*   *   *

Danny Chavasse had been gone three days. The church fête was in progress in the village of Benildon, and Sir Gerald Tarrant stood at the hoop-la stall with Modesty Blaise beside him, watching him throw the wooden rings. He paid for six more and sighed inwardly, reflecting that he would have been greatly enjoying himself if he had not been suffering from a rare attack of guilt. His job was one in which he often had to put his people at considerable risk. Sometimes they were given tasks which resulted in death for them. This was something to which he had been compelled to inure himself, though he sometimes feared that he was simply postponing any response to some future day, to retirement perhaps, when all the horrors would descend upon him together.

At this moment he was feeling guilty about the girl beside him who was licking an ice-cream cornet and carried a basket full of bottles, jars, cans of food and sundry other items either bought or won at great expense. She was no employee, but twice she had carried out missions for Tarrant, and in the *Sabre-tooth* operation had come close to dying for him.

Since that time, what had been acquaintance had become something closer, and he had been delighted when she invited him for a long weekend at her country cottage. They had fixed a date three weeks ahead, but only two days after making the arrangement Tarrant had been called in by the government minister to whom he was responsible. Intelligence reports from sources abroad and from other UK organisations had been passed to Tarrant, and he had been required as a matter of urgency to investigate and deal with a possible criminal matter of great delicacy involving foreign citizens and their governments. Evidence was patchy to the point of being nebulous, but he was told that speed in settling the matter was essential.

After long hours of increasingly uneasy consideration Tarrant had come to the ineluctable conclusion that no legal authority had the power to do what would be necessary if he was to achieve the task laid upon him. He had also concluded that there were two people who, being independent, could act more freely than any he could employ. They were also widely experienced in criminal matters, and above all had ways of thinking that he regarded as unique. So it was possible, just possible, that they might find a way to the heart of the nebulous matter and uncover what lay there.

Impossible simply to ask Modesty Blaise and Willie Garvin for their services again. He would have to involve them tangentially, and this he had now taken steps to arrange, which was why he felt heavy with guilt as he threw the last of the hoop-la rings and watched with horror as it settled neatly round a small but very ugly green frog. This prize proved to be of painted lead and was presumably intended for use as a paperweight.

Modesty choked off a laugh, crunched the last of her cornet, wiped her lips on a tissue and said, 'Well done.' She looked about her. 'Where did Willie disappear to?'

'Over there.' Tarrant nodded to a stall where Willie was throwing darts at rows of playing cards fastened to a large board.

Modesty stared. 'He can't do that!' She took Tarrant's arm and moved briskly across to the stall as Willie prepared to throw a final dart. 'Willie! Don't you *dare* win prizes at that, it's not for—' she swallowed the word 'professionals' and made it, 'for people like you.'

The motherly lady in charge said, 'Oh, it's all right, dear.' She pointed to the row of small, evil-looking gnomes on a shelf above the board where the playing cards were pinned. 'He hasn't hit any spots yet, but he's just broken three of the prizes and he's very sorry, so he's going to pay five pounds for each of them.'

Willie said, 'I can't get the hang of this, some'ow.' He threw the last dart, and a fourth gnome shattered with the impact. 'There, see what I mean?'

Modesty nodded thoughtfully. 'Yes . . . another time you could try aiming a bit lower, perhaps?'

'Might be the answer,' Willie agreed. 'I'll think about it.' He handed a note to the lady in charge. 'Twenty pounds, Mrs Bailey. Will that cover the damage?'

'Handsomely, thank you, Mr Garvin, they're only a pound each. And you're not fooling me for a moment, you know.'

Willie grinned, winked at her, then turned away with Modesty and Tarrant. 'What's that you've won, Sir G.?'

'It's a large emerald carved in the shape of a frog,' said Tarrant. Inspiration struck him, and he seized the moment. 'Should I seek protection, do you think? A bodyguard?'

Modesty said, 'I'll ask the Boy Scouts.' And before Tarrant could continue his theme she went on, 'I think we've done our bit now. Let's go home and have tea.'

Willie said, 'I'm dying for a cup. Let's 'ave the basket, Princess.'

As they moved towards the field where the car was parked Tarrant said, 'Talking of bodyguards—' he stopped as she gave him a puzzled look.

'Bodyguards? Oh, you mean just now. Yes, sorry, go on.'

Hiding his discomfiture Tarrant continued, 'If you'll forgive me for talking shop briefly I'd just like to ask if you could recommend a really good bodyguard.'

After a little silence Modesty said, 'We never dealt in that line of business. Surely you have access to a wide selection of likely people?'

'We need somebody rather special,' said Tarrant. 'The person to be guarded is inclined to be difficult.'

'And you can't tell us who it is?'

'In confidence, yes. It's Mr Howard A. Keyes. It's possible you may have heard of him.'

Willie said, 'Keyes? He's been in the news a bit. Owns a chunk of Texas and a chain of supermarkets.'

Modesty said, 'Is he the American the city pages call the Mystery Tycoon, who's planning to build supermarkets here?'

'And to take over one of our major supermarket chains,' said Tarrant. 'Yes, that's the man.'

They had reached the car, and as Willie opened the door for her she said, 'Who does he need protection from?'

'I'm afraid we don't know,' said Tarrant, 'but *what* he needs protection from is murder. And Keyes isn't particularly mysterious, just eccentric. He hates publicity.'

Willie said, 'Then he won't much like being murdered. It's bound to make 'eadlines.'

'I've been given the job of preventing that.' Tarrant took the back seat with Modesty, and Willie got in behind the wheel. As they moved away Modesty said, 'Why are you involved?'

'Because he's over here now, my dear. I've been instructed to protect him but he won't submit to normal security measures.'

Willie said, 'Lousy job. All the initiative's with the other side. And you've no idea who wants to knock 'im off?'

'We're not even sure that anybody *will* try to do so.'

'Jesus, you don't know a lot about this, do you, Sir G.?'

'Sadly, no. What's happened is this. Computers have come up with a pattern concerning several very odd and seemingly accidental deaths over the past year or so. They've found a common denominator, which is that the victims have all been foreign captains of industry involved in taking over British companies. In each case the person's death has aborted the take-over.'

Modesty said, 'I thought we were keen on investment from overseas.'

'Economics baffle me, but I suppose there's a difference

between investment and takeover, and I've been told to work on the theory that the deaths were in fact murder and that a group of Little Englanders feel so strongly about what they see as bits of their country being sold off that they're going to any lengths to prevent it.'

'And you think this American tycoon Keyes is a prime candidate for their attention?' Modesty asked.

'If an attempt is made, it will be very convincing confirmation of that theory.'

'You're not suggesting that Willie and I should turn bodyguards?'

'Oh, good Lord, no.'

'That's all right, then.'

Tarrant brooded for a moment or two. Then, 'We don't want Mr Howard A. Keyes dead, but he's a very difficult character. He won't agree to have bodyguards or submit to any security arrangements.'

Willie said, 'Then what's the point in asking if we can recommend anyone? I don't know what we're talking about, Sir G. D'you want us to come to the funeral or something?'

'I was simply hoping you could suggest someone Mr Keyes just might find acceptable as a protector. Or perhaps I should say protectors since Modesty raised the question of your participation.'

'*What?*' she said indignantly. 'I did no such thing and you're a wicked old gentleman. Only the other day a good friend of mine said I should stay away from people like you because you're likely to get a girl into trouble.'

Tarrant sighed and leant back in his seat, consumed by guilt. 'Very true,' he said gloomily, 'but please don't take his advice to stay away. I promise I'll never ask you again, and as an earnest of my good intentions I . . .' he took out his diary and flicked over the pages, 'I invite you both to dine with me at my club on Thursday next, if that's convenient?'

Modesty said, 'Well, that's very contrite of you. Yes, please. Are you clear, Willie?'

'No problem. You know, Princess, for a moment there he

sounded so apologetic I thought he was going to give you 'is frog.'

* * *

Tarrant belonged to several clubs. The one he had chosen was not of the kind where members died quietly in deep leather armchairs without anybody noticing the change, it covered a wide spectrum of professions and age-groups. When Modesty and Willie arrived at the appointed time they were immediately greeted by a steward who apologised for Tarrant and explained that he had phoned to say he would be a few minutes late. 'He hopes to join you in the lounge shortly, madam, and I am to ask if you would like an aperitif or glass of wine.'

Modesty and Willie were seated in a corner of the quiet lounge, talking together as they waited for their drinks to arrive when a voice said, 'Well, dang me if it ain't Miss Modesty.'

She looked up in astonishment to see Gus standing there, dressed much as he had been that day by the pond. 'Gus! What a nice surprise! What are you doing here?'

'Supposed to meet a feller, but I ain't too keen. He's been a-pestering me all week.' Gus looked at Willie with a touch of suspicion. 'Howdy.'

She said, 'Oh, this is Willie Garvin. Willie, this is my friend Gus. I told you about him.'

Willie rose and put out his hand. ''Allo, Gus. You kick 'em in the belly and I'll stomp 'em.'

The leathery face split in a grin as they shook hands. 'Ain't no need with Miss Modesty around. You shoulda seen her, son.'

'I've seen 'er. Sit down and 'ave a drink while you're waiting, Gus. We've got a generous host arriving soon.'

'I'll take whisky neat, please.' He sat down and looked from Modesty to Willie. 'You two sparking?'

She said, 'Willie and I? Oh, we've been around together too long for that.'

Gus sighed and shook his head. 'Sure wish I was thirty years younger.'

'I'm so sorry to be late . . .' It was Tarrant, hurrying towards them. 'Do forgive me.' As he reached the table he stared in surprise. 'Oh, you've met?'

Modesty said, 'Met?'

Gus said, 'You know this young lady?'

Tarrant looked embarrassed. 'Why yes, I—um—hoped to be here earlier so that I could explain, but in any event allow me to make formal introductions. Modesty, this is Mr Howard A. Keyes. Mr Keyes, this is Modesty Blaise and Willie Garvin.'

Modesty looked blankly at the old westerner. 'Gus? Howard A. Keyes?'

He shrugged uncomfortably. 'Augustus. My second name. Howard's kinda prissy and it don't shorten like Gus.' He looked at Tarrant and tugged at one ear. 'Danged if I can figure this, Miss Modesty. You something to do with this feller?'

She said, 'This feller's just an old and untrustworthy friend. You said you kept a store, Gus. You've got hundreds of them, plus oil wells in Texas.'

He looked at her anxiously. 'Never was one for big talk. I offended you some?'

'No, of course not. But this feller Tarrant—' She stopped speaking as a steward brought a chair for Tarrant and took orders for two more drinks. When he had moved away Tarrant said, 'I had the simple idea that if I brought you together you might take to one another. I could hardly know you'd already done so.'

Gus said to Modesty, 'He's some kinda sheriff and he's frettin' about some dirty side-winders aiming to dry-gulch me.'

Her eyes were troubled as she said, 'Yes, I know. And he tells me you won't have any protection.'

Gus gave a snort of contempt. 'Bodyguards! I seen 'em on the movies. You figure I want to spend all day hidin' behind a coupla big oxes with guns under their arms? Ain't no way for a man to act.'

There was a little silence. She looked at Willie for a moment or two, then at Gus again and said gently, 'Willie and I wouldn't want you to hide behind us. We'd just want to be around. Would that make a difference?'

He stared at her for long seconds, then grinned suddenly as her meaning dawned on him. 'You? Holy Moses, that'd make a difference, long as you was really willing. Oh, you didn't ask Willie yet, though.'

She smiled. 'Yes, I did. You can both stay at my place for the rest of your time here, Gus. There's plenty of room and it's fully secure, so if anyone wants to come at you they'll have to do it in the open.'

Gus beamed with delight. 'Then we'll git 'em!' He nodded towards Willie. 'He as good as you when it comes to pickin' 'em up and bouncing 'em?'

'Every bit as good, and he does it from higher up.'

Gus exploded in a gust of laughter that left him breathless. 'We'll kick the goddam plums off'n 'em—' he cackled, then stopped short, contrite. 'Sorry, Miss Modesty. Askin' your pardon. Bunkhouse talk ain't fitting for a lady.'

She laughed. 'Now now, Gus. No flattery, please.'

The steward arrived with drinks, and as he set them down Willie Garvin reflected on the strange workings of chance. Modesty would never have considered doing a bodyguard job, even for Tarrant, of whom she was becoming quite fond. But chance had set Gus on the spot at the moment when she found herself in a brush with two unpleasant men. He had walked into trouble for her, and so won her friendship, which as Willie knew was boundless once given.

*   *   *

In the days that followed, Howard A. Keyes proved to be an undemanding guest. He was happy to talk, or to sit with a pile of newspapers and magazines to read, happy to play poker for small stakes of an evening or to spend time in his room working on what he called 'business things'. He greatly admired Weng's cooking, and would sit cheerfully in the kitchen watching him prepare and serve dinner, happy to talk but careful not to distract.

Sometimes he would go out with Modesty or Willie, sometimes

with both, never alone. He enjoyed stage musicals and film comedies, but best of all for him were Laurel and Hardy videos. He also enjoyed playing what he called checkers, and was very good at it, usually beating Modesty or Willie but going down to defeat against Weng.

One long weekend was spent at Modesty's cottage in Wiltshire with the hope that this might tempt any would-be killers to strike—if indeed they existed—but there was no hint of trouble. They visited Willie's pub, *The Treadmill*, where they had lunch and Gus played an excruciatingly bad game of darts; and on another day they spent an hour or two on an out-of-town site where Gus was financing the building of a pigeon-hole carpark for a shopping precinct which would include one of his supermarkets. From time to time both Modesty and Willie were certain they were under surveillance, but they were unable to pinpoint it and nothing happened.

On the tenth day of Gus's stay at the penthouse a board meeting was held in offices off Threadneedle Street. It was chaired by John Beckworth and there was only one item on the agenda. Beckworth said, 'There's been a delay in the matter of dispatching Howard A. Keyes and I'll ask Sumner to give details.'

Sumner looked round the table and said sourly, 'Not much detail to give. We contracted with the Carter group and they've been keeping the subject under observation, seeking an opportunity for completion. However, it seems Mr Keyes is aware of his danger and has protection.'

Timmins said, 'How would Keyes be aware?'

Sumner frowned, and Harriet Welling said mildly, 'We can hardly expect Brigadier Sumner to know that.'

'Is it police protection?' Beckworth asked.

Sumner shook his head. 'No. A woman called Modesty Blaise assisted by a man called Garvin. Their reputation is such that Carter has now withdrawn his tender for the job. We have to decide on an alternative.'

Beckworth looked amazed. 'One man and one woman? You can't be serious.'

'Carter's serious enough,' Sumner said bluntly. 'I'm not privy to underworld reputations, but he is, and he won't touch the job now.'

Harriet Welling said, 'The Dark Angels, then?'

'Yes, Mrs Welling. I've placed them on standby, and I simply require the board's authority to activate them. However, I have to tell you that in this matter the Angels will not accept our standard veto against causing harm to other persons.'

Beckworth frowned. 'Why's that?'

'Because other persons in this context are likely to be Modesty Blaise and Willie Garvin. If they choose to place themselves between The Dark Angels and our chosen target, they will die. It may also not be possible to arrange a convincing accident. The guarantee is simply that Mr Keyes will vanish without trace, as will Blaise and Garvin if they intervene.'

The others looked at each other, then Timmins said, 'The Angels seem greatly impressed by this pair.'

'Indeed they are, which is very sensible of them. They are also eager to match themselves against them professionally. Very eager and totally confident. They have no doubt of the outcome, and hope to complete within two days.'

'Two days?' said Beckworth. 'That's remarkably quick, surely?'

'It is,' Sumner agreed. 'But they take the view that this Modesty Blaise person, who seems to be the senior partner, will react to a challenge if it's properly presented. I am of the opinion that if we fail to agree to what the Angels ask, then we cannot hope to kill Mr Keyes. For this reason I now ask the board for authority to activate them.'

Beckworth looked round the table. 'Sumner proposes to use The Dark Angels under the conditions just stated.' He shrugged. 'Needs must, so I second. All in favour?'

*   *   *

In the penthouse that evening an hour after dinner Modesty was teaching Gus the rudiments of chess and Willie sat working on a circuit diagram for a new electronic gadget he had in mind.

When the phone rang, Weng answered it in the kitchen, then came through to announce, 'A call for you, Mr Keyes. A Mr Smithson, who says it's urgent.'

Gus looked puzzled. 'Who's Smithson? He say what it's about?'

'I did not ask, sir.'

Modesty said, 'Better find out, Gus. Take it in your room if it's private business.'

'I got nothing private from you, Miss Modesty.' Gus got up, moved to a side-table and lifted the phone. 'I'm Keyes, who's this talkin'?'

He listened, frowning, and after a few moments said, 'Look, feller, I don't know how you come into it, but if there's trouble at the site you jest tell the guys I pay to handle it.' A pause of several moments, then, 'Come down *now*? You crazy?'

Again he listened. Watching him, Modesty and Willie saw his expression slowly change, his eyes narrowing warily. At last he said in a voice quieter than usual, 'Yeah. Okay, I got it. Hang on while I talk to my friends.'

He pressed the secrecy button on the unit and looked across the room. 'Feller says he handles insurance on that shopping precinct. Says there's trouble, subsidence he called it, an' that big carpark's like to fall down. Wants me to go an' look at it. Now.'

Willie said incredulously, 'They can't expect us to fall for that. It's phoney as a glass eye.'

Gus nodded. 'Sure. And he knew dang well he warn't foolin' me. Talked funny, kinda insulting.' He looked at Modesty. 'Know what I figure? They can see we know the score and they got tired of pussyfooting around. They reckon maybe we got tired too, so they're sayin' come out an' get it settled.'

Willie said, 'For all they know we could set up a cordon of fuzz round the place, Princess. Or you and I could go and leave Gus 'ere. But they don't reckon we'll do that.'

'No. They'll have eyes on the job, Willie, and if we don't play it their way they won't be there.' She thought for a moment, gazing at the chessboard. 'And if we just sit tight they can wait till Gus goes back to the States and try to nail him there. They don't fancy a long-haul job so they're offering a showdown.'

There was a silence. Gus looked from Modesty to Willie and back again. 'Then let's go get 'em,' he said quietly.

*   *   *

It was an hour before midnight when a Cessna Skymaster moved steadily through the darkness at ten thousand feet over Surrey. Within, The Dark Angels sat in silence, ram-air parachutes strapped in position, focusing their minds on the task that lay before them. Performance-enhancing drugs were at work in each bloodstream.

The aircraft banked gently, skirting the pool of light from a town below. Two miles to the west the darkness was pierced only by a red lamp on top of a tall structure, the iron skeleton of a partly built carpark.

The pilot spoke, and without a word the three black-clad figures in their ski-masks rose and moved to the door, Asmodeus first, followed by Belial and Aruga, each deep in the role he was playing, each with surging confidence in his more than human powers. Seconds later they were gone, dropping in free fall and moving laterally as they fell in echelon at a speed increasing to a hundred and twenty miles an hour.

The carpark was in the shape of a capital E with the middle stroke missing—a long centre span with two wings. As The Dark Angels came to within two thousand feet of the red lamp they diverged from one another and pulled the rip-cords. Black ram-air 'chutes blossomed into curving rectangles, easily distinguished against the starlit sky and the almost full moon, but they were in view for no more than a few seconds. The Angels had reconnoitred the site in daylight, and Asmodeus touched down beside the western wing, exactly where he intended. On the far side of the structure Belial landed gently beside a mobile crane. Aruga, to his anger, missed his chosen spot by several feet as he touched down midway between the two wings of the structure.

On a partly finished floor near the top of the building Modesty and Willie stood near the middle of the main span with Gus. Both wore black slacks and shirts, camouflage paint on their faces. Willie wore twin knives strapped on his chest, two small weighted clubs in loops on his belt. Modesty carried the kongo in a pocket near one shoulder and wore a holstered Colt .32 at her hip.

There had been some argument as to what part Gus should play. After Willie had checked carefully to make sure they were first in the field, he and Modesty had proposed finding a hidey-hole for Gus until the action was over. Gus had protested vigorously, pointing out that as bodyguards they were supposed to guard his body, which they couldn't do if he wasn't around. In the end they had taken him up with them on the platform of the power-driven hoist that rose on the outer side of the central span.

They had hardly heard the sound of the aircraft passing a mile away, but it was enough to alert them to a possibility, and they were watching when the 'chutes opened briefly on the final approach. Gus whispered, 'Three of 'em. By air. Jee-sus!'

Willie said softly, 'Fancy stuff, Princess. But they're good.'

'Yes. I wish now we'd slipped Gus a mickey and tucked him away safe somewhere.'

Gus sniffed in disapproval. 'I'd be real put out if you had, Miss Modesty. What we gonna do? Wait for 'em to come at us?'

'Better them on the move than us. Easier to spot.' She looked about her at the network of girders and stanchions forming the skeleton of the structure. 'These stanchions throw shadows. Stand close against one, Gus, and don't move unless I tell you to.'

Several floors below, Asmodeus was climbing a rope he had cast with a grapnel tipped with solid rubber, now caught over a higher girder. It had been agreed between the Dark Angels that there could be no pre-planned combination moves such as those they had devised for the Kaltchas contract. They would be engaged with opponents of high reputation who were expecting attack, and in this chosen arena of the half-built carpark all action would have to be improvised with each man acting on his own initiative according to the way the combat developed.

This was new for the Angels, and intensely exciting. It also introduced an element of competition, for each was eager to claim either Modesty Blaise or Willie Garvin as a victim, or better still both. One thing the novelty of the coming confrontation had not done was to diminish their confidence in the slightest degree, for it was established in their psyches that they were superior beings to whom defeat and death could not come.

One floor below where his quarry waited, Asmodeus stood by a stanchion rising from a nine-inch I-girder and put miniature night-glasses to his eyes for the fourth time. After a few seconds he smiled, lowered the glasses, pulled goggles down over his eyes and took a small CS gas bomb from a pouch at his hip. It was a long throw across the angle between the east wing and the main span to the floor above, but Asmodeus felt no shred of self-doubt as his arm swung.

The missile landed on the concrete platform a few paces from Gus and began vomiting gas. Within two seconds Willie was there, kicking it out over the edge. Gus was coughing, hands clutched over his eyes as Modesty reached him, holding her breath but with her own eyes streaming. Gripping his arm she hauled him across to the hoist platform, pushed him so that he sprawled on to it, then drew her Colt and knelt to press it into his hand as she whispered, choking a little, 'When you get below find a hole and *stay* there, Gus—shoot anyone who gets in your way.'

She groped for the switch-box, found the start button, and felt the hoist sink away from her as the engine below came to life. When she turned away from the edge Willie was beside her, crouching, knuckling an eye, a knife held by the blade. She said. 'Split. On the run till we can see straight.'

They had both seen the canister hit the concrete and bounce, and could judge the direction from which it had been thrown. Together they moved the opposite way, diverging. Each carried an empty sack picked up from a pile at the foot of the hoist. Using her folded sack as protection for her hands, Modesty slid down two stanchions to a lower floor, gripping the flange on each side of the stanchion to control the speed of her descent.

At the back of her mind she was very conscious that she and Willie had been prodded into action with no time for serious preparation, while their three opponents had taken whatever time they needed to choose the arena and equip themselves for the occasion. She had seen them only as dark figures at a distance when they landed, but knew they were very special operators, highly skilled and organised.

She sought to get closer to their minds, recalling that whoever had thrown the CS bomb must have located one of them, probably Gus himself judging by where the canister had landed, yet there had been no shot, no attempt to kill. Did this mean they carried no weapon to kill beyond arm's length? Or were they hoping to maintain their practice of faking an accident? Or were these men so sure of themselves that they felt able to play cat-and-mouse with their victims?

One floor down and in the west wing, Willie Garvin had an unhappy feeling that he was cornered. Somebody was stalking him, and his eyes were not yet working well enough to pick out a shape in the deceptive starlight. From where he stood a long scaffold pole extended across a corner formed by the inner side of the wing and the main span. It would take only four seconds to swing along that, he decided, and tucked under his belt the sack he carried.

Among other hobbies, Willie Garvin was part owner of a tenting circus that travelled Europe, and he would sometimes spend a few weeks with it, doing a knife-throwing act under the name of El Cazador and Conchita, who was his target. There were one or two occasions when Modesty had played Conchita, with Willie hamming outrageously in Mexican garb for the entertainment of friends in the audience. Willie had also been the stand-in catcher for a trapeze act, and to swing hand over hand along the scaffold pole was easy for him. He was halfway along when he saw the man appear at the end he was approaching, a tall man all in black and wearing a ski-mask. Where the mouth showed, the man was smiling. At the moment his arms were folded and he held no weapon.

Willie looked back and saw a duplicate figure at the end he

had just left, again simply watching, seeing no cause for hurry to dispatch a helpless opponent. Willie looked down at the ground sixty feet below, then at the floor he was facing, one level down from where he hung. The man on his right spoke softly. 'We are The Dark Angels. I am Belial.'

The man on his left said, 'I am Aruga. You will be the first of our victims ever to know who destroyed you.'

Willie thought, *They're psycho. I'm in with a chance.* He began to swing back and forth, talking amiably. ' 'Allo, I'm Willie Garvin. I've 'eard of Belial but I thought Aruga was one of those islands in the Dutch West Indies . . .' He went on talking as the man called Belial drew a knife from the back of his belt and flicked it over to catch it by the blade. By now Willie had increased his swing almost to the horizontal, and a glance the other way showed that the other man was also preparing to throw.

Willie made the final swing forward, putting all his strength into the move, turning in an open back somersault to land on the very edge of the floor below but with residual impetus, diving forward as two knives struck steel or concrete to either side of him. Next moment he had rolled on and come to his feet under the shelter of the floor above, out of sight of The Dark Angels.

Three floors higher, Modesty lay prone, looking down at the corner where Willie had vanished. She had heard his voice, and reached the edge of an unfinished floor just in time to see him escape the knives. Her gun was with Gus, or she could have brought down at least one of the men. Now they had gone, perhaps to follow Willie, perhaps to seek other quarry, herself or Gus. Later, if there was to be a later, she would be furiously scathing with herself for ineptness in approaching the challenge she had accepted, but this was not the moment for dwelling on it.

She edged back, slid down one floor and saw a mortar tray with a spade propped against a nearby stanchion. A length of rope was attached to the tray, perhaps for hauling it across the rough floor. She eyes the spade thoughtfully for a moment or two and decided to stay for a while.

Willie Garvin was also profoundly annoyed with himself and had decided it was high time to take some sort of initiative. To this end he was on the ground now, having slid down a succession of stanchions using the sack to protect his hands from friction. Knife in hand he moved towards the foot of the hoist, thankful that his vision was clear again. It was as he passed the heap of sacks that he heard a soft 'Pssst!' and dropped to one knee, turning ready to throw.

One of the top sacks was flipped back and Gus's head and shoulders emerged from the pile with a hand holding Modesty's gun. His voice held a tinge of disappointment as he whispered. 'On'y you. I hoped it was one o' them parachutin' critturs. How's it goin'?'

Willie breathed, 'I rate three out of ten so far, but I'm 'oping to improve.'

'Where's Miss Modesty?'

'Up top somewhere, I think.'

'Then what the hell you doin' down here? Let's git to helping her.'

He started to clamber out of the pile, but Willie pushed him back and whispered fiercely, 'You stay buried or I'll break your legs. You promised Modesty.' He flipped a sack over Gus's scowling face and moved on to the foot of the hoist.

Several floors above, Belial moved like a shadow through a lattice of girders and stanchions to a section of concrete flooring. In one hand he held the butt of a whip. Its thong was five feet long tipped with a further foot of razor-wire. There came a slight sound ahead and to his right from behind one of the broad steel stanchions. He froze, then edged forward. The lash leapt out, curling round the stanchion at head height, and in the same instant two feet smashed into Belial's back as Modesty launched a high drop-kick from behind.

He was flung forward, his head hitting the face of the unforgiving steel, and he slumped unconscious. Modesty listened for any hint of sound nearby, then moved forward. A spade lay behind the stanchion. It was attached to a length of rope she had used to create the small sound that had decoyed the man into position for her attack. She searched him for weapons, was disappointed to find no gun and only an empty knife sheath, then used the rope to tie his hands behind him with feet doubled back and lashed to the hands.

When she pulled off the ski-mask she saw the face of a man in his middle twenties with blood welling from a cut forehead. In the fall, a medallion on a chain round his neck had emerged from under his shirt. Using a pencil torch and carefully screening it she saw that the medallion bore a winged human figure. Arched above this were the words *The Dark Angels*, and below it the word *Belial*. She switched off the torch and knelt unmoving for a moment, marvelling as she thought, *My God, they're fantasy role-players—but for real!*

She had just risen to her feet when there came from below the sound of the engine that drove the hoist. She moved quickly across the girders to a point where she would be able to watch its progress, not knowing who had started the hoist or what it signified, but with an instinctive feeling that this was probably a Willie Garvin initiative, which was comforting.

On a floor below, Aruga crouched with a dart-gun aimed. The hoist ran in a framework of steel scaffolding and was located so that on each floor it could be halted at a point where a section of flooring had been run in. Aruga heard the engine note change as the platform came to a halt at each of the floors before moving on. Now it was approaching the floor where he waited only eight paces away. It came into view, halting just above the level of the floor, but the platform was empty except for one or two sacks lying on it.

Aruga stood up, moving forward to investigate. As he did so a man's head and shoulders rose from the farther edge of the platform and an arm swung. Startled, Aruga jerked the gun up, but even as he began the movement a knife drove into the muscle of his gun-arm. The weapon fell. Aruga staggered with shock and dropped to his knees. Making a huge effort he rose and lurched forward, reaching towards the dart-gun with his sound arm, but then the man was there, a big man with fair hair he had last seen hanging helpless from a scaffold pole. Now he was holding a second knife with its point touching Aruga's throat. A voice with a Cockney accent said softly, 'You'll 'ave to tell me more about The Dark Angels . . . but not just now.' A hand with an edge like teak struck behind Aruga's ear, and he fell sideways.

Willie Garvin felt slightly less annoyed with himself as he moved into some shadows and waited to see if any attention had been attracted. He had hung from the outer edge of the hoist with one foot in a loop of rope and with the control box detached from its mounting so that he was able to stop the platform at each floor in the hope that at some stage one of the ungodly would approach to investigate. And one of them had.

Looking across from the corner of the east wing, Modesty had been able to make out enough of the scenario to feel that Willie had probably eliminated one opponent, which left only the third man in contention. She moved off, walking on one of the long girders, arms spread for balance, reflecting that the odds were more favourable now but there was still nothing to be complacent about. The last man had to be found and—

He came from behind a stanchion ten paces ahead. She had moved from the girder on to a floored section when he emerged, his arm swinging horizontally in a throw, which told her the missile was not a knife, and as she ducked sideways she glimpsed the razor-sharp ninja star flashing past, its steel edge slicing a shallow cut in her arm just below the shoulder instead of finding the intended target of her throat.

Then he was upon her with a karate attack and she was off-balance, blocking, backing, using all her combat skills to evade a crippling strike, but unable to use her unique ability to fight aggressively while in swift retreat, for the floor edge was behind her with an eighty-foot drop waiting below. Driving him back for a moment with a glancing foot-strike she felt for the last stanchion behind her where the long girder began. By moving fast along it, by *running* along it, she would have the advantage at the far end if he followed.

She had taken only one stride when her foot slipped on a small pool of blood that had run down her arm from the cut in her shoulder and she sprawled forward, clutching at the girder as she fell, her legs slipping over the edge, their weight dragging her body over so that she hung only by the grasp of her two hands on the upper flange of the girder.

The man moved forward on to the narrow steel, treading lightly and with perfect balance, halting near her right hand and looking down at her, teeth showing in a smile. 'We are The Dark Angels,' he said, 'and I am Asmodeus, your destroyer.'

He stamped at her fingers, but she snatched the hand away and transferred her grip to the lower flange of the girder, following suit with the other hand. Now if he tried to stamp on her fingers he would be unbalanced and vulnerable. He made no move to do so, but laughed and took a step forward, turning to stand with legs astride, firmly balanced as he looked down from directly above her.

'I am Asmodeus,' he repeated, and slowly drew a knife from the sheath at the back of his belt.

She had been hoping for this, focusing energy on her stomach muscles, and now with explosive speed she chinned herself and brought her legs up behind him, thrusting her feet between his straddled legs, hooking her heels beneath his knee-caps, then pushing back. He swayed, uttered a wordless cry of shock, then fell, clutching futilely at space. One of his feet caught her ankle, almost tearing her loose from the girder, then he was gone and she heard a scream cut short as he hit a girder, a voiceless impact as he struck another, and a soft sound from far below.

With a huge effort she dragged herself up and crawled to the safety of the flooring to sit with her back against a stanchion, a hand gripping her cut shoulder. It was perhaps a minute later that Willie's voice whispered from the shadows, 'Princess . . . ?'

She said, 'Did you get any?'

'Only one.'

She relaxed. 'That's all right. We're clear. The one who just took a dive was my second.'

He emerged from the shadows, peering at her. Even in the

pale light he could see that her face was grazed, her shirt torn, her shoulder hurt. He said apologetically, 'Sorry to lumber you with most of it. I made a right cock-up to start with.'

'I made one both ends. Christ, Willie, we'd better get our act together. We walked into this as if it was going to be a tea-party.'

He nodded. 'I know. Too cocky. But so were they, only worse. What 'appened 'ere, Princess?'

'I'll tell you while you get a dressing on this shoulder. It took a bit of a cut from a ninja star.'

*   *   *

Fifteen minutes had gone by. A cement mixer was churning below. On a section of the fourth floor Aruga and Belial lay without masks, hands tied behind them, faces empty with shock. Aruga's right shirt-sleeve had been cut away and there was an emergency dressing on his upper arm.

Using the hoist, Willie had just brought the two men here from where he and Modesty had left them bound. He had not been pleased to find the whip tipped with razor-wire that Belial had used as a weapon. Modesty stood with arms folded, a bulge under the sleeve of her shirt just below the shoulder where Willie had fixed a dressing. Gus stood grim-faced, smoking the last of a cheroot having asked Modesty's permission.

Willie walked to where the concrete flooring ended and looked down through the steel skeleton of girders, then he moved to where the two Dark Angels lay and studied them as if trying to come to a decision. From the time he had brought the first of them here, Aruga, not a word had been spoken, and even now the ominous silence continued as Gus dropped his cigar butt and trod it out while Willie adjusted his knives and buttoned his shirt over them.

Another full minute passed before Modesty spoke. She said, 'I'm going to keep this simple. We're going to assume you know who sent you to kill Mr Keyes. If you don't know, it's going to be hard luck.'

Willie took Belial by the hair, hauled him to his feet and

backed him to the edge of the unfinished floor. 'We're mixing some concrete for the road,' he said. 'Asmodeus is already down there making a nice bit of 'ard-core foundation, and we thought you'd like to join 'im.'

Modesty said without much interest, 'Or you could just tell us the names.'

There was a silence. Belial glared defiantly. Willie said, 'He thinks we're bluffing, Princess,' and hit Belial hard under the jaw with the heel of his hand. Unconscious, the man fell back limply into the darkness below.

Willie stepped to the edge and looked down. 'That's amazing,' he said with interest. 'D'you know, he missed every girder going down. Didn't bounce once.' He turned with a grin. ' "Yea, he did fly upon the wings of the wind." Psalm eighteen, verse ten.' He hauled Aruga to his feet and pushed him back to the edge. 'Wonder if I can do it again?'

Modesty said, 'Just the names.'

Sweat was pouring down Aruga's face. He had suffered defeat, and a wound, and the world he lived in had been destroyed. Holding him by the throat Willie said, 'I expect you and your dead mates were going to mix up a bit of concrete for *us*, eh? Still, you can't say we never gave *you* a chance.' He lifted an eyebrow hopefully. 'No? Well, you go and tell Belial 'ow brave you were.'

He shaped for the blow, and Aruga broke. '*No!*' His head sagged and he mumbled, 'Sumner. Brigadier Sumner. Beckworth, Timmins . . . a woman, Harriet Welling . . . that's all I know.' As Willie pulled him away from the edge his legs gave way and he collapsed.

Gus moved forward and looked down over the edge. Belial lay ten feet below in a heavy loading net spread between the girders. Gus sniffed. 'The goddam net held,' he said sourly, and moved away to face Modesty. Taking a handkerchief from his pocket he held it against the weeping graze on her cheek, and saw her skinned knuckles as she took it from him. 'You took some bad lumps for me, Miss Modesty,' he said in a low sad voice.

She smiled. 'Fewer than I deserve. But we stomped 'em, didn't we?'

'Yeah. You an' Willie did. It all worked out okay.' He turned from her and stood with hands thrust deep in his pockets, looking out at the night sky with forlorn eyes. 'It worked out just fine.'

*   *   *

Twelve hours later John Beckworth, OBE, was standing by the big fireplace in the lounge of his Pall Mall club, glancing at the *Financial Times* and expecting that at any moment a steward would tell him he was wanted on the phone. The caller would be Brigadier Sumner, who by now would have received a report from The Dark Angels.

Looking up from the newspaper he saw that a fellow member had risen from a nearby armchair, a member with whom he had only slight acquaintance. Beckworth nodded a greeting and said, ' 'Morning, Tarrant. How's the Civil Service these days?'

'Oh, hoping to please, I think,' said Tarrant.

'Glad to hear it.' Beckworth frowned and stared past Tarrant with some annoyance. 'Good God, there's a chap come into the club wearing a rollneck shirt under his jacket. Doesn't he know the rules?'

Tarrant said, 'He's not a member. He's Chief Detective Inspector Finn, and he's with me, here on business.'

Beckworth stood very still for a moment or two, then laid the newspaper down on a coffee-table. 'Well . . . I'll let you get on with it.'

Tarrant said quietly, 'I'm afraid it's to your address, Beckworth. One of the Dark Angels is dead, the other two are in custody having talked. Sumner, Timmins and Mrs Welling were picked up an hour ago.'

'Ah, I see.' Beckworth stood in deep thought for a few moments, then managed a wry smile. 'I sometimes wondered precisely what your job was, Tarrant. I'd be greatly obliged if we could go to the Secretary's office and then leave before your chap actually arrests me.'

Tarrant's eyebrows lifted in query, and Beckworth went on

anxiously, 'I simply want to settle my bill and hand in my formal resignation. Better for the club that way, surely?'

* * *

At ten o'clock next morning Willie Garvin came into the penthouse kitchen where Weng was making bread. 'Let's 'ave Miss Blaise's orange juice, Weng,' he said.

The houseboy looked surprised. 'But she told us she would sleep till noon and to hell with it. She is restoring herself, Mr Garvin.'

'I know.' Willie waved a sheet of paper. 'But this just came through on the fax. It's from Mr Chavasse. Take a look.' There was nothing exceptional about his showing it to Weng, who handled all Modesty's affairs during any of her absences from home, which were sometimes quite long.

After fifteen seconds Weng blinked once then handed back the paper. Rolling the dough he had kneaded into a ball he wrapped it in plastic and put it in the freezer. 'I will have her orange juice ready in a moment, Mr Garvin.'

She roused when Willie tapped on her door and entered. 'Hallo, Willie love. What is it?' She knew the time was well before the hour she had set herself to wake.

He handed her the orange juice as she sat up. 'Tell you in a minute, Princess. How's the shoulder?'

She wore no nightdress, and looked down at the neat stitches put in by a police surgeon in the small hours of the day before, following the night of The Dark Angels. 'It's fine,' she said. 'I'll be ready for a workout with you in a week.'

He waited until she had drunk the orange juice and set down the glass, then he said, 'Gus has gone.'

She stared. 'Gone? You mean left?'

'Vanished. No note, nothing. Must 'ave slipped out before Weng was up. Weng told me when I came for breakfast, but I didn't see any point in waking you up.'

'No. But . . .' she shook her head, bewildered, 'it's out of character, Willie. Gus is so . . . courteous.'

'That's what I thought too, Princess, and maybe he is, but d'you remember Danny Chavasse rang you from Boston soon after he got there, and you told him old Gus turned out to be Howard A. Keyes, supermarket tycoon?' She nodded, and he handed her the sheet of paper, 'Well, this fax just came through from Danny in Miami.'

The fax read: *I suppose it takes one to know one. Your friend Gus is a double-phoney. When he said 'Jumpin' Jehoshaphat' twice in ten minutes I felt I was watching an old B-picture western. Didn't mention any doubts then because it didn't seem important, but when I rang from Boston you told me about Howard A. Keyes, so now I'm faxing you to say if Howard tries to sell you a gold brick, don't buy it. I'll be on Paxero's yacht with my good friend Julie Boscombe when it sails tomorrow, and meantime I've been mixing with some of the top tycoons in the US of A. They assure me there ain't no such person as Howard A. Keyes, owner of a vast supermarket chain and bits of Texas. The story fed to selected newspapers and magazines was a well-organised ploy. My rich friends suspect connivance by more than one government, which I find puzzling, but there it is. Anyway, the Breguet is wonderful. You shouldn't have, but thank you.*
Love,
Danny

She laid the paper down on her lap and said, 'Tarrant.'

Willie nodded. 'Who else? He set up that roadside fracas with noble old Gus standing by to do his stuff.'

'Which is why he rang to find out which route I'd be taking.'

'Adrian and Tarquin were phonies too. Tarrant's people. I like their choice of names though, Princess.'

She had been sitting tight-lipped, but now she suddenly grinned at him. 'Yes. You can't help admiring the old bastard, Willie. It was brilliant. He hadn't got a lead on these dubious accidents the computers came up with, so he set up a stalking horse as bait, namely Gus. Then he suckered *me* into the game with Gus turning up as my defender, which meant getting *you* in on it because he knew that's how it would be. And we did the job for him.'

Willie was happy to see her eyes sparkling with amusement. He said, 'Crafty old sod. I wonder who Gus is?'

'Yes, that's a question. But whoever he is he's got guts, Willie. He's no chicken, but he was there with us when The Dark Angels came down out of the sky to kill him, and that took cold nerve.' She thought for a moment. 'I wonder why he's run away?' She picked up the bedside phone. 'Let's see what Tarrant has to say.'

She dialled and gave her name to the switchboard operator, but it was Tarrant's assistant, Fraser, who came on the line. 'Sorry, Modesty, he's out of the office. Left for Heathrow ten minutes ago. Anything I can do?'

'I don't think so, thanks, Jack. Is he going abroad?'

'No, just seeing a VIP off.'

'Like Mr Keyes, the phoney tycoon?'

There were several seconds of silence, then Fraser sighed and said, 'I won't ask how you found out. Tarrant's in mourning over conning you, but I'm not. We had lives to save, and we don't have people like you on our books to call on.'

'Excuses, excuses. All right, Jack. Tell him I'll call tomorrow. Take care.'

She put down the phone, threw off the bedclothes and made for the bathroom. 'Two can play at withholding information, and I don't want him calling Tarrant to warn him. We're going to Heathrow, Willie. They have ten minutes start, but I'll be out of the shower in three and dressed by the time you've brought the Jensen round to the front, so we won't be far behind. Let's go.'

*   *   *

Sir Gerald Tarrant and Howard A. Keyes sat with coffee at a table in the café area of London Airport's main concourse. They had been speaking occasionally but had now lapsed into an unhappy silence, each lost in his own thoughts.

A Cockney voice nearby said, 'D'you mind if we join you?' Both men froze, then turned to see Willie Garvin with two coffees on a tray, Modesty Blaise beside him. They rose, their faces filled with dismay and apprehension.

She was in slacks and a thin rollneck sweater, wearing not a scrap of make-up, her hair loose and tied back with a small piece of ribbon. She seemed smaller now than either of them remembered, and they found it hard to conceive that this was the same girl who had fought the power of The Dark Angels for them only two nights ago, fought to the death for them. It made the sick pain they already felt even harder to bear.

After a moment or two Tarrant gestured and managed to mutter, 'Yes, please sit down.'

Willie set down the tray, held a chair for Modesty, drew up one for himself facing her, and gestured politely for the others to sit. Modesty opened her little carton of cream and poured it in her coffee, opened the packet of sugar and tipped it in, all without haste. She stirred the coffee thoughtfully, laid down the spoon, and looked at the American for the first time. 'Well, who are you, Gus?'

He spoke in the voice of an educated man and with a milder southern accent, a voice deeply troubled. 'The name's right, ma'am, and my friends do call me Gus. The rest was lies.'

'You don't own a string of supermarkets in America?'

He shook his head. 'I own a small hardware store in Montana.'

'So how did you get into this?'

'I was with the CIA for twenty-odd years, ma'am. Did a lot of undercover work. Seems they owed your friend Sir Gerald a favour, and when he told them what he wanted they remembered I retired a few years back and they gave him my name. Said I might fit the bill and go along with it. So the stories about the big supermarket tycoon were planted, then I came over, and . . . we set you up.'

'Yes, I know that bit now, and I know the reason why my—what did you call him?—my friend Sir Gerald did it. But you were there with us, up the sharp end with three very smart killers gunning for you. Why did *you* do it, please?'

'Me? Well, I did it for fifty thousand pounds sterling.'

'That's just money. There has to be a reason behind the money.'

'I did it, ma'am, that's all. No excuses.'

Tarrant coughed and said diffidently, 'I feel bound to reveal that Mr Keyes had a wife who was in a local hospice for three years before she died. The hospice now has to raise substantial funds for refurbishment or it will close. Mr Keyes asked that the consideration due to him for his services be paid to the hospice.'

After a moment Willie said, 'Post'umously if necessary?'

Tarrant smiled a small grey smile. 'Of course. But thankfully that doesn't arise.'

Gus Keyes said sombrely, 'We've been sitting here arguing about which of us hates himself most. We could have got you killed, ma'am. Oh, Willie too,' he added hastily.

Willie grinned and said, 'Thanks.'

Modesty drank some coffee, gazing reflectively from one man to the other. At last she said, 'Where did the Jumpin' Jehoshaphat character come from?'

The American gave her a hesitant smile. 'He was easy for me. That Gus was my grandfather, and I can conjure him up any time.'

She looked at Willie. 'He was a nice man, wasn't he, Willie? We liked Gus.'

'They don't make 'em like him any more, Princess.'

Gus Keyes flinched. 'Sure. I don't think he'd like his grandson too much.'

Still speaking to Willie she said, 'On the other hand lives have been saved, killers put away, and our Gus would certainly have wanted to do his best for the hospice, wouldn't he?'

'I just 'ad the same thought. He'd even 'ave done it for the measly fifty grand.'

She frowned. 'It was a hundred grand, Willie. You can't have been listening properly.' She looked at Tarrant. 'That's right, isn't it, a hundred thousand sterling?'

Tarrant sighed. 'Yes, of course.' He looked at Willie and said severely, 'Do listen more attentively, please.'

After a short silence Gus Keyes said, 'You're heaping coals of fire on my head. I don't know what to say.'

'You can tell me why you ran out on me this morning.'

He met her gaze with troubled eyes. 'For shame, ma'am, you

must know that. For shame. The longer it went on, you and me and Willie, the worse I felt.'

'But you agreed to spend a week with us down at the cottage before you went back. A week with no worries.'

He shook his head. 'I couldn't do it, living lies for another week. I couldn't.'

'Well, that won't apply now, will it? The invitation still stands.' She smiled suddenly, and it was a smile that warmed his heart and made him catch his breath as she said, 'But I won't be offended if you turn me down. I know you have a store to run.'

He sighed, and tension seemed to drain out of him. 'The store can wait,' he said. 'You're a very generous lady and I'm deeply beholden to you, ma'am.'

'Good. Now you can stop calling me that.' She looked across the table. 'Will you take care of Gus and his luggage please, Willie? I'll join you at the car in a couple of minutes. I just want a quick word with Sir Gerald.'

'Sure, Princess.' Willie rose and picked up the suitcase beside Gus. 'Come on, old-timer, let's get them oxen harnessed.'

When they had moved away Tarrant said, 'I'd rather you were angry with me than hurt.'

She looked at him, puzzled. 'I'm neither. I was annoyed with myself for being suckered, but that'll help keep me on my toes. Why didn't you simply ask me?'

'You mean tell you the full story and ask you to take part, knowing Gus was a fake? I couldn't believe you'd agree. Why on earth should you?'

She sat thinking for a few moments, then said slowly, 'Yes, you could be right. There had to be someone I cared about involved.' She shook her head and laughed. 'You'd better remember that another time.'

Tarrant looked away. 'My dear,' he said gently, 'I remembered it this time, didn't I? There'll never be another.'

OLD ALEX

On her tenth day in the cave Modesty Blaise roused as usual an hour after dawn from the comatose state in which her life processes were slowed to the essential minimum. She made no attempt to test her condition or remaining strength, for to do so would serve no purpose but would consume a few scruples of precious energy.

She had been walking in the Pyrenees, in the remote area west of the department of Ariège, when she heard the soft report and felt the sharp pain in the back of her thigh as the dart struck. She turned quickly, seeking her attacker, but within seconds she knew what had happened and that she had little hope of defence. Yet still the ferocious instinct for survival that had been bred in her throughout her childhood made her sink to the ground and slump as if unconscious before the tranquilliser had in fact taken hold.

She lay very still, slowing her heartbeat to lengthen the time it would take for blood carrying the drug to reach her brain. She had worked with a vet on a game reserve in East Africa, and knew that if the dart carried imobilon she was dead. Imobilon was for elephants and rhino. More likely it carried a mix of meditomidine and ketamine. Whoever had fired it, he or they would come to complete whatever their purpose might be, no doubt carrying the tranquilliser gun but perhaps a handgun also, and perhaps . . . perhaps she could . . .

Her senses were swimming, and she fought to hold back oblivion. Perhaps she could . . . do something . . .

But there was no sound, no rustle of sun-dried grass beneath approaching feet before darkness closed about her.

When she roused from a stupor her reliable internal clock told her that some three hours had passed. She was lying in a cave, a small cave some twelve feet deep and with a ragged arch of an opening no more than half the size of an average door. But this opening was blocked by a boulder rolled hard against it, a boulder that would have required mechanical aid or at least two men with crowbars to manoeuvre it into position. Outside it was still day, but the only light in the cave came through a few narrow gaps at one or two points round the edge of the opening where the boulder did not quite fit.

She waited until her senses were clear, then sat with her back to the cave wall near the boulder to assess her situation. Three days ago she had set out on this walk-about. It was something she still did from time to time, an escape from ease and comfort, a reminder of the childhood years when she had wandered for thousands of miles through the Middle East and North Africa. Sometimes now she joined Aborigine friends in the Australian outback, but usually she went alone, walking barefoot, wearing only a cotton dress, carrying a small pack with a bottle of water, some packets of dates and nuts as emergency food, a few toiletries and a change of underwear—a luxury compared with the wardrobe of her early days.

She was highly skilled at living off the land, and according to Willie Garvin was well able to eat things no hyena would touch, but here in the Pyrenees food had presented no problems. Certainly this stretch of land through the slopes of the foothills was remote, but there was always a small farm within six or seven miles, and occasional villages on tributaries of the Salat and Ariège rivers. She carried a little money with her, but the French farm families were intrigued by her, and hospitable, and she had found it hard to pay for whatever food they provided.

As she sat in the cave on that first day, watching a narrow beam of sunlight fall across her thighs, she knew that she had been imprisoned here to die slowly. Somebody had put out a contract on her for an aggravated killing, and whoever was handling the contract had planned it carefully. Only Willie Garvin and Weng, her houseboy, knew what she was doing and where.

So she had been followed from London, which called for considerable organisation, and then tailed expertly to Lacourt, where she had left her car, and on into the mountains until the contractors had found the right moment to strike.

It had been skilfully done, and clearly there had been teamwork with radio communication, for somebody had reconnoitred ahead and found the cave. She did not wonder what other method of aggravated killing might have been chosen if the cave had not presented such a perfect opportunity, for that was unimportant. The contractors and whoever employed them were also unimportant. They could wait till later—if there was to be a later. Nothing mattered now except survival.

Her pack had been taken. She had no food, no water, nothing but the clothes she wore—bra, pants and a cotton dress. The boulder was immovable. A search of the cave had produced little of use; dust, gravel, scattered pieces of rock, feathers, a skeleton of a bird, animal droppings, two or three sticks, and—the only sign of human existence—the empty cigarette packet of a long extinct brand.

Unless somebody freed her by moving the boulder she would die. The chance of anyone passing nearby, a local or walker like herself, was remote but not impossible. The problem would be to know if this happened, and even through the widest gap between rock and cave-mouth, perhaps two inches, she could see only a narrow segment of thinly grassed earth extending for some twenty yards before sloping down out of her sight.

Willie Garvin would be concerned if she failed to contact him after two weeks. He would call the small hotel at Lacourt where she had left the car, then come out to find her, but she had followed no particular route, and the chances that he would stumble upon the cave were infinitesimal; except that he was Willie Garvin, who had a remarkable intuition for anything concerning her, who might well follow the route she had taken, and who would instantly be curious about a large boulder in an unnatural position.

But that, if it happened, was many days in the future. Her sole task must be to remain alive for as long as possible, so that the infinitesimal chance might grow to become minute. To do this she would need all her mental skills and all the abilities she had learned from Sivaji, the ancient guru in the Thar desert north of Jodhpur, for without a controlled slowing of heartbeat and breathing no human could survive more than a few days without water.

So it was that on the tenth day, when she roused from the coma she had lain in from dusk to an hour after dawn, she sat up slowly and waited for body-heat to return. She was wearing only bra and pants, for her dress had been pushed with a stick through a ground level gap to one side of the cave-mouth. She drew the dress in carefully through the gap and began to suck from it the heavy dew it had collected overnight.

When she had taken all the moisture it would yield she laid it aside and began to work on the task she had begun eight days ago, moving very slowly and with minimum mental and physical effort, listening carefully for any sound from outside.

One of the sticks was of cane, and with a sharp stone she had cut about four inches from one end of it. Now, using the quill from a feather, she was boring out the central pith from the cut piece. Most of this was now hollow, and she had cut a thin notch close to the open end to make a whistle. She did not know how effectively it would work, but it had been good for her morale to do something undemanding but positive during her listening-out periods. These were from early morning till mid-morning, then from mid-afternoon till dusk. The rest of the day and night she was comatose.

She worked with a blank mind, without hope, without despair, and at about eight o'clock when the whistle was finished she tried it once, and allowed herself a moment of pleasure at the shrill sound it produced. Beside her lay the rest of the cane with a piece torn from her dress tied to one end. *Got the whistle and the flag now, Willie*, she allowed herself to think. *Come soon.* Then she withdrew her mind from all thought and stimuli except for the listening.

It was two hours after dawn next day when a sound triggered her to wakefulness. At first she was unsure that she had heard

anything, but then it came again, a crunching as of wheels on a
rocky track, from somewhere to the right of the cave-mouth and
drawing nearer, but below the slope where the ground dipped.
Normally she could produce a taxi-hailing whistle of ear-splitting
quality with fingers to her mouth, but not with parched lips and
drained energy. This was why she had contrived the little cane
instrument.

Now she pushed her flag through the gap at the top of the
cave-mouth and knelt with her face close to the gap. It was a
huge effort to blow, and to keep blowing, to use the other hand
to wave the flag from side to side and to crane her neck in an
effort to see through the gap. After perhaps fifteen seconds she
paused to listen, chest heaving and weakness flooding her limbs.

The crunching sound had stopped. Again she began to whistle
and wave her flag. She could see nothing through the gap, nothing,
and could feel despair gathering to pounce when, startlingly near,
she heard a gruff voice speak with rising astonishment. '*Il-y-a
quelqu'un là? Dedans?*'

She could manage only a husky whisper as she said in French,
'M'sieu, I am trapped in a cave behind this boulder. Can you
hear me?'

Part of a face came into her view on the far side of the little
gap, an old and weatherbeaten face beneath a shock of thick grey
hair. '*Une femme?* How in the name of God—?'

She broke in. 'Please, m'sieu. I have been here for some days
and I am very weak. Please bring help to move the boulder.'

The grey head nodded. 'Wait, mam'selle, a few moments only.
Napoleon and I will see to it.' The face vanished, but the voice
continued briefly and she had the odd impression that the man
had said, 'Bloody hell!' in English.

Slowly pulling on her dress, she knew that she must be disorientated and had misheard. It was not surprising, for the last
two minutes had produced the effect of shock in her, and she
was reaching within herself now to regain control.

The man had referred to 'Napoleon', a friend presumably, and
had spoken of a 'few moments only'. This she could not understand. It would take four strong men to roll that boulder away

without implements for leverage. She was mentally preparing what she would say to him on his return when there came a clanking sound and strong, work-worn fingers pushed a length of chain through the gap.

The voice said, 'Pass it round the rock, mam'selle, and back to me through the little space on the other side.' A throaty chuckle. 'It is good fortune that I came to haul timber today.'

She took the end of the chain and drew it across the boulder, relaxing now in the knowledge that the man knew what he was doing and she could leave it in his hands. A second chain was fed through to her, and after a few moments she saw them both tighten round the boulder. From outside she could hear him talking to somebody, encouraging, cajoling, and it was suddenly clear to her that this was Napoleon, a beast of burden.

There came a heavy thudding sound from close outside, and with strange certainty she knew that he was using a pickaxe or heavy crowbar to dig away the ground by the outer base of the rock so that it would move readily. After a few minutes the thudding stopped and part of his face reappeared at the gap. 'Soon, mam'selle. Soon now.'

'Thank you. Please tell me your name.' She wondered if she inwardly feared hallucination and was seeking his name to give him reality.

'Me? I am Old Alex, mam'selle. Alex Mirot, from the Mirot farm. And you?'

'Modesty Blaise. From England.'

'Enchanted to make your acquaintance, mam'selle. You speak very good French.' She saw part of a smile on the brown face, then he was gone and she heard him shouting, urging Napoleon on.

The rock shook, and its base shifted a few centimetres. A crowbar was thrust through the gap, levering against the edge of the cave-mouth, then sunlight blazed suddenly in upon her as the rock rolled and settled, leaving an ample gap on one side. She crawled through into the open, got slowly to her feet and stood with head tilted back, eyes half-closed against the light, breathing deeply.

Old Alex was taking the chains from round the boulder. Napoleon, a massive ox, stood waiting patiently to be re-harnessed to the long cart that stood a little way off. Slowly she absorbed the scene, and realised that the cart must have been moving over a patch of gravel at the foot of the gentle slope when she heard it.

She swayed, and Old Alex dropped the chains and moved towards her. Weakness was mounting in her now, but her mind was strangely clear and perceptive. She saw that this grey-haired French farmer was as fit as a lifetime of hard work and contentment would make a man. He was of medium height with a square face, blue eyes and a gentle manner, concerned for her now as he said, 'You must rest, mam'selle. There are sacks in the cart for you to lie on. I will take you home.'

She knew her face must be gaunt, her cheeks sunken, and her appearance had worried him, but she managed to smile as she said, 'Thank you, Old Alex. Thank you from my heart.'

Then abruptly her strength was gone and she would have fallen if he had not caught her. He stooped to slip an arm beneath her knees and straightened up, cradling her with her head against his shoulder, her eyes closed in deepest sleep. He spoke a word to Napoleon, and moved towards the cart, looking down at the pallid face. '*Ah, la pauvre petite,*' he said softly, and shook his head in bewilderment. 'Bloody hell . . . !'

*   *   *

The Mirot farm stood between woodland and pasture, a kilometre from the cave and three kilometres from any other habitation. From it, a cart-track led down through the subalpine terrain to a lateral road through the foothills. Four generations lived in the rambling farmhouse and outbuildings, and in the four days since she had been brought here Modesty had seen them all but had little idea of who was related to whom.

Of the oldest generation there were only two—Old Alex and Matilde, a quiet, sharp-eyed woman, perhaps a year or two younger than Alex and presumably a spinster since she wore no wedding ring.

There were two men and three women in their late forties and early fifties. Of these, Pierre Mirot was evidently the head of the family, and it was his wife, Beatrice, who had taken upon herself the task of looking after Modesty, bringing her very small dishes of bread and milk every hour or so for the first two days, then moving on to eggs, meat and fish, again in small portions.

Modesty had no idea who the other man and two women were, but had learnt their names and thought one of the women was the man's wife. The third generation consisted of two boys and two girls ranging from eighteen to twenty-four or five, offspring of Pierre, Beatrice and the others. These young ones had themselves produced three small children, two boys and a girl.

It was soon apparent to Modesty after she roused from her first long sleep that her arrival was the most exciting event the Mirot family had known for a long time. In turn they all came to see her in the little bedroom she had been given. None showed any hint of peasant dourness, and she was touched by the courtesy they displayed in asking no questions they felt might distress her.

She had told Pierre the simple truth, that she had been walking along when she had been hit by a dart she found in her leg later, and that when she came round she found herself in the cave. She also told him she had no idea who would wish to do such a thing to her, which was true in particular but not in general, for she had no wish to speak of her background. She suspected that the family felt she had been only three or four days in the cave rather than ten, and she made no attempt to correct this belief, for again she had no wish to explain how she had managed to stay alive for what seemed an impossible time.

The Mirot family appeared to get on remarkably well together. Like Beatrice, they all took to calling her Modesty, and showed unfailing consideration. On the second day Pierre asked if she wished to inform anyone of her safety and whereabouts. There was a village with a telephone only three kilometres down the track, and he would gladly drive her there tomorrow if she felt well enough. The farm owned a car, he informed her, a Citroën, old but with some mileage left in her. Money? She was not to concern herself. She was a guest of the family, and Old Alex would be greatly upset if she distressed herself about a few francs.

So it was that on the third day she was able to phone Willie Garvin and tell him something of what had happened, but she cut short his startled questions. 'No, leave it, Willie. Details when I see you. I'm fine now, but if you're free I'd be glad if you'd come out here in about a week's time. I'll ring the hotel at Lacourt and tell them you'll pick up my hired car and deliver it to the garage. Then there's something special I'd like you to do for me as a thank-you to these good people . . .'

From the fourth day onward she was up and about, eating with the family in the big kitchen, gaining lost weight and restoring muscle-tone. Janine, one of the younger girls, had lent her a few clothes, and shoes were no problem for she had gone unshod throughout the years of her childhood. She particularly enjoyed the evening meal in the kitchen. The Mirot family were much given to argument and there was invariably a babble of voices raised in dispute on any subject that might come up either on the radio or in the newspaper collected daily from the village.

Old Alex intrigued her. He was the oldest member, certainly not married to the elderly Matilde she realised as time went on, and apparently none of the others was his son or daughter or grandchild, yet he was clearly much respected and treated with affection by all.

To her surprise she now knew that he had in fact said 'Bloody hell!' that day at the cave, for she had several times heard him use it again as an interjection. Occasionally other odd English words emerged. A grumbling 'dim view' was familiar to her, but something that sounded like 'wizard prang' rang only the faintest of bells. The rest of the family took these oddities for granted, they were just things Old Alex had always said.

Her fifth day at the farm was a Sunday. Pierre drove Beatrice and the three children to the village church. The rest of the family, apart from Matilde, walked the three kilometres. For the first time Modesty found herself alone on the farm with the old lady, sitting with her at the kitchen table as she started to prepare a great mound of vegetables for the Sunday dinner.

Modesty said, 'Can I help, Matilde?'

A brisk shake of the head. 'You must rest, child, rest. Old Alex will be cross with me if I allow you to work. He will start with his bloody hells.'

Modesty smiled. 'We'd better not have that on a Sunday. I wonder where he picked up such words. Has he been to England?'

Matilde shrugged. 'He came to us here when I was a girl of eighteen. He has never been away.' She began to scrape some carrots, her eyes distant, remembering. 'It was from June to February before he spoke. There was more English then. He was not well.'

It was not easy to follow the old lady's rambling comments. Modesty said, 'In what way was he not well?'

'It was his head, of course. He had fallen down a little cliff near Pic de Zarra and cracked his head. My brother Maurice found him,' she looked up over her spectacles, 'as Old Alex himself found you . . . how long is it now? Fifty years later.'

'So he was not of the family?'

'Not then, no. But naturally he became so.'

Modesty sat very still, a strange suspicion growing within her. She said quietly, 'Did he tell you his name, Matilde?'

'Ha! It was impossible not to know that, for he said nothing else through all the early days that I nursed him except his name, Alex something, and a number.'

'I see.' Now the suspicion was becoming conviction. 'Are you the only one left who remembers that time?'

'I suppose so. My two older brothers are dead, my older sister married and moved to Pamiers. My nephew Pierre, who is Maurice's son, was only just born.'

'So Alex came, and stayed, and nobody since has wondered where he came from?'

Matilde put the carrots aside and began to peel potatoes. 'Why should they? For them he has always been here, a part of the farm.'

'Yes, of course.' Modesty was silent for a few seconds. Then, 'Do you remember what he was wearing when your brother brought him home injured?'

The old lady peeled two potatoes without speaking, then put down the knife, wiped her hands on a tea-towel and stood up. 'Come,' she said, and moved towards the stairs. Modesty followed, intrigued yet strangely reluctant, half-wishing she had never asked the first question about Alex. When she hesitated at the door of Matilde's bedroom the old lady beckoned her in, closed the door and moved to a big chest of drawers. Kneeling creakily, she opened the bottom drawer and lifted out several layers of clothes wrapped carefully in tissue paper.

Again she beckoned, and Modesty moved forward to look down into the drawer. Lying at the bottom was a jacket, torn and stained, deliberately stained it seemed, with the buttons removed. But it had once been blue and was of military cut. When she looked more closely she could see where the wings insignia had been removed from above the breast pocket.

Matilde looked up. 'He was wearing this,' she said.

Modesty knelt beside her. 'This was during the war? He was an English airman, shot down over France and trying to escape across the border into Spain?'

'Who knows? He remembered nothing.'

'But surely you must have—' She broke off, unwilling to complete the question. 'Has he never recovered his memory, Matilde? Even in some small way?'

She shook her head slowly. 'After some time he began to work with us. Then to speak. It was like a child learning to speak, in French of course. After two years he was one of us.' She hesitated, then reached beneath the collar of the jacket and drew out a tape with two small flat discs on it. 'I took this from his neck on the day my brother brought him home.'

The work-worn old hand trembled a little as Modesty took the tape and read what was stamped on the discs. After a few moments she handed it back and said gently, 'Did you never show him this? Or the jacket?'

Matilde replaced the discs and ran a palm over the jacket to smooth out a fold. 'I hoped he would marry me,' she said. 'For years I hoped, but he did not wish. Bloody hell. Now it has long ceased to matter.'

Modesty knelt gazing down into the drawer. 'Oh, my God,' she thought. 'Oh, my God.'

*   *   *

On the eleventh day of her time at the farm Willie Garvin arrived driving a new Range-Rover and with a suitcase of her clothes and shoes. It was around mid-morning. Apart from Beatrice and the two young mothers and the three children, all the family was out working. Willie was fluent in French, his accent far better than in the Cockney English he chose to maintain. Moreover he had a gift for being at home on any level and for being liked by being himself. It had been explained by Modesty that he was neither husband nor partner, simply a close friend of long standing. To Beatrice this was baffling.

'Why are you not married?' she whispered as she stood with Modesty and watched the two young mothers talking eagerly with him, laughing at something he had said. 'There is some problem?'

Modesty smiled. 'Not really, Beatrice. It's just that we're happy as we are.'

'Ha! You English!'

It was an hour before she could get Willie away from the women and children to go with her on the walk she took morning and afternoon now that she was herself again. He was desperate to know what had happened to her, and she told him as they walked to the cave where Old Alex had found her, a kilometre from the farm. When she had finished, and he had seen the cave and the boulder, he leant against the rock wall beside the cave-mouth, arms tightly folded, eyes like blue stones, fighting to control the huge fury that possessed him.

She had known it would be so, and that no words could ease his reaction, it would have to run its course. She patted his arm, kissed him lightly on the cheek, then moved away a little and sat on the grassy slope, looking down towards the wooded valley where Alex and Pierre would be working now. After a minute Willie came to sit beside her, taking her hand and touching the knuckles to his cheek. He was a little pale, and his smile was forced, but the rage had been absorbed and dispersed.

'Well, sorting out whoever set this up'll keep me out of mischief for a bit, Princess,' he said, still holding her hand. 'You got any ideas?'

'Nothing concrete, Willie. Somebody hates me pretty badly, but you could form a club from those people. Most of them you can discount because they're no longer in a position to have me put down. I'd say it's a contract job, but who paid and who took the contract is anybody's guess.'

Willie said, 'Salamander Four? You cost them fifty grand when you made them cancel that contract for an obscene killing of Steve and Dinah after the Kalivari caper. The money's nothing but they don't like losing face and it's not the first time you've hurt them.'

'Salamander's a possible,' she agreed, 'but I've no idea who they might have contracted to do the job. Could be any one of a dozen groups, there are plenty about these days. They'll be in the Yellow Pages soon.'

Willie gazed absently down into the valley. 'It's got to be settled, Princess. Will you leave this one to me?'

'No, Willie love, I won't. I agree it has to be settled, but we'll take a lot of care and thought over it. When it's known I survived they'll expect trouble, so let's wait for them to drop their guard a bit. Meantime let's both watch ourselves. Nobody who knows us is going to put me down without being damn sure they have to put you down too.' She paused, frowning, then gave a little sigh. 'Anyway, there's something else that needs sorting first.'

'Something else?' He looked at her curiously. 'Here?'

She nodded, troubled. 'When we go back for the mid-day meal you'll meet Old Alex, the man who saved me. He's a lovely character, about seventy-four or five I think, but tough as hickory and with years left in him.' She drew a deep breath. 'Willie, he's also English, part of a bomber crew I imagine, I don't know the details. They were probably shot down over France around June 1943, and I don't know what happened to the rest of the crew.

What I do know is that Alex, probably aged twenty or twenty-one, was trying to get across the border into Spain when he took a bad fall.'

Willie was staring at her incredulously. 'Blew 'is memory? All those years back?'

'Yes. He suffered a head injury that brought on total amnesia. The brother of Matilde, that's the old lady you saw at the farm, he found Alex unconscious and brought him home. The boy didn't speak for months, except to give his name and number, but even that soon faded. Matilde nursed him, he picked up French, became one of the family. He's been here ever since. That's the bones of it, Willie.'

Willie Garvin shook his head as if to clear it. 'God Almighty,' he said softly. 'What a story. How d'you find out, Princess?'

She pressed his hand. 'Let's start walking back, I'll tell you as we go.'

He rose and drew her to her feet. As they began to walk she said, 'It's not a family secret. Old Matilde is the only one of her generation left, the only one who was alive when Alex came. It's strange, he still uses an English word or two as a kind of exclamation. The day he found me I thought I heard him say "Bloody hell!" and I couldn't believe it. But he does say that, and sometimes he says "wizard prang!"—isn't that one of those wartime RAF expressions for something good happening?'

Willie nodded. 'Heard it in old late-night war movies. It goes with the handlebar moustaches the RAF used to wear.'

'I thought so, but at first I just assumed he'd been in England for a time—with the Free French, perhaps. The family takes no notice of his little interjections. I don't think any of them know or care where Alex came from, apart from Matilde. For them he's always been there, part of the farm. But last Sunday I was alone with Matilde, the others had gone to church, and she spoke of Alex and his bloody hells, so I asked if he'd been in England. That's when it began to emerge, Willie.'

She told him of the strange conversation with Matilde, of going to her bedroom and seeing the jacket and discs. 'It was an RAF jacket. He'd torn off the buttons and wings and the rings on the sleeve, and he'd stained it with God-knows-what so he could pass for a peasant at a distance, I suppose. And there was this thing the forces wear round their necks, with discs giving their name, number and religion.'

Willie stopped short to look at her. 'She'd got 'is identity discs?'

'Yes. She let me handle them, and then she showed me a letter he'd been carrying in one of his pockets. She'd never been able to read it, of course. It was from a girl called Elaine.'

As they moved on again Willie said, 'And she'd never *shown* 'im the letter?'

'She was eighteen when they found him, and after nursing him she hoped he would marry her one day, but he didn't.'

Willie blew out his cheeks in bewilderment. 'Well, weirder things 'appen in wartime, I suppose. Anyway, so now you know who this Old Alex really was—really is?'

'Yes, I know,' she said reluctantly. 'He may be entitled to a different name now, but when he was trying to escape through the Pyrenees in 1943 he was the Honourable Alexander Sayle. I think that means he was the son of a peer. A lord or an earl, maybe.'

'Oh, Jesus!' They walked on in silence for a few moments, then he said, 'What are you going to do about it, Princess?'

She sighed and took his arm. 'I wish I knew, Willie. I wish to God I knew.'

*   *   *

Twenty-four hours later Willie Garvin said, 'Could you run us down to the village, Pierre? I can phone for a car from there.'

The farmer stared. They were standing outside the farmhouse, a little apart from where Modesty was saying her goodbyes to the family. 'A car? But you have this, Willie, the beautiful Range-Rover.'

'Ah, well, I'm leaving that. We thought it might be useful round the farm.'

Pierre blinked, then frowned. 'We do not want payment for the little we have done. It has been our pleasure to have such a welcome guest.'

Willie put a hand on his shoulder. 'I know that,' he said very quietly, 'but it's not payment, Pierre, she's just saying thank you. So am I. Alex saved Modesty's life, and all the riches of Versailles mean nothing to me beside that. Please don't turn us down, Pierre. It's not from the pocket, it's from the heart.'

Pierre stood in thought, running a hand over the Range-Rover's wing. Then he smiled. 'Old Alex will love this,' he said.

*   *   *

'More tea?'

'If you please.' Sir Gerald Tarrant passed his cup. He had left his office in Whitehall where he headed a Special Intelligence Group and was sitting with Modesty Blaise and Willie Garvin in the big drawing-room of the Hyde Park penthouse that was her home. Three days had gone by since her return with Willie. She had telephoned Tarrant at once, for her regard for him was almost filial, but he had not seen her till now, and was relieved to find her looking fit and well after the appalling ordeal Willie had described to him.

She was wearing a summer dress in pale yellow, and her hair was up, exposing the lovely column of her neck. Tarrant noted that Willie's eyes rested on her, not watching, just gazing with dreamy content. It was, Tarrant felt, a rewarding occupation. Sometimes, alone, he was swept with shame at the memory of other ordeals she had endured of which he had been the cause, and one of which he had been the occasion, when he had watched, helpless, as she fought unarmed and naked in the great crystal cave to save him from death. Those searing moments would live in colour for him for the rest of his life.

Yet whenever he saw her the shame was washed away by the smiling affection with which she always greeted him.

As he took his cup from her he said, 'Would you like me to run over my report again?'

She shook her head and gave him a somewhat rueful look.
'No, I think we've got it. The Honourable Alexander Sayle was
the elder of the two sons of Viscount Sayle of Casterlaw, now
deceased. In late May 1943 he was captain of a Halifax bomber
that failed to return from a mission. The crew baled out over
France and were taken prisoner. They reported later that the
aircraft had been badly damaged. Alexander, as captain, presumably baled out after the crew had gone, but he was never captured
and never heard of again. He was first reported missing, and later
missing believed killed.'

She looked down at her tea, prodding the slice of lemon in it.
'Alexander's brother Mark, younger by four years, inherited the
title twenty-five years ago. He is married with children and grand-
children, and occupies the family manor house in Kent. He is
renowned for his charitable work, and well respected in the city
and in the country.' She stopped and looked a question at Willie,
who nodded.

'That's it, Princess.'

She turned to Tarrant. 'So?'

'So what are you going to do about this obscene attempt to
kill you slowly? I understand you made no report to the French
police.'

She shook her head impatiently. 'Don't change the subject.
We're watching our backs and we'll deal with it ourselves. What
could the police do anyway? What I want now is your advice on
what I should do about Old Alex. Oh, I'm sorry, I haven't thanked
you for digging out all these details. I'm very grateful.'

'Not at all. May I say I've never before known you to seek
advice as to what you should do in given circumstances.'

She gave a small laugh. 'Most of the decisions I've had to
make were pretty basic. This one isn't.'

'I can see that, which is why I'm hedging. But since you press
me I think you should make the survival of Alexander Sayle
known to his family.'

Willie said, 'Alexander Sayle doesn't exist any more, Sir G.
He's someone else now. Has been for fifty years.' He looked at
Modesty. 'But I still think you can't just leave things, Princess.

I know it's going to be a traumatic 'appening, but for God's sake, Lord Sayle's got a right to know. Old Alex is his *brother*.'

'In fact,' Tarrant said gently, 'Old Alex is Lord Sayle, and his younger brother is simply the Honourable Mark Sayle.'

Modesty said, 'I don't care about all that. I care only about Old Alex.'

Tarrant nodded. 'And with good reason, for although in truth it was your own abilities that saved you, he was the man who heard and responded. You fear what effect revelation may have upon him, but should you therefore deny him knowledge of his own birthright?'

She sat gazing into space for perhaps a minute, then sighed and looked at Tarrant. 'No, I can't deny that knowledge, either to him or to his family. But you have to keep my name out of the newspapers. You can tell his brother in confidence, because he may want to talk to me, but as far as the media's concerned Alex saved an unknown woman who was injured near a remote farm in the Pyrenees, and this revelation . . . emerged. Dress it up any way you like.'

Tarrant sat up straight. '*I'm* to dress it up? You expect me to break this to the Sayle family?'

Willie said, 'Who else? You've got the clout to make 'em listen to what seems a barmy story, and anyway you *owe* the Princess. Jesus, she's left skin and blood all over the place pulling chestnuts out of the fire for you.'

Tarrant winced. 'Don't remind me.' He looked at Modesty. 'All right, my dear, I'll do what I can. But even with Willie's assessment of my clout it won't be easy to convince Sayle that the brother he's believed dead for fifty years is still alive.'

Modesty opened the handbag beside her and took something from it. She rose, moved to Tarrant's chair and bent to kiss his cheek. 'Thank you,' she said. 'You're not a bad old gentleman really, and you won't have any trouble. Just show Lord Sayle these.' She dropped the identity discs into his hand.

Tarrant stared down at them, then looked up. 'You were able to bring them back with you?'

'Yes. Because Matilde gave them to me. I think *she* believes he's entitled to know of his birthright at last.'

* * *

Professor Stephen Collier said, 'Well you certainly managed to hit the headlines without actually getting your name in the papers. Have you seen him since his brother brought him home?'

'Once,' said Modesty. 'Apparently he kept asking for me, and I went down to Sayle Manor to see him. They were all being very kind, but he looked so . . . so out of place with his nice suit and a clean shave instead of stubble.'

Three weeks had passed since Tarrant's visit. Steve and Dinah Collier, closest of all friends to Modesty and Willie, were with them in the penthouse roof garden on a late afternoon of a warm day. Their glasses were almost empty and Modesty's houseboy, Weng, had just brought a fresh jug of fruit juice and another of meursault and soda.

'Was the old chap unhappy?' Collier asked.

Modesty shrugged. 'I don't know. I was so afraid he'd be angry with me, feel betrayed, but he was so pleased to see me and he seemed as . . . as jolly as ever. But I'm not sure he wasn't putting on a show for me.'

Dinah turned her sightless eyes towards where Modesty sat beside her and said, 'Look, honey, you have to stop fretting. You did what you had to do, and it's something for the Sayle family to work out now. You can argue points on this for hours and get nowhere. I know, because old Collier there kept me awake for about three hours the other night with his ''on the one hand this, and on the other hand that''.'

Collier grinned and flickered an eyelid at Willie. 'I'd been secretly reading an article in *Cosmopolitan* about making the matrimonial bed more exciting, and I thought that a stimulating discussion of moral issues would be a sure-fire success. Unfortunately all I got from my beloved was some neanderthal grunts culminating in a threat to tie my leg in a knot if I didn't shut up. I think it was my leg.'

Dinah gasped. 'He just makes it up, Modesty! He's a terrible liar! That's not how I shut him up in the end.'

'My darling,' said Collier, 'you don't imagine these two experi-enced people ever believe me, do you? Now let's move on to this cave business.' He looked at Modesty. 'You're in a rut, you know. You got a knockout needle in your bottom only last year, and now you've done it again with a dart. I trust it was the other cheek?'

'I'm sorry, Steve, I can't remember.'

'You must try harder, darling. Balance is all. I suggest a small cross tattooed on the puncture next time.'

'He's jabbering like that because he's likely to explode any moment,' said Dinah. 'You watch.'

'Yes, I bloody well am,' said Collier, his lean intelligent face suddenly taut with anger. 'Do you know who those cave bastards were, Modesty? And if so, then what? Or even if not, then what?'

'We don't as yet know who they were,' said Modesty. 'As to "then what?" I'm not making any announcements even to you, in fact especially to you, Steve. You'll only go all bitter and bad-tempered about taking risks and so on. We never take risks we don't have to.'

'I'll do no such thing,' said Collier grimly. 'My heart's desire is that you go and find these unutterably evil buggers and make sure they're never seen or heard of again. I ask for nothing lingering. I'm not a vengeful type. But such creatures aren't fit to live, so please see they don't.'

His voice was shaking as he ended, and Dinah said, 'Easy, tiger. The girl's safe home with us again.' She turned to Modesty. 'Oh God, you should have been at our place when I first told him. Willie had rung and given me the whole story of you in the cave, then Steve came home and I told him. We were in the kitchen, and when I finished I could hear him sort of gibbering, then he actually flung a plate against the wall and smashed it to smithereens.'

'I was throwing it at Dinah,' declared Collier, himself again, 'to stop her snivelling about what had happened to you, but I missed.' He shrugged. 'Nobody's perfect. I remember Cetewayo saying that very thing to me during my last but one incarnation, when I was with his renowned Silver Assegai Impi during the Zulu Wars. I threw my assegai at a redcoat but it went the wrong way and hit Cetewayo in the foot. "Don't worry, Umbopo," he told me as he limped up to me, "nobody's perfect." Then he caved my head in with his knobkerry. I'll never forget it.'

By the time Collier had finished it was tacitly accepted that the cave and Old Alex were not for further discussion, and conversation moved to other matters. At six o'clock the Colliers left to spend a few days with friends in Cambridge. At seven-thirty Modesty and Willie were taking a pre-dinner swim in the pool beneath the penthouse block when the attendant came from his cubby-hole and called, 'It's Weng on the phone, Miss Blaise. Urgent, he says.'

'Thank you, Charlie.' She pulled herself from the pool and moved towards the cubby-hole, dabbing herself with a towel. Willie followed.

'Yes, Weng?'

'I have Mrs Collier on the line, Miss Blaise. She's at Kempton Road Hospital.'

Watching, Willie saw her eyes widen then go suddenly hard as she listened. He was familiar with every nuance of her expression and body language, and knew she was controlling a surge of fury. After perhaps thirty seconds she said, 'I see. Where's their car now?' A pause. 'All right, Weng. Tell her we'll be with her as fast as we can get there and we'll take care of everything.'

She put the phone down. Willie was already holding her wrap for her to put on. As they moved to the lift she said, 'Steve's been beaten up. Pretty badly, I think. Dinah's at Kempton Road Hospital with him.'

Willie's face lost a little colour. He said, 'Is Dinah hurt?'

'Not physically. There was a traffic diversion and Steve lost his way somewhere in the East End. Went into a pub to ask directions, and a man beat him up.'

'Did Dinah say why?'

'No. She told Weng she was with Steve because he didn't want to leave her alone in the car. Somebody jostled her and Steve protested, saying she was blind. Then it happened. She could only *hear* it, of course.' Modesty swallowed hard. 'Oh Jesus, Willie.'

With aching heart he recalled all that he knew of the Canadian girl with honey-coloured hair and a gentle nature who had come so strangely into his life. Since then he and Modesty had twice seen her face lethal danger with unfailing courage, and their affection for her was boundless. Willie imagined her listening helplessly in darkness, crying out, pleading in vain as the husband she loved was savagely beaten, and a wave of rage and nausea swept him.

As they emerged from the private lift into the penthouse foyer where Weng awaited them, Modesty said, 'Do you know how Mrs Collier got him out of the pub and called an ambulance, Weng?'

'She did not say, Miss Blaise. I think she was finding it hard to speak. But she did manage to say that the pub was *The Black Horse* in Waverly Street. Professor Collier told her that, so he must have been conscious. Their car was parked about fifty yards from the pub, she said. If there is anything I can do, I should be most happy.'

They had started to move towards the bedrooms, but now Modesty paused, thinking. After a moment or two she said, 'Phone Inspector Brook and tell him what's happened. Say I'd be grateful for anything he might be able to tell me about *The Black Horse*. We'll leave in five minutes. I'll drop Mr Garvin off to pick up their car and follow me to the hospital. We've no keys but he can hot-wire it. Make sure the guest bedroom is ready for Mrs Collier.'

She looked at Willie. 'I know how you feel, but don't go near that pub. Maybe this is a casual bit of violence but it feels like something more deliberate, so let's find out where we're at before we do anything about the bastard who did this.' She turned to move on to her bedroom. 'Then we'll do something about him, by God.'

*   *   *

The young doctor looked tired and angry. 'Two ribs cracked, damaged knee, query broken nose, heavy facial bruising, internal cuts to the cheeks from his own teeth, and an old-fashioned black eye.' He grimaced. 'The usual expert beating-up.'

Modesty glanced at Willie, then returned to the doctor. 'Usual?'

He hesitated, then, 'We get a casualty like this from *The Black Horse* every few weeks. Don't ever go in that pub unless you're one of their regulars.'

Willie said, 'You mean it's a gang job?'

'Oh, no. It's a crony job. There's a man called Pike, I don't know if it's a first name, surname or nickname, but he reigns in that area like one of the old Glasgow razor-kings. The rest are boot-licking cronies. Maybe he runs some sort of protection racket, I don't know. I only know he likes to maintain a rule of fear . . . and we get the examples here as casualties.'

Modesty said, 'Does nobody ever bring charges?'

The young doctor laughed shortly. 'He can always produce a dozen witnesses to swear he wasn't there, and anyway there's always a threat to the victim's womenfolk. I'll wager your unfortunate friend had a word or two whispered in his ear before he was dumped out on the pavement.' The doctor squeezed his eyes shut for a moment. 'And there's that wife of his. Blind. Don't quote me, but I'd like to get a few volunteers from my rugby club and beat that bastard to a pulp.' Bitterness infused his voice. 'And you know what would happen? We'd all be charged, probably lose our jobs, have to pay compensation and Christ knows what else.' He shook his head and ran a hand through his hair. 'Sorry. I got a bit carried away. Will you be taking care of his wife?'

Modesty said, 'Yes, we're close friends and she can stay with us.'

'That's fine. We'll keep him in overnight but he'll probably be discharged tomorrow. Will she be able to look after him for a few days?'

'Yes,' said Modesty, 'but there's no need. They can both stay with me. Can we see him now?'

'No problem.' The young doctor stood up. 'I'm glad you'll be taking care of Mrs Collier. I only wish somebody would take care of that bloody man Pike. Excuse the language.'

Modesty said, 'That's all right. We feel much the same way.'

Stephen Collier lay in bed in a small room. What could be seen of his face between bandages looked like a bruised plum. Dinah sat holding his hand, turning a tear-stained face to the door as Modesty and Willie entered.

'It's us, Dinah.'

'Hallo, honey.' Her voice was croaky. 'I'm sorry to drag you out.' Modesty took her in her arms as she stood up, holding her close.

Collier surveyed them with his one good eye, then looked at Willie. 'I'm not sorry about dragging you out,' he said, articulating with difficulty. 'I just hope you've missed your dinner. I can't stand people who aren't suffering when I am.'

Willie hid a sigh of relief. 'Is it worse than when Cetewayo clobbered you with 'is knobkerry?' he asked.

Dinah began to laugh and cry at the same time, then recovered herself and whispered an apology. Collier said, 'Willie, I'd be vastly obliged if you'd take Dinah to the canteen or whatever they have here and buy her a cup of tea and a wagon-wheel. This has been much tougher for her than for me, and you're good for her nerves. Tell her stories of your indecent past while I have a quick word with Modesty. Nothing special, but I know I'm going to be pestered about what happened and I'd like to get it over with and then go to sleep.'

Dinah hesitated. Collier said, 'Please, sweetheart.'

Willie said, 'Come on, love,' and took her hand. 'I'll throw in a packet of crisps if you're a good girl.'

When the door closed after them Modesty took the chair where Dinah had been and said, 'Go on, Steve.'

'It was all such a shock,' he said slowly, and there was no humour in his eye now. 'We got lost in the East End. Stupid me. Went into this pub, *The Black Horse*. Took Dinah with me rather than leave her alone in the car. It was so weird, Modesty. There were about fourteen or fifteen men standing around or sitting with drinks. One barman, no women. And the moment we entered there was silence. Everything stopped. I moved up to the bar and said very amiably that we'd lost our way and could they tell me the best way to get to the M11.'

He closed his eye. She saw that his bandaged hand was shaking and took it gently in her own. 'Take your time, Steve.'

He nodded feebly, and after a moment continued. 'Nobody answered. Then a man moved away from the bar and walked past Dinah. He was a biggish chap, square face, black hair cropped short, huge chest, very light on his feet. As he passed Dinah he jostled her with his shoulder so she almost fell. I said something like, 'Please be careful, my wife is blind.'

Collier drew a quivering breath, then winced, a hand to his ribs. 'That was all I said, Modesty, and then he turned on me suddenly, raving at me. Insults. Abuse. Who the effing hell did I think I was? He'd bloody well teach me to give him his props— whatever that might mean.'

'Proper respects. It's top-thug talk. Go on, I've got the picture.'

'Well, I tried to move past him to take Dinah out, and that's when he hit me the first time.' Collier shook his head slowly. 'I've never been really hit before. I was dazed, and I fell down. After that it's all a blur. He kept hitting me, kicking me some-times, hauling me up and knocking me down again.'

Collier stopped speaking and gazed into space as if mentally reliving those moments. When he went on, his voice was a whis-per. 'There were two terrible things. One was that the other men seemed to be . . . excited, stimulated. They watched, and giggled, and said approving things in a sycophantic sort of way. Nobody spoke a word of protest. But worse . . . far worse, I could hear Dinah calling out, begging them to stop what was happening. Begging the man to stop. She couldn't see, of course, but she didn't need to. God, I was so scared for her. I kept trying to call out to her to go. I thought this madman might turn on her, and I couldn't protect her . . .'

His voice tailed away and tears welled from the eye Mod-esty could see. Quickly she moved to dab them away with her handkerchief. He swallowed, fought for control and croaked, 'Oh Christ, darling. Can you imagine it? My poor Dinah.'

'We've been imagining it, Steve,' she said quietly. 'Now just do some deep breathing until you steady up.'

'Sure. Can't breathe too deep with these sodding ribs.' A ghost of a laugh and a wince of pain. Two minutes later he said in a steady voice, 'I won't apologise for the exhibition. Not the first I've done for you, is it?'

She bent to kiss his cheek, then sat down again. 'Are you up to telling me the rest?'

'There's not much left. I think they dumped me outside the pub and pushed Dinah out with me. I vaguely remember her supporting me, trying to get me to the car. When I came round a bit more I was sitting half in the car with my feet on the ground, and passers-by were giving us a wide berth. I couldn't drive and Dinah couldn't do *anything*, but then a builder's van stopped to ask what was wrong. He had a mobile phone and rang for an ambulance. His name's Dan Ringmer, of Ringmer Contractors— remember it for me, Modesty. I must get in touch to thank him. I guess that's about all.'

She studied him thoughtfully. 'No. What is it you wanted to say that you don't want Dinah to hear?'

'Oh God, yes. That's the important thing. The *only* thing that really matters.' He put out his hand to her. 'I'm not going to the police about this because I'm sure it's a waste of time, and I know what you and Willie will be thinking but I don't want you to do anything. Anything at all.'

'Because you're afraid for Dinah? I know how it works, Steve. The doctor told me.'

'All right, maybe it's all a big bluff, but I can't put her at risk, Modesty. I *can't*.'

'Do you think Willie or I would? She's very precious to us, Steve. Look, do you trust us?'

He stared. 'Of course I bloody do. Christ, you've seen us through all kinds of lethal shit.'

'Then you can be sure that nothing we do will create a threat to Dinah. Okay?'

He sighed. 'I've never yet won an argument with you. Okay, then.' He closed his eyes. 'God, I'd like to see that animal get his come-uppance.'

'So would that doctor and a lot of other people. We'll see what can be done. Now I'll just fetch Dinah to say goodnight, then we'll take her home, and if you behave yourself we'll probably be able to collect you tomorrow. All right?'

He opened his eye and looked at her quietly, remembering many things they had shared. 'In some ways you're not too bad,' he said. 'Not too bad at all.'

* * *

At nine-thirty that evening when they were at the coffee stage of dinner at the penthouse there came a phone-call from Sayle Manor. Lord Sayle would like to speak to Miss Blaise if convenient to her. It was Old Alex, and she left Dinah and Willie to talk, taking her coffee through to the drawing-room. Old Alex had nothing in particular to say, yet after half an hour he was still speaking, remembering the occasion of his finding her in the cave, reminiscing about his life on the farm, practising a little of his returning English, and describing the wonders of his life today, of London, of his caring family, of his visit to the House of Lords.

At ten Inspector Brook phoned from reception to ask if it was too late to call with some information he had gathered. Willie said, 'No, come on up, Brookie. She's talking to one of 'er upper class friends but she won't mind coming down-market for a copper.'

By the time Brook reached the penthouse foyer she was waiting for him. 'Hallo Brookie, do you mind if we talk at table? Weng's just making some fresh coffee.'

'I'd love some, thanks.' He kissed her cheek.

'And our friend Dinah is with us. You've met her a couple of times.'

'Indeed. Not a lady I'm likely to forget. I'm an admirer.'

In the dining-room when he shook hands with Dinah he said,

'I'm deeply sorry about what happened to your husband, Mrs Collier. This has been a great ordeal for you.'

Her smile was tired but genuine. She said, 'Thank you, Inspector. If you'll excuse me I'll leave you to talk with Modesty and Willie alone.' She turned her head to Modesty. 'Look in on me later, honey. I won't be asleep.'

'I'll do that.'

Brook watched as she walked to the door and turned into the passage without hesitation. 'How does she do it?' he said softly.

'She knows the layout,' Modesty answered, 'and we're careful to keep everything in place while she's with us. But in a strange area she can locate any sizeable object by making a high-pitched whistle on the edge of human hearing and picking up the reflection.' Her lips tightened. 'It didn't help her at *The Black Horse*. When I think—' She broke off. 'Never mind. What have you got for us, Brookie?' She gestured to Dinah's chair and began to pour coffee.

Inspector Brook said, 'This evening I went over to see Harry Lomax, my oppo who covers that area. He knows all about *The Black Horse* and Pike, and he reckons Pike is the enforcer for a pretty powerful group.' He took the cup Modesty passed him. 'Thanks. Possibly Salamander Four.'

She stared in surprise. 'Salamander Four? Oh, surely not. They're into high-class big money projects, not East End thuggery.'

'Yes, I know you've crossed swords with them once or twice, and my first reaction was the same as yours, but Harry Lomax doesn't exaggerate and he says things have changed. There's a hell of a lot of money sloshing about in the East End these days, and the mobs are getting more sophisticated all the time. Salamander Four always contract out. Okay, if they want an industrial espionage job done they'll give it to a suitable up-market specialist. If they've taken on a killing they'll pick the right hit-man for it. But think of the loot that's gone missing from bank robberies, ram-raids, security van hold-ups over the last few years. Those jobs call for basic thuggery, hard men with iron bars, the lowest layer of the criminal world. So the big-boys are taking over that area, controlling it, sub-contracting. And for that they need enforcers, men who create intense fear, who can intimidate witnesses, intimidate people on juries. Sadistic psychopaths like Pike.'

Brook had been speaking ever more quickly, now he stopped abruptly and shook his head.

Willie said, 'You got a bit carried away there.'

Brook drank some coffee and leant back in his chair. 'Sorry. I must have picked up some of Harry Lomax's frustration about it.'

Modesty said, 'There's nothing he can do?'

'Like what, for God's sake? We can't move without evidence, you know that. If people won't bring charges and won't give evidence we're hog-tied. Will your Professor Collier bring a charge of assault?'

'I'm afraid not. He's scared for his wife.'

'There you are, then.'

There was a long silence. At last Modesty said, 'Well, thanks for calling in, Brookie. If you haven't eaten, Weng can put up a simple supper, or you can stay and have a general natter with some background jazz.' She smiled and touched his hand. 'You're always welcome.'

'Thanks, but I'll be getting home.' Brook sat frowning for a moment, then went on, 'Let's get this clear. I'm a copper, and I don't approve of anything in the way of vigilante action.'

Willie Garvin looked hurt. Modesty said, 'Neither do we. But if I'm attacked I'm entitled to defend myself, surely?'

Willie said, 'And if the attacker doesn't bring charges there's nothing to answer, is there?'

Brook got to his feet. 'Let's leave it at that,' he said. 'Thanks for the coffee.'

*   *   *

Two weeks later Collier stood by the great picture window of the penthouse looking out over Hyde Park. 'They're up to something,' he said. 'I can smell it.'

Dinah came up beside him and slipped an arm round his waist. 'If you can smell, that's good,' she said. 'The nose feels normal now, but it's great to know you've got it working again.'

'*All* the Collier organs are in working order,' her husband announced with dignity, 'as I'm prepared to demonstrate. How about going to bed?'

'Any time, honey. But it's only seven of a summer's evening and maybe we should hold off the demonstration till after our hostess returns.'

'You've been reading books on etiquette. Moreover, you too can smell that they're up to something and you're dying to know what. All right, I'll give you a thrashing at backgammon while we wait. Come on.'

Collier had spent three days at the penthouse after leaving hospital, then he and Dinah had gone down with Modesty to her cottage in Wiltshire for a further ten days. Now they were back at the penthouse and planned to return to their home in Surrey tomorrow. That morning Willie had come up from *The Treadmill*, his pub on the Thames. An hour ago he and Modesty and Weng had left on unspecified business.

'Do you think it's to do with us?' Collier said quietly as he set up the backgammon board. 'I mean with what happened to us at *The Black Horse*?'

Dinah picked up the cup and dice. 'I don't know. Modesty tells me just about everything, but she's said nothing about that.'

'They never do when it's a caper,' he observed. 'Neither before nor after unless you drag it out of them. Come to think of it, we might just as well go to bed.'

She laughed. 'I'll get something out of Willie. Oh golly, it's good to see you back in form, tiger.'

He reached out to take her hand. 'I want to tell you something strange, sweetheart. It's hard to put into words and it sounds crazy, but I have a curious sense of . . . of relief, of satisfaction almost, at having endured a beating-up. I'm a card-carrying coward and the thought of being the kind of victim they some-times show you on television makes my stomach churn. But now

it's happened, and it's past, and I've come out on the other side.'
He laughed suddenly. 'God, I wouldn't want it to happen again,
but . . . I don't know, I've sort of joined the club of those who've
been through it, and I feel a bit braced up by that.' He shook his
head. 'What's a nice girl like you doing, married to a total prat
like me?'

'I can't remember now,' Dinah said thoughtfully, 'but I guess
I had nothing better to do that day. Let's give it a bit longer
anyway. I think I've started a baby.'

Collier stared, then nodded. 'Yes. As a professional statistician
and lustful maths expert I was beginning to suspect something
of the sort.' He took her hand and touched it to his lips. 'That's
wonderful, sweetheart.'

'Yep. Good old fertile Collier.'

'Oh, come now. You were there too, as I remember.' He
released her hand. 'My word, I do lead an interesting life. Do
you know this will be the first time I've ever beaten a pregnant
woman at backgammon.'

'Cocky sod,' said Dinah amiably, and threw the dice. 'Not yet
you haven't.'

*   *   *

Weng sat in a hired car parked a short stone's throw from *The
Black Horse*. During the past week he had checked that the man
called Pike came regularly between half-past seven and eight,
and stayed for about an hour. This evening Pike had arrived ten
minutes ago, and Weng had used his mobile phone to report this
fact. Now he watched with interest as a man and a woman on
foot turned the corner and moved towards the pub.

The man was grey-haired, quite tall but paunchy and round-
shouldered, wearing a dark, rather shabby suit and a clerical
collar. The woman was also grey-haired and running to fat. Incon-
gruously she wore a white T-shirt with *Jesus Saves* on it and
green corduroy trousers. As they passed the car Weng saw that
the man had sad, hangdog brown eyes and carried a concertina
hung round his neck. The woman had blue eyes, wore grey cotton

gloves and carried a small haversack with some papers sticking out of it. In the mirror Weng watched them enter the pub and prepared to follow.

As the door swung to, the clientele of *The Black Horse* fell suddenly silent, all eyes on the newcomers. Some glanced sidelong to where Pike stood drinking with three or four of his close cronies. Here was unusual fodder for Pike, and they wondered how he would react. Pike favoured younger, possibly tougher prey, but all was grist that came to his mill for the propagation of his image as the hardest of hard men.

The couple gazed benignly around, then the man played a long chord on his concertina. 'Good evening, brothers,' he said with a strong Scottish accent. 'Ah am the Reverend James McNally but Ah'd be much pleased if you'd call me Jamie, and here's my wife, Jeannie. We come not to preach but to lift your hearts with songs of praise to the good Lord.' He looked towards the barman. 'You've no objection, brother?'

The barman, a dour man in his fifties, looked a question at Pike, who gave a slight shake of his head and set down his glass. Moving as if to the door, he walked past the woman, jostling her with his shoulder so that she stumbled sideways and almost fell. Her husband said in severe tones, 'Have a care, friend. It's no' polite to be near knockin' a woman doon.'

Pike turned to him. 'Oo the bloody 'ell d'you think you are? We don't want no bible-thumping jocks 'ere.' His fist flashed out in a hook to the head, and the man staggered back, yet even as Pike prepared to follow up he had an odd feeling that his blow had barely connected and it was therefore strange that the vicar or whatever he was had gone reeling back across the bar-room to fetch up against a table near the door.

Pike had taken no more than a pace after his victim when the woman was suddenly there confronting him, eyes blazing.

'Ye'll no' abuse ma husband when he's speakin' for the Lord!' she cried angrily. 'Repent before the Almighty, ye great cowardly bullyin' creature! Doon on yer knees, wull ye? Doon on yer knees an' beg forgiveness, ye fallen brute sinner!' Somebody laughed. Nobody noticed the young oriental who slipped through the door and stepped lithely up on to the table where the Reverend James McNally now stood.

Then it happened. Pike swung an open hand to slap the woman aside, but by the smallest of movements, seemingly unintentional, she evaded the full force of the blow so that it became little more than a light slap across the face. Then one gloved hand swung in a seemingly casual fashion to hit Pike in the face with the little-finger edge, and it was as if he had been struck by an iron bar. He reeled back, blood streaming from his nose, shock and fury exploding within him. Then he launched himself at her.

Throughout the next thirty seconds the woman never ceased talking. At first she moved back in a small circle, seeming ever and by chance just beyond reach of Pike, yet hitting him incessantly with her gloved hands and sometimes with a flickering movement of a sensibly shod foot. After fifteen seconds it was Pike who retreated, trying to escape her, limping, clutching at his ribs, cowering with an arm crooked above his head.

And all the time her penetrating voice hammered at him. 'Have ye no shame, man? Wull ye lay wicked hands on a poor wee woman who did'nae ask but that ye put aside the ways o' violence an' repent before the Lord? For yer ain soul I'm beggin' ye to remember the worm that dieth not an' the fire that burneth for ay. Up, man! Up!' He had fallen, and she hauled him to his feet by an ear. 'I'll have ye fall on yer knees from yer ain guid wish to repent, not from weakness o' the flesh!'

Only one man noticed the young oriental with the cam-corder to his eye, and moved towards him. As he approached the table, the vicar with the concertina gave him a friendly smile. An arm shot out, and the man remembered nothing more until he woke under the table several minutes later. Another crony ventured to intervene between Pike and the woman, reaching out to grab her arm. It seemed almost an accident when she back-heeled him in the crotch. He gave a screech of pain and sank to his knees, clutching himself. The rest simply watched, transfixed, bereft of all initiative.

Then, in the closing seconds of the woman's exhortation, when

Pike was croaking, 'No . . . please . . . no,' the atmosphere among the spectators changed from one of dazed incredulity to something akin to awestruck pleasure. The monster they had long feared and fawned on was being destroyed, and like human jackals they found relish in this.

Pike was on his knees, barely conscious, hands held up before his face. The woman stepped back and took some sheets of paper from her haversack. 'Right, Jamie,' she said with a glance towards her husband, 'Let's have a wee song.' She moved around, thrusting papers into reluctant hands, and looked coldly at the barman. 'We're stubborn folk for the Lord, and it's a song we'll have now from you good people, else it'll mean our comin' back each night till we've stirred the spirit in yer souls.'

The barman had drawn breath to protest, but her last words changed his mind. Stupefied by the concept that this visitation could afflict him nightly, and unable to think of any other action he could take, he looked balefully round at his clientele and muttered hoarsely, 'Sing. Sing, for Christ's sake!'

The concertina wheezed an introduction, then launched into the verse of *Yes, Jesus Loves Me*. Led by Jamie and Jeannie, too dazed to resist, the pub regulars began to sing, feebly at first, but then, exhorted by the barman and under the woman's menacing eye, with greater effort. Pike still knelt, the singers grouped roughly behind him. The woman pinched his ear hard. 'Sing up, ye glaikit tattie-bogle!' she commanded stridently, and Pike began to open and close his swollen mouth in wordless mime.

After one chorus she gave orders for him to be carried outside. The young oriental followed, saw him dumped on the pavement, called for an ambulance on his phone, then listened happily to the renewed singing within for a few moments before making for his car. Two minutes later the grey-haired couple emerged from *The Black Horse*, walked to the corner and disappeared.

Weng waited, but nobody followed, and as soon as he heard the ambulance arriving he drove off.

At nine o'clock that evening Modesty Blaise and Willie Garvin called at Kempton Road Hospital. They had changed their clothes in a hotel room and removed padding, wigs, and coloured contact lenses they had worn as Jamie and Jeannie McNally. Modesty had removed the thin strips of lead she had worn inside her gloves along the little finger edges of the hands.

Dr Ramsey said, 'Aren't you the couple who were here a week or two ago when that poor blind girl's husband got beaten up at *The Black Horse*?'

Modesty said, 'Yes, that's right. We happened to be passing tonight and called in to say that Professor Collier's doing very well and to thank you. We'd like to make a contribution to your staff fund, or to anything for the hospital. Can we leave you and Sister to decide?'

She handed the young doctor a cheque. He looked at it and whistled. 'This is very generous, Miss Blaise.' Suddenly a huge grin spread across his face. 'As a matter of fact we're having rather a good night-shift tonight.' He glanced at Sister beside him, who nodded, then went on, 'This is off the record. We're over the moon because that *Black Horse* thug himself was brought in an hour ago, and somebody's beaten the—the living daylights out of him. You'll never believe this, but apparently it was some old religious bird who duffed him up.'

Dr Ramsey shook his head in disbelief. 'Pike didn't tell us, he hasn't said a word—oh, not because he's stoic, he's just plain traumatised! But when our ambulance chaps picked him up a couple of his cronies were standing around outside where they'd dumped him—ex-cronies maybe, because they seemed quite psyched up about it and weren't doing a thing for him. Anyway, they said this old couple had come in to sing hymns, and Pike hit the man, then slapped the woman and she went for Pike and fairly beat the—er, you know . . .'

'Beat the shit out of him,' said Sister happily. 'He has just about the same injuries as he caused your friend. It's amazing.'

Dr Ramsey lowered his voice. 'And Pike's *crying*,' he said with delight. 'She's broken the bastard.'

Modesty and Willie looked at each other in astonishment, then at Dr Ramsey. Willie said, 'Well, I'm sure that will help speed up our friend's recovery.'

'And we can tell him tonight,' said Modesty. 'He's staying with us. Thank you very much, doctor.'

At noon next day Inspector Brook was in his office with Inspector Harry Lomax watching the tape and listening to the sounds for the third time running. When Brook turned the TV off Lomax wiped his eyes and said, 'It's my best day since I joined the force, Brookie. Tell her if she ever wants to murder someone she can come and do it on my patch for free. What in God's name is a glaikit tattie-bogle?'

Brook said, 'According to Willie it translates as a clumsy scarecrow, but it's much more scathing than that in the vernacular. A Glaswegian called Jock Miller ran her transport section for *The Network*, and Willie says she picked it up from him.'

'Well, give 'em my very best,' said Lomax. He nodded towards the screen. 'But I can't tell my boys who they really are?'

'No way, Harry. That was Jamie and Jeannie McNally, who came and went, nobody knows where from or to. Wasn't it bloody marvellous, though?'

Lomax grinned. 'Pike's deader than if they'd killed him. He won't dare show his face in the East End again. Look, can I have copies of that tape? I could push them around a few pubs on my patch where they'll love seeing Pike getting duffed up. Could do us a bit of good.'

'I'll ask her,' said Brook, 'but if she says no, that's final, Harry.'

Lomax lifted a hand. 'It's final. I owe her more than that.' He hesitated. 'Any chance of meeting her?'

Brook looked doubtful. 'She doesn't like a lot of attention, or thanks either. I can't go to her and say my old mate Harry Lomax is dying to meet her. But ... well, if ever something crops up, a window of opportunity as they say, I'll do what I can.'

'Thanks. But don't forget.' Lomax got to his feet and stood gazing at the blank screen thoughtfully. 'You can tell her one thing, though. She'll know it, but tell her anyway. Whoever the big boys behind Pike are, they won't have to guess who Jamie and Jeannie were. By now they'll know exactly what happened, and they'll know those two were Modesty Blaise and Willie Garvin. Nobody can disguise style, Brookie, and what happened at *The Black Horse* reeks of their style.'

*   *   *

It was ten days later when Modesty rang Willie at *The Treadmill*. He was working out solo in his combat room behind the pub, and her call was put through to him there.

' 'Allo, Princess, what's new? Has it been confirmed about Dinah's baby?'

'Yes, and I'm so pleased for them after what happened last time.'

'Me too. We'll stand guard this time, no messing. You still getting calls from Old Alex?'

'Three last week. He says everybody's very kind, but there's no hint of his memory coming back and I don't think he's happy.'

'Fishes out of water usually aren't.'

'I know. But listen, Willie, I've rung because something pretty weird happened an hour ago. I had a call from Sir Angus McBeal.'

'*What?*'

'Yes, what indeed.'

McBeal was a very rich man, a director of a number of companies. His activities were closely watched by the City, for if McBeal decided that a particular investment was a Good Thing then the City was inclined to follow. What was known to perhaps only three other people in the world beside Modesty and Willie was that Sir Angus McBeal was also one of the four directors of Salamander Four, probably the world's most formidable criminal group outside the Mafia.

There had been a time when Salamander Four accepted a contract for the obscene killing of the Colliers from a client seeking leverage over Modesty and Willie. It was a Dead Man's Handle contract, unstoppable even though the client had been killed. Modesty had confronted McBeal and told him that his life would be forfeit if the Colliers were harmed, also the lives of his three European co-directors, Chard, Gesner and Pereda. The same applied, she had said, if any attempt were made to dispose of her or Willie Garvin, pointing out that she and Willie were highly experienced in not getting killed, while McBeal and his colleagues were not.

McBeal had never admitted his connection with Salamander Four, but the contract had been cancelled and the fifty thousand-pound fee sent to Modesty for the Colliers as confirmation that it was no longer running. That was over a year ago. Now, out of the blue, McBeal had made contact and Willie was amazed.

'It couldn't 'ave been for a social chat, Princess. What did he want?'

'I don't know yet. Well, I know he wants to meet me, with you present if you and I so wish. He wants me to name a day and time next week, but I needn't tell him the place until just before we meet. The only thing he asks is that a telephone be available.'

There was a long silence. At last Willie said, 'Weird isn't the word. When you said he wanted to meet you I started thinking he aimed to set you up for a hit, but he's covered that by letting you fix the time and name the place at short notice.'

'Right. So what can he have to say to us?'

'Beats me, Princess, but we'd better find out.'

'I have the same feeling. I thought of making it noon next Tuesday if you're free then. He lives in Belgrave Square, so I can ring him there half an hour before and tell him to come to the penthouse. He might anticipate that, but I can't see that it matters. We'll be watching him, and anyway he's no hit-man, he's a head-office man.'

Willie said, 'Tuesday's fine. All right if I come up Monday evening?'

'Yes, I'd like that. Come to dinner.'

'Thanks, Princess. See you then.'

At noon precisely, five days later, Weng took a call from the porter in reception and was told that Sir Angus McBeal had arrived to see Miss Blaise by appointment. He was alone. 'As arranged,' Weng reported, 'Hudson informed me that Sir Angus

was carrying only his hat, umbrella, and a small document case.
I have said he was to be sent up.'

Modesty and Willie were in the penthouse drawing-room. She
said, 'All right, Weng. Show him in, then lurk in the kitchen.
The intercom's on so you'll hear whatever's said.'

When McBeal arrived in the foyer he gave hat and umbrella
to Weng but retained the slim document case. Modesty and Willie
were standing when he entered the drawing-room. She thought
he had aged since she had last seen him a year ago. He still wore
the old-fashioned boardroom uniform of dark suit and wing
collar, but it seemed to hang looser on him. His thin grey hair
was thinner, his long neck more scrawny, and he looked ten
years older than a man in his fifties and in normal health should
look.

Modesty said, 'Good morning, Sir Angus. This is a surprising
visit.'

'These are surprising times, Miss Blaise,' he said in the rather
high-pitched voice she remembered. 'I have come here to thank
you and to do you a service.'

'To thank me? I can't imagine for what.'

'It would be quite impossible for you to do so, Miss Blaise,
but I shall be happy to explain. May I sit down?'

She gestured towards an armchair and seated herself on the
chesterfield, facing him across a coffee table. He gave her a stiff
little bow and moved to the chair. Once he was seated, Willie
settled himself beside her on the chesterfield. McBeal cleared his
throat and said, 'I have discovered that you were the person who
recently found Lord Sayle living as a peasant on a farm in the
Pyrenees, having suffered total amnesia following the occasion
when the aircraft he was piloting crashed in France in 1943.'

McBeal paused, looking over his glasses at her as if giving
her the opportunity to comment, but she simply looked at him
impassively. After a moment or two he went on, 'Yes, I know
your name was never mentioned in the newspapers, but I happen
to know that you were in that area at that time and I suspect that
Alexander Sayle or another resident of the farm had some hand
in your escape from slow death in a cave.'

She felt Willie go stiff beside her, and fought to prevent the abrupt shock of McBeal's last words showing in her face or body-language. Her voice was mellow as she spoke. 'Are you saying that was a Salamander Four contract?'

McBeal nodded. 'Yes. An in-house operation. There was no client. I hope you will believe that I protested most strongly and was out-voted.'

She looked at Willie, who said, 'We might need convincing.'

'I hope,' said McBeal, 'to satisfy you on that score later. For the moment may I say that a considerable schism has developed between my colleagues and me. They have never forgiven the loss of face suffered when forced to cancel the Collier contract and pay the contract price to the Colliers as proof of cancellation.'

Modesty said, 'You took a different view?'

'Certainly. I have dealt with you face to face, Miss Blaise, they have not. I am less given to emotional reaction than are my colleagues. I pressed the view that you were no threat to us, that if we left you—and any friend of yours—alone, then you would leave us alone. This did not suffice for them. Hence, after a prudent delay, the contract for your slow death, for the execution of which we engaged a South American team of three who had very good references. They are comparatively new on the criminal scene. Have you heard of Las Sombras?'

She looked at Willie, who shook his head. 'The Shadows?' she said. 'No, but we'll certainly take note of the name.'

'You need not trouble to do so, Miss Blaise. They died shortly after we heard of your safe return. We do not usually terminate sub-contractors, but in this instance it was necessary to avoid any possibility of your tracing, through them, the participation of Salamander Four in the enterprise.'

Willie Garvin sat with a look of polite interest, trying to conceal the fact that he was struggling to collect his scattered wits. Here was this man, a principal of the most successful criminal group outside America for the past twenty years, sitting before a woman they had tried to kill, and retailing the manner of the event as if presenting a report on the half-year results to a company boardroom.

Modesty said quietly, 'Do you remember what I said we would do about Salamander Four if any attempt was made to kill either of us?'

'I do indeed, and vividly, Miss Blaise. You said you would kill us, the four principals, to prevent any further attempt, and I believed you. It was a very rational proposition.'

'Be advised that it still holds, Sir Angus.'

McBeal looked at his watch. 'As to that, I shall shortly offer an alternative I hope you will find acceptable and may even deem a substantial service. Meanwhile may I proceed to the other purpose of my visit?'

'The other—? Oh, to thank me for something. Yes, I'd be most interested to hear about that.'

'It refers to my opening remarks concerning your discovery of Lord Sayle, believed killed in action over fifty years ago.' McBeal began to unzip the document case on his lap and Willie reached under his jacket to where twin knives were sheathed, but when McBeal's hand emerged it held only a bundle of a dozen or so letters, the paper on which they were written now yellowing with age. He laid them on the table before Modesty, and when he spoke his voice had changed. The words came hesitantly, as if he were shaken by emotion.

'These letters were sent to my mother during the war,' he said. 'Her name was Elaine McBeal, and she died when I was five. Her parents brought me up. They are long dead, and I have no other family.'

Utterly bewildered and now making no attempt to hide it, Modesty said, 'You wish me to read them?'

'At least one or two, if you please. All of them if you so wish.'

She picked up the top letter. It was dated September 1942 and bore the letterhead of Sayle Manor, Fenstone Green, Kent. A touch of prescience sent a shiver of strange anticipation through her. She drew a deep breath and began to read. The letter was only two short pages, and in it the writer hoped that he and Elaine would be able to make their leave coincide next time round, and that Elaine would spend at least part of it with him at the manor. There was more, for it was a very loving letter.

She read it carefully, passed it to Willie and picked up the next. It was, she supposed, a typical wartime letter subject to censorship, giving nothing away and consisting only of small personal hopes and news. She heard Willie mutter 'Jesus!' and waited for him to finish both letters before she spoke.

'I won't read any more, Sir Angus. These are love letters written to Elaine McBeal, serving in the Women's Royal Air Force, by Flight Lieutenant the Honourable Alexander Sayle.'

'Who was my father,' said McBeal.

Incredibly, there were tears in his eyes now. He swallowed, and made an effort to keep his voice steady as he went on, 'I am illegitimate, of course. He went missing six months before I was born. I was in my late teens before my grandparents told me what had happened and gave me the letters. My mother never told him she was pregnant. They said she feared he would think she was trying to force him into marriage. But this is why I have come to thank you, Miss Blaise, for finding my father.'

There was a silence while she tried to unravel her tangled thoughts, to understand his motive, to find the right questions. At last she said, 'I didn't find your father, Sir Angus. He found me, and saved my life.'

'You were the instrument of his being found, Miss Blaise. I cannot tell you how grateful I am.'

She said tentatively, 'Have you come to me because you wish to see him? Do you feel you have some right of inheritance—?'

'No!' For the first time they saw passion in his cold eyes. 'No, no, no! He must never know that I exist. He would be so ashamed of me if he . . . if he knew the truth about his son.'

Willie rubbed his eyes with finger and thumb, wondering if he were dreaming. Modesty made a helpless gesture and said, 'I'm at a loss, Sir Angus. For long years you've remembered your father as a hero who died for his country. Why should the discovery that he's alive make you . . . let's say, take a different view of yourself?'

He looked through her with blank eyes for long seconds, and at last he said in a small voice, 'So hard to explain, even to myself. But because he is alive he could . . . form an opinion of me. An opinion that fills me with shame. I can only say that it has changed everything for me.'

Head bowed, he gazed down at the floor in silence for a few moments, then suddenly sat up straight and looked at his watch. His voice was flat and businesslike again as he said, 'May we revert to your own situation now, please?'

Modesty gathered up the letters and handed them to him. 'In what respect?'

'I said a short time ago that I would provide an alternative to the ultimatum you so rightly presented to Salamander Four and which they ignored.'

'They? You exclude yourself?'

'As I have said, I was the sole objector.' Again McBeal looked at his watch. 'At this moment my three colleagues are gathered at a house in a somewhat remote part of Sussex that we use for board meetings in this country. Shortly before arriving here I telephoned them to say that I was being delayed by traffic and would be about thirty minutes late in joining them. They will now be expecting me shortly.' He took a mobile phone from his pocket, dialled a number, listened for a moment and said into the phone, 'Stand by.'

Still holding the mobile, he glanced towards a side table and said, 'I would like to use your telephone now, and I see you have an amplifier. May I switch that on for you to hear?'

Modesty said, 'Go ahead.'

McBeal rose and picked up the phone. He dialled a number and switched on the amplifier. After two rings a deep voice said, 'Yes?'

'Hallo, Chard. I'll be with you in a few minutes. Are Gesner and Pereda there?'

'We are all here waiting for you,' said the voice impatiently. 'What the devil are you thinking of, using names on an open line?'

McBeal said, 'One moment please.' He put the mobile phone to his lips and said, 'Now.'

The deep voice was speaking. 'Hallo? Are you there? Hallo—?' The line went dead.

McBeal switched off the amplifier, cradled the phone and listened on his mobile. After a few seconds he said, 'That is very satisfactory. I will put through the balance of the agreed sum as arranged.' He switched off, put the mobile in his pocket and returned to his chair.

Modesty said slowly, 'What exactly have you done?'

McBeal took off his spectacles and began to clean them on a small square of cloth. 'I have retired,' he said. 'I have retired from alternative business. Salamander Four has ceased to exist.'

She came to her feet, staring. 'The house in Sussex——?'

'There has been an explosion caused by escaping gas accumulating in a cellar,' said McBeal patiently. 'It was arranged and triggered by an expert who observed the effect from a safe distance and just reported to me that the whole house has collapsed and is burning. I believe this will save you a great deal of trouble and danger, Miss Blaise, and I hope you will be convinced that I personally am no threat to you or to Mr Garvin.'

She looked at Willie, who had risen with her, and it was the first time he had ever seen her open-mouthed. With an effort she collected herself and turned back to McBeal. 'Christ!' she said. 'What would your father think of *that* little effort?'

He blinked at her sadly and put his spectacles on. 'They were very bad, dangerous men. I think that for your sake my father might well approve.'

She turned away and walked to the big picture window, thinking, *Yes. Old Alex just might.* Willie Garvin was wandering aimlessly around the room, trying to stop feeling disorientated. McBeal sat looking fondly at one of the letters. After a while Modesty said, 'Well . . . you've said your thank-you and you've done us a service, which is what you came for, Sir Angus. Is there anything else?'

He looked up from putting the letters away in his case. 'Yes, there is, Miss Blaise, and I urge you to give it serious thought. The man Pike was in our employ—not that he knew who his employers were, of course. After events at *The Black Horse*, and after discharge from hospital, he decamped to Liverpool and was killed in a brawl there by arrangement. We don't, or perhaps I should say we didn't, permit our lowest stratum of employees to cause us to lose respect without their suffering the consequences.'

'What's your point?'

'My colleagues and I had a report of the event, and knew at once that you and Mr Garvin were the principal protagonists. For myself I felt only professional admiration. My colleagues, however, were incensed that yet again you had damaged our organisation. They at once agreed that a further attempt on your life should be made without delay. I protested but was again overruled.'

McBeal closed the document case and stood up. 'Gesner proposed a simple assassination by sniper rifle, hiring the world's best practitioner for the purpose.'

Willie said, 'Skendi? The Albanian?'

'The same. It was suggested that the best opportunity as regards location would be Miss Blaise's cottage in Wiltshire. At this juncture of the meeting I was required to withdraw since I was opposed to the operation, so I cannot tell you whether the proposal was acted upon. Skendi was in South Africa at the time, and as you are aware, we work through cut-outs so it would take several days at least to conclude the contract. I can only tell you that perhaps from this very day you may well both be at risk from long range, and there is now nothing I can do to cancel the contract—if it exists. In that event Skendi will have been paid half one hundred thousand pounds in advance, the rest to be paid on completion. He will not know that this balance cannot now be paid.'

McBeal paused, thinking. 'I believe there is nothing more I can usefully tell you,' he said. 'Thank you for your time.' He made no attempt to shake hands, but gave another little bow and moved towards the foyer. Weng appeared with his hat and umbrella, handed them to him and opened the lift door. McBeal started to enter, then paused. 'May I offer you a word of advice, Miss Blaise?'

She laughed shortly. 'After all you've said so far I'm hardly likely to decline.'

'It's of little importance really, but should you survive Skendi's

attentions, as I sincerely hope, I recommend a substantial pur-
chase of Bearstead Holdings. There will be an agreed takeover
in about six weeks and the shares will double in value.'

He nodded, stepped into the lift, and the door closed after
him. Weng, who was probably the world's richest houseboy, said
thoughtfully, 'Bearstead Holdings . . .'

Willie sat down on the chesterfield, leaned back and closed
his eyes. Modesty joined him and followed suit. A long minute
later Willie said, 'I just 'ad a very funny dream, Princess.'

'So did I. This man called, and sat there chatting about various
people he'd had killed. Then he got us to listen while he killed
off some more over the phone, his colleagues actually. Oh, before
that he thanked me for discovering his father, lost for fifty years,
and got tearful about how ashamed his father would be of him—'

She broke off at the sound of Weng setting a tray down on
the low table. When they opened their eyes they saw that he had
brought a half-bottle of champagne in an ice-bucket, and two
glasses. As he poured, Willie said, 'You have great perception,
Weng. We needed a pick-me-up.'

'Thank you, Mr Garvin. The bit I liked best,' Weng had to
pause, struggling to contain his mirth, 'was when he said he had
retired from . . . from *alternative business!*'

He choked on the last word, overwhelmed, and fled from the
room with a wailing cry of apology. Following the tensions of
the past twenty minutes it was infectious. Modesty collapsed
against Willie, beating a hand against his chest as he heaved with
laughter.

After a little while, breathless, they picked up their drinks.
Modesty said, 'Well . . . at least he's saved us some agonising
decisions over what to do about Salamander Four. We've never
gone in for assassinations, but I wasn't going to wait around to
be killed.'

Willie said soberly, 'There's still Skendi.'

She nodded. 'He's very good, very careful, but he doesn't hang
about on a contract. If he's taken it we can expect something
within ten days or so.'

'He'll know he's got to get both of us,' said Willie. 'Whoever's left 'll go after 'im.' He thought for a moment. 'Small chance of taking us together, though. He'll settle for one at a time if he has to.'

'We'll set it up that way.' She drained her glass and put it down. 'He's wanted for murder in New York, isn't he?'

'They've 'ad special agents trying to nail 'im for a couple of years since he shot that Sanford heiress and then 'er husband made a death-bed confession soon after, saying he'd paid for the hit.'

'Well . . . as I said, I'm not standing still for it. We'd better do something about him.' She sat gazing into space, and after a while gave a little sigh.

Willie looked at her curiously. 'What was that for, Princess?'

She half-laughed and gave him a wry look. 'Just a silly moment, Willie love, and it's McBeal's fault. I've never thought of it before, but I was just wondering if my father, whoever he was, would be ashamed of me.'

*   *   *

Willie Garvin flew to Paris the next day. He then disappeared and was not to be found at any of his usual haunts. In Hyde Park the following day Modesty Blaise took a fall from her horse. She happened to be riding with a police surgeon of recent acquaintance, supplied by Inspector Harry Lomax. The surgeon had her taken to the hospital at which he was a consultant and she was discharged that evening with one leg in plaster, Weng pushing her in a wheelchair.

Next morning her friend Dinah Collier came to look after her, and it was then decided that Weng should drive them both down to Modesty's cottage near the village of Benildon in Wiltshire. Stephen Collier was reluctantly absent for his own sake. Willie Garvin, speaking on the phone from wherever he was, had said, 'Modesty won't 'ave you near the cottage, Steve. We reckon Skendi might think you're me at long range, even with a sniper-scope, and we don't want you knocked off. Dinah thinks there's a bit of mileage in you yet.'

'Jesus, Willie, how the hell could anyone take me for you? I'm handsome and debonair, with opposed thumbs, and I move beautifully—'

'I know, Steve, I know. But Skendi might go in for a bit of wishful thinking, because he'd love it to be me. Or he might blow your 'ead off out of sheer male jealousy.'

Collier had laughed. 'There's always that. But Dinah's safe?'

'Skendi's a pro. He'll only kill the girl in the wheelchair.'

Morning and afternoon at the cottage in the valley Weng pushed the wheelchair with its passenger out into the garden for an hour to doze in the sun. Sometimes Dinah would emerge to sit with her for a while or to see that she was comfortable, adjusting the pillow on the stool supporting her hurt leg. Sometimes Weng emerged to speak with her briefly, but for the most part she seemed content to sit and read, or doze, or watch the occasional hang-glider that floated lazily across the sky between Furze Hill and Benildon.

Skendi came after dark on the fourth night. He left his hired car at a garage miles away and hired a mountain bike which he hid in thick woods near the ridge that ran north of the cottage. At first light he lay within the edge of the woods and studied the lie of the land and the position of the cottage in the valley below. He had brought food and water in a haversack with him, and throughout the morning he watched through binoculars.

Once or twice he saw the houseboy and the fair-haired girl he had been told about by his advance team watching the London penthouse, but it was not until eleven that the subject of his mission was pushed out in her wheelchair to sit in the garden. She was facing south, towards the ridge on the far side of the valley which was pasture land and offered no cover for him. A hang-glider was moving out from the hill beyond, and Skendi noted that he would need overhead concealment in choosing his position for putting a bullet through the subject's head.

After studying the terrain for half an hour he made his choice. There was a place where the ground rose in a little hummock to a broad hedge fronted by a patch of tall nettles. He could not check it out in daylight, but could do so shortly after dusk with little chance of being seen, for after crossing an area of pasture he would enter a field of corn on the other side of the hedge, and he could approach under cover of that.

He wriggled back deeper into the woods, then rose and walked to where he had left his mountain bike with its pannier containing a small bivouac. Skendi was a wiry man of less than medium height, in his late thirties and with thinning hair, a forgettable appearance and a phlegmatic manner. He felt no pride at knowing he was considered the best in the world at his job. He was interested only in the money. He sat reading a paperback till dusk, occasionally eating a sandwich from some packets bought earlier, and drinking water, then he walked back through the woods, crossed the pasture and crawled through the cornfield to reach the spot he had chosen. With secateurs he cut a narrow hole through the base of the hedge and lay within it, looking over the hummock at the lights of the cottage below, three hundred yards away.

For ten minutes he remained there, getting the feel of the position and making a thin mattress of straw to lie on. There had been no wind worth mentioning today, and the forecast was settled. It would be an easy killing. He moved back through the cornfield and the woods, set up his tent, climbed into a sleeping-bag, set a small travelling alarm clock near his head, and went to sleep.

Half an hour before first light he roused, packed the tent, put it in the pannier of his bike, and picked up a flat box he had brought with him strapped to his back, a wooden box perhaps one-third the size of a card-table. Fifteen minutes later he was crouched by the hedge, hidden by the corn as he carefully assembled the parts of his custom-made rifle with its telescopic sight. He slid an expanding bullet into the breech, then crawled into the hole beneath the hedge.

For a few minutes he sighted on various targets at the range he would be using, then turned on his back, settled himself on the straw mattress with the rifle lying beside him, and took the paperback from his pocket.

Through the first hours of daylight he read and dozed. At ten o'clock he turned on his front and began to watch the cottage. It was shortly before eleven when the young oriental pushed the wheelchair into the garden accompanied by the fair-haired girl who spent some time making the subject comfortable. There seemed to be a suggestion that a sun umbrella be set up, but this was evidently declined and the two went back into the cottage.

Slowly Skendi lifted the rifle to his shoulder and sighted. He could see the back of the subject's head clearly above the top of the wheelchair. There was hardly any tension in him as he brought the cross-hairs to the middle of the head and gently squeezed the trigger.

The report was not loud. Skendi saw the head burst open, spraying blood, then he was wriggling back, lying low in the corn, beginning smoothly and without haste to disassemble the rifle and pack the components in the padded box. Glancing up, he saw a hang-glider drifting over the far ridge. No problem. He had only to crawl across the corner of the cornfield and the down-slope would hide him as he moved over the pasture to the woods.

In the cottage Dinah and Weng had heard the report. Weng was sitting by the window, watching the dummy in the wheelchair. As the head shattered he noted the direction in which the fragments of plastic and sponge had been flung, and lifted a hand-radio to his lips. 'From the north ridge, Miss Blaise. Go, go, go!'

Dinah, making coffee in the kitchen, called 'Weng! Was that it?' She came hurrying through to where he sat, her face pale.

Weng stood up and said grimly, 'He blew the head apart. I'm glad you did not see it, Mrs Collier—' He caught himself and winced at the gaffe. 'Forgive me, please. You know what I meant.'

'It's nothing.' Her voice shook. 'We're wound up so tight, waiting. Thank God it's over. Oh Weng, is it really over? Can we be sure?'

He looked out of the window again at the headless dummy and the fake blood spattered round it. 'It is almost over, Mrs

Collier,' he said, 'but I regret that Miss Blaise has to observe certain legalities.' He sighed and shook his head. 'A pity it could not be left to Mr Garvin to conclude the matter. He has a very positive way of dealing with people who try to kill ladies.'

Remembering moments when men had sought her own death, Dinah said soberly, 'Yes, Weng. Yes, I know.'

*   *   *

Holding a hand-radio and sitting in the passenger seat of a car parked half a mile away in the lay-by off the road running along the ridge, Inspector Harry Lomax said to the driver beside him, 'All right, Sergeant, let's go. It's the north ridge so we're nice and close.'

Three days ago Lomax had taken a week's leave and was spending it at *The Plough* in Tunbury, a village two miles from Benildon. Most of each day was devoted to his favourite pastime of fishing, but for an hour every morning and afternoon he sat in this unmarked car with the Detective Sergeant from the local force, listening out on the radio and occasionally catching sight of a hang-glider drifting high above the road leading to Benildon. His friend Inspector Brook had been going to carry out this surveillance, but in an act that Brook himself deemed the height of selflessness he had asked if Lomax might be invited to take his place.

A minute after Weng's message to Modesty came through on the radio the car drew up where a footpath led south through a tapering neck of woods. At that moment Skendi was emerging from the cornfield adjoining the wide pasture on the far side of the wooded area. Pausing to scan the ground ahead, and finding it empty, Skendi rose to his feet and began to walk towards the woods, carrying the case holding his rifle. He was halfway across the pasture when a cruciform shadow passed silently over him. His pulse quickened as he saw the hang-glider less than a hundred feet up as it moved ahead of him, turned, then slanted down to land.

Shock hit him like a blow under the heart as the pilot touched

down lightly, released the harness, moved clear of the wing and
stood looking towards him, hands on hips. It was a woman, a
dark-haired woman, and even at a distance of fifty yards or more
he knew that this was Modesty Blaise, knew that his contract to
kill had been blown, that he had walked into a well-placed trap,
and that he was nearer to sudden death at this moment than he
had ever been.

He dropped to one knee, fighting to keep his hands steady as
he opened the flat box and began to assemble the rifle. Sweat
broke out on his brow as the chill of fear gripped him, for this
was Modesty Blaise. When he glanced up he saw that she had
started moving unhurriedly towards him. Breech and barrel were
now fitted together. No need for the telescopic sight, for she
would be at point-blank range. With new horror he realised that
he also would be at point-blank range, for she wore a holstered
gun and it was said that she was lethally fast and accurate.

Such was Skendi's concentration on the rifle and the advancing
figure that he was utterly unaware of the second hang-glider
dropping down fast from the thermal it had been riding, swooping
round in a gentle curve to arrive directly behind him at fifty feet,
drifting quietly towards him. Skendi had slipped a cartridge into
the breech and was lifting the rifle to his shoulder when a black-
jack thrown from only twenty feet hit him hard on the back of
the skull and dropped him senseless.

Modesty relaxed, and lifted the hem of the hip-length dark
tunic she wore to drop it over the Colt .32 holstered at her hip.
It would not be needed now. She had never known Willie to
miss a throw, but the timing of his arrival had been critical and
they both regarded the taking of unnecessary risks as bad practice.

He landed to one side of her and stepped clear of the wing,
his face showing no pleasure. 'I could've rigged it to look like
an accident,' he said plaintively. '*He* could've been hang-gliding
and got his neck broken when he crashed 'ere. No problem.'

'Oh, shut up, Willie love,' she said amiably, 'we've been
through all that.' She lifted the radio hooked to her belt and spoke
into it. 'All over, Weng. Tell Mrs Collier we're fine—except that
Willie's having a bit of a sulk.'

Weng's voice said, 'Wilco, Miss Blaise. So am I.'

Willie grinned and looked towards the woods. Two men were emerging from the trees. As they drew near, Inspector Lomax called, 'Miss Blaise and Mr Garvin, I believe? The Sergeant here tells me you're the regular hang-gliding folk locally.' He produced his warrant card. 'I'm Inspector Lomax and this is Detective Sergeant Baker. We saw you come down and thought you might be in trouble.'

Modesty said, 'Well, no, Inspector. We were gliding over the ridge and we saw that man lying there.' She pointed. 'He seemed to be unconscious, so we landed to see if we could help.'

'Very kind of you, Miss. We'd better take a look.'

Together they moved towards Skendi, and Lomax said, 'My word! Just look at that, Sergeant—it's a rifle!'

'And not a sporting rifle, sir,' said Baker with the stilted air of a man remembering lines. He pointed to the weapon and then to the open box in which the telescopic sight and spare cartridges were clipped. 'That's the sort of weapon *assassins* use!'

'So it is!' exclaimed Lomax. 'Lucky you happened to bring that sheet with you, Sergeant. There'll be fingerprints all over the box and the rifle. Wrap them up carefully, then put your 'cuffs on this fellow.'

'Right, sir,' said Baker. 'I wonder what he was doing here?'

'Practising, I'll be bound,' said Lomax confidently. 'But he must have tripped and hit his head on . . .' He looked about him and pointed to a huge flint a dozen yards away, '. . . on that rock. Staggered over here and collapsed.' He fingered his chin thoughtfully. 'You know, I've seen that face on some wanted pix that were circulated recently.'

As the Sergeant bent to his task Lomax turned to Modesty and Willie and went on solemnly. 'It's quite possible that this rifle has been used for assassination elsewhere. If so it can be identified by bullets taken from the bodies of any previous victims.'

Willie Garvin said, 'Gosh! Really?' and Lomax had a brief choking fit before he could speak again.

'I hope,' he said, looking at Modesty, 'I hope this hasn't been too much of a shock for you, Miss?'

'No, I—I'll be all right,' Modesty said bravely. 'Mr Garvin will see me home.'

Lomax nodded and turned away, standing in silence for a few moments with clenched jaws. He relaxed and said to Baker as he rose from handcuffing the unconscious man, 'Get that gear back to the car, Sergeant, then radio for an ambulance. I'll wait here.'

'Right, sir.' Baker gathered up the sheet-wrapped rifle and box very carefully and moved off towards the footpath. When he had disappeared into the woods, Lomax turned and said quietly, 'Thanks very much. It's a particular pleasure for me to meet you, and I'm sure you'll know why.'

Modesty smiled. 'I hope you won't feel you've wasted some well-earned leave.'

'Oh God, no!' Lomax looked down at Skendi, who was beginning to stir and make faint sounds. 'It's outrageous, but I'll get the credit for this. I understand there's been some sort of advance consultation at high level in anticipation of Skendi being nailed, and the American Embassy have extradition papers already prepared. This cold-blooded bastard is either going to spend the next ninety-nine years in stir, or he'll get the hot-seat.'

'Needle,' said Willie. 'It's New York State.'

Lomax nodded. 'That'll do nicely.' He looked at Modesty. 'May I call later—officially to take statements confirming what you've said to me and to Sergeant Baker?'

'Yes, of course, Mr Lomax. We're very grateful for your help. Come about eight o'clock and join us for dinner if you're free.'

Lomax laughed. 'The name's Harry,' he said. 'And thanks, I'm free all right.'

*   *   *

It was mid-afternoon six days later when an old man came into reception at the penthouse block and spoke haltingly to the porter. Eight floors above, Modesty Blaise was in her lapidary workroom, cutting *en cabochon* one of two large rough emeralds Willie Garvin had last year dug from the emerald-bearing shale of abandoned mines in Colombia, working among the *guaqueros*, treasure-seekers who would have slit a dozen throats to lay hands on his find.

As she worked she recalled with a smile his falsely contrite air as she trounced him for taking such a risk. The fact was that Willie enjoyed bringing her unusual presents and would do so whenever an idea seized him. This afternoon Weng was off-duty, playing bridge at a club where the stakes were high and where he invariably made several thousand a year. When the house-phone rang she switched off the slitting saw, laid down the dop-stick with the emerald cemented to its head, and moved from her chair to pick up the phone.

'Yes, George?'

The porter said, 'I've got a foreign gentleman here who wants to see you, Miss Blaise. Says his name is Alex something, I couldn't quite get the surname.'

She was taken aback. 'Is he alone?'

'Yes, Miss.'

'All right, George. Put him in the lift and point out where the up-button is, will you?'

'Certainly, Miss Blaise.'

She moved to the foyer and waited by the lift gates, wondering, remembering. Alex was the key to all that had happened since the day he had found and saved her. It was he who had frustrated Salamander Four, thereby ensuring that she was alive later to deal with the thug who had savagely beaten Steve Collier, the man who unknown to her was a Salamander Four enforcer. Because she had shattered this enforcer's power they had set up another attempt to kill her. But Old Alex, unknown to himself, was the father of Sir Angus McBeal, one of the four Salamander directors, and McBeal had first destroyed his three colleagues, then warned her of the Skendi contract. And it had all begun and continued with Old Alex.

The doors opened and he stood gazing at her anxiously. He wore a beautifully cut suit with a silk shirt and tie, contrasting strangely with his weatherbeaten face and gnarled old hands.

'I do not inconvenience you, mam'selle?'

He spoke in French, and she answered in the same tongue. 'Alex dear, you could never be an inconvenient visitor. Come in, come in and talk with me.' She took his hands, drew him into the foyer and kissed him on each cheek. 'But why are you calling me mam'selle? It was always Modesty, both on the farm and when we spoke on the telephone.'

'I don't know. I think because I am afraid.'

She led him down the three steps to the drawing-room and sat beside him on the chesterfield, holding his hand.

'What are you afraid of, Alex?'

He shook his head helplessly. 'Of . . . of each day. They are kind, Modesty, very kind. And I have tried . . . tried hard to learn and remember and become as they would wish. But it does not march. They are unhappy because they think they fail in a duty. I am unhappy because . . . because I am alone always, even when we are all together. I think about the farm, the vines, the family eating together in the kitchen. I want to harness Napoleon and haul logs. I don't know what I once was, Modesty, but I know what I am now, and it is not the same. Bloody hell.'

He turned his head to look at her, his old eyes desperate. 'I cannot bring myself to ask them for what I truly want. It would be cruel, for they know I am of their blood and are doing all for me. But to me they are strangers. I cannot ask them, so I come to you. I have the address.' He touched his breast pocket. 'I have money. I walk to the station and take a train to London. I show the address to the taxi man and he brings me, and you are here, thank God. So I ask you . . . please take me home. Please.'

She patted his hand, feeling a wave of pity and relief sweep through her. 'Of course I will, Alex. You'll stay here tonight and I'll take you home tomorrow. Nobody can stop you if you want to go, but I do have to telephone your brother at once, to let him know you're safe with me.'

His eyes shone with tears of joy. 'Tomorrow?'

'I promise, Alex. Tomorrow. Now just sit and rest while I phone.'

A minute later, on the phone in her workroom, she was saying, 'Lord Sayle? This is Modesty Blaise, and I'm calling to say that Alex is safe here with me.'

Mark Sayle's voice said, 'Oh, thank God for that. When he went for a walk and didn't return we feared his memory was playing tricks and that he might have met with an accident.'

'No, he's quite all right. But I think he's been under much greater strain than anyone realised, and I'm afraid his mental capacity could well be impaired if it continues. The fact is, he wants to go home. He's desperate to go home, to the home where he belongs. He couldn't bring himself to ask you because he says you've all been so kind and he felt it would be cruel. So he came to me, I suppose because he feels closer to me than to any-one else in the country, and I've promised to take him home tomorrow.'

There was a brief silence, then Mark Sayle said quietly, 'Now that it's happened I'm not surprised. We've really tried hard, you know, and Alex is a lovely chap, but . . . try as I may, I haven't been able to see him as the brother I grew up with. I'm sorry if that seems heartless.'

So there would be no opposition, and new relief touched her as she said, 'That isn't heartless, it's honest, and Alex quite simply *isn't* the brother you grew up with. After fifty years I don't believe there's anything left of that young man except an occasional bloody hell or wizard prang. It's heart-breaking, but there it is.'

'Well . . . I can only say I'm very grateful to you, Miss Blaise. Do you wish me to send his clothes or any possessions? My chauffeur could bring them this evening. It's probably better for Alex if I don't try to say goodbye.'

'I think that's a kind decision. Please don't worry about clothes. I'll take him out and buy him the sort of clothes he'll feel comfort-able to go back in, then he can stay with me tonight and we'll fly to Perpignan tomorrow.'

Mark Sayle said, 'Thank you. I'm sure he'll be very happy to have you take him home. Will it offend you if I offer to cover your costs?'

She laughed. 'It won't offend me, but no thank you. I felt guilty about causing Alex to be brought here, and I'm relieved to be taking him home.'

'You're very kind.'

'I hold him in great affection, and not only because he saved my life.'

'Yes, I understand. At an appropriate moment please ask if I might one day visit him and his family on the farm, when he's had plenty of time to settle in.'

'I will. And I look forward to visiting them myself.'

She said her goodbyes, put down the phone and returned to the drawing-room. Old Alex looked up anxiously. She gave him her best smile and said, 'It's all settled. I'll phone now to book our flights for tomorrow, then we'll go and get you some proper clothes. You don't want to arrive home in that suit, do you?'

He rose and embraced her wordlessly, then stepped back, grinning in the cheerful Old-Alex way she remembered. 'If I go back like this,' he said, 'perhaps Matilde will marry me after all!' He chuckled happily.

Modesty stared. 'You mean she refused when you were young?'

'Refused? Ah, no. I was nobody from nowhere. With nothing. How could I ever ask?'

She exhaled a long breath and gazed at him wonderingly. 'Oh Alex,' she said, 'this is a funny old life, isn't it?' She studied his worn, happy face and straightened the tie he had pulled loose at the neck. 'I'm sure Matilde would have married a handsome man like you, if you'd asked.'

'Handsome? Me?' He was genuinely amused.

'Of course.' She took his arm and moved to the foyer, picking up her handbag from a side-table. 'If you were younger by fifty years or so I'd keep you myself for a toyboy. Come on, let's go and buy you some clothes.'

She had used the English word toyboy, knowing of no French equivalent, and Old Alex echoed it, puzzled. 'Toyboy? What is that?'

As they went down in the lift she explained. A few moments later the porter watched her crossing the reception area, arm-in-arm with an old man who looked like a peasant and was dressed like a lord. He was grinning broadly and kept saying, 'Toyboy! Bloody hell!'

THE GIRL WITH THE BLACK BALLOON

Poised sedately on his motor-scooter, Simon Bird kept to a speed he thought suitable for a man of the cloth as he moved along the winding Cornish lane. From time to time he ran a finger round the new clerical collar he wore, and from time to time he reached under his jacket to feel the butt of the Colt .357 in the Berns-Martin shoulder holster under his black jacket. He touched it not because he was in any way apprehensive, but because he was obsessed by it with all the passion of an ardent lover.

It was years since the lane had known any repair, but neither had it suffered more than occasional use. After winding for half a mile through thin woodland it became a rising track that led up across open greensward to a granite headland towering above the Atlantic. Here stood *Poldeacon*, a folly built a century before by a quick-tempered tin magnate who had later cut his wife's throat and bludgeoned to death the man he believed to have cuckolded him. This proved to be a false belief for which the tin magnate expressed deep regret before being hanged.

The incident gave *Poldeacon* an unsavoury reputation. By chance, later residents met with a variety of misfortunes and rarely remained for more than a few years. Local people in the village of Mallowby, a mile away, believed that a curse lay upon the pile. Those less superstitious attributed such misfortunes to the theory that anyone who wanted to live in an unimaginative heap of granite confronting the savage force of the Atlantic in winter must be less than fully sane and therefore prone to self-inflicted misfortune.

As he emerged from the woods into noonday sunshine Simon

Bird gazed with affection at the dark towers rising beyond the new wall that surrounded the folly. He neither knew nor cared that the wall had been built by a government department ten years ago for a scheme abandoned eight years ago. His heart and mind were already with the companions he knew he would find within that bleak dwelling.

The heavy wooden gates in the outer wall stood open. He rode through into the courtyard and pulled up beside a short row of cars parked against the western wall. Dismounting, he took off his crash-helmet and replaced it with a low-crowned black hat from one of the saddle-bags. As he moved towards the main doors he saw that they were closed, and that at a window above stood a very large man in clerical garb with an impressive mane of white hair. Simon Bird halted. The man at the window made a regal gesture indicating that he should go round to the back of the mansion. Bird raised a hand in acknowledgement and moved off.

A back door stood open, and as he approached it Bird saw that against the wall to one side was the crude figure of a man, cut from plywood and backed by sandbags. A happy smile touched his round cherubic face. He halted six paces from the figure and with a courteous air took off the flat black hat with his right hand, holding it close to his chest.

For a moment he was still, eyes flicking up to a window above where now appeared the same large man with two companions also wearing dark suits and clerical collars. Simon Bird's eyes returned to the wooden figure. The hat slipped from his fingers, then the Colt was in that same hand, firing once, and he stooped only slightly to catch the hat by the brim with his left hand before it reached the ground. The bullet had ripped a hole through the middle of the target's face.

Bird looked up and inclined his head as he slipped the gun back into its holster. The figures at the window clapped politely, unheard. Bird made a slight bow, then moved towards the door. A minute later he was passing through a large room on the ground floor, dreary in design, its decor sadly run down from long neglect. Four apparent vicars were playing poker at a card-table. Three more sat watching a blue video, slumped in boredom.

Bird said, 'Christ, do we wear these togs all the time?'

One of the poker players spoke without looking away from the game. 'Mountjoy says we stay in character while we're here. Was that you shooting just now?'

'Who else? Where do I find him, Jacko?'

The man nodded towards a door at the far end of the room. 'Through there, and second on the left. Paddy and Silver are bringing the patient up.'

Bird nodded, went through into a wide passage and took the second door on the left. It opened into a spacious study. Mountjoy was seated behind a large old desk. He rose ponderously and moved round it to shake hands with Bird. 'Simon, my dear fellow. Your arrival is most admirably timed.' The white hair swayed as he nodded towards a pair of bolt-cutters lying across a corner of the desk. 'As you see, our visitor has arrived.' The face framed by the thick white hair was younger than might have been expected, but broad and unrevealing, an enigma of emptiness.

'Yes, Jacko told me.' Bird took off his hat and threw it on a chair, then slipped a hand under his jacket to feel the butt of the Colt for comfort. He could never understand what it was about Mountjoy that made him feel strange twinges of fear. 'Are we all here now?' he said.

'You are the last, Simon. As you were attending to the business in London, Jonathan brought your luggage down as requested. You will find it in your room.'

The door opened and two more vicars entered, both strong-looking men, both a little breathless, one pushing a trolley bearing a large and obviously heavy wooden crate bound with thick galvanised wire. Several holes were bored in two of the sides. The other man nodded to Bird and said, 'You never came all the way from London on that scooter, did you, Birdie?'

Bird shook his head. 'Only from Exeter. Got a sore arse at that, Paddy me boy.'

Mountjoy said to the man with the trolley, 'If you please, Silver.' The man tipped the trolley forward and the crate fell with a crash. Paddy and Silver heaved it over so that the hinges of the lid rested on the floor. Mountjoy looked at Bird and gestured with a graceful movement towards the desk. Bird moved across, picked up the bolt-cutters and snipped through the three bands of securing wires.

The lid fell open and a huddled man rolled out. He was in shirt-sleeves and without shoes, his wrists manacled and attached by a short chain to shackles round his ankles. He was a rugged-looking man with a strong face, but now he was in agony with cramp, his face bruised and bloody, his hands swollen and blue. He lay on his side panting, staring up at the men about him, trying to hold down his fear.

Very carefully Bird cut through the short chain. The man extended his tortured legs painfully. Bird smiled and crooked a finger, telling the man to stand. It took thirty seconds for him to struggle to his knees, but he could move no further. He knelt there sweating, chest heaving from the effort, glaring up at his captors.

Mountjoy said in his rich, solemn voice, 'Your real name is unknown to us, but we do know for whom you work, and we feel it necessary to make an example of you.'

*　　*　　*

Sir Gerald Tarrant sat in his Whitehall office on a fine sunny morning and made himself look at the photographs once again. Sick at heart, he put them aside and leaned back in his chair, gazing wearily across the desk at his assistant, Fraser, who stood blinking owlishly at him through unfashionable glasses. After a little silence Fraser cleared his throat and said diffidently, 'I feel this is a very serious development, Sir Gerald.'

'For God's sake, Jack, you don't have to tell me that!' There was anger and frustration in Tarrant's voice, and the use of Fraser's forename was a signal telling him to drop the pose of anxious timidity that was second nature to him. It had served Fraser well during his active years as an agent, and had been the death of several highly competent enemies, but there were times when Tarrant found it nerve-racking, and this was just such a moment.

'So what are we bloody well going to do?' said Fraser. 'If those bastards murder Tor Hallenberg, Nobel Peace Prize winner no less, the press is going to demand the return of public hanging for the Home Secretary personally, which is fine by me except that it'll just about blow The Department to hell and gone.'

'We'll have to get another man inside,' said Tarrant. 'I don't know how, and I dread how long it may take, but it's the only option.'

Fraser nodded towards the photographs. 'After what they did to Nash, you'll have to make it a volunteer job anyway, and we're not going to get knocked over in the rush.'

Tarrant looked at him balefully. 'So suggest something better.'

Fraser hesitated, then said warily, 'We need a different approach. A way of getting to these people fast. *We* don't see any way, but we know somebody outside The Department with a knack for that kind of thing. She *thinks* differently from the way we do—'

'Forget it!' Tarrant said sharply. 'Just forget it, Jack. She's left blood and skin and God knows what else all over the place for me, and it's enough. I can't even begin to think about getting her into this bloody mess.'

Fraser chewed his lip. 'She has this knack,' he said carefully. 'And she wouldn't be on her own, would she? Both she and Willie Garvin are in the country just now. I'm having lunch with them at *The Treadmill* on Saturday. Honest to God, they're the only people I know, or even know *of*, who might get in fast and do the job. You wouldn't have to ask her. Just show her those pix you've been looking at.'

'I've no right,' Tarrant said quietly. 'I've never had any right. We've sent people to their deaths over the years, God forgive us, but that was always on the cards in the job they were paid to do.'

Fraser sighed. 'The thing is, we have to operate The Department.' He gestured towards the photographs. 'I'm worried sick about the effect of this killing. We can keep it away from the press and public, but not from our own people. They already know what happened to Johnny Nash, and can you imagine what it will do to morale if we don't nail these buggers fast?'

'I can imagine,' said Tarrant. 'But there are some things even I can't bring myself to do, and what you suggest is one of them. Let me have a list of available volunteers on Monday and we'll take it from there. That's all for now.'

Fraser got slowly to his feet and peered over the top of his spectacles with an air of nervous apprehension, a mouse of a man. 'Very well, Sir Gerald,' he said meekly.

*   *   *

The Treadmill stood a long stone's throw from the Thames and a few miles from Maidenhead. Between the pub and the river was a long low building without windows and with a single door at one end. This was Willie Garvin's combat room. It contained a miniature gymnasium, a dojo, and a range with targets for pistol, knife, and short-range archery. There were racks of weapons, ancient and modern, two shower cubicles, a dressing-room, and a separate workroom lavishly equipped for almost any task from micro-engineering to wrought-iron work.

Willie was under one of the showers. For the past two hours he and Modesty had been working-out in several combat disciplines. He glanced at her now as he turned off the shower and began to towel himself. She had taken off her combat slacks and tunic, and was standing in front of the long mirror beside the open cubicles. Her body still gleamed with sweat from the work-out, her feet were bare and she wore plain black pants and bra with a shoulder holster rig that held a Colt .32 just below and forward of her left armpit. She was drawing the gun and returning it to the holster again and again, sometimes slowly, sometimes at speed, her face a mask of concentration.

Willie finished drying himself, pulled on shirt and slacks, and moved across to watch closely. She sighed and turned to him with an apologetic air. 'I'm sorry, Willie. I know you've put hours of work into designing this rig, but I can't make it work. I'm losing a fifth of a second.'

Willie nodded and checked the position of the holster carefully. 'Do it in slow-motion a few times so I can see, Princess.'

She moved her hand to the butt slowly, and drew. After the third time Willie grimaced. 'Your left knocker gets in the way,' he said.

She laughed. 'They're both part of the set, Willie love.'

'So three cheers. I thought we might 'ave a problem there, but it was worth a try.' He took the rig from her as she slipped it off. 'Better stick to the old hip-holster. You're only tooled up when we're on a caper, and the tunic hides it then.'

'Yes. But thanks for trying.' She moved to the other shower, took off bra and pants, put on a shower-cap and turned on the water. 'We're respectable citizens now, so it's pretty well academic. Anyway, in all the years there were only three or four moments when I had to get a gun out fast.' She began to soap herself, then paused and moved her head clear of the water to look at Willie. 'But you never know, so let's take care not to forget first principles. If you do get into a gunfight there's no prize for coming second.'

'Only a wooden overcoat,' said Willie. He turned away and sat down to put on socks and shoes, grinning to himself. It never failed to amuse him that she genuinely regarded herself as being immensely cautious.

Five minutes later she was dressed and running a comb through her hair when the intercom on the wall buzzed and a woman's voice said, 'Mr Fraser's here, Mr Garvin. Shall I tell him you'll be over soon?'

Willie pressed the intercom button, said, ' 'Ang on, Mavis,' and glanced at Modesty with a lifted eyebrow.

She said, 'Have him come here for a few minutes, Willie. He loves browsing around your collection, and I want to put a bit of make-up on.'

Willie spoke briefly into the intercom, then moved to the end of the combat room to unlock the door. Fraser arrived, growled a surly greeting, and mooched around the various weapon displays for a while, responding with little more than a grunt to any comment from Willie. At last he said abruptly,

'Modesty's here, isn't she? I thought that was the arrangement.'

Willie stared. 'Yes, she's 'ere. Look, are you all right, Jack? You're looking a bit pasty.'

Before Fraser could answer, Modesty appeared from the dressing-room section at the far end and came towards them, smiling. 'Hallo, Jack, it's good to see you.'

Shoulders hunched, mouth turned down, he watched as she approached and stood before him. 'Christ, you look great, girl,' he said dourly. 'Since the day you went legitimate I've got twelve years older. You've just stood still. If you ever feel like taking care of a miserable old sod with no money in his declining years, just call me. I wouldn't mind marrying you.'

The midnight blue eyes held mingled laughter and puzzlement as she studied him. 'You certainly know how to touch a girl's heart, Jack. But that was a bit heavy, even for you. Is anything wrong?'

He hesitated, then exhaled and said, 'Sorry. Can we talk here for a few minutes before we go to lunch?'

'Of course.' She gestured to a corner where there was a bench locker and two chairs. Fraser had left his bowler hat and umbrella there with a large envelope. As they sat down she said, 'Are you speaking for Tarrant? And is it about the Hallenberg snatch?'

Fraser said grimly, 'I'm certainly not speaking for Tarrant, but there's a connection with the Hallenberg snatch.'

She waited, sensing his indecision and puzzled by it, for it was out of character. Tor Hallenberg, winner of the Nobel Peace Prize, had come to London on a lecture tour and been kidnapped seven days ago. The government was working with the Norwegian Embassy and releasing nothing to the press about ransom demands or police activity in the hunt for the missing celebrity. It would not have surprised her to be asked if her knowledge of the underworld, and Willie's, could offer any pointers to whoever might be behind the kidnapping.

Fraser said, 'The Royal Lithuania Movement snatched Hallenberg. They've sent proof of holding him.'

Willie said incredulously, 'Royal Lithuania?'

'That's right,' said Fraser. 'They want the Grand Duchy of Lithuania restored.'

Modesty said, 'I didn't know there'd ever been a Grand Duchy of Lithuania.'

'Before your time, little girl. About six hundred years before. It stretched from the Baltic to the Black Sea.'

'Are you serious, Jack?'

'Never more so, lady. What's not serious but ludicrous are the ransom demands. Recognition of the Duchy in Exile. Promise of arms for subversion. A ban on trade with Russia and Poland, their old enemies. And half a million in gold.'

Willie said, 'They're barmy.'

'They would be if in fact the Royal Lithuania Movement had anything to do with the snatch, but in fact the movement is only about twenty strong, and the youngest is a man of seventy-three.'

Modesty said quietly, 'You're stalling, Jack. You don't want to get to the point. Come on, what's this all about?'

Fraser scowled, took off his glasses and began to polish them. 'You're right, and I'm sorry. Well, what it's about is a big scam. The Basque Liberation Group had nothing to do with the snatch in Spain two months ago. The Amboines had nothing to do with the snatch in Holland before that. We now know that five out of the last six snatches haven't been made by these fringe political groups at all. A professional mob's running the scam.'

Modesty nodded. 'That begins to make sense. How does it work in detail?'

Fraser put on his glasses. 'They pick a suitable candidate and grab him. Their demands, as Willie just said, are barmy and they know it. Then comes negotiation. It's done by phone and always from another country, so it can't be traced in time. Eventually the kidnappers yield on all points except the money.'

There was a little silence. Fraser saw Modesty and Willie looking at each other absently, and suspected that in some strange way their thoughts were merging. At last Willie said, 'So they've picked up a few mill in the last eighteen months.'

'Quite a few. The only failure was Brazil. They wouldn't pay for De Souta, and he was found in pieces. It'll be the same for Hallenberg now, and in less than forty-eight hours. The Norwegians won't pay on principle, neither will we.'

Another silence, and again Fraser sensed that nebulous measure of communication. At the same moment that Willie shook his head Modesty said, 'Starting from cold there's no time to do anything useful. But surely you're not starting from cold, Jack. Tarrant must have been trying to get a man inside this mob for months.'

Fraser nodded. 'We put a man on the job, and he got in. You know Johnny Nash?'

Modesty smiled. 'Yes, I know Johnny well. Nothing heavy. We're good occasional friends.'

Willie said, 'If Johnny's inside, you ought to wrap it up pretty quick now. He's as good as anyone you've got.'

Fraser drew in a long breath and picked up the envelope that lay by his hat. 'He was very good. But he must have got blown somehow.' He took two photographs from the envelope and handed them to Modesty. 'Before they killed him they gave him a manicure. With bolt-cutters, we think.'

She sat holding the photographs, one in each hand, looking at them, her face wiped clean of all expression. After a few moments she passed them to Willie and stood up, holding her elbows as she paced away before turning to come slowly back. Willie laid the photographs face-down on the locker beside Fraser. His face held no more expression than hers as he said, 'Where did you find 'im?'

Fraser said, 'In our private carpark, in a sack. As from the Royal Lithuania Movement.'

Modesty came to a halt, looking down at Fraser, understanding the strangeness in him that had puzzled her earlier. 'You're certainly not speaking for Tarrant,' she said quietly. 'He'll kill you for showing me those photographs, Jack.'

Fraser shrugged, looking up at her with an attempt at a smile. 'He'll certainly fire me. But . . .' he touched the photographs with his fingertips and the effortful smile became a savage, self-mocking grin. 'You know how it is, lady. A man's gotta do what a man's gotta do. Christ, girl, I'd go back on the job myself if I thought I had a cat in hell's chance, but I'm long past it now.' He shook his head wearily. 'And anyway I wouldn't know where to start.'

Modesty stood gazing absently into space. Willie sat watching her quietly, waiting. He knew several things now beyond all doubt. She would seek whoever had performed that obscene killing of Johnny Nash. She would hope to find them, and hope for a confrontation that would provide an opportunity to destroy them in hot blood. She would not take Willie's support for granted, even though she knew he would declare it. And she would be aware that as soon as they began their search Tarrant would know that Fraser had shown her the photographs.

It was Fraser who broke the silence, sounding happier now that he had committed himself. 'I'll tell the old man when I get back to town. No point in hanging about.'

Modesty nodded, and her remote gaze faded as she looked at him. 'Yes, phone him today. He knows Johnny was a friend, so tell him that if I'd found out about this later I'd never have forgiven him for keeping it from me.'

Fraser said bleakly, 'That just might save my bacon, except that I just might be getting you killed, in which case I wouldn't want my bacon saved.' He picked up the photographs, put them in the envelope and glared at her sullenly. 'For Christ's sake don't get killed, girl. I've still got a few years left maybe, and I don't want to be carrying that with me.'

She gave him a small affectionate smile. 'I'll bear it in mind. Did you get anything at all from Johnny Nash before they killed him?'

Fraser grimaced. 'Almost nothing.'

'Almost?'

'The managing director of the mob running the scam will be attending a gathering at a house in Belgravia this evening. But since we have no name and no description, and there are going to be a hundred and fifty others there, it's not much help.'

'Can you get us in?'

'No problem.'

'There's nothing else? No clues on Johnny or the sack he was in?'

'Forensic checked but got nothing useful. Oh Jesus, no, wait a minute, there was something in the sack but it still wasn't useful. I don't know why I bothered to bring it.' Fraser opened his brief-case and took out a small transparent plastic bag containing a white cotton glove, holding it up for Modesty to inspect. 'It wouldn't have fitted Nash even before they worked on him, so presumably it was worn by somebody who helped put him in the sack. Somebody who just might be at the gathering.'

Modesty said, 'Has it been handled much?'

'Only by forensic in rubber gloves. Why?'

'Can you leave it with me?'

Fraser gave a snort of humourless laughter. 'Why not? I've shown you the pix, so how the hell can I get into worse trouble?' He handed the bag to her, then blinked and gave a baffled stare. 'God Almighty, you can't take a bloodhound to this gathering. It's the Prison Abolition Society and they're actually campaigning for the abolition of prisons if you can believe it, but even a bunch of nutters might think it a bit odd to have a bloodhound sniffing around.'

Modesty said, 'They might not notice a heavily disguised bloodhound.' She looked at Willie and said doubtfully, 'Too much for Dinah?'

Dinah Collier and her husband Steve were their closest friends. Blind from childhood, Dinah had a remarkable sense of smell, and could recognise people by their scent if she knew them well enough to have registered the characteristics. Often she described the scent by reference to other senses, so that to her Modesty's was like the taste of brandy, Willie's like the sound of a muted trumpet, her husband's like the feel of suede.

Willie shook his head. 'Dinah couldn't match a person to what she could get from that glove, Princess. No chance. You'd need an Abo for that—' He broke off and sat up straight.

Modesty said, 'Yes, you told me you had a call from Bluey Peters. He's in London?'

Willie nodded and got to his feet. 'Staying at the Waldorf and he's got Jacko with him, as usual.'

Her eyes sparkled as she turned to Fraser. 'Then we have our bloodhound.'

Fraser stared. 'You're saying an Aborigine can do it?'

She moved to sit beside him, and he sensed the relaxation in her. 'An Aborigine can do it, Jack, and we have one who's an old friend. Outside his tribe he's called 'Orace, and I've been walkabout in the bush with 'Orace and his people more than once. They can follow a three-day-old scent across miles of rock and desert and scrub.' She paused for a moment, thinking. 'Look, there are no guarantees, but whereas I thought it might take us weeks to get near the people who killed Johnny Nash, I now hope we may be able to get that far tonight. In which case there's a slim chance that we could get Hallenberg out before they kill him.'

Fraser touched her hand. 'Oh God, that's great. Make sure it's before they kill *you*, lady.'

She said with a touch of impatience, 'I don't think like that, Jack. Just tell Tarrant about the Hallenberg possibility when you make your confession, and say I might ask for back-up if need be.'

Willie said, 'I'm in, Princess.'

She smiled. 'Thanks, Willie.' Then to Fraser, '*We* might ask for back-up. But we'll let you know.' She stood up. 'Now let's forget it and have lunch. I'm starving.'

*   *   *

What Willie Garvin liked most about cocktail parties of this kind was that they were so horrible. The worse they were, the more he enjoyed them because they presented such a variety of unbelievable characters for his amusement. This one was quite satisfactorily horrible in these terms, but he could not enjoy it fully because he had other matters to hold his attention.

The room had once been the ballroom of the large house in the corner of the square. A wide archway on one side opened into an annexe where tables were set with canapés and various confections on cocktail sticks. There were fewer than a hundred and fifty people present, Willie calculated, but still well over a hundred, a mixed bunch of free-loaders, cranks, police-haters, and slightly dazed-looking people who had perhaps been raked in without quite knowing what it was all about.

Modesty was with an earnest bearded man. He had a drink in one hand and was leaning against the wall with his other arm over her shoulder, more or less pinning her there as he talked energetically between quick attacks on his drink. She was in a good position for surveying the room, and had given no sign of wanting to be rescued.

Willie stood on the other side of the room, protected on one side by a pillar, an untouched drink in hand, keeping a casual eye on two men who had arrived together twenty minutes ago. Bluey Peters was a big, rugged Australian with short-cropped ash-blond hair. His companion, 'Orace, was tall and slender with shiny black skin and a shock of black curly hair. They were moving slowly, casually, from group to group, Bluey playing the extrovert with self-introductions, 'Orace showing white teeth in a big smile, his broad nose flaring as he exchanged greetings. On his own, Bluey might have found himself coolly received, but with 'Orace in tow there was no danger of that. Any such gathering would above all be Politically Correct.

Both men had worked for Modesty in the days of *The Network*, running one of her motor fishing vessels in the Mediterranean for smuggling or any other purpose she might require. 'Orace was a pure Aborigine and had spent the first sixteen years of his life in the bush. His people were the best trackers in the world, and not only on their own territory. Willie had known 'Orace to track Bluey three miles through a city to find him in a bar.

An hour ago 'Orace had sniffed the cotton glove for a full thirty seconds before announcing that it held four different human scents. One was a dead man's scent. Of the others, the strongest by far was inside the glove. Now Willie estimated that 'Orace had checked three-quarters of the people in the room. He watched as the contrasting pair moved away from a group. Bluey cocked an inquiring eye at his friend, who gave a quick shake of his head. Willie sighed inwardly. The chances of the glove-man being present were growing slimmer.

At his elbow a voice said, 'Look, I hope you don't mind my sort of accosting you, but I'm feeling a tiny bit lost, really. I don't actually know anybody here.'

She was in her middle twenties, with short dark hair and an earnest manner. Her eyes were large and brown, her face round and pleasant, her figure truly excellent. Again Willie sighed inwardly, knowing that he could give her only part of his attention. Sometimes life was very perverse. Putting aside his regrets he gave her a welcoming smile and said, ' 'Allo, I'm Willie Garvin. Why d'you come if you don't know anybody?'

'Well,' she paused to sip her drink, 'well, Daddy wrote and said would I, so I did, because he's been rather sweet about buying me a new balloon. Oh, I'm Lucy, by the way. Lucy Fuller-Jones.'

Willie thought, *I've got a weirdo here.* Aloud he said, 'What colour balloon?'

'Well, actually it's black.'

As she sipped her drink again, Willie shot a glance round the room. Modesty was still with the bearded man. Bluey and 'Orace had moved across one end of the room and were starting slowly down the far side.

'Black's not very festive,' said Willie. 'I like red balloons better. But only if I can't 'ave three or four different colours all tied together. They're best of all.'

She stared at him blankly for a moment, then her eyes widened and she gave a chuckling laugh. 'Oh golly, I mean a *big* balloon. One you go up in.'

Willie put a hand to his head with a wincing expression of apology. 'Sorry, Lucy, I thought—well, never mind. How did a girl like you get to be a balloonist? When I say a girl like you I don't mean—'

She broke in eagerly. 'It's *extraordinary* that you should say that, Mr Garvin—'

'Willie, please.'

'Willie. Because actually it's *because* I'm a girl like me that I became one. I mean a balloonist.' Her manner became apologetic. 'It's my glands, I'm afraid. They seem to produce a lot of awfully excitable hormones that make a girl get rather addicted to . . . well, to *chaps*, you see.'

Willie suppressed a fervent wish that he was not otherwise occupied at this moment, and covered another survey of the room with a kind of eye-rolling expression that might have indicated astonishment. 'Addicted to chaps? Isn't that good, Lucy?'

'Oh, it's absolutely no good at all if you want to achieve what the Swami Gumarati calls the Golden Plateau of Serenity.'

Willie breathed deeply and said, 'That sounds fascinating. Is it a sort of yoga?'

'Well, it's more than that, really. I'll lend you Swami Gumarati's book if you like.'

'I'd rather 'ave a ride in your balloon, Lucy.' A puzzled lift of his head covered another glance round the room. 'Wait a minute, though. What's the balloon got to do with your gland troubles?'

'Ballooning sublimates the *earthly* aspects of our nature, which was my trouble, of course, the earthly aspects. I wrote to the Swami, and he went into a trance and wrote back to say I should take up ballooning. So I did, and it works.' She paused, frowning a little. 'Well, I think it does.'

Willie said, 'I sometimes get a bit of that gland trouble myself. Could I phone you sometime so we could meet and 'ave a chat about it?'

'Well . . .' She pursed her lips doubtfully, 'we'd have to be careful *where* we meet, wouldn't we? I mean, with our glands.'

'Ah yes, I'm glad you thought of that Lucy. Somewhere public. Maybe an art gallery or . . . or the zoo. D'you live in London?'

'Oh yes.' She relaxed, smiling. 'I've got a flat in Chelsea, and I'm in the phone-book. Lucy Fuller-Jones.'

'Well, that's fine. I've got a few things to attend to just at this time, but I'll certainly give you a call.'

'Jolly good. I say, there are some rather peculiar people here, aren't there?' She gazed slowly round the room.

'Talking to you, I'd 'ardly noticed,' said Willie, and thankfully joined her inspection. Towards the top of the room on Modesty's side two men in clerical collars were speaking with a large, gushing woman. Bluey and 'Orace were moving slowly towards them. One of the clerics was a very big man with a mane of white hair. The other was smaller with a round cherubic face.

Bluey glanced at the group, was clearly not interested in its composition, and passed behind the clerics. 'Orace followed, looking disconsolate, then stopped with a hint of surprise. Even across the room Willie saw the nostrils flare behind the smaller man. 'Orace smiled happily, his gaze moving from Modesty to Willie. Then he lifted his untouched drink and drained the glass before moving on.

Lucy was saying, '. . . if you'd really *like* a ride in my balloon, I expect we could arrange something.'

Willie beamed at her. 'I'd love that. Will you excuse me, Lucy? I've just remembered I promised our generous host that I'd get a few comments from different people for the *Prisoner's Friend* magazine.'

'Oh. Yes, of course. You go ahead.'

The gushing lady was leaving the two clerics as Willie moved towards them. Glancing to his right, he saw Modesty and 'Orace leaving together. The man who had been talking to her was still in the same position, propped by one arm against the wall but with head turned and a puzzled air. Bluey ambled by, and without looking at Willie murmured, 'She says make sure they stay put for a couple of minutes.'

Willie had expected this. She would be fixing a radio bug on any car that 'Orace identified as bearing the scent of the clerics. He collected a fresh drink from a passing waiter and strolled towards his quarry. All around him the buzz of conversation was growing louder and more shrill as liquor loosened tongues. The two men eyed him benignly as he began to move past. He halted, gave them a rueful look, and spoke in one of the cultured voices he could produce so accurately.

'"For they stretch forth their mouth unto heaven, and their tongue goeth through the world."'

They looked at him blankly, and the smaller man said, 'I beg your pardon, sir?'

'Psalm seventy-three, verse nine. I felt it an apt comment on the sound of a large cocktail party, but perhaps the allusion is rather strained.'

The big man said, 'Ah, I see. Are you in holy orders, sir?'

Willie shook his head regretfully. 'I saw the light too late in life, I fear.' He extended his hand. 'Francis Pennyquick, youth club leader.'

The white head was inclined courteously as the man took Willie's hand. 'How do you do? My name is Mountjoy, and this is my spiritual confrère, the Reverend Simon Bird.'

'A pleasure,' said Willie, and shook hands with the man 'Orace had identified.

Bird's cherubic face was innocent and welcoming. 'You do important work, Mr Pennyquick. Are you a student of the psalms?'

Willie smiled deprecatingly. 'Only in a very amateurish fashion, I assure you.' He did not feel it would be fruitful to admit that he knew them by heart as a result of spending six months in a Calcutta gaol in his younger days with only a psalter to read. 'You're interested in the Prison Abolition Society, Mr Mountjoy?'

Mountjoy pondered the question. Then, 'Obliquely, Mr Pennyquick, obliquely. The first necessity is of course to eliminate crime, thereby obviating the need for prisons. I take it your own efforts are to that intent?'

With long practice in front of a mirror Willie had found that by pulling his chin in, folding his lower lip under his upper lip, curving his mouth in a smile, and causing his head to wobble slightly as he spoke, he could create an appearance of great stupidity. He had been building this effect since first speaking to Mountjoy and Bird, and had given it full rein while Mountjoy was speaking. Now he said, 'We youth club leaders are in the front line of that battle, Mr Mountjoy.'

Bluey Peters appeared in the doorway, one hand holding a lapel of his jacket, thumb pointing up. Willie looked at his watch

and registered surprise. 'Good heavens. I had no idea. The time,
I mean.' He pointed to his watch as if to clarify the matter. 'Do
excuse me. I promised young Kevin I'd go with him to see his
probation officer . . .' He allowed his words to fade into incoher-
ence, and hurried away.

Mountjoy and Bird watched him go with well-concealed contempt. Smiling about him, Bird said in a low voice, 'Twenty
years ago I had a probation officer who was almost as dumb as
that dickhead.'

Mountjoy said softly, 'Don't knock it, Simon. We like dumb
people. I'm only sorry the Brits and the Norwegians aren't quite
dumb enough to pay up for Hallenberg.'

'There's still time,' said Bird, 'and you never know. They
might crack in the last few hours. But I don't think we'll get
anything out of this evening's jaunt. Nobody's going to believe
in a militant wing of the Prison Abolition Society going in for
kidnap and murder.'

'I'm aware of that, Simon. But it's at gatherings like this that
one meets all kinds of single-issue weirdos who might provide
ideas for future use. That Greek woman who button-holed us is
a case in point.'

'Jesus, she wanted a Ladies Only Olympics! We can't use
that.'

'I wouldn't rule it out entirely. But in fact it made me think
about the Greek-Albanian situation. There might be something
for us in that.'

'We've got another chat coming up,' Bird murmured, watching
the dark-haired girl approach. 'Nice piece, too. She'd certainly
give me a few ideas if I weren't a man of the cloth.'

Lucy Fuller-Jones said, 'Oh, do excuse me, but did you see
where Mr Garvin went? He was with you a few moments ago,
and then somebody spoke to me, and when I looked again he'd
gone.'

Mountjoy said slowly, 'Mr Garvin?'

'That's right. The gentleman you were talking with just now.
He told me his name was Willie Garvin.'

Bird was staring at her fixedly. Mountjoy said, 'Ah, yes. The gentleman who was with us just now. We must have failed to hear correctly when he introduced himself.' He spread his hands in a gesture of regret. 'I'm afraid he's left, my dear. We had exchanged only a few words when he remembered he had an urgent appointment.'

Lucy looked crestfallen. 'Oh, what a pity. He's such a nice man. Well, thank you.' She gave them a smile and moved away. Mountjoy and Bird looked at each other with no outward sign of agitation. Bird said in a whisper, '*Garvin*, by Christ! You know what that means?'

Mountjoy nodded and said without emotion, 'Yes. It means Modesty Blaise is in the game. The authorities are playing their aces, and we must take immediate steps to trump them.'

Together, inclining heads benevolently to any who caught their eye in passing, they made their way through the chattering throng to the door.

*   *   *

The rather elderly Rover moved at a rather elderly pace along the Cromwell Road. Eighty yards behind, with one car between, Modesty sat at the wheel of a Mercedes. Beside her Willie said, 'Well, we shouldn't lose 'em, unless we get 'ad up for loitering.'

She said, 'I hope they're not going far. It's more difficult to make this sort of tail look natural than one at normal speed. Still, we didn't have to hang around for them till that cocktail do ended. They almost followed you out.' After a few moments she said, 'Was that just coincidence?'

'I don't see it could've been anything else, Princess.'

'I suppose not. Still . . .' She let the nebulous thought fade unspoken, for the Rover had turned left down Earls Court Road. Five minutes later it drew up opposite a small and seedy hotel where no lights showed except for a dim lamp over the entrance. Mountjoy and Bird got out, crossed the road and went in by the front door.

In the Mercedes, halted well back from the hotel, Modesty said, 'It looks deserted.'

Willie unfastened his seat-belt. 'We just passed a pub. I'll go and ask about it.'

The hotel lobby was bare of furniture except for one shabby chair in which a man with thin sandy hair sat reading a tabloid newspaper and smoking. The remains of a take-away meal lay on the counter. As Mountjoy and Bird entered, the man got hastily to his feet, stubbed out his cigarette in some tomato ketchup decorating a cardboard plate, and showed signs of ingratiating unease.

Mountjoy ignored him and moved to the counter. Picking up the phone there, he dialled a number. Bird stared at the caretaker without expression. After a few seconds Mountjoy said, 'Tabby? Good. Now listen. I want four men at the contact point within twenty minutes.' A brief pause. 'No, don't tell me you'll *try* to fix it, Tabby. Not *me*. There'll be some merchandise to pick up for delivery as before. Two units of merchandise, and they'll need cautious handling, you understand? Good. Just don't make any mistakes, Tabby. Any at all.'

He put the phone down and looked at the caretaker. 'We shall leave at once by the back way, Charles. In a few minutes you'll almost certainly be having visitors. Now listen carefully while I tell you what to do. It's much the same as before.'

A stone's throw from the entrance, Willie returned from the pub and spoke to Modesty through the open window of the Mercedes. 'The 'otel's closed, Princess. Went bust. Empty now except for a caretaker to keep squatters away.'

They both gazed along the road towards the dimly lit entrance, calculating possibilities. After a few seconds Modesty said, 'I wouldn't think they'd keep Hallenberg there.'

Willie nodded agreement. 'Maybe they're on to us. Went in the front, out the back and took a cab.'

She considered. 'Hard to see how they could be on to us.' For half a minute neither spoke, then she looked at her watch and opened the car door. 'It's been ten minutes now. We're not going to find out anything like this. Let's go and take a look.'

Charles the caretaker was reading his newspaper again when they came into the lobby. He glanced up briefly and said, 'We're closed.'

Willie moved towards him. Modesty stood in the middle of the lobby, looking about her. There was a lift with stairs running up beside it, a closed door opposite the lift, a partly open door to the left of the reception counter, a corridor leading off to the right.

Willie said to the caretaker, 'I want a word with the two gents who came in a few minutes ago.'

Charles returned to reading his newspaper. 'What gents?' he said without interest.

Willie took a twenty-pound note from his wallet. 'Clerical gents. Vicars. Remember?'

Charles looked at the note. 'Who wants 'em?'

'Me and my auntie. We're in their confirmation class.'

Charles reached out a grubby hand to grasp the note, but Willie didn't release it. 'They've gorn,' said Charles impatiently. 'Went down the 'ole.'

'What 'ole?'

'The *'ole*! What used to lead down to the subway. It was for air-raids in the war.'

Willie glanced at Modesty, then released the note. 'Show me.'

Charles scowled and got reluctantly to his feet. 'Along 'ere,' he said, moving into the corridor. 'Down through the store-room.'

Less than a minute later he opened a door and put on the light in a large, windowless room. Empty steel shelving was fixed along two walls. The only furniture was a single ladderback chair with a hole in its cane seating. The floor was littered with rubbish—bundles of newspapers, a galvanised iron bucket with a large dent in one side, a broken broom, and a cluster of small oddments and trash. Nothing was new except four large crates stacked in one corner. In the opposite corner lay a square of dirty threadbare carpet.

Willie stood by the door, watching the way they had come. Modesty was in the room, her eyes on the caretaker as he pulled the piece of carpet aside to reveal a large trap-door secured by two coach-bolts. He drew the bolts and lifted the trap, resting it back against the wall.

'There,' he said with the air of a man who had performed far beyond the demands of duty. 'You go down the 'ole, across the cellar, then through the passage, and you come out in a branch of the subway. Never used now, but there's only a rope across it.'

Modesty took a small torch from her handbag and flashed it down into the darkness. A lightweight metal ladder rested against the thick beam at the fore-edge of the trap. She turned and began to go down, shining the beam about the empty square cellar below. Charles sighed resignedly and lit a cigarette.

The cellar was about twelve feet along each side, and ten or eleven in height. In one of the walls was an arched doorway. Modesty moved towards it and shone the torch along a passage that ended in a right-angle turn. She called softly, 'All right, Willie.'

In the store-room above, Willie moved to the open trap. Charles shrugged and slouched towards the door. 'I can't 'ang around all night,' he said plaintively. 'If you come back this way you shut it yourself.'

Willie paused at the top of the ladder. 'The rate you've been earning since we got 'ere works out at about two thousand quid a day,' he pointed out.

Charles sniffed. 'It's all relative,' he said surprisingly, and went out.

The walls of the passage leading off the cellar were rendered with concrete. With Modesty leading, they moved slowly forward. Twice in the twenty-yard length she halted to listen. The only sound was that of their own breathing. When they came to the right-angle turn she moved swiftly across the width of the passage, shining the light on the inside corner while Willie stepped quickly into the centre of the new passage with his back to the wall.

Nobody was lying in wait. Modesty said, 'We'd better follow this through anyway.' She turned the beam along the passage and heard Willie mutter an oath. Twelve feet from where they stood, the light shone on a solid wall. The passage had been bricked up.

Willie was racing back the way they had come, and she was

on his heels. A second before they reached the cellar there came the crash of the trap falling shut and the lesser sound of bolts scraping home. The ladder was gone.

Modesty exhaled and said quietly, 'I wasn't too clever, calling you down.'

Willie shrugged, gazing up at the trap. 'He 'ad me fooled, Princess. Worth an Oscar, that was.'

They were both staring up, gauging the height. She said, 'I think you named it, Willie. They're on to us, God knows how. But they didn't work this just to shake us off. I think this may be how they nailed Johnny Nash.'

Willie's head snapped round to stare at her in the gloom. 'Those crates we saw upstairs?'

'I think they expect to use a couple of them for us. We'd better not hang around.'

'I'll vote for that. Seeing what's 'appened so far I reckon they've got some hired muscle pretty close. Probably on its way to get us crated.'

As he spoke she handed him the small torch and her handbag, and unfastened her skirt. 'What about the Oscar winner, Willie?'

'Off to the pub till it's all over. He wouldn't want to see the nasty bits.'

'Are you carrying anything?'

He opened his jacket to show the twin knives sheathed on the inside left breast. 'You?'

She threw the skirt aside. 'Just the kongo on the handbag.'

He put the torch in his breast pocket so that the beam shone up, and together they moved to stand beneath the fore-edge of the trap, facing each other. She kicked off her shoes and put her hands on his shoulders. He reached out to grip her arms above the biceps and bent one leg slightly to offer her a knee to step on. Her foot was there for less than a second before she was gone with a little spring, doubling her body at the waist then extending her legs upwards so that she was standing on her hands on his shoulders, well supported by his grip on her upper arms.

Their combined height in this position was a fraction under twelve feet, but her legs were bent with the trap-door only six inches above her feet. She drew in a deep breath and smashed her feet against the trap in the area she had judged one of the bolts to be. These were feet unshod for most of her childhood years, feet on which she could still walk unshod for any distance over any terrain.

The door lifted slightly and shuddered. Her head almost touched the top of Willie's head with the recoil, but then their arms straightened and she kicked again. On the third strike she felt something give, and one corner of the trap lifted an inch or two. Willie said a little breathlessly, 'That bolt's gone, Princess. Ripped the screws out of the keeper section.' He moved sideways a little, and again she launched a hammerblow with the flat of her feet against the position of the other bolt. It gave on the second strike, and she kicked the door back to rest against the store-room wall above. Doubling at the waist, she lowered her feet to Willie's shoulders, straightened up, and with her back to the fore-edge reached up to hook fingers over the edge before lifting her legs to circle her body up and over on to the store-room floor.

The metal ladder, in two short sections, lay near the trap. As she got to her feet her handbag and skirt were tossed up from below. She said, 'The ladder's here, Willie. Won't be a moment, it's in two bits.'

She was bending to bring the two sections together when the door opened and a man stepped into the store-room, a thin, neatly dressed man with dark hair sleeked back, a long jaw and watery eyes. He stopped short, staring at her, and the three men who were following crowded in the doorway behind him. Two were of medium build, the third a big man, all hard-faced and well-muscled, with the confident air of experienced minders.

The big man gave a sudden laugh and said, 'Well there's a turn-up. Nice legs, eh Tabby?'

Tabby moved aside, blinked watery eyes and said, 'Get her, Dave. Quick.'

As the man moved towards her she spread her hands and said ruefully, 'Okay, there's four of you, so let's not get heavy about this.' On the last word, timing his pace accurately, she spun round and delivered a vicious back-heel to his crotch. He squealed, staggered sideways, and sank down against the wall, panting and clutching himself, face pale with shock.

Tabby said in a voice suddenly shrill, 'Christ! Get the bitch!' One of his two remaining companions was dark and stocky, the other was younger with a shaven head. A half section of the ladder was in her hands as they moved forward together. With one end of it she hooked the ladder-back chair to send it skidding across the floor and down through the open trap. Continuing the swing, she dropped the two furthermost rungs over the shaven head and sent the man cannoning sideways into his companion. They fell in a tangle together, and she snatched up her hand-bag, clutching the kongo that formed part of the clasp, jerking it free.

In the cellar, Willie held the chair by its topmost rail, the legs pointing upwards. She had let him know that there were four men to cope with and in one brilliant stroke had given him the way out. The sounds from above suggested that she was managing so far, but he was well aware that in such a confined space she would be at a great disadvantage. He bent at the knees, concentrated for a second, then jumped. The seat of the inverted chair hooked over the edge of the trap, and at once he began to haul himself up the ladderback.

As his head cleared the opening he saw a big man clutching his crotch and trying painfully to get to his feet. A second man sat with his neck trapped between the rungs of the ladder and his head covered by the galvanised iron bucket. Its handle was caught over one of the projecting ends, making it very difficult for him to get the bucket off. Modesty, kongo in hand, faced a dark stocky man with a knife and was using all her footwork skill to keep him between her and a thin man by the door who held a gun.

Halfway out of the trap, knife in hand, left forearm braced on the floor for support, Willie threw. The blade sliced across the top of the gun-hand, and the weapon flew wide with the violent reaction of the nerves. The man gave a muffled scream, clutched his gashed hand, and started forward as if to recover the gun.

Willie held his second knife poised. He said briskly, 'Leave it, Tabby, or this one goes right through your pudding-chute.'

The stocky man was distracted. Modesty stepped inside an ill-judged thrust and dropped him with a strike from the kongo. Tabby focused on the figure climbing out from below, and the blood drained from his face. He backed against the door, wounded hand clutched under his armpit now, trying desperately to force a smile.

'Oh Jesus, I didn't know it was *you*, Willie!' he croaked. 'I mean, we were just doing a job for someone, that's all. I'd never 've *touched* it if I'd know it was *you*! I mean, would I?'

The man with the bucket over his head gave up trying to remove it and sat very still. Modesty moved to pick up the fallen gun and the stocky man's knife. Evidently Willie and the man he called Tabby had met in the past. Tabby was plunging on now, trying to be jocular. 'It's a real turn-up, this, innit, Willie? I mean, with you down the 'ole *I* couldn't know who it was, could I? I mean, I never seen Modesty before——'

He broke off with a yelp of terror as a knife grazed his ear and stood quivering in the door. Willie moved towards him, grim-faced. 'You referring to *Miss Blaise*?' he demanded. 'Just don't take bloody liberties, Tabby, it upsets me, see? You might need specs one day, so you don't want to lose your ears, do you?'

Modesty suppressed a smile. She knew that Willie's anger was quite genuine. It always baffled her that he could accept with equanimity the notion that people might try to kill her but was infuriated if they showed any sign of disrespect. Tabby was looking at her now, sweating, ducking his head in apology and saying huskily, 'Sorry, Miss. No offence.'

She said, 'You've done this before, haven't you, Tabby? Picked up a man here. A man with thick dark hair and a scar over one eye.'

Tabby swallowed. 'I—I might 'ave. Miss.'

She said, 'He's dead. So are you now. He was an SIS man, and his friends will sign you off when we hand you over, so you won't live to need spectacles.' She began to turn away, then paused. 'Unless we can come to some arrangement.'

Tabby almost choked in his eagerness to get the words out. 'Anything, Miss. Anything,' he gabbled. 'I mean, whatever you say. Oh Christ, I just want out. I 'ate that Mountjoy.' He glanced in terror at Willie. 'I don't know much, honest, Miss. But I'll tell all I know.'

Willie said, 'Will Mountjoy phone you tonight?' Tabby nodded. 'So you'll tell him everything went according to plan?'

Tabby said desperately, ' 'Course I bloody will! You don't reckon I'm going to tell 'im I blew it, do you? He'd 'ave me gutted! You going after 'im, Willie, you and Miss Blaise? I mean if you don't nail 'im he'll 'ave me gutted anyway, soon as he finds out I blew it.'

Modesty said, 'Did you deliver the crate last time, or was it collected?'

Tabby looked away. 'My boys delivered it,' he muttered. 'Just delivered it.'

'So you know where. That's good. When would you expect to deliver *us*?'

Tabby winced. 'He'll ring and say. Most likely it'll be tomorrow night. Not before.'

'All right.' She glanced round the room. It was clear that all three men had to some extent come to their senses, but all were unmoving. Impossible to see the face of the man with the bucket on his head, but the other two seemed to be listening dazedly. She said, 'Can you answer for your boys? Answer to Willie for them?'

'Oh God, yes, Miss. Yes. No sweat.'

She looked at Willie. 'Can you screw the keeper sections of those bolts back in place so the caretaker won't wonder?' He nodded, and she turned back to Tabby. 'For the same reason, you take two of those crates when you leave here. When Mountjoy has phoned and you've told him all's well, you and your boys disappear. Go anywhere as long as you're well out of distance. Watch the newspapers. If you read that Hallenberg is safe, then you won't need to worry about Mountjoy. Or his friend.'

*　　*　　*

At ten that evening, in his apartment overlooking the Thames, Sir Gerald Tarrant took a phone-call from Modesty Blaise. 'Yes,' he said quietly. 'Fraser told me what he had done. I was very angry indeed, but then he gave me your ultimatum.'

'No. Just my message telling you how I feel. It wasn't a threat to sever relations.'

'Even so, after all I've put you through in the past I don't think I could bear to have you unable to forgive me for failing to tell you about Nash.'

She said gently, 'Well, that doesn't arise now. What are you going to do about Jack Fraser?'

'Nothing. I'm terrified of offending you.'

He heard laughter in her voice. 'I'm very glad about that, and now I need your help. There's a big old house in Cornwall called *Poldeacon*, perched on cliffs and quite a long way from the nearest village, which is called Mallowby. I'd be very glad if you could use your considerable resources to find out all you can about it, without letting it appear that inquiries are being made.'

'That doesn't sound too onerous. When do you need this information?'

'Tomorrow morning would be very nice. I don't want to talk about it on the phone, but I'm not asking as a personal favour. It's to do with the hope I expressed to Fraser this morning, and which I'm sure he passed on to you.'

Tarrant said, '*What?* How can you possibly—?'

She broke in. 'I know it's only a few hours since he told us, but we got lucky at that Prison Abolition function this evening. Can you come and see us tomorrow morning? Willie's here with me.'

There was a brief silence, then Tarrant said, 'Is there really a chance that you might save some Scandinavian bacon for me?'

'That's what we're hoping for. We'll expect you for breakfast.'

'My dear . . . thank you.'

Tarrant put down the phone and moved to gaze out of the window, torn between hope and fear. In time past he had used her ruthlessly, and knowing the extent of her abilities he felt a surge of hope that she might indeed save Hallenberg. But although he would never have confessed it, his affection for her now could not have been deeper if she had been his daughter, and it chilled his blood to think what might happen to her if she made the smallest mistake in going up against the men who had killed John Nash so horribly.

At half-past eight next morning he sat down with Modesty and Willie to a classic English breakfast served by her houseboy, Weng, and at nine moved with them into the big sitting-room overlooking Hyde Park. Modesty's hair was loose and tied back with a ribbon. Like Willie, she wore just a shirt and slacks, for they had been swimming in the pool below the penthouse block before Tarrant's arrival.

Now he said, 'You're extremely civilised, banning all serious discussion during breakfast. I'm sure it enhances the digestion.'

She gestured for him to take an armchair, and said, 'I don't think as well as I might when I'm eating. That's probably because I enjoy it so much.' She moved to another chair and picked up some embroidery on a tambour-frame from a small table at her elbow, studying it for a moment with a frown before taking the threaded needle from where it had been lodged in the canvas.

Willie watched her start to work, seemed to understand some unspoken requirement, and sat down facing Tarrant. 'Okay, Sir G., what've you got for us?'

Tarrant picked up the slim brief-case he had brought with him, opened it, and took out a photograph and a piece of paper, handing the photograph to Willie. 'I had a man flown down to Cornwall last night. He had to get one or two people out of bed, but he managed to put together a good report on the situation. However, that picture and most of the background information were available from Ministry of Defence files.'

Studying the photograph, Willie said, 'This is *Poldeacon*?'

'And immediate surroundings. The picture isn't new, but the place hasn't changed in a century.' Tarrant looked at the paper he held. 'There's a wooded area that ends a couple of hundred yards from the front of the house. Cliffs drop down to a bay at the rear.'

'Ideal place for 'em to be 'olding Hallenberg.'

'Better than you can imagine, but we'll come to that in a moment. How did you and Modesty pinpoint this place?'

'Fraser told us Johnny Nash said the top man would be at that nutty do in Belgravia last night. He got us invitations and gave us the glove that was found with the body. It had the scent of a clerical gent called Bird, who was with another clerical gent called Mountjoy.'

Tarrant stared. 'Had the *scent*?'

'We've got an Aborigine friend with an ace hooter. He picked 'em out. We followed them, and they 'ad a good try at getting us crated like Johnny Nash. I don't know what the Church of England is coming to these days.'

Tarrant said, 'So you were blown?'

Willie nodded. 'But they think we're crated and awaiting delivery to *Poldeacon*.' He explained briefly what had happened at the empty hotel and how Tabby had been persuaded to tell what he knew. 'So we reckon *Poldeacon* is where they've got Hallenberg, and the sooner we get 'im out the better. What does your report say about the place.'

'A few years ago the Ministry of Defence were going to use it for one of their research laboratories. They built an outer wall round it and set up a radar alarm system. Then the idea fell through and the place became a white elephant,' Tarrant looked up from the report, 'until it was rented two months ago by a Mr Mountjoy. He has some ten men in residence there with him.'

'Plus Hallenberg, that's for sure now. What's their cover, Sir G.?'

'Holy Orders. Mountjoy purports to have set the place up as a retreat for overworked clerics.'

'Blimey. A whole *team* of the ungodly playing at vicars?'

Tarrant shrugged. 'Bizarre, I agree. But clever. And I've been saving the bad news, Willie. *Poldeacon* was built over the ruins of a medieval castle with the usual primitive sanitary facilities. In this case a vertical shaft drops down to a good way below sea-level, where there's an influx of sea through the workings of a tin mine that was abandoned in the last century. The effect is that anything dropped down the shaft is carried out to sea by an undertow.' He put the piece of paper aside. 'The shaft is capacious enough to accept a body, and is believed to have done so more than once in the past, so Hallenberg could be gone within a minute of their alarm system warning them of a raid. In these circumstances I don't see how we can get him out alive.'

'You reckon they'll 'ave put all the radar circuits in working order?'

'Yes. Why else choose that place? They're very efficient people.'

'And that's it? The lot?'

'It's all I can tell you.'

'Ah, well.' Willie got up and moved to stand gazing out of the great picture window. After a while Modesty sighed, held her embroidery out at arm's length to study it, and said, 'I try. I really do try, but it looks awful. I don't know what I'm doing wrong.'

Willie moved from the window, took the embroidery she held out for him, and examined it carefully. 'It's the stitches,' he announced at last. 'You do the stitches wrong.'

'Oh well, if that's all . . .'

She got up and moved to the window where Willie had been standing, holding her elbows as she looked absently out across the park. Tarrant drew breath to speak, caught Willie's warning shake of the head, and let the breath out quietly. A full minute passed before she turned from the window, and now there was a sparkle in her eye. 'Willie, can you get hold of the weird girl you were rubbing chests with at that gathering last night? The girl with the urgent glands?'

Tarrant saw sudden contentment in Willie as he put down the embroidery he had been wryly studying. 'Sure, Princess. I've got 'er number.'

Modesty said, 'I think maybe she spoke to the vicars after we'd left, and blew us accidentally. But if she's got a black balloon she could be just what we want.'

*   *   *

An hour before noon Willie was sitting with Lucy Fuller-Jones on a park bench and she was saying, 'You do understand why I couldn't ask you to the flat, Willie?' She gazed sadly across the Thames. 'I'm sure you're a very nice man, but it's with *nice* men that I don't quite trust myself.'

Suppressing a powerful urge to take her by the ears and turn her head to face him, Willie said, 'Sure. Fine. I love it 'ere in the park, Lucy. Love it. Okay? Now, did you listen to what I've just been *telling* you?'

Now she turned her head to regard him with large, doe-like eyes. 'Yes, of course I did, and it's a dreadful story, honestly, absolutely dreadful. How can people go around just killing other people like that? I mean, that poor Swedish man. I don't like to think about him.'

Willie started to say, 'Norwegian,' then decided it didn't matter. Instead he said gently, 'They 'aven't killed 'im yet, Lucy, and you don't have to think about 'im. Just help us get 'im out.'

A touch of curiosity entered her gaze. 'Are you a sort of policeman?'

'I'm sort of on their side.'

She bit her lip, frowning in concentration. 'Well . . . I know Daddy's frightfully keen on law and order, that's why he told me to go to that abolition thing to see what they were up to. I mean, he feels there are all sorts of people who ought to be hanged, and he's certainly been awfully sweet about buying me a new balloon, so I think I ought to.'

'Ought to help?'

'Well yes, silly. It might be rather difficult but I'm sure we'll manage if you really can arrange transport and a launching team.'

Willie offered up a silent prayer of thanks. 'Anything you want, Lucy, including a military 'elicopter if need be. Anything.'

She eyed him with anxiety. 'But I won't be *alone* with you in the basket? Being up in a balloon is frightfully erotic, you know.'

'We'll 'ave a chaperon. A girl. Honest.'

She smiled brightly and stood up. 'Well that's all right, then. I suppose we'd better hurry, hadn't we?'

He took her arm and began to walk briskly towards the park

gate. 'Yes. I expect Mr Hallenberg would like us to get a move on. He's due for the chop at dawn tomorrow.'

She winced. 'I'd rather not talk about him, Willie.'

'All right. What do you do when you're not ballooning or meditating?'

'I go swimming a lot. Long distance swimming. It's much more lasting than cold showers.'

Willie shook his head. 'One day, Lucy,' he said kindly, 'I must 'ave a serious talk with you.'

*   *   *

Two hours after sundown Tarrant stood in the narrow road that led through woods to *Poldeacon*. He was watching a jeep move slowly in reverse. A man holding a hand radio walked beside it with Fraser at his elbow. From a winch bolted to the floor behind the driver a thin wire cable ran out sideways from the jeep, rising at an angle of forty-five degrees, vanishing into the moonlight above the woods.

The radio squawked. The man holding it spoke to the driver and the jeep stopped. The radio man spoke quietly into the instrument and a brief exchange with a female voice took place. When it was over, the radio man spoke to Fraser, who moved to join Tarrant by the car in which they had both travelled from the heliport at Plymouth. A great deal had been achieved in the last ten hours, and Tarrant was thankful that the government minister he answered to had used his authority forcefully during that time.

Fraser said, 'Okay so far. They went up a thousand feet and the wind took them across the top of *Poldeacon*. They were winched back, but ended up a bit east of the place, so the jeep's just towed them west.' He sniffed grudgingly. 'I had that Fuller-Jones girl tabbed as a card-carrying idiot, but she's been man-oeuvring in three dimensions, fore and aft, laterally, up and down, and she's done a bloody good job. They're in position now and the wind's holding steady. Full moon, clear sky, and you can see a hell of a way. I don't know whether that's good or bad.'

A hundred feet above the roof of *Poldeacon* Modesty and

Willie watched with mingled surprise and respect as Lucy Fuller-Jones juggled with the burner and the hot air release valve. They were both in black combat rig: calf-length boots, slacks, Willie with his shirt unbuttoned for quick access to the twin knives sheathed in echelon on his chest, two small weighted wooden clubs clipped to his belt; Modesty with a tunic that fell to her thighs and covered the holstered Colt .32, the kongo in a pocket, her hair tied back in a short club, a small haversack on one shoulder.

Lucy said, 'Even if the wind doesn't veer, there's bound to be drift. I'll try to hold still, but you mustn't count on it, Willie.'

'We know that, Lucy. No sweat.'

Modesty said, 'It would be nice if we *could* get Hallenberg out this way, Lucy, but if not we'll call in the cavalry.'

'Oh, jolly good. What cavalry?'

'There's a squad of armed policemen standing by. Once we're in, and find Hallenberg, we should be able to keep him intact for ten minutes or so while they get here.'

'Oh, I see. Jolly good.'

In the glow of the burner Modesty saw Willie roll his eyes skyward. Lucy peered down, and the balloon sank gently towards the roof, which was partly gabled with flat areas between. At forty feet she said, 'I don't think I can risk any lower.'

Modesty dropped a light rope-ladder over the edge of the basket. 'That's fine, Lucy. You've done a great job.' She swung a leg over and began to descend.

Lucy said thoughtfully, 'Willie . . . have you known Modesty very long?'

'Quite a few years now.'

'Oh. Well, I was just thinking, this sort of thing isn't very *usual* for a girl, is it? I mean, do you think this is her way of sort of sublimating her, you know, urges?'

Willie grinned and shook his head. 'She doesn't believe in sublimating them, Lucy.' He climbed over the edge of the basket and on to the ladder. At the bottom, ten feet above the roof, he hung by his hands and dropped beside Modesty, the balloon lifting as his weight was lost.

Above, Lucy adjusted a second time for the extra lift, then picked up the hand radio that hung from her neck. 'This is me reporting,' she said. 'They've both landed safely.'

On the roof, Modesty crouched by a door set in the stairs bulkhead that gave access from below. Willie watched as she probed gently in the key-hole with a lock-pick. She shook her head, and he handed her a different probe from a set of six in a small leather wallet. Thirty seconds later the lock yielded, and when she eased the door open it made no sound.

She looked at Willie, saw him grimace in the moonlight, and could read his thoughts for they matched her own. Landing on the roof and getting into *Poldeacon* had been deemed that part of the operation which could most easily go wrong, yet it had all gone smoothly. From experience they both knew that when the hard parts went well it was likely that one of the easy parts would go sour on you. She shrugged, flickered an eyelid at him, and moved through the door.

For ten minutes they prowled silently through the dark top floor, using a pencil torch, seeking any indication of where Hallenberg might be held. They saw and heard nothing except distant music from below. Somebody was listening to a pop programme.

Three minutes later, on the floor below, they moved along a dark passage illumined only by a light from the far end where it joined a wider passage. At the corner Modesty took a small mirror on a thin metal arm from her haversack and edged it slowly out beyond the wall. Fifteen paces away a man in clerical wear sat in an easy chair facing a door with a light above it, reading a magazine.

She drew back, put her lips to Willie's ear and whispered, 'One man guarding a room. Profile shot.' He nodded, and took a sling from a thigh-pocket. Three slingshots were carried in a tube slotted into a narrow pocket down the seam of his slacks. Each was the size of a plum and was made of lead-shot moulded in wax. Willie Garvin, ever fascinated by weaponry, had made a study of the sling and its usage from earliest times, and had discovered by long practice that it could be remarkably accurate.

He eased a shoulder and half his head round the corner, sighted the man in the chair, and started to spin the sling. After a moment or two, as expected, the whisper of noise or a glimpse of movement made the man turn his head. An instant later the shot took him squarely on the brow, just above the bridge of the nose, disintegrating as it struck home. Modesty was out in the wider passage and running soundlessly, the kongo in her hand ready to follow up, but the man sagged back limply in his chair and lay still, the girlie magazine slipping from his hand.

As Willie came up she pulled the man into a half lying position and pushed an anaesthetic nose-plug into one nostril. She was beginning to go through his pockets when Willie said softly, 'The key's in the door, Princess. It's a red carpet caper so far.'

She rolled her eyes, miming wariness at such good fortune, and moved to the door. It opened into a comfortable bed-sitting room with a large alcove containing a bed. Curtains were drawn back on each side of the alcove. Opposite the door was a window set in a deep bay with a built-in cushioned window-seat. An iron grille covered the window and the outer shutters were closed. In one corner of the room was a small wardrobe, a chair beside it; in the centre a table with a tray bearing a meal of cold meats, cheese, tomatoes, bread rolls, and a pot of coffee.

At the table, pausing in the act of buttering a roll, sat a tall grey-haired man with an air of quiet dignity who regarded his visitors with mild surprise.

Hallenberg. His photographs had been in every newspaper for the past few days. Willie closed the door, a prickle of unease creeping up his spine. So they had found Hallenberg just like that. No snags, no set-backs. Very ominous.

Hallenberg said, 'Yes?' and resumed buttering his roll.

Modesty said, 'Don't talk, please. Just come with us and try to move very quietly.'

The man surveyed them both and clearly understood their presence but showed no sign of relief. He said, 'Who are you?'

Willie thought, 'Here it comes.' This was the easy part going sour. He was much too experienced to offer any mental reproach to his second favourite female, Lady Luck. When she decided to torment you, you just had to smile at her whims. Resentment annoyed her deeply.

Modesty said, 'Does it matter who prevents you from being murdered, Mr Hallenberg?'

He considered the question. Then, 'Yes, I believe it does.'

'You want credentials? Banker's references?'

Hallenberg put the roll on his side-plate and began to cut a piece of cheese. 'Have you read any of my works, young woman?'

There was an edge to her voice as she said, 'I'll start tomorrow. Will you stop eating and come with us now, please?'

He sighed regretfully. 'If you had read my works, you would know that I deplore the ethos of opposing violence with violence. The men here have treated me with courtesy and respect. One of them guards that door. What have you done to him?'

'He's unconscious.'

Hallenberg gestured as if his point had been made. She said, 'But he's still alive. In a few hours these men will kill you. Is that what you want?'

'No,' he said patiently, 'but I will not betray my beliefs. Are you so different from these men?'

'You see no difference between what they intend to do and what we're trying to do?'

Wearily patronising, Hallenberg said, 'It is the means, young woman. The *means*. Do not confuse motive with means. Dear God, I have spent thirty years trying to make the world grasp that simple truth.' He put bread and cheese in his mouth and began to munch.

Modesty wiped out the anger that was trying to possess her and made a swift appraisal. They had a genius to cope with. A genius with a massive ego and all the common sense of a cockroach. It was impossible even to admire his courage, for clearly he could not imagine that he was to be killed. It was simply unthinkable that this could happen to him. Mountjoy and company had been treating him well. He might even be rather enjoying the situation, convinced that either the ransom would be paid or that his captors would release him because he was so wonderful. Well, one way or another she intended to take the man out of *Poldeacon*, but perhaps . . .

Willie reached the same conclusion at the same moment and said in Arabic, 'Easier if he comes quietly. Worth gambling a few minutes if you can talk him round.'

She gave a little nod and said to Hallenberg, 'I'm sorry the world hasn't grasped your simple truth, Mr Hallenberg, but there's another simple truth. The dead stay dead, and the world urgently needs Tor Hallenberg alive.' She smiled respectfully at him, took the other chair to the table and sat down facing him. 'Could we talk about your latest work, please?'

Willie opened the door quietly and went out, moving along the passage to where a broad staircase led down to the ground floor. There he found a place in the shadows from which he could watch the empty entrance hall below and the two interior doors leading off the hall. *Lovely job, that Hallenberg character*, he told his second favourite female admiringly. *Great fun. I don't know 'ow you come up with these ideas.* You had to woo Lady Luck to win her favours, not whinge.

A hundred feet above the roof Lucy peered down in surprise. A scooter was chugging briskly up the track towards the house, an unmistakable figure in the saddle. She lifted her radio and said, 'Excuse me, but there's a policeman coming towards the house on a motor-scooter thing. I think he must have seen my balloon.'

On the road through the woods Fraser said to the radio man, 'Bloody hell! How did *he* get there? I thought your men had the road sealed off.'

The radio man said, 'They have, or he'd have come through here.'

The jeep driver said, 'There's a bridleway that cuts off the loop in the road. Maybe—'

Tarrant broke in sharply. 'Never mind how. Tell the girl we have to get her away from the roof and we're letting the cable out.'

The driver turned and hit the winch brake release. The cable raced out and they all heard Lucy's cry of protest over the radio. 'I say! Steady!'

Fraser snarled, 'Gently, you prick!' He snatched the radio as the driver eased on the brake. 'Lucy? Lucy, are you all right?'

Tarrant unclenched his fists as her voice came through. 'Well, golly, only just! I mean, there was a frightful lurch and I'm miles away from the roof now, well, not really miles away, but out over the sea actually, and I think the cable's got caught round something on the roof. Whatever's happening?'

Fraser said, 'Sorry, but we had to get you away in a hurry, Lucy. Just stand by while we sort things out. If you're well away from the roof now you're quite safe.' He released the switch and said grimly to Tarrant, 'Or let's hope so. What now? That copper's going to blow the operation any minute and we can't give a warning. Willie's only got a matchbox transmitter for calling *us*. One-way communication. Do we tell the weapons team to move in now?'

Tarrant shook his head. He had already calculated the pros and cons. 'No. They don't appear to have found Hallenberg yet. That's the vital thing. They'll signal when he's safe in their hands.'

'They can't get him out by the roof now.'

'And we can't solve their problems for them,' Tarrant said sourly. 'She taught me that a long time ago. They don't *expect* a free ride. ' He turned and walked away.

In the common room at *Poldeacon* Mountjoy had been playing chess with Simon Bird when the light began flashing in the alarm panel on the wall and a buzzer sounded. Mountjoy picked up the house phone at his elbow. 'Yes?' A pause. 'I see. Nothing else showing on the screen? Very well.' He put down the phone. 'A uniformed policeman is about to arrive. He's alone.'

Bird stood up and reached under his jacket to feel the butt of the gun he loved so dearly. Mountjoy said, 'I'm sure that won't be needed. We'll stay in character, Simon.'

Two minutes later Bird opened the front door. Mountjoy smiled benevolently at the police sergeant who had rung the bell at the outer gate. 'Oh, good evening to you, officer. Can we be of help?'

The sergeant was a well-built man with a brisk manner. 'Evening, sir. I was passing along the valley road and I saw this thing over your house. A balloon, sir.' He waited, and when the two vicars stared at him blankly he added, 'I mean a big balloon, with a basket.'

Mountjoy blinked, then smiled in sudden comprehension. 'Ah, the *balloon*. Yes, of course. I thought the local weather station would have informed you about it.'

On the landing above, every word came clearly to Willie Garvin. He moved silently back as the policeman said, 'I don't think we've had anything from them, sir.'

'Really? Well, perhaps they didn't think it necessary. The experiment will only be lasting a few hours, I understand.' A kindly smile. 'But thank you for taking the trouble to call, sergeant.'

In the room above, Hallenberg was pouring coffee for himself and saying, 'Your argument has a false premise, young woman—' when the door opened and Willie said quietly, 'We're blown. They're on to Lucy so the roof's no good. We've got a couple of minutes, with luck.'

Modesty's hands shot across the small table to grip the collar of Hallenberg's jacket, wrists crossed, fists turning inwards to force knuckles into the jugulars. She stood as he half rose, his eyes bulging with shock and fear. One hand tugged feebly at her wrist, the other groped on the table, found a knife and raised it to strike. Willie took it from him a second before his body went limp.

'I must 'ave a chat with 'im sometime about opposing violence with violence, Princess.'

'You're welcome,' she said bleakly, and lowered Hallenberg to lie across the table. From her haversack she took a slim box containing a hypodermic and barbiturate ampoules. 'Call in Tarrant's posse, Willie. We've got a busy ten minutes ahead, and the more distraction the better.'

Willie took from his shirt pocket a piece of thick plastic. From one corner he drew out a short aerial, then spoke with the plastic close to his lips. 'Bo-beep calling. Move in now.' He repeated the words three times, put the miniature transmitter away and grimaced. 'Bo-beep,' he muttered in disgust.

In the hall Mountjoy pressed the remote control button to close the big gates after the departing policeman. Two other men in clerical wear had now joined Bird. Mountjoy said, 'You and I will start from the roof, Simon.' He looked at one of the other men. 'Alert the rest of our flock, Roger. Check Hallenberg's room first and leave a man with him—if he's still there. If not, we search the house.' He looked at the second man. 'Patrol the courtyard, Terry. If we have visitors on the premises they can't be in the courtyard yet or they would have made contact with the policeman, so they're in the house. Kill anyone who tries to get out.'

A minute later Mountjoy and Bird stepped on to the roof, Bird with a gun in his hand. The balloon cable was easy to see, glinting in the moonlight. It extended from the front of the house in one direction and towards the sea in the other, trapped under a heavy bracket that had once supported an aerial on the roof. Mountjoy pointed seaward, where the cable rose gradually for two or three hundred feet to a huge black balloon hanging above the sea.

Bird took up a stance with feet astride, both hands on the gun, taking careful aim, but Mountjoy laid a restraining hand on his arm. 'No, Simon. Much more urgent to deal with any visitors who may have landed.'

In the room where Hallenberg had been held, two of Mountjoy's vicars gazed at an overturned chair and the coffee-pot spilled across the table. A minute later, on the floor above, they met Mountjoy and Bird returning from the roof. One of the men said, 'They've got him. They've taken Hallenberg. Looks like he made trouble. There's been a rumpus and we found one of his shoes in the passage.' The man's voice was strained, and there was the dawning of fear in his eyes.

Mountjoy said without emphasis, 'If you start running scared, Roger, I'll kill you. They haven't got him out yet, so let's find them, and fast. They probably have back-up standing by, but once they're down the long chute with Hallenberg, *and* our guns, we can be singing hymns when the back-up arrives.'

On the last word there came a small sound of impact followed instantly by the rattle of lead-shot falling to the floor. Roger's head jerked forward with the impact and he sagged to his knees before toppling sideways, unconscious.

Bird said, 'Christ Almighty!' and fired into the shadows at the end of the corridor. On the floor below, Modesty heard the shot. It was not unexpected. She and Willie had split to wage guerrilla war against the enemy, and she guessed that Willie had just done a hit-and-run job.

At this moment, here on the first floor, three men were working their way along the passages which ran north and south between two wider ones running east and west. The men were calling to each other from time to time, and one was shortly due in the narrow arched passage where Modesty was braced against the high ceiling, her feet against one wall, a shoulder against the other, her body curving up into the arch.

The man turned in from the wider passage and she dropped as he passed beneath her, catching him by the shoulder from behind to get her feet down first, and striking to his neck with the kongo as she landed, jerking him back towards her so that she was able to catch the gun as it fell from his hand. She laid him on his side, emptied the cylinder of the Smith and Wesson .38 Terrier, and put the cartridges in her haversack. Kneeling, she opened the man's jaws, slid the two-inch barrel into his mouth and closed it again, then moved to the wider passage with her mirror to seek fresh prey. She had given Willie the remaining anaesthetic nose-plugs, but thought he would be pleased with the gun-in-mouth tactic. It was weird and chilling, and would give a morale-crushing impression of superiority.

Four minutes later she joined Willie at an agreed point where back stairs led down to the ground floor. They spoke in whispers.

'We're keeping 'em busy, Princess. I've dropped a couple.'

'Plus two for me. Where do these stairs go, apart from down?'

'Don't know, but we can—' He broke off at the sound of voices drawing closer. Two men, and no facility for taking them by surprise when they turned the corner twenty paces away. Modesty jerked her head and they moved quickly down the stairs.

At the bottom a well-lit passage ran left and right. The voices were nearing the top of the stairs now. Modesty pointed and they ran to the right, passing a door on one side before reaching a second door at the end of the passage. Then they were through, closing the door behind them.

The light was on, revealing a large kitchen with tiled walls, well furnished and supplied but in a messy state. Unwashed crockery was piled in the sink. Jars, cans and bottles lay about on the units. The window was barred, the exterior shutters closed. There was no other door. They had reached a dead end.

Modesty said savagely, 'What clown built this dump? *All* kitchens have back doors. You play dead, Willie.' He nodded, picked up a bread knife, slipped the blade in the crack of a drawer and snapped it off an inch from the hilt. Stabbing what remained of the blade into a cake of soap on the draining board, he snatched up a bottle of ketchup and splashed it on his shirt-front and neck. Modesty said, 'Fine.' She was still looking about her. Willie could play dead, but there was no place for her to hide unless . . .

She saw the mincer. It was of the kind that fixed to the surface of a work unit by the rubber suction disc forming its base. As she turned the lever to release it she heard faint sounds from along the passage and guessed that the two men were checking the first room off it.

Willie saw the mincer in her hand and followed as she moved to the door. He still held the knife stuck in the cake of soap. She took his free hand, stepped up on his bent knee and swung round to step up again so that she was on his shoulders. Crouching there, she pressed the mincer against the tiled wall, close to the ceiling, and turned the lever to operate the suction disc.

Carefully she placed the edge of one foot on the edge of the door-frame lintel, lifted the other foot behind the first, and crouched there holding the mincer to prevent her toppling sideways.

It was less than a minute later that the door opened. Guns in hand, two vicars stopped short. Willie Garvin lay on his back by the sink. A bread-knife, rising from the cake of soap buttoned beneath his shirt, appeared to be stuck deep in his chest. There was much blood on his shirt and neck, a trickle of it from one corner of his mouth. His half-open eyes were glazed and still.

One man said, 'Who's that? Who *stuck* him for Christ's sake?' He moved forward and bent to peer at Willie's face. A hand flashed up in a blur of speed and tore the gun away. The man screamed as a finger broke in the trigger-guard. In the same instant Modesty dropped behind the second man from above the door and struck with the kongo to the nerve-centre in the back of the neck. He was falling even before his brain had registered what was happening, and only milliseconds before his companion's scream was cut short by Willie's foot-strike delivered from the floor.

Modesty began to empty cartridges from the two guns. Willie wiped his face and neck on a tea-towel, and watched with pleased interest as she slid gun-barrels into mouths. 'That'll spook 'em, Princess. I like it.'

She said, 'It may not matter much now, Tarrant's posse ought to be here any minute. I'm worried about Lucy, though. Let's go up and check.' She paused, calculating. 'Yes, the clerical brethren are down to seven now, so we shouldn't have too much trouble.'

'I take it you didn't run into Mountjoy or Bird when we were keeping everyone busy?'

'No, goddammit and more's the pity. Not much chance now before Tarrant takes over.'

They were on the roof, having met no opposition on the way, when the big wooden gates were smashed open by a bulldozer and a dozen men came running into the courtyard. A voice from a loud-hailer announced the presence of armed police and began to give orders.

After a glance at the situation in front of the house Modesty and Willie moved to the back where the balloon cable ran over the edge of the low parapet and was now angled downwards, passing over the outer wall and the cliff-top to the sea beyond. The moon was brilliant, bathing the whole area in light that was enhanced by reflection from the sea. A hundred yards out, Lucy's balloon had descended and now hovered with the basket just above the surface, light glinting on the balloon-wire cable that angled down above the edge of the cliff.

Willie said, 'She'll be okay. She's a long-distance swimmer for sublimation purposes.'

Modesty said, 'There's a small door in that back wall and it's open.' She touched Willie's arm and pointed to the right of the cable. Beyond the wall two figures were moving briskly towards the edge of the cliff where a simple wooden railing seemed to indicate the top of steps or a path leading down to the bay. Even in silhouette the figures were easy to recognise. One was a very big man, moonlight gleaming on his white hair. The other was small, wearing a flat clerical hat.

Willie said, 'Mountjoy and Bird. They've done a runner. Must 'ave a boat down in the bay. I reckon we've lost 'em.'

'No.' Modesty bent to pull up one trouser leg and unzip the calf-length boot. 'You stay and cover Hallenberg. I'll see to these bastards myself.'

Her voice was quiet, but there was a metallic quality in it, a quality he had heard on very rare occasions before and which made the hairs on the back of his neck bristle, for he knew she was carrying the memory of Johnny Nash, horribly mutilated, in her mind, and was seeking a kill-or-be-killed opportunity to destroy. He said as she wrapped the leather upper of her boot round the balloon cable, 'I was pretty close to them in London, Princess. Don't know about Mountjoy but I think Bird's carrying an armpit gun for a right-hand draw, and I got the feeling he just might be a bit of an ace.'

'Good. Thanks, Willie.' She stood on the low parapet, both hands gripping the leather wrapping, and hooked the heel of her booted foot over the wire. It sagged only a little under her weight as she began to slide down the long slope. Willie turned and moved to the stairs bulkhead. He could now hear the loud-hailer bellowing its warning somewhere within the house.

At the cliff-top the cable ran only a few feet above the ground. Modesty touched down and surveyed the bay. A small landing-stage with a motor-boat moored to it lay to her left. To the right she could see across the curve of the cliff to steps that wound down to the bay. Mountjoy and Bird were more than halfway down. Directly ahead, Lucy's basket was partly sunk in the sea now, with the balloon collapsing to one side of it. So much the better. It would provide a better anchor for the far end of the cable.

She tested the tension, decided it would do, and again began to slide down the wire, hanging by hands and one foot. This was a steeper angle, and the leather boot was smoking as she came to within a few yards of the sea's edge before dropping to the sand. Turning, she saw Mountjoy and Bird halt for a moment at sight of her, then they came on.

She lifted the hem of her tunic to clear the Colt .32 holstered beneath it on her right hip, and pulled the drawstring round the hem tight to hold it securely. Then the whole of her being focused on the approaching men, with no other thought or awareness intruding upon her concentration.

They halted six paces away. Mountjoy's hands were empty, his large face unreadable. Bird was smiling a little, a sparkle of eagerness in his eyes. Mountjoy said, 'I have to point out that you are in our way.'

She kept his hands within the cone of her vision, but her eyes were on Bird. She said, 'Which of you is the expert with the bolt-cutters?'

Bird's smile widened. He lifted his right hand very slowly to take off his clerical hat, held it across his chest and said, 'My pleasure.'

Modesty said, 'You're not fit to live, but they'll let you, of course. Just turn round now and we'll go back the way you came.'

Bird gave a resigned shrug as if of compliance, then let the hat fall. His gun was out and the hat was at thigh height when her bullet grazed the thumb-joint and ripped his heart open. The impact rocked him back, and his gun fell to the sand as he went down. There were seconds of silence, then Mountjoy looked down at the dead man and said, 'Poor Simon. It's just as well you killed him. His pride could never have survived defeat by a woman.'

She studied Mountjoy for a few seconds, and knew the man

carried no gun that he could reach swiftly. Bird's gun lay well away on the far side of his body. Stepping forward three paces, never taking her eyes off Mountjoy, she bent to lay the Colt on a small patch of flat rock showing through the sand.

'Or you can spend the next twenty years in gaol,' she said, and stepped back, waiting.

The moonlight was on her face, and what Mountjoy saw in her eyes told him that if he moved he was a dead man, for she would be upon him long before he could reach the gun. He had male strength and was twice her weight, but he knew beyond doubt that she would be infinitely more skilled and carried death in her bare hands.

Mountjoy looked about him, at the sea, the cliffs, the sky, then at the woman before him. 'Madam,' he said, 'will you permit me to see myself out?'

She looked at him without expression and said nothing. Very slowly he put thumb and finger into a waistcoat pocket and withdrew them pinched together. He put them to his lips, then lowered the hand with thumb and finger spread wide. For a moment he gazed at Modesty with open contempt. 'I despise you, madam,' he said. 'Had the boot been on the other foot you would have died screaming.'

His jaws clenched as if crunching something, then his head jerked back and his mouth gaped as he choked and panted convulsively. The big body crumpled to the sand face-down, twitched for perhaps ten seconds, then was still. Modesty moved forward, picking up the Colt. Gun aimed, she set her unshod foot on one of Mountjoy's wrists, then bent to feel with her free hand for the pulse in his neck.

There was nothing. The man was dead. She straightened up, holstering the gun, then turned as she heard Lucy's voice calling, 'I say . . . !' Lucy was wading in through the shallows, pushing wet hair back from her face. 'I'm frightfully sorry not to be on the roof, Modesty, but they suddenly let the cable run and it must have got caught up there somewhere and I was absolutely *stuck* out over the sea, and then it sank, I mean the balloon did, so I thought I'd better swim ashore.'

She came splashing out on to the sand, water streaming from her clothes. Modesty said, 'You're all right, Lucy?'

'Well, I'm a bit miffed about the balloon. I mean, I hope we can get it back, or I don't know what Daddy will say.' She stared at the two bodies, frowning. 'I say, was that a vicar I saw trying to shoot you just now?'

Modesty said gravely, 'I don't think he'd actually been ordained.'

'Well, I should jolly well hope not. I mean, it would be a bit much, wouldn't it?'

Modesty felt laughter and an unexpected affection for Lucy rising within her. She took the girl by the arm and began to move towards the cliff steps. 'Come and tell Willie about it being a bit much,' she said. 'He'll love it.'

*   *   *

Two men wearing flak-jackets and carrying guns came into the room where Willie Garvin sat on the window-seat facing the door, a knife in his hand. One of them turned and called down the passage, 'Here, sir!'

Tarrant appeared, followed by Fraser. The two armed men went out. Tarrant looked about the room, then at Willie. 'We've found only two men capable of resistance,' he said, 'and they decided against it. Where's Modesty?'

Willie looked surprised. 'I 'ad an idea you'd ask about Hallenberg first,' he said, and slid the knife back into its sheath. 'Mountjoy and his reverend brother did a bunk down to the bay. Modesty went after 'em.'

Tarrant glared. 'Then why the hell aren't you with her?'

Willie stood up. 'Because, my little old civil servant, she told me to stay and look after your goodies.' He pushed the cushion off the window-seat and opened the lid. Tarrant and Fraser moved forward to look down on Hallenberg lying unconscious inside. 'He wouldn't come quiet,' said Willie. 'She tried to persuade him but then we got blown, so we gave 'im a shot and dumped the silly bugger 'ere while we 'opped about creating diversions for you. We figured the last place they'd look for 'im was in 'is own room.'

Fraser nodded approval. 'Better than being lumbered with him while you were hopping about. Why has he only got one shoe on?'

Willie smiled. 'We left it just along the passage, where they'd find it and reckon it came off while we were taking 'im away— which they did.' He shook his head. 'That was the Princess. You can't believe 'ow fast she thinks when it's all 'appening.' He looked down at Hallenberg and let the lid fall. 'You're welcome to 'im.'

*   *   *

It was just before dawn when Willie slowed the car to a halt outside the penthouse. Modesty was asleep beside him, her head on his shoulder. He patted her cheek and said, 'You're 'ome, Princess.'

She opened her eyes, yawned, sat up, reached for her handbag. She wore a duffel coat over her tunic now. Willie made a move to get out but she put a hand on his arm. 'Thanks, Willie love. Don't get out.' She turned to where Lucy sat sleepily in the back. ' 'Bye, Lucy, and many thanks. We'll arrange about a new balloon and equipment.'

'Well, jolly nice of you, Modesty. Thanks.'

Modesty opened the door, paused, looked back. 'Willie, I've got tickets for the Royal Ballet on Thursday if you're not doing anything.'

He nodded. 'That's great. I always 'ave a good laugh at the ballet.'

She smiled, reached out to ruffle his hair, then got out and closed the door. Willie said, 'Right. I'll drop you off 'ome now, Lucy.'

Ten minutes later he was opening Lucy's front door for her. In that time she had not spoken and was clearly deep in thought. Willie handed her the key and said, 'You don't fancy asking me in for breakfast?'

She gazed at him with large, longing eyes. 'I'm sorry, Willie, but I *am* trying to achieve the Golden Plateau of Serenity, and I *know* how one thing leads to another because of my glands.'

He patted her shoulder reassuringly. 'Sure, Lucy, that's okay. Thanks for 'elping out, you've been great.'

He had started to move away when she said, 'Willie, aren't you and Modesty . . . ? I mean, well, you know. You and Modesty?'

He shook his head with mock solemnity. 'Definitely not.'

'But . . . I mean, why not, if you don't mind my asking? It seems frightfully strange.'

'Not to us, Lucy. It's just not on the cards.'

'Oh.' She was still baffled. After a moment she said, 'Well, goodnight Willie. It was all jolly exciting, and I do understand about Official Secrets and all that. I'll keep absolutely mum, honestly.'

'Good girl.'

He had only gone half a dozen steps when she came hurrying after him, beaming happily. 'Oh gosh, I really am a bit slow sometimes, aren't I? Do come in and have a bit of breakfast with me, Willie. It's quite all right.'

*   *   *

It was during the interval at Covent Garden two days later that Willie said, 'I was a bit slow meself, Princess, and I didn't catch on till we were up in Lucy's flat. Then I realised that because of you and me, she reckoned I must be gay.'

Modesty choked slightly on the glass of wine she held. 'You? Oh, Willie, she didn't.'

'Straight up, Princess.' He gazed into space with a reminiscent smile and sighed happily. 'Lucy's glands didn't 'alf get a lovely surprise.'

COBRA TRAP

Professor Stephen Collier ran a hand through his greying hair and mentally cursed himself for doing so since he was trying to appear unworried. 'Ease up, you stupid bastard,' he told himself, surreptitiously relaxing taut muscles.

Collier was sitting in the office provided for him in Government House, in the Central American Republic of Montelero. His Canadian wife, Dinah, blind since childhood, sat with him on the settee, holding his hand. She was listening partly to the distant sound of artillery fire, which at the moment she alone could hear, and partly to Willie Garvin speaking on the phone.

It was twenty-odd years since she had first heard that gravelly voice speaking to her out of the darkness. That was on a day in the Pearl Islands, when he had saved her from abduction and destroyed the two men who had murdered her sister in cold blood. She had heard that voice with huge affection on many occasions since, and was thankful to be hearing it now, especially as he was speaking to Modesty Blaise.

'It should be all right, Princess,' Willie was saying, 'but I'll keep this short because we could get cut off any minute. I'm with Steve and Dinah now. These rebels call themselves the Montelero Cobras and they're about ten miles from the capital, maybe less. The government's pulling out, using a three-carriage train and heading for the Panama border. Because of the work Steve's been doing for 'em these last few months we've got places on the train. If all goes well we'll be at the border sometime early tomorrow.'

He paused, then spoke again. 'Yes, the government lot reckon they'll be allowed in, but could you get through to Sagasta and tell 'im we're with the party? He'll see that we three don't 'ave any trouble at the border.'

He listened, then smiled, looking at Dinah. 'Of course I'll take good care of 'er. Look, she's worried about the children because she knows *they'll* be worrying, so could you get a message to Dan at the medical college? Steve says you've got the number. And tell Dan to call Sue, okay?'

After several seconds: 'Sure. Leave it to Weng, and we'll reckon to see you—' He jerked the phone away from his ear, wincing at a blast of static, then listened warily again before dropping the instrument back on its cradle. 'The line's down,' he said. 'Weng will organise letting Dan and Sue know, and Modesty's on 'er way.'

Collier sat up straight. 'On her way where?'

Dinah sighed. 'Here, dum-dum,' she said, patting the hand she held. 'You know what she's like.'

'I do indeed,' Collier agreed, 'but my normally computer-like speed of thought ran into the buffers at the idea that she could be on her way here when she was speaking on the phone in Benildon.'

Willie said, 'John Dall's staying at the cottage with 'er for a few days, and he'll 'ave a private jet at Heathrow. I reckon it'll be airborne for Panama in a few hours.'

'Billionaires have their uses,' Collier said, 'and John is my favourite of that ilk. What will she or they do when they get to Panama? I mean, apart from enlisting a little help from that admirable police chief.' He remembered Sagasta well, for it was in Panama long years ago that Collier had first met Dinah, at a time when she was under threat from a criminal group of chilling power. Modesty had put Dinah in Collier's care while she and Willie, with Captain Sagasta's help, had fought a savage and bloody battle against the Gabriel group.

Willie said, 'Sagasta's not a policeman now, he's Minister of Defence, so he'll be watching the situation 'ere with a very beady eye, and that could be useful.'

Dinah said, 'You mean if anything goes wrong, and this train with us on it doesn't get to the border.' It was a statement rather than a question.

'That's right, love.' Willie knew her quality too well to indulge in empty words of reassurance.

Dinah stood up and moved to stand close to him, feeling for his hand. 'What did Modesty sound like?' she asked.

Willie exhaled a long breath, thinking. 'On top of the world,' he said at last. 'Sort of . . . eager. I don't know why.'

'Eager?' said Collier, frowning. 'Oh, nonsense. You're going senile, Willie. She always acts like a mother-hen to Dinah, and she must undoubtedly be frantic with worry about *my* safety, as any woman would be, so how can she sound on top of the world when we're surrounded by hordes of trigger-happy cobras?'

'There aren't hordes and we're not surrounded,' said Dinah. 'This is a picnic compared to that blood-and-guts Mayan affair in Guatemala—'

'I know, I know,' Collier broke in hastily. 'Let us not dwell on our past involvements with the Blaise/Garvin axis, it's bad for my bladder.'

Dinah turned sightless eyes to Willie and pressed his hand. 'At least we've been spared any information about the effect on his sphincter this time.'

'I'm saving that for on the train,' said her husband grimly.

*   *   *

John Dall leaned back on the chesterfield, watching Modesty Blaise. They were in the living-room of her cottage in Wiltshire and she was speaking on the phone, a large-scale map spread on the table in front of her. Weng, her houseboy, had sent the map-section through by fax from her penthouse in London, where many unusual items were stored.

Ten minutes earlier Dall had been on the phone himself, giving instructions to his PA. In four hours the private jet would be ready to leave Heathrow having taken on board a parcel of equipment that Weng would deliver to the airport in good time. In three hours a helicopter would land by the cottage to take Dall and Modesty to Heathrow.

It was only a short time ago that Dall had arrived, expecting to spend ten days with the woman he had loved for more than twenty years, and now he was trying not to feel frustrated. He was glad to find that at least he felt no resentment. Her friends the Colliers were in possible danger, so she would go to them, just as she would have gone to Dall in similar circumstances.

At this moment she was talking to Miguel Sagasta in Panama, a finger on the map as she spoke and listened.

'But won't Montelero object to your sending two reconnaissance aircraft over their territory? Ah ... you have a point, Miguel. Do you know why their government is getting out by train rather than by air? I see. Would it be possible to monitor the train without compromising your own interests? Well, never mind, it was just a thought. What was that? Oh, thank you, I'm truly grateful, Miguel. Yes, we should be arriving about 09.00 hours your time. Hope to see you then.'

She put down the phone and stood up, gazing into nothingness with unfocused eyes, arms across her waist, holding her elbows. It was a posture Dall knew of old, and he also knew that for the moment he had ceased to exist for her, but the knowledge did not trouble him. This was an aspect of Modesty Blaise, and he would not have wished her different in any way. He was well content simply to look at her, remembering, and to marvel at how lightly the years had touched her.

She would be ... about fifty-two? Impossible to be sure, for all memory of her early childhood had been wiped clean, but today her body would have passed handsomely for thirty, her face for the early forties. The legs were still those beautiful dancer's legs, and she still moved like a dream. There were more lines at the corners of the eyes now, and the jaw-line was perhaps less lean, but the column of her throat held firm and never failed to draw his eye. Not only his, for in memory he could hear Willie Garvin's voice as he gazed upon the mahogany carving Dall had commissioned, 'I told Alex Hemmer just before he finished it ... I could look at 'er throat for hours.'

Now, as he sat watching her, Dall saw the far look fade from
the dark blue eyes to be replaced by a momentary expression he
could not define for it was so full of contradictions: urchin humour
and troubled concern, hope tinged with regret, eagerness tem-
pered by uncertainty. This was a blend Dall had never seen in
her before, but in a moment it was gone as if it had never been,
and she was looking at him with wry apology. 'I'm sorry, Johnny.
Really I am.'

He smiled. 'I know.' The smile faded. 'And I know you have
to . . . do whatever there is to be done, but for God's sake don't
let yourself get hooked again. Hooked on risk and danger. Come-
backs are stupid, Modesty. You're too *old*, for Christ's sake!'

She laughed and came to sit beside him. 'Don't worry. This
old broad isn't aiming for a come-back, I promise.'

'Okay. So what's the situation? All I know about Montelero
is that it's about the size of Wales with a population of less than
half a million. The only reason neither Panama nor Colombia have
taken it over is that it's a pretty useless chunk of real estate, mainly
scrub and jungle, and the residents are sort of Central American
Sicilians, never happy unless they're killing one another.'

She nodded. 'That's more or less what Miguel said. They have
no airforce or airline, and the government's being evacuated by
train because they want to bring out all records and documents
to set up a government in exile. They can't do that using private
light aircraft even if any were available. Miguel says this lot are
pretty civilised, and he thinks they'll be back in control within
a year as long as they get out before the other lot cut their throats.'

'So he's on their side?'

'Up to a point. He knows a bit about the rebel leaders, and
they're not nice. He says one or two villages have suffered total
massacre.'

'How does he justify having recce aircraft over Montelero
territory?'

She smiled. 'He claims it's in case missions of mercy are
called for. If anybody objects, he'll take note of it. I hoped he
could monitor the train that Willie and Dinah and Steve will
be on, but he says he couldn't get that past his government

colleagues.' She shrugged. 'Still, he's promised to meet us when we land in Panama and he'll help in any way he can.'

'Like what?'

She hesitated. 'Well, he said he'd have a light aircraft available for me to hire.'

'So *you* can go train spotting and do whatever you think needs to be done?'

'Johnny, I can't help by just sitting in Panama City.'

'So how *can* you help?'

'I've no idea. I just have to get there and find out.'

He sat remembering other times when she had gone into situations blind, relying on her skills and experience to improvise whatever action might be demanded. There had been no guarantee of a safe outcome then, there could be none now.

Dall sighed and looked at his watch. 'Three hours before the chopper comes for us. Do you have things to do, or am I going to take you to the cleaners at gin rummy?'

She was silent for a few seconds. Then: 'There's nothing I have to do. We've eaten, and we can eat again in flight. Weng will deliver all the gear I want to take with us, and he's fully competent to handle any and all matters for me while I'm away.' She stood up, took Dall's hands and drew him to his feet. 'I thought we might go to bed, Johnny.'

He took her gently by the waist, his strong face with its redskin ancestry sober as he regarded her. 'I didn't come here just for that.'

'I know you didn't. But it would be a happy thing for us to do, wouldn't it? Unless you've given up going to bed with old broads.'

John Dall laughed and gathered her into his arms, his pulse quickening as if twenty years had been wiped away.

*　　*　　*

'When I was a temple virgin in Baalbek,' said Professor Stephen Collier, 'in the time of Antiochus the Third, the temple priests had a rather intriguing way of testing us for virginity.'

They had been on the train for several hours now, moving at a crawl, drawn by an ancient locomotive through the thin jungle that characterised the northern part of Montelero. There were twenty-eight government members aboard, with three times as many relatives including some thirty children. One of the three coaches carried luggage and government files. Ten soldiers provided the armed escort, some travelling on the roofs of the coaches. Progress was slow because the single track with passing places was in a poor state of repair and there were several long steep gradients to be overcome.

Willie and the Colliers had a compartment to themselves, with their luggage. This privilege had been secured by Willie's convincing claim that the influence of his powerful friends in the Panamanian diplomatic service could well affect the reception of the refugee government at the border.

Dinah sat in a corner with her back to the engine, facing Willie, her husband beside her. It was five in the morning, and they had been dozing through the night hours. For safety the train was showing no lights, but now the darkness was turning to grey with the coming of dawn. Because the others might be sleeping, none of them had spoken for the past few hours, but now Collier had broken the silence with his dubious reminiscence of a previous life.

Dinah lifted her head from his shoulder and said, 'This temple virgin persona was one of your earlier incarnations, I guess.'

Collier kissed her ear. 'It's the first I can remember after spending a few brief years as Ug the Caveman before being eaten by a tyrannosaurus. There may have been other appearances in between.'

'I'm going to regret asking this,' said Dinah, 'but what was intriguing about the way the priests tested you virgins for *intacta*?'

'I'm glad you asked, sweetheart,' said Collier. 'You never know when these scraps of useful information may prove to have some practical application. Once a year we virgins were required to sit on one of those large Ali Baba sort of containers half full of the local wine. Then the high priest would smell our breath, and if he could smell the wine we were fired. I mean fired like Joan of Arc. Ex-virgins *flambées*, as you might say.'

Willie said, 'How did you make out?'

'Very well,' said Collier. 'The girls with the largest bottoms did best, because they sealed the perimeter of the container, and so prevented alcoholic fumes escaping. I was among those so blessed.'

'You'd do pretty well today, porky,' said his wife. Then, to Willie, 'My God, where does he get these disgusting ideas?'

Willie said, 'I hate to defend him, but according to legend that's just what the Baalbek priests used to do. I can't vouch for Steve being one of the virgins around at the time.'

'Oh, don't *you* encourage him,' said Dinah. 'It's bad enough having Dan and Sue always egging him on.'

'Our children have a lively appreciation of their father's historical expertise,' said Collier. 'Now, as we hurtle across northern Montelero at five miles an hour, let us devote a few golden minutes to serious discussion. Here we are, two intelligent people, three if you count Willie, threatened with hours of boredom, so let us pool our thoughts on the subject.'

Dinah paused in wiping her face with a damp tissue. 'What subject, honey?'

'The subject we were just talking about, dozy. What happens to one when one shuffles off this mortal coil—or has it shuffled off for one? Does one return? Is one reincarnated? Or not? And if not, then what?'

Dinah blinked. 'That's a bit heavy for five a.m., isn't it?'

'Quite so. It will fully engage our attention, which you may remember is highly recommended by the Blaise/Garvin consortium for the prevention of adrenalin fatigue in stressful situations. You start, Willie.'

With an effort Willie drew in tendrils of attention that he had been giving to areas of possible developments he felt he might have failed to anticipate. Throughout the night he had been uneasy about his responsibility for Dinah and Steve. There would probably be no danger to cope with, but you could never be sure,

and he was realistically aware that he did not quite have the edge
of years gone by.

Perhaps Steve had sensed his unease, and this had prompted
him to quote the maxim he had learned long years ago from
Modesty Blaise and Willie Garvin concerning adrenalin fatigue.
Whether or no, it was a timely reminder, Willie decided. He had
done all he could to prepare for whatever might arise, and he
should now switch off until something happened.

'Let's start with a profound thought,' he said cheerfully.
'There's plenty of options on offer, but what 'appens next after
we pop our clogs 'ere is anyone's guess. So that's the profound
thought—it's anyone's guess.'

Collier sniffed. 'You get one and a half out of ten for that,
young Garvin. But continue, lad. Name a few options.'

'Well, sir, please sir, when the Grim Reaper calls your name,
either you come to a dead stop or you go on. If you stop, that's
it. If you go on, there's the problem that you're no longer in
Time, and in our present state we're not smart enough to be able
to imagine existing in some sort of eternal Now. Then there's
the question, are you still *you*? And aware of it? Or are you just
part of what someone once called a Gloomy Merging? I think it
was Noel Coward of all people, but never mind. If you *are* still
you, and aware of it, what do you do all day in your new situation?
Except that without Time that's a silly question because doing
something involves a sequence. So maybe you get the Baalbek
option, and keep coming back as a caveman and a temple virgin
and a balding statistician, or you get the Christian option, which
is very nice but a bit vague, or the Islam option, which is either
hellfire or a pleasure-palace mainly for men—and even that lot's
just for starters. Who's next?'

'Blimey, Willie,' said Collier, 'you've given it a bit of thought,
haven't you?'

Willie looked mildly surprised. 'Not really. It's all a guess, so
I figured I'd just wait and see. Or not, as the case may be.'

Dinah said, 'You and Modesty spent time with that old Indian
guru in the Thar desert, didn't you? And he imparted a lot of . . .
I don't know, mental abilities, yoga powers. We've seen you

both do things we wouldn't have thought possible. What did he say about being dead?'

Willie shrugged. 'Only that it was a foolish question. "Can a beetle fathom the ways of the universe?" Old Sivaji never said much about anything. You used the right word, Dinah. He imparted. But he certainly reckoned he was going through a long cycle of incarnations, aiming for perfection so he could finally get off the wheel of rebirth.'

'And attain Nirvana?' said Collier. 'But then what? Eternal bliss? Wouldn't you get sick of it?'

Willie smiled. 'I've always preferred contrast meself. But the Buddha never described Nirvana. He said it was a state of being that couldn't be expressed. I suppose that puts it with all the other heavens on offer that nobody can imagine.'

Dinah said, 'What does Modesty think? I know people don't get to talking about this kind of thing much, but surely the subject must have come up between you two.'

Willie reflected for a few moments. Then he said, 'Not in a big way, just the odd comment in passing. We've talked about old Sivaji quite a bit, and one thing he did speak of was what he called the interim. The time between incarnations. Modesty once said if he was right about all that, then she hoped there'd be something worth doing in the interim. She didn't fancy listening to cherubim and seraphim singing their 'earts out till the next incarnation came round.'

Collier chuckled. 'That wouldn't suit either of you. But what about the absence of Time in which to *do* anything?'

'Oh, she reckons if we do go on there'll be a substitute for Time. And for bodies.'

Collier looked out of the window at the scrawny jungle set back no more than forty paces from the track. 'Some of these near-death experiences you read about are fascinating,' he said. 'Being drawn along a tunnel towards a bright light seems to feature in several accounts. Of course, the doubters say that's just a final flicker of the brain closing down, but who knows? As you said, it's anyone's guess.'

Willie said absently, 'It could be a bit individual. I didn't see any tunnel——' he broke off. 'Sorry. Just thinking out loud.'

Dinah said, 'I'm not having that.' She got up and moved to sit beside Willie, feeling for his hand. 'Hey, did you have one of these near-death things?'

'It's boring, Dinah. Like when people tell you their dreams.'

'You tell us about it right now, Buster, or I'll beat you up something rotten.'

Willie sighed. 'I bet you were the school bully.'

Collier said, 'You didn't find yourself walking through a drift of clouds, with check-in desks manned by angels in double-breasted suits and ties?'

Willie grinned. 'Like in a Hollywood movie? No, I didn't get that far.'

Dinah said, 'I'm not letting go on this. Please, Willie, tell us.'

'Well . . . it was back in *The Network* days. A vice mob under a scumbag called Karnak started some terror killings so he could take over a lot of girls working independently. Modesty decided we'd take 'im out, and we did. It was an easy job compared with some, but I got unlucky and took a ricochet that opened an artery in me thigh——the only shot fired in the whole operation. They got me to our own Network 'ospital in Tangier with not much blood left, and that was only because Modesty got to me in the first ten seconds and rammed 'er thumbs in the wound till Krolli could get a tourniquet on——are you all right, Dinah?'

She said softly, 'Yes, I'm fine, Willie. I guess I jumped a little because . . . well, it suddenly hit me, the way we've all been sort of interwoven even before we knew one another. I mean, if Modesty hadn't been quick enough getting to your artery that day, then you wouldn't have been around to save me from Gabriel in the Pearl Islands years later, and I'd never have met Modesty, my best ever girlfriend, or Steve, or . . . oh golly, you never realise what a knife-edge you're walking. A minute late or a minute early and something could change your whole life.'

Collier said, 'There's always the theory of parallel worlds. You know, alternative universes where it all happened differently. One where the alternative Modesty was a bit slow with her thumbs, and——'

'Just cut the fantasy stuff and be glad you're in this world, Professor,' his wife broke in firmly. 'And don't interrupt when I'm listening to Willie.'

Collier sat up straight. '*I* didn't interrupt!' he said indignantly. 'It was you coming in with all that "if this and if that" rubbish! But I won't complain. It's my own fault for marrying beneath me. Go on, Willie lad. You have my full attention.'

Dinah said, 'Yes, go on, Willie. I'll deal with old Collier later. You'd lost a lot of blood and you were in *The Network* hospital.'

'I don't remember anything much of what 'appened after Modesty grabbed me leg,' said Willie. 'Danny Chavasse told me later that she sat by my bed for three days after they'd pumped a new load of blood into me. All I remember is being . . . somewhere else, like in a dream, but much stronger, and different. Different in new ways you could never imagine. I was walking down a slope of grass, except it wasn't like any grass I've ever known, and at the bottom of the slope, in the valley, there was . . .'

Willie paused, giving Collier a look of wry exasperation. 'I could say a sort of silvery path, or maybe a river, running off . . . somewhere. But it wasn't either. It was different. Look, people who use hallucinogenic drugs say they see colours and hear sounds that don't exist in the real world. Well, everything was like that, yet it was all perfectly natural and right in its own way. I said I was walking down a slope, but it wasn't a slope and I wasn't walking. It was all new and different. I can't even visualise it now, and even if I could there aren't words for it. But I was still me, and more . . . more fully aware of meself than I've ever been, before or since.'

Collier said, 'Were you aware of any other presence?'

Willie shook his head. 'No. I was alone.'

Dinah said, 'It seems to have left memory-traces but no visual recall.'

'That's about it.'

She closed her blind eyes. 'Or aural recall?'

It was a long time before he answered. During that time Collier could see and Dinah could sense that he was struggling for expression. At last he said reluctantly in a low voice, 'You can 'ear the songs the stars sing.'

After another silence Collier said gently, 'Can you expand on that a bit, Willie?'

He shrugged. 'No. It doesn't make sense to me either, now, but it's the nearest I can get in words. You can't really tell *any* of it in words.'

'So there's no way of knowing whether it was a near-death hallucination or . . . whatever?'

'There never will be. It'll always be anyone's guess.'

Dinah said, 'It doesn't seem like a dying brain-flicker to me, Steve. I mean, he didn't die, did he?'

'No, which is just as well for us. Willie, this silvery path or river you saw—did you feel that it led somewhere?'

Willie exhaled gustily. 'It's 'ard to give straight answers. I think I just felt it led to whatever comes next.'

Dinah said, 'But you came back. How did that happen?'

'I've no idea, love. All I can remember is waking up very slowly, 'earing Modesty's voice, very soft and gentle, saying nice things like 'ow much she needed me and so on. Then I could feel 'er hand 'olding mine, and a bit later I realised where I was and managed to open my eyes.' Willie patted Dinah's hand. 'Well, that was it. I never told anyone till now, except Modesty.'

Collier said quietly, 'Well thanks, Willie. I'm not going to make one of my usual insulting comments.'

Dinah said, 'You'd better not, or you'll get a knuckle sandwich from the little woman. Hey, listen, Willie, if it turns out that we all come back, you'll keep an eye open for us, won't you?'

Willie considered. Then, 'All right. As long as you come back as a girl.'

Collier laughed and was about to speak when the train jerked to a sudden halt, almost throwing Dinah to the floor. Willie caught and steadied her. Collier said, 'You haven't lost much speed, Willie. Thanks. I'd have said somebody pulled the communication cord, except we don't have one.'

With a hand on Willie's chest, Dinah felt a shape she recognised from long ago under the light leather windcheater he wore.

She opened her mouth to speak, then closed it and said nothing. Willie stood up, and she heard him open the door. 'Hang on,' he said. 'I'll go and see what's 'appening.'

Moments later he was moving along beside the track towards the locomotive, which was only partly in sight on a bend. Some of the soldiers were milling around excitedly. One or two men from the government contingent were with them, others were descending, some busy preventing older children getting off the train. Then Willie saw the track a few yards ahead of the loco- motive and his heart sank, for both rails were buckled. It could only have been done by explosives, and well before the train's arrival here, for there had been no sound as it approached.

Willie was still fifty paces from the small crowd when he stopped abruptly and moved across the strip of bare ground between the track and the jungle. Five seconds later he had dis- appeared. In the compartment Collier stood looking out of the window. Dinah said, 'What's happening, Steve?'

Collier shook his head. 'God knows. The track curves just here, and I was watching Willie, but he suddenly oozed off into the jungle.'

'Maybe—'

'No, I'm damn sure he wasn't going for a leak. There was something about the way he moved. Something familiar, but I can't recall why.'

Dinah came to his side. 'He knows something the rest haven't realised,' she said. 'That's what it is.'

'What the hell can he know—' Collier broke off and put his arm round her. 'Sorry, sweetheart. You're right, of course. I've seen him and Modesty in action enough to recognise the aspect they take on. That's what was familiar.'

Dinah said, 'He's wearing his knives. I felt them.'

'I never doubted he would be, my darling. He sees us as his responsibility. You in particular. But what the devil can he be up to?' Collier's voice sharpened suddenly. 'Oh Christ, of course! Somebody's blocked the line, and they must be *here* to have done it! So now they're tucked away in the bush, ready to open fire when they get the right target—the President and half the government most likely. Willie saw it right away.'

'Oh my God, the children!' said Dinah. 'Run and *tell* somebody, Steve—tell them to keep under cover!'

Collier swore, opened the door, and dropped clumsily to the ground, almost falling. Then he began to run.

Willie Garvin moved warily through the trees and tangled bushes, moving in a half-circle that would bring him towards the railway at a point where the cover was thickest, the best position for an ambush. He thought the Cobra team would be small, no more than an advance party of a few men, otherwise they would have attacked by now. Very sensibly they wanted to minimise risk and make their first strike conclusive—a massive killing.

It was a long time since he had worn his knives except for practice, but he had brought them to Montelero in the knowledge that trouble threatened, and was thankful that he had done so. The leather jacket was unzipped. He carried a knife in one hand, held by the blade, the other was still in one of the twin sheaths strapped in echelon on his left breast. In his free hand he carried a rock he had picked up, the size of a cricket ball.

The ambush was where he had anticipated, three men with a Browning machine-gun mounted on a tripod, hidden from the railway by a carefully constructed hide of leafy branches. One man sat at the gun ready to fire. A second knelt beside him with several spare ammunition boxes, each with its 250-round disintegrating link belt. The third man was a few paces nearer to Willie, his back to the machine-gun, peering into the jungle. He held a sub-machine gun at the ready, aimed from the hip, and Willie knew that when he left the train he must have been seen and was expected.

He said under his breath, 'Send me good vibes, Princess,' and stepped out from behind the tree that hid him. The rock hurtled fast from his hand as the muzzle of the gun swung towards him, finding its mark before the trigger could be pulled, striking squarely on the centre of the forehead. The man went down without a sound, but as he fell the Browning began to chatter.

Willie swore viciously and a knife flew, the second knife following as the first struck home. The chatter of the machine-gun stopped abruptly. About one and a half seconds, Willie thought as he moved forward, and with a rate of 500 rpm that would mean only about twelve rounds fired, and probably well bunched. It could have been worse.

With sudden realisation he flung himself flat, diving behind a shallow ridge in the ground, barely in time to escape the fusillade of shots that came from the railway, ripping through the jungle fringe, tearing away leaves and twigs. The soldiers were firing blind with their Sten guns.

Beside the train, Collier raced towards the scene, bawling like a madman. '*Stop, you bastards! Stop!*' One soldier and one government man lay on the ground, either dead or wounded. Collier swerved round them, still shouting, switching to Spanish and waving his arms frantically in an obvious cease-fire sign. The shooting dwindled and died, more because magazines were empty than from Collier's action, but it gave him the chance to get in front of the small bewildered group, still shouting and waving at them.

No shots came from the jungle, and the soldiers looked uncertainly about them for guidance. Collier turned and bellowed, 'Willie! Are you okay?'

A voice came clearly from the jungle fringe. 'Only bloody just! Tell them I've got two dead rebels 'ere, plus one possibly live rebel and a machine-gun! And I'm not even going to *stand up* till all those Stens 'ave got the safety-catches on! Tell 'em, Steve!'

Collier heaved a sigh of relief, wiped sweat from his brow, and turned to speak to the soldiers.

*   *   *

In the Security Office at the Panama City airport John Dall sat holding a mug of coffee, watching Miguel Sagasta and Modesty Blaise as they studied a map spread on the table. Modesty wore a camouflage jacket and trousers. She had slept for most of the time during the flight from Heathrow. Dall had been unable to sleep, and was tired now. They had arrived only minutes ago to receive news that he felt she had reacted to oddly. At first she had seemed anxious, but this had quickly passed to be replaced by a sparkling eagerness, as if the challenge had brought her a surge of exhilaration.

'Your friends and all on the train with them are trapped,' Sagasta was saying. 'The track is destroyed, the telephone line also.' He looked at Modesty curiously. 'When you called from England, why did you ask if I could have listening watch kept on those lines at the border exchange?'

She shook her head with a touch of impatience. 'I don't know, Miguel. It just seemed right.' She pushed back a wisp of hair from her brow. 'The lines on this side of the break are probably sound, so they offer a possible avenue of communication. I must have felt it might be useful.'

Sagasta smiled. 'You have a great instinct, my dear, and now logic has caught up with it. Willie Garvin seems to be on the same wave-length, for when he left the capital he took one of the office phones with him. This is now connected to the lines on this side of the break and a hundred metres or so from the train,' he laid a finger on the map, 'about here, not far from the 125-kilometre post. That is how we know the location.' He looked up. 'So I have spoken directly to Willie. The border exchange patched him through to this office. Do you wish to speak with him, Modesty? It will take a few minutes. He has returned to the train but left a man by the phone who will call him if need be.'

She hesitated, then, 'If he's taken charge there, he could have his hands full. First let's hear what he told you.'

'Very well. A party of three rebels blew up the line and lay in ambush, ready to attack with a machine-gun when the people descended from the train. Willie forestalled this. One of the three was left alive and made prisoner. While Willie was away connecting the telephone, the man was questioned by the Montelero escort of soldiers. Questioned intensively, I fear, for he did not survive. It was revealed that a rebel force some two hundred strong is approaching from the west, and that he and his late comrades were sent on a day ahead of that force to halt the train and kill the refugees.'

Modesty said, 'All of them?'

'So he admitted, shortly before he died. Every soul on the train was to be destroyed, leaving no witnesses. That task will now fall to the main body when it arrives, which can be no more than a matter of hours now.'

When Modesty looked up from the map Dall saw that her eyes were blank, her face without expression. 'Will they do that, Miguel?' she said.

'Without question, my dear. A government in exile is the one threat to their hopes of many years in unchallenged power.' Sagasta leaned forward to run a finger across a small section of the map. 'The Cobra force is moving from the west along this road, south of these two parallel ridges. There is a narrow pass through the first ridge, here. They can then continue along a track that runs up over the second ridge and down to the railway line.'

She said, 'How strong is the Montelero escort and what fire-power do they have?'

Sagasta looked up, grim-faced. 'The escort has decamped. They disappeared into the bush with their weapons, heading away from the rebel approach. In due course they will either declare themselves for the rebel cause, or attempt illegal immigration over our border.'

Modesty looked at the scale of the map. 'That's about seventy miles to the nearest point, going across country. Even Willie can't get a whole mob of men, women and children to the border through that jungle terrain.'

Sagasta said, 'But there is perhaps something he can do. He wants to take up two sound rails from behind the train and use them to replace the buckled rails in front of the train. Once it is moving again, the rebel force cannot overtake it.'

Dall said softly, 'The old bastard hasn't lost his touch, Modesty.'

But she was watching Sagasta. 'You don't look happy, Miguel. What's the snag?'

'I'm sorry. He needs a tool to effect the change. He needs a fish-plate spanner, a spanner a metre long. Without it he cannot unbolt the rails and replace them.'

Dall said, 'Oh, Jesus. Can you get one to him?'

Modesty made an impatient gesture. 'Not just one, Johnny.'

Sagasta smiled at her. 'Of course not. Two would halve the time. I have managed to secure three at short notice, and they are with the aeroplane I have hired for you. It is for you to get them to him, Modesty. I am already beyond the limits of my authority.'

She touched his arm. 'I know that, and I'm grateful. I'll file a flight plan for Santiago, so whatever happens it can't be laid at your door. Will that do?'

Sagasta spread his hands. 'Perfectly. Now, do you wish to speak with Willie or will you leave at once?'

She had already made that decision. 'I'll go now. He'll be doing everything I might suggest, and I mustn't waste any time. Just pass the message that I'm on my way, please Miguel.'

Dall got to his feet as she moved towards him. He said, 'No good asking to come with you?'

'Oh, Johnny. You know that's out of the question.' She took his face between her hands, studying him. 'You're tired. Now give me a kiss, then go and rest. And thank you for everything.'

Dall kissed her, holding her close for a moment. 'Come back safe,' he said. 'You hear?'

She laughed softly. 'I've never been able to promise that, have I? But don't fret, Johnny, I'll be okay.'

He let her go and she moved to the door Sagasta was holding open for her. There she paused, rested a hand briefly on Sagasta's shoulder, looked at Dall for a moment, smiled, flickered an eyelid at him and was gone.

*   *   *

Willie Garvin sat in a corner of the compartment, his eyes closed. He was alone. Collier and Dinah had climbed the ladder to the coach roof above him. With her highly acute hearing, Dinah would be the first to pick up the sound of Modesty's aircraft as it approached.

A few of the government men had set off along the track on

foot with their wives and children. Willie had not tried to dissuade them. They could not hope to make the journey before being overtaken by the rebel soldiers, but once the track was repaired the train would soon catch up with the walkers and take them aboard, for all the difficult gradients were behind, and the driver had said that the rest of the run to the border was over flat ground which would allow reasonable speed.

For Willie it had been a busy morning. He had spent the last half-hour using yoga techniques to restore his mental and physical energy. Now he reflected quietly on what he had done, and decided there was nothing more until Modesty arrived. It would be impossible for her to land here, but that simply meant the aircraft would be a write-off. No doubt it was fully insured.

She was on her way, Sagasta had told him, with fish-plate spanners, weaponry, field glasses, two-way radios, and whatever other items she had decided might be of use.

Willie sat relaxed, slowly distancing himself from the present and from all about him, letting his mind drift back to when he had last seen her. That was at her cottage in Benildon, ten days ago, shortly before the fighting broke out in Montelero. He had been lying in a lounger on the terrace in the warm July sunshine, idly assessing the pros and cons of getting up and fetching himself a cold beer from the kitchen.

It was a finely balanced decision. On the one hand Modesty always kept an ample supply of his favourite beer at the cottage, and it would be bliss to feel the ambrosial liquid swilling around his taste-buds before it made the happy descent down his throat. On the other hand, as lawyers so often said, one had to consider adverse factors. The lounger was very comfortable, and the fridge in the kitchen was a good thirty paces from the terrace where he reclined.

'And,' Willie reminded himself solemnly, 'you're not as young as you were, Willie-boy.' He grinned to himself at the thought, and was about to get up when two bare arms slid down over his shoulders to rest across his chest, and a soft cheek was laid against his.

Surprise touched him gently, for this and other small gestures

of affection she had been showing lately were something new—
not that her affection for him had ever been in doubt, but through
all the long years it had been tacit and rarely displayed. He found
the change very pleasant even as he wondered at it.

Opening one eye he saw that a tankard of beer now stood on
the little table beside his chair. Modesty Blaise said in his ear,
'I have this amazing telepathic power.' She straightened up,
ruffled his hair, and moved to sit on the swing-seat to his left.
Her feet were bare, and the long slender legs rose to faded denim
shorts topped by a sleeveless silk blouse. The legs, Willie decided,
were as good as ever, a joy to contemplate.

He said, 'Thanks, Princess. I bet you got this telepathic power
when you were in the woods at dawn one day and saved a little
pixie who was caught in some brambles, and she gave you three
wishes.'

She looked at him in surprise. 'How did you know?'

He took a long pull at his beer. 'I've met 'er myself. It's Mabel.
She's always getting in trouble and giving three wishes to people
who get 'er out. I once saved 'er from a killer rabbit, and she
gave me the Derby winner.'

'That was useful. What about the other two wishes?'

'I've forgotten now. I think one of them was to do with girls.
What about your other two?'

She was silent for several seconds, gazing absently into space,
then seemed to emerge from a reverie. 'Oh, sorry. My other two
wishes?' She shook her head. 'I passed. From what I've read
about people who take up these three-wish offers they usually
wish they hadn't. There's always a nasty sting in the tail.' She
paused, frowning. 'Did I tell you John Dall's coming here at the
end of next week to spend a few days with me?'

Willie said, 'You told me last week, Princess. Give 'im my
best. I'd like to 'ave seen John, but I'll be in Montelero.'

She nodded. 'Yes, of course. I'm glad you're going. Things
seem to be getting a little tense out there, and I always worry
about Dinah.'

A few days ago a typical letter from Collier had arrived,
pointing out that for ten weeks now he had been hotly engaged

in statistical analysis for the Montelero government, and that
Dinah was alleging neglect and becoming mutinous. She had
therefore demanded that he require the presence of the notorious
hooligan, Modesty Blaise, to keep her company for the final
weeks of his commission. Dinah's demand had been emphasised,
he claimed, by skilfully timed rights to the jaw and threats of
knee-capping if he failed to assuage her loneliness. The presence
of that ill-favoured member of the lower classes, Willie Garvin,
would be tolerated providing he remained silent and wore a stock-
ing over his head at all times.

To Willie's surprise Modesty had said, 'You go, Willie love,
I can't make it just now. I have John Dall coming, and then
Weng's getting stroppy because he says there's a lot of business
paperwork I've neglected.'

It was no doubt true about Weng and the paperwork, thought
Willie as he took another pull at his beer, but it was unlike her
to be concerned about such things.

She said, 'I've cabled them to say I'm sorry I can't make it.
Anyway, Dinah loves having you around, so does Steve, whose
insults are code for endearments. They won't mind if I'm not
there this time.' She rose from the swing-seat. 'Give a shout if
you want another beer.' She patted his cheek and moved away
towards the cottage.

Steve and Dinah would mind though, Willie thought as he
watched her go. They would both be disappointed, as he was
himself. He sighed inwardly. How long was it now? Over thirty
years since the day she had come into his wretched life and
remade his world. Leaning back, he closed his eyes and gazed
down the long slope of the years. In the beginning was *The
Network* and the days of high danger. When Modesty wound up
the organisation and they retired, there was an unexpected but
not unwelcome continuation of risk and challenge in what Willie
always thought of as the Tarrant era.

Sir Gerald Tarrant was head of British Intelligence in that time.
Modesty and Willie had worked for him only twice by design,
but there were later occasions when he had been involved in a
number of the conflicts into which they had been drawn. It was

now eight years since Tarrant's death following five years of retirement. He had suffered a heart attack while staying with Modesty at Benildon, and died quickly, quietly, contentedly, in the ambulance on the way to hospital, holding Modesty's hand.

Throughout the Tarrant era and the years that followed, time had slipped by barely noticed, for their lives were full. They sought trouble no more than the iron filing seeks the magnet, but were drawn to it no less inevitably. There had been new enemies to face, new dangers to be met, but these occasions were short-lived periods of intense experience, and served only to heighten their enjoyment of all that lay between, sharpening their appreciation of the good fortune that fate had laid upon them.

Their adrenalin addiction, whether gift or burden, had also been laid upon them by the tapestry woven in their early lives, and they were aware of this, accepting it as a facet of their destiny. But with the passing years it grew less demanding, and this seemed to reduce the aura that made them so readily subject to the attraction exerted by the force-field of danger. It was four years now since they had been in serious action, but regular training in their various skills was a lifetime habit they still maintained.

And that was just as well, thought Willie as he came back to the present, because this could turn out to be a very dodgy caper. He opened his eyes, got to his feet and was about to open the compartment door when Collier shouted from the roof above him.

'Willie! She's here—Dinah can hear her!'

Two minutes later they were on the strip of open ground between track and jungle, standing among the chattering refugees as a Piper Tomahawk circled above them, quickly losing height. 'She's checking the wind-direction by the locomotive stack,' said Willie. 'I got them to chuck some green stuff on the coal to thicken it up.'

Collier said, 'Why is she—?' and broke off. The plane had moved upwind and was turning in a slow roll. Something fell, and immediately blossomed into a small parachute which slanted back towards the train as it descended. 'Very considerate,' said

Collier. 'She doesn't want us to have to climb trees.' He took his wife's hand. 'There's a small parachute with a little package coming down, and it's going to land pretty close. How did she get it out of the plane, Willie? You can't just open a window, can you?'

'There's a roof door on the Piper Tomahawk,' said Willie. 'It's open now. That'll be a hand radio she's dropped, with a bit of weight for stability.' He began to move forward, calling in Spanish to the little group of men watching, telling them to remain where they were. Since he had achieved the miracle of summoning help his authority had been unquestioned, for these were very frightened people. It was on his instructions that the children were now confined to the coaches and in the care of the women.

The parachute came down just ahead of the locomotive and close to the jungle fringe. Willie cut the padded bag from the shrouds and took out the little radio. Above, Modesty had banked round and he could see her looking down. He waved and received an answering wave before the circuit took her from his view. Walking back to join Steve and Dinah he checked that the batteries were firmly connected and drew out the short aerial. At once her voice came clearly to him. 'I'll be dropping the container next, Willie. Three fish-plate spanners, some weaponry and sundries. How long will you need to get that train moving?'

With the sound of her voice his heart lifted and the whole world became brighter, for he felt suddenly complete. *Three* spanners! He was grinning with relief as he spoke into the integral microphone. 'A couple of hours if we hit no snags, Princess.'

He had rejoined the Colliers now, and they were listening as she spoke again: 'Then we'll need a holding operation. At the moment you have only about half-an-hour. Have you been up on that east-west ridge to look at the approach, Willie?'

'Sure, Princess, first thing after I'd got through to Sagasta. It's not good. There's a track leading up from the pass to the railway, meeting it about a quarter-mile west of where we're stuck. But with you and me up on the ridge with a bit of fire-power we could hold 'em quite a while. Long enough, I reckon.'

'Not that simple, Willie. I made a sweep south before I came here, and I've seen the Cobra column. They're going to reach the pass in less than half-an-hour. What their late comrade didn't tell his inquisitors is that they have two armoured cars. The stuff I've brought will stop foot-soldiers but not armour. Are Steve and Dinah listening?'

'Yes. Sorry, Princess.'

'No, that's fine. I just want them to know it's all going to be okay. Now here's the plot. I'll drop the container next circuit. You get the driver and fireman and any other likely man busy with the spanners. Show Steve exactly what has to be done, and put him in charge. Have him wear one of the revolvers from the container to establish his authority, then you meet me on the ridge, just east of that stand of tall trees. You'll have to hump the rifles and as much ammo as you can carry, but you can take it slowly. I'll bring the first aid kit and the radio. Leave your radio with Dinah so we can keep in touch. We'll want to know when the train's ready to go so we can disengage. All clear?'

'You'll be coming up the ridge from the far side?'

'Yes. With you being so loaded, I'll probably be there before you. Okay, stand by for the drop.'

Again the Piper moved upwind along the railway. Again it rolled, and this time as the parachute opened a large cylindrical canvas container hung from it. Willie said, 'Lend a hand, Steve, and bring Dinah with you.'

Collier took his wife's arm. As they moved with Willie towards the area where the container would land Dinah said, 'Why is she going to bale out so far away?'

Collier said in a startled voice, 'Bale out?'

'Well, what else, honey? She can't *land* here.'

'Oh God, no, of course she can't. But what about the plane?'

'She'll think of something,' said Willie. 'Waste not, want not.'

'Eh?'

They had reached the container, and Willie ignored the question as he dropped to one knee and began to unfasten the straps. 'Help me sort this stuff out, Steve. You 'eard what Modesty said.

I'll show you what's to be done, then I'm off. The rest's up to you.'

Collier said miserably, 'Jesus, I'm useless at this sort of thing. I'll make a colossal cock-up of it.'

Dinah put her arms round him and kissed him on the chin. 'You said the same thing twenty years ago when you were looking after me in Panama, and you've been saying it ever since, but you always turn up trumps, Steve.'

'This is different—'

'Shut up and listen. You're not required to do anything manual, you simply use your voice and your terrifying personality. You're going to strut about giving orders in a loud, hectoring manner. I know that's not you, but I also know you can ham it up. You're great at that. Now come on, give me a snarl, tiger.'

Collier bared his teeth. 'Grrrrr! Like that?'

'Promising, but could do better. Now work yourself into the skin of the part while you're helping Willie. It's an act, Steve, and it's right up your street, so bloody well do it.'

Willie lifted an M-16 rifle from the container and sighed inwardly as he glanced at the blind girl. There were times, before Steve, that he never allowed himself to think about now. She was still lovely, and he had never ceased to admire her quality. He laid the rifle aside and lifted out the great spanners. 'Let's get to work,' he said.

Ten minutes later he stood beside the track where the rails were buckled. The container was now slung across his back and secured by the straps, leaving his hands free. In it were two M-16 rifles with ten 20-round staggered-row box magazines, one Colt .45 revolver, two pairs of field glasses, some plastic explosive with detonators, four grenades and a coil of nylon rope. A small haversack at his hip held a bottle of water, chocolate, packets of dates, and some amphetamine tablets.

Collier, in shirt-sleeves and with a revolver holstered at his hip, was barking out orders to the driver, fireman, and ex-Minister of Agriculture who were using the fish-plate spanners. Other men were filling holes blown in the flint-stone base of the track. Above, the Piper was still making wide circuits out beyond the ridges and back, with Modesty reporting progress of the rebel force. Dinah stood beside Willie, listening to the medley of sounds.

He said into the radio, 'It's all going okay 'ere, Princess. I'll be on my way now.'

Her voice came back. 'Me too, Willie love. We'll need time to pick a good spot. See you soon.' The Piper banked away, climbing.

As Willie put the radio in Dinah's hand she said, 'What did you mean about Modesty and the plane when you said "Waste not, want not"?'

'Well, she's got to bale out, but she'll try to work it so—' Willie broke off as Collier came towards them, face set and gleaming with sweat, jaw jutting, eyes narrowed, a man transformed. He was gazing south, to where the Piper had climbed high above the ridge and was beginning to dive. They could hear the rising scream of the engine at full throttle, and now the Piper was vertical, hurtling towards the ground like a dive-bomber.

Collier said savagely, 'What the bloody hell is she playing at?' Nobody answered, and he exhaled with relief as he glimpsed a small black object above the aircraft. A parachute opened and began slanting north as it descended. The Piper flashed on down. A split second after it had vanished behind the ridge there came the heavy bellow of an explosion.

'. . . try to work it so she blocks the pass,' Willie resumed.

A thick black cloud of smoke rose in the distance, and as the parachute sank lower her voice came over the radio, a little breathless. 'She hit the north end and she's burning nicely. I need both hands to steer this 'chute, so over and out.'

The men working on the buckled rails had stopped to stare. Collier whirled and bawled obscenities at them. As they hastily returned to their work he glared at Willie. 'She's done *what*?'

'Crashed the plane in the pass. It'll burn for a while and be too 'ot to 'andle for a lot longer. They can get past on foot by climbing up the west slope a bit, but they won't be able to get the armoured cars through. That's what matters.'

Collier grinned wolfishly, watching the parachute and its

passenger vanish below the line of the ridge. 'The Blaise touch,' he said. 'You can recognise it anywhere.' His expression changed to one of frowning indignation. 'How did *you* know what she was going to do?' he demanded.

Dinah said, 'Boy, are you dopey, you've seen it all before. He just knows how she thinks, doesn't he? Now go on, get back to your slave-driver act.'

'Watch me,' said Collier. He punched Willie gently on the arm. 'Give her my love and bring her back safe.' He turned to stride back to the working party, shouting. 'Come on, you idle bastards! Get those holes levelled up! You're not Minister of Culture now, Santana, you're *all* ministers of labour, and it's sweat or die! You hear?'

Willie said, 'He'll do all right, Dinah. He always does.'

She nodded. 'It would kill him to let you down. Can you manage all that weight?'

'Sure. It's not too bad.'

'Well, you take care. And give a girl a kiss before you go.'

He laughed, gathered her in his arms and held her quietly for a moment before kissing the corner of her mouth. 'Don't worry. We always come back, don't we?'

'You'd better. Give her my love, too.'

'I won't forget.' He released her, turned and began to move west along the railway to where the jungle track led up the ridge and on to the pass in the valley beyond.

*   *   *

The slope up from the railway was wooded except where the narrow track ran through it. Beyond the ridge, the ground fell to a valley, and here the jungle ceased, giving way to seamed rock and scrub. The incline down to the valley was long and gentle, the valley itself narrow, for soon the ground rose again to a higher ridge, bare and rocky, to drop almost sheer on the far side.

This second ridge was split by a sharp V, forming a pass which became the track leading on over the nearer ridge and down to the railway. An hour had gone by, but the remains of the Piper still smouldered and the wreckage blocked the pass. The Cobra rebels had outflanked the wreckage on foot by climbing some way up the west slope of the V, and were now deployed in the valley, pinned down by sparing but very accurate fire from the northern ridge before them.

Modesty Blaise and Willie Garvin lay in the shallow depression on the crest, a sandy hollow rimmed on its southern edge by a screen of foliage they had cut and dragged into position. From this vantage point they could look down upon the area where the rebels had taken cover two hundred yards below. An early attempt to rush the summit had been broken up well before the leading attackers were halfway up the slope. Since then there had been outbursts of small-arms fire, achieving no result, and an attack using mortars. Nine bombs had fallen along the ridge, the nearest on rocky ground some thirty feet away, but the hollow had given good protection. Only a direct hit would have any effect.

Willie lay resting. Modesty was on watch, gazing through a gap in the foliage. Willie thought she looked more relaxed and serene than he remembered for several weeks past. She had greeted him warmly, giving him a hug when they met, and had been talking easily and happily between the short periods of attack.

'If they've got any sense,' said Willie, 'they'll send someone to climb the far side of the ridge across the valley. From that peak at about eleven o'clock from 'ere he'll 'ave us in view. Range about two-fifty. He could just spray us.'

Modesty nodded. 'I had a look at the far side from the Piper. It's steep but climbable. I think they'll make it in another half-hour.' She turned her head to smile at him, and it was the rare smile he always held in his mind's eye, warm and humorous and intimate, the smile that made him feel he could pluck the moon from the sky for her, and was for him alone because of all they had shared through the long years.

She returned to her task, watching the valley below, and Willie settled himself more comfortably, closing his eyes, waiting for his turn to take watch in another ten minutes if no emergency occurred before then. She was extraordinarily relaxed, he thought.

Once the rebels put a man on that peak, quite apart from being able to fire down on the hollow he would also be able to signal any attempt by the defenders to disengage, which would give them only a two hundred-yard start in reaching the train. That was too little, for the old locomotive would have to move very slowly over the repaired section of track, and in any case would take some time to reach more than walking speed.

Willie was fully aware that Modesty knew all this as well as he did, yet she was clearly unworried about the problem of disengagement. 'She'll have something in mind,' he decided comfortably. 'She always does.'

Half a mile away, Collier moved to where his wife sat near the track on a cushioned seat taken from the train. 'What's new, sweetheart?' he said, dropping down beside her with a grunt of relief.

'Looks pretty good,' said Dinah. 'We're not making small-talk, but Modesty came through ten minutes ago to say there's been no fresh attack since that last mortar-bomb effort. I don't think she's conning me, because I've heard no firing. How's your team doing? I haven't heard you bawling at them lately.'

'No need,' said Collier. 'There's nothing like being scared spitless to boost your output. From the moment that firing started they've been working like demented beavers.'

'No snags?'

'Plenty. There are twelve sleepers to each section of track, and two fish-plates on each sleeper. Every fish-plate is bolted to the sleeper and to the rail. We've unbolted the buckled rails and replaced two busted fish-plates with two from the track behind the train. We've unbolted one good rail from behind and bolted it in front. Now we're working on the second rail. We've also had to replace a smashed sleeper and repair bits of track—I mean the stones the sleepers are bedded in.'

'So plenty of snags but you're coping?'

'Yes. Rather well, to be honest. I just pretend I'm Modesty or Willie and come up with an answer.' Collier shook his head, frowning. 'It's bloody patronising of them if you ask me. I shall have words with them on their return.'

Dinah smiled and felt for his hand. 'No. You'll just rave at them for leaving it late and taking needless risks and so on, the way you always do.'

Collier pressed her hand, then got to his feet, grinning. 'They'd start worrying about me if I didn't,' he said.

* * *

Another thirty minutes had gone by. Willie lay prone on watch. Beside him, Modesty lay on her back. There had been one sneak attempt by two men to crawl within grenade range of the hollow, but Willie's grenade range on the down-slope combined with his unique power and accuracy was almost three times theirs and they were now dead.

There was hardly any wind, and it was very quiet on the ridge when Modesty said softly, 'Willie . . . give me a kiss.'

He was startled, as he had not been when Dinah used almost the same words. 'Eh? Oh . . . my pleasure, Princess.' He edged towards her to kiss her cheek, but she put a hand to his chin and moved her head a little so that her lips were laid gently on his for a moment, and for the first time.

Then she was smiling up at him, patting his cheek and saying, 'Back on watch, Willie, and don't look away from that peak while I talk. There's something I have to tell you.'

He stared across the valley, stomach suddenly taut with anxiety, trying to concentrate on his task. 'What's up, Princess? I mean . . . did something 'appen I don't know about?'

She said, 'I want you to go back now, Willie. Back to the train. Dinah just said they'll be ready to move in twenty minutes, and I want you there from the start. I'll be staying on to cover you. I won't be coming back.'

He said hoarsely, 'Christ, no! It's not on, Princess! I know disengaging could be tricky, but we'll manage. Even if the train goes without us we can make it through the jungle, you and me. We'll do it easy—'

She broke in. 'Don't argue, Willie, we haven't much time. Believe me, this is the best thing that could have happened for

me, it really is. If I went in for praying, it would be what I'd
pray for. No, don't take your eyes off that peak. Just listen. I've
been worried sick about you for weeks now, trying to figure how
to tell you, but now it's simple.'

Without moving his head he said in a whisper, 'Tell me what?'

'About three months ago I started getting headaches. That's
new for me, but it wasn't just headaches. I began to feel there
was something wrong in my head. That's when I went off to
New York for a week or two, because I didn't want to worry
you.' He felt her hand on his arm, and swallowed incoherent
words that were jumbled in his throat.

She said, 'I'll keep it short, Willie. I went into the Royston
Clinic. They took X-rays, made scans, and decided something
needed checking. They drilled a little hole in my head, took a
sample from inside, and discovered that I've got something nasty
there that they can't do anything about. It's too late. It was always
too late.'

She was silent for a few moments, letting him absorb the shock.
Willie said nothing, for no words could cope with the huge horror
that filled him. She said gently, 'I know it's a shock, but be glad
for me, Willie. I've had a marvellous life, you know I have. Now
time's up, and for the last few weeks I've known that I'll soon
be starting to die—but that first I'll stop being me and become
pretty much a vegetable. In a way I suppose that wouldn't matter
much for me, because I wouldn't know, but I couldn't bear it
for you, and I've been at my wit's end trying to think whether
to tell you, or just disappear, or . . . whatever.'

She pressed his arm, then took her hand away. 'But when this
Montelero thing happened I had a feeling that somehow I'd have
a chance to go out the way I'd want, the way we both thought
it likely we'd go during all those years when we somehow managed to miss it by a whisker. I didn't dream it could work out
quite so well as this. I mean, we *can't* disengage until that train's
on the move. Apart from Steve and Dinah there are . . . how
many children aboard? Thirty, didn't you say? Well, one of us
has to stay till they're on their way, and I'm first choice by a
mile. You can't argue, Willie. I have to go on the big walk-about

soon, and I'd so much rather go with a bang than a whimper, doing something a bit useful. This is the very best thing that could have happened to me.'

He lay for a long minute, holding back futile protest, a part of him seeking desperately for a way out, an alternative, yet knowing there was none. Now he understood the open affection she had shown for him these past weeks, the small physical contacts, the almost maternal regard, and the moments when she had seemed far away in a world of her own. Now too he understood the eagerness for action he had sensed so strongly during the phone-call from Government House yesterday, and he knew that she had come here gladly to die.

He heard her laugh softly, and she said, 'It's been a great bonus, living this long, Willie. Don't make it hard for me now. I want you to start back right away. I'll tell Dinah about it on the radio, so you won't have that job to do when you see her. All right?'

It was an effort to speak, for his throat had almost closed, but he croaked, 'All right, Princess.' The last word had barely left his lips when he saw a figure stand up on the peak across the valley, a rifle aimed. With instant reaction he sighted and fired. The man went down, and as he did so Willie heard a quiet sound close beside him, followed a fraction of a second later by the brief chatter of firing from the peak, delayed by distance and no more than four or five rounds.

He said, 'I got 'im just as he fired, Princess. Looks like he was on 'is own.'

Her hand pulled feebly at his arm, and when he turned his head he saw that she was lying on her side now with blood welling from the hollow behind the collarbone, and he knew that a chance bullet had driven down through that hollow, deep into her chest. She said in a gentle voice, 'Well, there now. I'm sorry. Do what you think best, Willie love.'

She turned on to her front, head pillowed in the crook of her good arm, her face hidden. Seconds later her body went limp. Willie reached out to rest a hand on her neck. Two fingers felt the last fading pulse of the carotid artery, and he knew he was

alone. Beside her the radio squawked and Dinah's voice said,
'We've got up steam, Modesty, and the driver says only ten
minutes now. You and Willie start running. Please, honey, don't
wait.'

Before Willie could reply he heard the sound of mortars from
down in the valley. Moments later, when three bombs landed,
he was huddled down in the hollow, the radio beneath him for
protection, an arm across Modesty for no reason. The bombs
exploded, the nearest fifteen yards from where he lay. He said,
'No damage, Princess,' and was lifting his head to watch for the
expected attack when a piece of rock the size of a melon came
down from thirty feet on to his ankle.

After the first gasp of agony he focused on the pain, closing
his mind to it as he peered down the slope. Four men were
moving up at a crouching run, weaving as they came. He waited
a little, ignoring Dinah's anxious voice from the radio, then
picked off the leading two. The others turned back and he let
them go. Using the Sivaji technique, he opened himself to the
pain, letting it wash through him as water through a net, distancing himself from it until it faded to insignificance. Then he picked
up the radio and said, 'Dinah?'

'Oh God, I heard them start that bombing again, Willie. Are
you both okay?'

He said, 'I've got something important to tell you, Dinah.
Modesty was going to tell you 'erself, but it's too late now. She
just died.'

'Oh Willie, *no*!' Her voice cracked on the word.

'It's what she wanted. Exactly what she wanted. She told me
why, only a couple of minutes ago. Now listen . . .'

A little way from where the second rail was being bolted to
the last of the fish-plates, Dinah stood white-faced and drawn,
the radio close to her ear. A minute later, cheeks wet with tears,
she said shakily, 'But why didn't she *tell* us? Oh, I'm sorry,
that's stupid! She wouldn't lay that on us. But . . . but . . . oh
God, I can't think. Can *you* get away now? She'd want that,
Willie, you know she would. We'll be ready the moment you
get down here.'

His voice over the radio was easy and untroubled. 'She told me to do what I think best, so here it is, Dinah. With one of those last bombs, a bloody great chunk of rock came down on my ankle and it's bust. Now listen and don't argue. There's no way I can come with you. I'm staying 'ere till I see the train on its way. When it's about 'alf a mile from where you are now I'll be able to see the smoke until you go be'ind that low ridge where the track takes a long bend.'

'Willie, please—'

'Just listen. Once you're away I'll move off. I'll be a bit slow, but with any luck I'll be able to lie low or get clear one way or another. Then I'll take the jungle route to the border. I can rig a crutch with the rifles, and I'm good in the jungle, you know that. This is what Modesty would want, so this is what I'll do. Okay?'

She said in a small voice, 'Yes, Willie.'

'That's a good girl. Don't let Steve make a song and dance about this, will you? I think that's all. See you later, love, but I might be a while so don't wait up for me, eh?'

'All right, Willie. Good luck, and a big hug from me.'

She lowered the radio and called, 'Steve! Steve!'

Two minutes later, grey with exhaustion and grief, Collier said, 'Oh, dear God. We'll be breathing on one lung from now on.' He put his arms round Dinah and held her close. 'Do you think he'll make it?'

'He'll . . . sort of do his best. But for Willie there's no longer any point in making it now. That's the difference.' She drew a deep breath, stepped back and wiped her damp grimy face. 'Come on, tiger. We've got a job to finish. I couldn't bear to let them down now.'

Fifteen minutes later Willie saw smoke from the locomotive appear above the trees to the east. He watched with satisfaction as it moved steadily on for several minutes before vanishing behind the ridge. There was no further attack in that time, but he suspected that a small party had split from the main body unseen during the last mortar attack and had moved along the valley to climb the ridge further west and so outflank him.

On reflection he decided it was time to tidy up and be gone.

He had strapped the broken ankle securely, and lashed the two rifle-barrels together, overlapping end to end so that they formed a makeshift crutch. Now he spent five minutes crawling round the edge of the hollow, setting small quantities of plastic explosive deep in the sandy earth beyond the rim, talking quietly to Modesty.

'I'm glad it worked out for you, Princess. Knocked me sideways at first, but ... I can see 'ow you felt. I reckon they're aiming to outflank me, so I'll be off soon. The train's away with Dinah and Steve and all the rest, so there's nothing more to be done 'ere. I 'ope you're okay. Funny thing, when we were on the train Steve got us talking about what comes next. Well ... it's anyone's guess, isn't it?' He put the last piece of plastic in place, then set a detonator in each before crawling away from the hollow to the edge of the wooded slope leading down to the railway. There he took cover, watching.

The explosions came as close together as he had hoped when setting the detonators, and as the echoes died he saw with satisfaction that what had been a deep hollow was now a mound of earth and sand. He said, 'Sleep well, Princess,' and began to hobble down the slope.

After five minutes he had covered no more than two hundred yards and had fallen twice. His hurt foot gave no support and the rifles made a poor crutch on the incline, tending to slip. Pausing for a moment, holding a sapling for support, he heard shouts from the ridge-top behind him. Chest heaving with effort, he pushed on. There came a louder shout from above, and he heard the whipcrack sound of a bullet as it passed a yard to his left.

'Getting a bit dodgy, Princess.' Holding in his mind's eye that smile of hers that was his alone, he stumbled on, well content, but had moved only a few more yards when he fell again and for a moment was numb.

Then he was on his feet once more, moving easily and unencumbered down the slope, without pain, the trees gone now. Timeless he moved down the slope of grass that in some way was not grass but perhaps the essence of it, down towards the valley where a silvery path or perhaps a river, though in some way neither, ran or perhaps simply was.

Somewhere he could hear the songs the stars sang, and with new senses he was aware in unimaginable ways of himself and everything about him, but above all and as never before knowing the totality of the familiar companion moving with him.